I0692686

# ALSO, BY R.W. MARCUS

R.W. Marcus

# MIRRORED DESTINY

*A Tale of the Annigan Cycle
in Three Acts*

## BOOK EIGHT

# R.W. MARCUS

## LAUGHING BIRD PUBLISHING
### GALAX, VA USA

Published by Laughing Bird Publishing
Galax, Virginia USA

Visit us on the web https://AnniganCycle.com

Cover art by Kilson Spany
Cover layout and design by Laughing Bird Publishing

Laughing Bird Publishing® is a registered trademark of Mark W Phillips

Manufactured in the United States of America
10 9 8 7 6 5 4 3 2 1


First Printing, 2024
ISBN 979-8-9877180-4-9

R.W. Marcus

*Dedicated to the memory of*
*Edgar Rice Burroughs...*
*with a wink and a nod to*
*Philip José Farmer &*
*Quentin Tarantino*

# CONTENTS

# ACKNOWLEDGEMENTS

Without a doubt a project of this size and complexity would have been nearly impossible to achieve alone. My humblest and most sincere gratitude go out to the members of what I affectionately have named, "Team Marcus."

As always, my loudest shout out is to my greatest love and partner in crime Cheryl Pepper, who is not always fond of R.W. Marcus and the cavalier manner in which he manages to kill off her favorite characters. Nevertheless, she still outstandingly acts as proofreader, replacing several inept so-called professionals.

To Mark Phillips, my closest and oldest friend, the guy with his thumbprint on virtually every creative project I've undertaken in the past forty plus years.

I couldn't do without my wonderful beta readers: Max Yrik Valentonis, Lynn Marie Firehammer, Ivy Maxine Elissa, and Dave Holman who also added his chemical expertise to the Marcus technical team. These folks are the first in line to detect anything amiss in the early manuscript.

The technical arm of Team Marcus also deserves praise for keeping me straight in the ways of science and anatomy: Jessica Pepper RN, Physicist Keenan Pepper and artist Kilson Spany.

Last but not least, in the appreciation department, is Laughing Bird Publishing who has taken care of me every step of the way.

I know I speak for R.W. when I say..." You all may live another day."

# WELCOME TO THE ANNIGAN

This mostly aquatic planet travels in a geosynchronous orbit around a small yellow sun. It's set far enough back in the solar system's Goldilocks Zone so that it maintains an atmosphere conducive to a wide variety of life.

Sentient creatures, terrestrial, marine or amphibious, share a hyper-fertility devoid of genetic boundaries. Any sentient creature may mate with any other and produce offspring.

Lumina basks in perpetual sunlight on one side of the Annigan. Humans dwell alongside many other sentient races thriving across its various continents and island chains. The fertility enriching rays of the sun, and the warmth of the Shallow Sea, support a vibrant and rich ecosystem.

Although life is abundant there, Lumina is hardly a serene place as you will see. Millennia of feuds, ruthless ambition and individual hatreds forged a fragile peace, barely sustained under the rule of the Great Houses.

Because of the incredible diversity of sentient creatures, all races, genders and hybrids in Lumina enjoy social equality, judging each as an individual based upon their own merits. Beneath the veneer of peace, however, dwells a hotbed of totalitarian torture, raider uprisings and a constant escalating cold war between the Great Houses.

Nocturn languishes in constant darkness on the other side of the Annigan. Only moonlight, starlight and bioluminescence illuminate the land of endless night. Without the warming rays of the sun, Nocturn's oceans are frozen over, but constant geothermal activity heats the land masses, creating a temperate and misty terrain teeming with exotic and predatory sentient races.

Imperialistic cat people rule aboveground and hive nations of humanoid mantises swarm beneath the surface. In the Ocean Deep, a race of sentient octopods dwell in vast underwater cities worshiping the ancient ones of the abyss. You are predator or prey in Nocturn's despotic societies.

The Twilight Lands reside at the fringes of the Annigan and remain in constant gloaming. Here, warm and cold air currents clash, generating a perpetually stormy climate.

Ruled by the amphibian Bailian race, the Twilight Lands serve as a neutral zone for cultures from every corner of the Annigan. Many encounter other races for the first time, and like the weather, their clashes can prove tempestuous.

Only the sun of Lumina keeps back the nocturnal predators of the dark side. Legends tell of a prophesied great eclipse stripping away all boundaries and igniting an apocalyptic war. Until then…

…these are the tales from the Annigan Cycle.

*A shift in the Annigan*
*A pass of the torch*
*A new generation begins*
*With ancients returning*
*And old foes reborn*
*The past falls away in the din.*

# ACT ONE

# A Gem of an Idea

Wakil de Banimi was a long way from home. His self-imposed exile was a recent development for the young Valdurian deep cover operative. He originally infiltrated the infamous Pa-Waga cult in Zor; however, since their banishment two grands ago, they made their new home, here, in the Free City of Tannimore.

As far as cities were concerned, the floating metropolis proved little different than other large communities. The mostly human population displayed all the congestion and crime associated with large urban spaces.

Most of the enforced laws in this city concerned themselves with the use of fire. All understood the importance of care in this regard, since the founders constructed the entire city from the wood of the bonded, decommissioned ships stranded in the Doldrums, the flat seas located in the southwestern Ocean Deep of Lumina.

The adherents of the Pa-Waga, the mawl God of greed, imposed all other laws, which mostly dealt with keeping the populace busy in the pursuit of making money. Ever since they turned Tannimore into a hedonistic playground for any who dared make the journey to its remote location, the influx of gold into the city's coffers remained constant.

Wakil, a tall, thin man with slightly elongated features, had a knack for blending in, no matter the crowd. His inconspicuous nature served him well in working his way up the ranks in the theocratic court of Wikk the First. It became his duty, as a trusted runner for the ruling assemblage, to be

1

unobtrusively present at their meetings and await orders from its members.

The conclave, which had just adjourned, proved most troubling for the Valdurian agent. They proposed plans which would significantly alter the very structure of power in the Annigan, especially for House Valdur. He considered it dangerous, but he must make contact with his handlers. They needed to know this intel, but he realized this single act could potentially blow his cover.

He traversed at a brisk, steady pace the wide, busy catwalks linking together the various interconnected buildings. They stacked the structures haphazardly, incorporating the various abandoned vessels forming the base of the city. Crossing over the central main wharf, situated between two massive flagships, he could see that another shuttle from the Goyan Islands had just arrived.

He worked his way through the throng of naked and near naked greeters, enthusiastically waving and calling down to the disembarking revelers. The mostly human males cheered and waved back, eager to spend their money on the many pleasures the city had to offer.

Making his way down to the third level he attempted to get lost in the incoming crowd of patrons solicited by nude prostitutes offering drinks and companionship. He knew he must be careful not to arouse the suspicions of the Piety Watch, which were everywhere.

Once he broke away from the pack heading for the various drinking and gambling establishments, he took a left at the next large intersection. This particular street led to his small neighborhood of apartments. His grouping of single person living quarters occupied a row along the north face of the city and actually provided an ocean view.

Wakil noticed his heavy breathing when he closed his front door behind him and secured the latch. Leaning against it, he took a moment to calm himself and mentally compose his message. It had to be concise. They could trace lengthy broadcasts and strictly limited all outgoing transmissions.

The single room dwelling measured twenty-foot square, with a narrow bed against the wall on the right side and a small seating area against the left side of the room. Directly across from the door, a table and two chairs sat below the solitary window. Outside, he could see the waning moonlight as the orb made its way westward towards the horizon. Soon, the only illumination would be the weakened rays of the sun fixed permanently in the western sky.

He lifted his mattress, reached underneath and pulled out a flat, inch thick rectangle wrapped in a swath of cloth. Sitting on the bed, he unwrapped the six-inch-wide Larimar communication tablet. With a touch of its milky white surface, the upper right corner of the Etheria pad came to life with a dull bluish glow.

Quickly going over the message he composed in his mind, he used his fingertip and began scribbling out his warning in the ancient language of Yassett. He no sooner wrote three lines, than a pounding on the door interrupted him. Startled, he snapped his head towards the commotion.

"Brother Wakil," came a gruff male voice. "Open the door immediately. We must talk to you!"

Wakil's heart pounded and he scribbled at a frenzied pace. "Just a moment," he called out meekly.

"Now, brother Wakil!" the voice demanded.

"I just need a moment," he pleaded, tapping the upper left on the screen.

The words disappeared, launched toward their intended recipient or so he hoped, just as the door burst open. Two large members of the Piety Watch, who appeared incredibly similar, stepped into the room.

They both stood six feet tall, with long dark hair pulled back into ponytails. Their cape's high collar, resembling cat ears, framed their scowling clean-shaven faces. Wakil felt his throat go dry and he fought the urge to piss himself while gripping the tablet on his lap.

"What do you want?" he asked, his voice trembling. "Why the need to break in my door?"

Both glared down at the communication device resting in Wakil's lap and then back up to the frightened runner.

"We couldn't help but notice you left the meeting in a rush," one said accusatorily, "and now we find you with an Etheria tablet. You can understand our suspicion."

"I understand nothing!" Wakil said indignantly. "I am violating none of the Lord's commandments!"

"Who were you communicating with?" the other asked icily.

"What business is that of yours!? I am a faithful follower of the Lord and a trusted member of court!"

"Save your indignation and answer the question," the first one replied. "We are well within our rights to ask it."

"I will not!" Wakil said adamantly.

With a brutal sneer they grabbed the much frailer Wakil by each arm and pulled him to his feet, sending the Etheria tablet clattering noisily to the floor.

"Nothing to say, huh?" the second one said with a sneer. "Perhaps some time in Mistress Ve-Qua's dungeon will loosen your tongue."

Six hundred miles northwest of Tannimore, the City of Penaber rests on the frigid windswept northern coast of the Narrow Lands. This remote outpost of House Calden hosts a large naval base which predominantly trains Brightstar sailors for their perilous final exam of rounding the Innaca

Deep just to the north. Because of Penaber's proximity to the giant Flavian Portal in the Innaca Deep, it often accommodates a wide variety of sentients from across the Middle Realms and multi-verse, making it more cosmopolitan than even the High Holy City of Zor.

In a small, nondescript building on the city's cramped west end, six mongrel mawls sat watching as many Larimar screens attached to the windowless walls. Whiskers and tails twitched continuously while the humanoid cat creatures monitored the magical communications for the enigmatic Order of Kaplan. This listening station, along with the others spread around the Annigan, eavesdropped on the entire area, especially Tannimore, the city of their sworn enemy.

"I tell you; I've found a place that has the freshest Maudo Grass this side of home," a black mongrel with white splotches said to a fawn colored one seated next to him.

"I don't know," the fawn mawl replied, not taking his eyes off the screen before him. "I'm always worried they're going to lace it with something nasty."

The black one chuckled. "I swear six, you must be afraid of everything new!"

"I don't think caution is a bad thing given where we are," Six defensively said, before his attention focused on an upper area of his screen. "Woah, what's this?!"

"What?"

Six swiped his hand downward, filling the screen. "I just caught a transmission out of Tannimore, headed for Zor. It's weak so it probably didn't make it."

The perplexed mongrel's tail twitched furiously and his head cocked from side to side as he attempted to make sense of the strange looking language.

"Looks like gibberish," he said, finally peering away. "Chief, I've got something here you might want to look at."

An orange Tiikeri in a gray tunic exited the only other room in the building and came up behind his charge. "What is it, Operator Six?"

The mongrel indicated the ten lines on the screen. "I just intercepted this dispatch from Tannimore bound for Zor."

"It's awfully weak," the chief noted, leaning over the operator's shoulder. "Do you think it made it?"

"No, sir, and even if it did, it looks like nonsense to me."

"It's supposed to, Operator Six. That's Yassett, an ancient human language only used for court intrigue and espionage."

"Looks like you may have caught a live one, Six." The Tiikeri stood up straight and placed a furry hand on the mawl's shoulder. "Good work! Let's bump this up the line and get it translated."

Taleeka found the hackney ride torturously slow and the blindfold only made it worse. She could hear her friends, mostly Nibira, tittering away giddily in the seats around her and she good naturedly played along. Despite recent rains, it had turned out to be a beautiful spring day in the High Holy City of Zor, the twenty-third cycle in the quinte Teine, her birthday. Not her real birthday, of course, that day was lost to the recesses of history, eighteen grands ago, in the slums of the mining city, Toriss, where she had been born.

In fact, her actual age still remained a mere guess, agreed upon by her adopted family. They delivered her from a life of poverty and misery to one of acceptance, love and adventure. In the past, her mom and dad had always marked the day with subtle revelry and a modest, yet thoughtful gift. Today, she had absolutely no idea what her friends had in store for her.

When the hackney finally came to a stop, the friends happily piled out with Noorim assisting the blindfolded birthday girl out of the cab and up a short flight of stairs. Once they passed between two large double doors, the sounds and smells betrayed her location as Air Station Three.

"Okay kids, what's going on?" she said, when she felt the first large gust of wind rush over her, indicating she stood on the flight deck.

"In both our cultures, patience is considered a virtue," Noorim said glibly.

"Says the one who's *not* blindfolded," Taleeka retorted.

Okay, we're here!" Nibira said, when they came to a halt and she felt Noorim's hands untying the eye covering.

"SURPRISE!" came the vivacious chorus the instant they removed the blindfold.

Taleeka's eyes went wide and she held both hands up covering her mouth which dropped open in joyous amazement. As perceived, she stood in the main hangar of the Valdurian Air Station next to a row of parked ships. Nibira, Barr-Ani, Noorim and Gidaria all stood in a semi-circle in front of her, looking pleasantly proud of themselves. Just off to the side, standing beside a Resistance Class Cruiser, Mal and Alto beamed with pride at their daughter.

"Mom! Dad!" she squealed, rushing into their arms."

"You didn't think we'd forget your birthday did you sweety?" Mal said, giving her a kiss on the cheek.

"Especially your eighteenth," Alto added.

When they broke from the hug, Alto gave her a quick kiss on the forehead and her friends excitedly gathered in close. With the initial shock over, Taleeka looked around with a puzzled expression.

"This is a great surprise," she said, scanning the five exuberant faces ready to burst, "but what are we doing here?"

"We thought this the ideal place for you to receive your present," Alto replied smiling slyly.

Mal looked up at the airship she stood next to and patted its side. "She's all yours, Kiddo."

Once again, Taleeka gasped in delight into her hands.

"Are you kidding me!?" she gushed, stepping over to the craft.

"I did mention you were gonna need a bigger ride, Boss," Gidaria said, watching Taleeka run her hands lovingly along the hull.

"It was Gidaria's idea," Nibira admitted. "We all chipped in. Well, it was mostly your folks. The parking slip comes along with it."

"I, I don't know how to thank you, all of you!"

"Just use it well and don't get fucking killed," Mal offered sardonically, rapping on the side. "And to make sure that doesn't happen, there's more."

Slowly, the large rear hatch lowered and Taleeka peered into her ship's freakishly massive cargo bay. Jixie stood smiling just inside the open hatch. The fourteen-grand-old still possessed a baby face, but he now carried an air of serene confidence. Fifty feet behind him, in the far corner of the cargo bay, she saw Gidaria's hackney with a leashed Brzo happily bounding from the passenger seat to the driver's seat, panting out the windshield at them.

"Hey Tally, happy birthday!" the young mechanic greeted cheerfully. "I've made some improvements to your new ride."

"I'd say so," Taleeka gasped, stepping into the unnaturally large space in awe. "Cavernite?"

"Yep, just like in your backpack, only bigger. I wanted to hit you with the *wow* factor."

"You sure did that," she said walking around, staring up at the twenty-foot-tall ceiling.

"They lined the walls with it," Jixie said proudly. "It can get even bigger, depending on how much PSI you pump into it. Speaking of which, you've got an extra-large Obsidian PSI battery and an independent backup just for this section. You definitely don't want to run out or this place shrinks back to its original size, which could be catastrophic."

By now everyone had joined Taleeka's private tour.

"I've also installed a Gyronite disk on the underside, just like Gidaria's hackney over there, only bigger. Staying upright shouldn't be a problem."

"How did you manage all this?" Taleeka asked, still in shock.

Jixie grinned broadly. "Your mom hooked me up with this blue skinned lizard fellow, Da... Da?"

"Da-Olman," Taleeka completed his sentence. "Yeah, I know him."

"Why am I not surprised? He's a whiz with Etheria, that's for damn sure. He set you up with two Trinilic weapons, fore and aft, on the underside of the hull." He then raised an amused eyebrow. "But the best part is in the cockpit."

"Oh?" Taleeka said warily, following him up to the command chairs.

The cockpit of the upgraded Resistance Class came with pilot and navigator's stations in front of the control panel, and captain's chair behind and between them.

"Put your hand on that," he said, pointing to a four-inch oblong blue, purple and clear crystal set into the dashboard at the navigator's controls.

Taleeka did as requested and a twelve-inch pale blue phantasmal globe projected from the clear part. Taleeka gasped in surprise seeing the continents of the Annigan displayed on its spectral surface.

"It's like Zau's eye!" she gasped. "How?!"

"I've only heard about your friend's eye," Jixie said patiently, "but this isn't as attuned to Flavian activity as hers. Da-Olman did, however, figure out the right combination of Etheria to make a pretty impressive navigational device. It's called a Croquis."

Taleeka stared at the globe for a few moments before releasing her fingers and the sphere receded back into the crystals. She glanced over at the smiling faces peering at her and blushed.

"I... I honestly don't know what to say," she managed to stammer out. "This is the best birthday ever!"

"Do you have a name for her?" Mal asked.

Taleeka pondered for a moment before nodding her head. "I think I'll call her, *The Vastus*."

"*The Vastus* it is," Mal confirmed heartily. "Now, how about a celebratory meal before we have to scoot."

Taleeka's face fell in disappointment. "You're not staying?"

Mal smiled sympathetically. "Sorry sweety, but there's this big event next cycle. Your dad's being honored by the Amarenian queen, and you sure as fuck don't want to keep the queen waiting."

*Fire,*
*Smoke,*
*Commotion, and the smell of roasting meat.*
*Lord Banavor's kitchens, the new girl, barely ten grands old, in her new green dress,*
*She could feel their eyes following her.*
*Frightening, but at least she knew she wouldn't go hungry again.*
*Kuhinja, the kitchen crone, firm but fair.*
*Her first job, washing dishes. The warm soapy water feels good on her hands.*
*Thick callused hands lift her dress from behind, makes her gasp, paralyzed in fear.*
*"Hey there, missy, the voice sounds gruff and male. "If you're gonna be working around here we gotta break you in right."*

*The same hands now cup her buttocks and slide between her legs.*

*"You just leave it up to old Nasilnik here. By the time you're ready to bleed, you'll be an old pro at fucking, and you'll have me to thank for it..."*

*The blow feels hard, the slap loud, and his hands immediately withdraw.*

*Kuhinja's voice, stern and reprimanding. "Nasilnik! What the fuck do you think you're doing?!"*

*Spinning, she faces her assailant.*

*Thin, mid-fifties, long greying hair and goatee on a pockmarked face, which he now nurses from the crone's blow.*

*"Your pot's boiling over!" Kuhinja admonishes harshly. "If you burn Lord Banavor's supper, he'll find a use for that withered old cock of yours. Now, get back to work!"*

*Kuhinja's face turns kind and conciliatory. "Don't you mind him. If he gives you any more trouble just punch him and he'll leave you alone."*

*Humiliation, degradation and building rage, glaring at him at his station across the kitchen.*

*He laughs at her with his coworkers, making lewd pelvic thrusts.*

*Watching her hands, trembling with anger, picking up the meat cleaver.*

*"Well, hey there, missy" he gloats reaching for the handle of a pot. "You change your mind about me breaking you in?"*

*The cleaver comes down on his forearm, severing it.*

*Screams, blood shooting everywhere.*

*The next blow lands in his side.*

*And the next,*

*And the next,*

*And the next.*

*Kuhinja's hand on hers halts the onslaught.*

*Breathing hard, staring down at the bleeding mutilated body.*
*The kitchen staff, standing frozen in horrified shock.*
*The front of her new green dress, covered in blood.*


"We're almost there ma'am." The voice of her driver snapped her back to the present.

Thank you Vozac." Mazie de Goya said, watching the ramshackle buildings of the Seven Sisters Slums go by from the back of her private hackney. It had been two grands since her father, Stovle's death and their Lord Banavor's disappearance. Two grands of coalescing her power within Banavor's shattered empire and holding it together. She now felt ready to step out, attempting what formerly would have been considered unthinkable, and it started here.

"Turn here," she instructed the large bald man behind the wheel.

He complied and the vehicle glided down a smaller side street where groups of slovenly, idle people sat around the doorways suspiciously watching her pass.

The hackney finally came to a stop in front of a large, abandoned warehouse, streaked with graffiti. Five rough looking characters stood in front of it talking in hushed tones. They paused the conversation and stared warily when Vozac got out and dutifully opened Mazie's door for her.

Sef de Sedam watched an expensive pair of black Kell skin boots step out onto the cobblestone street. White silk slacks followed, and he whistled softly when Mazie's shapely form, in a black low-cut blouse, came into view.

"Stay with the hackney and be ready," she ordered softly.

Sef ran his hand across his short, bristly white hair. He had to admit, she *was* a looker. He found himself unable to take his eyes off her curvaceous five-foot-six frame, topped off with long brown hair and a beautiful, coffee-colored complexion. She reeked of wealth and privilege. *What in the name of the gods is she doing here?*

She gracefully stepped around the sparce debris in the street and the group seemed genuinely surprised when she headed their way. She smiled slyly at their hoots and cat calls then stopped directly in front of Sef.

"You are Sef de Sedam, and this is your street?" she asked firmly but lyrically.

"Who the fuck wants to know?" Sef asked with a sneer, making his grizzled appearance even more hardened.

Mazie continued her smirk. "The person that wants to offer you a job."

The entire group erupted in laughter.

"Bitch, I don't fucking work for anyone!" Sef said with a condescending scowl. "I swing the big dick on this block. People work for *me*."

Mazie peered around at the squalor and sloth with an amused look. "So, I see."

"I got a better idea," Sef said, stepping forward aggressively. "What say I drag your pretty ass into that alley over there and have some fun with you then we take what we want. What do you say?"

Mazie's smile turned coldly confident. "I'd say all of you would be dead before you laid a hand on me."

"All of us?!" one of the others, a wiry young man with short brown hair and wild eyes, blurted out.

"Think of it as incentive to behave," she replied. "Now about that job?"

"Alright," Sef said skeptically. "Let's say I'm interested. What's the job and what's it pay?"

"I want you to contact the other street bosses. Set up a meeting right here in this warehouse. And it pays more money than you've ever seen in your life."

Sef's mouth dropped open in surprise. "Why the fuck do you want to do that?"

"I'm looking to bring everyone together under one umbrella... Mine. Everybody keeps control of their respective blocks, but we work together and stop the squabbling."

"Under you?" Sef asked in disbelief.

Mazie merely nodded, causing Sef to scoff loudly.

"Bitch, are you fucking kidding me?! The centi the guards get wind that we're trying to organize, we'll be ass deep in Red Division. That'll be the end of us all!"

"You let me worry about that," Mazie said confidently.

Sef scoffed again. "Bitch..."

The cleaver appeared in her hand before any could react. She brought it down hard on the top of Sef's head with a loud crack. The heavy bladed butcher's tool easily traveled halfway down his skull, finally stopping just before the top of the nose.

"Don't call me bitch," she said calmly, sliding the blade out from between his very surprised eyes.

The thug had no time to cry out, as rivers of blood began pouring from the wound and he toppled over. On his way to the ground, Mazie deftly ran the bloody cleaver against the sleeve of his shirt, cleaning it.

Flicking away a drop of blood on her cheek, she glanced over at the young man which had spoken up.

"You, what's your name?"

"Drugo?" he said meekly, looking at Sef's oozing body.

"Well, Drugo, what do you say? You up for the job?"

"Do I really have a choice?" he asked hopelessly.

"Of course, you have a choice," Mazie replied in surprise. "You can languish in this shit hole for the rest of your life, however long that may be, or you can take my offer and become rich and powerful."

"Well, when you put it that way," Drugo said resignedly.

"Good boy," Mazie praised, reaching into her pocket.

She pulled out a hundred secor gold note and offered it to the wide-eyed young man who stared in shocked disbelief.

"Take it," Mazie prompted.

Drugo did as told, fondling the large sum of money in his hand while staring at it.

"Hire some of the locals and get that warehouse cleaned out," Mazie ordered authoritatively. "Then, get with the street bosses. Set up a meeting here for this cluster, preferably within the next few cycles."

Drugo nodded his head, all the while his attention switched from the money he held to Sef's dead body.

"Relax," Mazie said, seeing the young man's trepidation. "Your friend is dead because he lacked vision. You have vision, don't you?"

Drugo quickly pocketed the Ukko wafer. "More than him."

Chen Arador, abandoned son of Stryder Aramos, held his Zorian hand-and-a-half bastard sword in the forward guard position and smiled, warily watching his five adversaries circle him. The self-assured Zorian swordsman stood at an even six-feet-tall with boyish good looks, shoulder length blonde hair and matching goatee. His blue, sweat soaked robes of the Zorian Sword Academy clung to his lean muscular frame like a second skin, accentuating his exemplary form.

When the first blow came, he was ready. Chen had no trouble intercepting the poorly executed, well telegraphed overhead strike. Instead of merely deflecting the blow, he allowed the opposing blade to travel down his blade, where six, one-inch-long teeth were set into the steel just before the guard. The protuberances cleanly trapped the other blade and, with a twist from Chen, snapped the opposing weapon cleanly in half.

He quickly spun and continued the momentum, slashing the edge across the chest of the startled, weaponless adversary. Still turning, he lashed out with a forward kick, catching a charging attacker in the stomach and sending him to the floor.

"You and you, out!" a commanding voice ordered from off to the side.

The martial maelstrom abruptly halted and an older man dressed in the same blue robes with a red sash around his waist stepped amidst the sparring class. His greying ponytail swayed and his wild blue eyes flashed in excitement pointing at the two disqualified students who had been struck. When they left the floor, the master clapped his hands and pointed to the remaining contestants, now down to three against one.

"Begin!" he commanded.

Chen struck first this time, catching one of his opponents with his sword tip before he could ready himself. Stopping just before impaling his classmate, Chen gave a victorious smile and the master's voice rose again.

"You, out!" he ordered, pointing at Chen's most recently vanquished foe. "*Keep fighting!*"

Chen, first to obey his master's instruction. dropped to one knee before the defeated student could leave the floor. He swung the bastard sword low and caught one of the two remaining students across both calves with the flat of his blade. The force of the blow swept the student off his feet and he landed on his back in front of Chen, who then drove the pummel onto his abdomen, winding him.

Still kneeling, he drove the tip of the sword upward at the chest of the second startled student. It stopped inches before penetration and the defeated classmate's shoulders slumped.

"Stop!" the master ordered, before calling the five bested pupils before Chen, where they bowed.

His look grew stern when addressing the defeated classmates. "You are all dead because you were not ready for combat!" He then pointed to the two last defeated. "You two are dead because you did not follow orders! I said, 'keep fighting,' not wait for the floor to clear. You were caught unprepared. Be thankful these are only practice swords, or the rest of your class would have to clean up the mess."

The levity of the master's last comment broke the tension of the admonishment and the class erupted in laughter. He then looked around at his twenty other charges sitting cross-legged around the walls.

"Line up!" he directed, standing regally at the head of the room with arms crossed.

The class scrambled into position, forming three lines, seated with backs straight, legs folded beneath them and hands resting on their thighs. Chen knelt in the first line, to the master's immediate left. With an extended hand, he called Chen to his feet and beside him. The two then faced each other and bowed.

"You fought well today," the master commended, "and have shown yourself worthy to wear the black sash of a full member of the Zorian Sword Academy."

Another of the black sashed instructors joined them at the front of the class. In his hands, he held a black sash and a brand-new sword.

Reaching down, the master untied the soiled white sash around Chen's waist and replaced it with the new black one. As tradition dictated, the master was always afforded the honor of tying the first knot, indicating his recognition of Chen's qualification to wear the rank.

Chen silently watched his master take the sword from the other instructor's hands.

"You will always need your practice sword for the training hall," the master said, ceremoniously handing him the sword with both hands, "but for your time out in the world, let this blade be your guardian."

Chen accepted the weapon with a broad grin. The beautiful instrument of death seemed to shimmer in its hard, black lacquered sheath. The distinctive, traditional maroon leather of the order wrapped the handle. Its design appeared identical to his practice sword, but this blade was very real.

"Thank you, Master Kuru," Chen said finally. "It is a dream come true to be inducted into such a time-honored society. I will always strive to uphold the dignity and reputation of the Order."

Kuru smiled proudly, then both silently bowed to each other before he called the class to its feet. With a closing oral salutation and bow, he dismissed the assembly.

With the lesson over, all crowded around Chen to offer their congratulations at his promotion. Master Kuru stepped up behind the Order's newest, full member and gently put a hand on his shoulder.

"Si Arador," he said softly. "When you're through here, I would like a word."

Chen nodded that he understood, and then returned to gracefully accept his comrades' felicitations. Once the hall had cleared, he made his way to the master's private chambers and knocked.

Kuru's spartan sanctuary contained only a low desk and bed roll as the primary furnishings. Kuru sat at the table writing and he put the pen down and offered Chen a spot on the floor.

"In addition to your promotion, you recently celebrated your eighteenth birthday. You do *know* what that means?"

"Yes, master."

"You have lived and trained with the Order since the age of five," Kuru said reflectively. "Thirteen grands is a long time. Now that your period of servitude is over, what are your plans?"

Chen looked thoughtfully for a moment at his instructor and father figure. "Being raised in the Order didn't feel like servitude, Master, you've been more of a father to me than Stryder Aramos ever was. The Order shielded me from the unpleasantries coming with the dubious reputation of having Stryder Aramos as my father.

"Shielded, maybe," Master Kuru agreed quietly, "but be aware that when you leave here, you will be back under his shadow again.

"Make no mistake, Chen, we did not rescue you. House Aramos sold you to us because they feared your father—not only him, though, but they also feared you. Even at the tender age of five grands they sensed the warrior in you. Normally, that would have invited your murder, instead, they sold you into servitude because of their fear. It is best that you remember this fear of you still exists."

"I'm not interested in House Aramos. I'm not my father. I seek no vengeance toward them. Nor do I seek their countenance because I'm no prodigal. Other than what I've learned here at the Academy, I really don't know what I am."

"You are more than just your father's son," Master Kuru reminded, "you are also a brother and a nephew. House Aramos sent your siblings off to live with your aunts. I suggest you seek them out and reunite as a family. Do not let your father's bad blood make you shun the connection of your bloodline. The answers you seek about who and what you are may well lie with them."

"I see the wisdom in that, Master," Chen admitted, thoughtfully. "I will seek them out, but whether or not they consent to be a family, I wish to return here as an instructor, with your permission."

Kuru chuckled knowingly. "In many of the Annigan's martial disciplines it is tradition for those newly promoted to full status, as you have been, to go on a quest, testing their abilities out in the world. While that is not officially one of our traditions, we respect the ritual. It sounds like a fine quest. I look forward to your triumphant return, where you would be welcomed into my cadre of instructors."

Chen, pleased with his master's response, couldn't help but feel a bit of apprehension. It had been a long time since he had seen his siblings and he had no idea what to expect.

Wikk Roncel, known to the faithful as Wikk the First, Lord of the Free City of Tannimore, didn't especially like visiting the barge containing the dungeon of his Minister of Judgement, Mistress Ve-Qua. Her appearance, while always disturbing, with her large pale blue breasts bolted together and vaginal lips hooked lewdly open, always seemed worse when she resided in her element.

The tenth level Kinjuto Dominator, however, proved to be the best he had ever encountered at gaining information and confession through creative ways of causing pain and agony. Torment, both physical and mental, increased the torture mage's prowess. Lately, ever since he abolished the death penalty and turned over all of the condemned to her, she had grown very busy and *extremely* powerful.

Descending the stairs into her triple deck barge, he couldn't help but note the anxious look on his Piety Watch bodyguard's face when he heard the first anguished cries. His eyes darted about nervously, catching the distinct odor of blood and fear permeating the air. The bodyguard's trepidation only grew when they passed between the scores of naked humans attached to a plethora of agony inducing devices dutifully attended to by the mistress' trainees.

Wikk made it a point to have all Piety Watch visit the labyrinth of pain to fully impress upon their minds the penalty for a breach of fidelity.

They finally found Mistress Ve-Qua in her private chamber on the first floor, standing in front of a very dead Wakil looking disappointed. She had literally nailed the Valdurian spy to a board through his shoulders and knees. Small weights attached to thin strips of his sliced flesh had slowly peeled the skin downward, when finally succumbing to gravity, and flayed all the flesh off the front of his body. The young corpse's face remained frozen in an eternal and silent scream.

"What did you find out?" Wikk asked abruptly, not wanting to spend any more time there than necessary.

"Well, hello Dearies," Ve-Quah said with a seductive smile. "I found out this worthless slab of meat had a lower tolerance to pain than I initially thought. I didn't even get a chance to start on his back. Still, his pain was delicious, I managed to cum at least a half a dozen times. So, at least that's something."

Wikk cleared his throat. "I meant something useful."

The naked Bailian laughed and the bodyguard morbidly stared at her connected breasts bouncing on her chest.

"Dearie, my orgasms are always useful." Her demeanor turned serious. "He was a deep cover Valdurian agent."

"Yes, yes," Wikk said impatiently, "The plan, did he divulge the plan?!"

"Doubtful," she said, indicating Wakil's Etheria communication tablet on a nearby table. "The psionic battery was weak. If the message made it out, it didn't get far."

The answer seemed to somewhat reassure the Pa-Waga leader, but he still remained skeptical. "We can't take any chances. I think we're going to have to arrange for some decoys just in case he got through."

The Kinjuto mistress' mood brightened once again. "Whatever you say, Dearie. Now, if that's all, I'm late for an impaling."

The Kan fog gradually rose over the High Holy City of Zor. In keeping with their daily ritual since moving in together, Mukavar and Rafel met at the Zorian Baths where they decompressed from their respective workdays. They would then stop at one of their favorite food vendors, pick up their evening meal, and then leisurely walk home.

They procured their residence, a spacious apartment in the upper end of the Northern Docks, for a modest price. Rafel insisted on getting it when they decided to cohabitate, even though his old place seemed more than big enough for the two of them. There were just too many memories of Hoyt trapped like an errant ghost within those walls.

Even though the two talked about the events and people they encountered, both of these Society of Whispers professionals reserved any sensitive conversations for when they were safely away from potential eavesdroppers. Rafel realized there were still things he couldn't speak of, specifically dealing with House Calden's secrets. However, Muuky's unwillingness to reveal anything about his personal past, especially former relationships, ate at him.

Rafel knew Muuky had run away from home and joined the navy to escape an abusive father. He also knew of his friendship, founded in the service, with the son of House Calden's patriarch, but not much more.

"So, how's it going with that mysterious trader?" Rafel asked, before taking a bite of his still steaming cottage pie.

Mukavar swallowed and pondered for a moment.

"Even more mysterious now," he said finally. "You know this guy, his name is Konesai, was so cautious, the only way I stumbled on him was by accident. I've only been following him for the past few clusters, but when I checked his trading logs, he's been at it every cycle for the last two grands. He sells off a block of commodities, sometimes at a loss, just enough to buy ten shares of Etheria notes. He then takes actual possession of the notes, puts them in an envelope and delivers them to the next outgoing shuttle to Tannimore. Every cycle, *every one*, except today. Somethings going on, I can feel it."

"It doesn't sound like he's broken any laws," Rafel said, reaching for his drink.

"Technically, no," Mukavar agreed. "It's just suspicious as all get out."

"Do you remember, eleven grands ago, when Stryder Aramos snatched the whole damn Zerian Forest and ransomed it off to the highest bidder?" Rafel asked, before taking a sip.

Mukavar chuckled. "Yeah, I was part of the Calden recovery flotilla when all that Ukko Wood poured out of the Innaca Deep."

"Did you know getting the wood back was because of the Konrad woman and her team, not the paying of the ransom?"

Mukavar set his fork down and stared intently at his lover.

"I did not!"

"Yes, there was a bit of divine intervention—a fire—and ten thousand, one hundred secor Etheria notes were presumably lost."

"Lost, how? Commodity notes are made of Ukko. It takes magical fire to burn Ukko *and* it floats."

23

"The Ukko may float," Rafel replied, "but the crates they're in don't. Rumor has it they're somewhere on the bottom of Ocean Deep."

Mukavar resumed picking at his food. "That must make you crazy, not knowing for sure."

"Sometimes," Rafel said with a sly grin. "And sometimes secrets can be... sexy."

"Really?" Mukavar's voice lowered its register.

He then gazed at Rafel's face, which had softened into a sensuous glow. Without a word Rafel got up from the table and disappeared into the bedroom. He returned a brief moment later, head bowed, reverently holding a thick leather belt out in front of him and naked from the waist down.

Mukavar smiled lecherously at the spymaster's small, but rampant erection in stark contrast to his meek, submissive demeanor. Rafel approached in a slow, seductive amble, then went down on his knees in front of Mukavar's much larger frame. Keeping the belt extended to him, he provocatively looked up at his dominant lover.

"Daddy, I've got a secret. I've been very naughty today."

Taleeka always held fond memories of the Zorian Forum. It had been here, eight grands ago, she and her parents received their bespoke name, bestowed upon them by Joc' Valdur, along with the prestigious title, 'Hero of the Realm.' She traversed the busy, oversized corridors on the congested route to the head Valdurian's office, taking in the heady sights and sounds of the most diverse meeting place in the Goyan Islands.

Making her way around two female EEtah's of House
Nur conferring with an Otick shaman in mid hallway, she
smiled, glad they designed the Forum, and indeed the entire
city, to accommodate sentients of all shapes and sizes.

She turned left at the next large intersection and arrived
at Joc' Valdur's new office. The former Valdurian
Ambassador to Zor became the family patriarch last grand.
Instead of returning to rule at the family's ancestral palace
in Dryden, he opted to govern from Zor, the real seat of
power. In his absence, he assigned a prime minister to attend
to the everyday running of the family business. However,
this meant he now required a larger office and staff. Taleeka
just had to get used to the new location.

She paused outside the formal looking door. When she
reached for the handle, it flew open and a young female
Picean, carrying a stack of papers, rushed past her with a
squeaky apology cast over her shoulder. An amused grin
crossed her face and she stepped into the busy outer office.

Two nondescript human females sat at desks straddling
the two corners on the right. One woman stared intently at a
large Larimar screen on her desk, while tapping away at the
edges with her forefinger. The other appeared busy, going
through a sizeable stack of papers and occasionally handing
one to another female Picean, who stood dutifully waiting.

The one studying the Etheria screen looked up at Taleeka
when she entered and smiled.

"Ah, Mz. Konrad, they're waiting for you."

Taleeka kept the grin but cocked her head. "They?"

"You can go right in," she said pleasantly, before
returning to her work.

Taleeka gave a quick knock, before opening the door and
entering the spacious office of Joc' Valdur. She expected a
few people to be present, but halted in her tracks when she
saw who was in attendance.

Joc' sat behind his wide ornate desk in the center of the
rear wall. Pierce Calden sat on a small sofa on the left, with

his number one mechanic, Mukavar, standing beside him. Most surprising turned out to be the white Tiikeri in blue silk robes seated in a chair off to the right.

"Ah, Mz. Konrad," Joc' said amiably. "Do come in and close the door."

Taleeka did as requested, stepping into the room with a questioning expression while everyone stood.

"I believe you know Ambassador Calden and Senior Lieutenant Mukavar," Joc' said formally.

Taleeka grinned and nodded. "Si. Ambassador, Muuky."

"This is Jo-Rakk, former ambassador to Immor-Onn."

"I've heard of you from my mom," Taleeka said, stepping up to the much larger humanoid tiger and offering her hand.

"I had the pleasure of meeting your mother on several occasions," the Tiikeri's voice resonated throughout the room. "A most formidable sentient. With quite the colorful vocabulary as I recall."

This caused Taleeka to chuckle. "Yeah, my mom elevated the use of the word 'fuck' to an artform."

This statement caused the three human males to grin knowingly and nod in agreement.

"Please forgive my surprise and my rather blunt questions, but I didn't think there were any Tiikeri left?"

A sad smile played at the man-tiger's mouth. "It's true, the Do-Tarr decimated the Tiikeri Empire. We were all but wiped out. The five hundred of us who survived retreated to the only safe place in the Annigan, The Unaligned City of Shun-Dra. It was there we remade ourselves. We no longer lust for the glory of empire, but rather seek to be a group watching from the shadows and effecting change as needed."

"That sounds slightly ominous," Taleeka said suspiciously.

"We call ourselves The Order of Kaplan," Jo-Rakk explained, "and the only thing ominous about us is our underlying mission statement. We seek the utter eradication of the group ultimately responsible for our empire's demise, the dangerous cult of Pa-Waga."

"Well, lucky for you they're now all in one place, Tannimore," Taleeka said glibly. "They should be fairly easy to finish off."

"We abandoned such crude measures along with the Singa shock troops," Jo-Rakk responded good-naturedly. "We prefer to work behind the scenes, which coincidentally is why I'm here."

"Yes," Joc' interjected. "The Order of Kaplan stumbled upon a most disturbing revelation."

Taleeka glanced over at the white Tiikeri. "And that would be?"

"Two cycles ago one of our listening stations in Penaber intercepted a weak message coming out of Tannimore," Jo-Rakk began.

"Wait, did you say, 'listening stations?'" Taleeka asked in astonishment.

"The message was bound for Zor," the Tiikeri continued, ignoring the question. "It seems they are preparing to cash in a very large amount of Etheria notes at the Imperial Bank in Immor-Onn within the next few clusters."

"Okay?" Taleeka said warily.

"A *very* large amount," Joc' reinforced. "So large it could potentially crash the Bailian economy."

"I've been keeping an eye on this trader by the name of Konesai," Mukavar said, sitting forward. "Over the last two grands, he's slowly funneled small amounts of Etheria notes out to Tannimore."

"That, however, wouldn't be enough to cause any noticeable effect on the Bailian economy," Pierce Calden added, finally joining the conversation. "We think the large amount in question is the ransom Etheria notes paid to Stryder Aramos for the return of the Zerian Forest.

"Ten thousand notes would do a real number on not just the Bailian's but the entire Imperial Banking system. All the branches across the Annigan would be forced to come to the Immor-Onn branch's aid."

"Rafel and I were just discussing this last Kan," Mukavar chimed in excitedly. "Those notes were in hundred secor denominations and up. They were thought to be lost until... well... *this morning*."

"Woah, hold on," Taleeka said, raising a hand. "I thought the Pa-Waga nut jobs were all about greed, making money, things like that. Collapsing an economy hardly seems in line with their values."

"I don't believe that's what they're trying to do," Joc' replied somberly.

"What then?"

"When a commodity note is presented to the Imperial Bank for redemption," Pierce explained, "the entity backing it is responsible for honoring the amount in gold, or, if the bearer wishes, the equivalent amount of the commodity.

"For the Bailians, gold would be no problem. However, they are also duty bound to be able to hand over the equivalent amount of Etheria. *Just one problem*, there isn't that much Etheria on hand, so it acts as an IOU for future Etheria production. That moves our group of religious fanatics to the front of the line."

"It would choke off the supply of Etheria for the entire Annigan for grands," Joc' followed up.

"So, where do I fit in?" Taleeka asked, eyeing the parties involved.

"Well," Joc' said coyly. "Technically the notes are ill-gotten gains. And your skills at, oh what shall we call it, procuring hard to get items is... well known."

Taleeka gave a wicked grin. "So, you want me to steal them?"

"More like, steal them back," Joc' corrected.

"Yes," Pierce quickly added. "Just name your cut."

Taleeka kept the grin and shook her head. "I don't collect money anymore. I've got plenty. I collect favors. And after this is over, all of you are going to owe me, *big time.*"

"So, exactly why did patrol say they wanted us to get involved?" Talib asked when the hackney pulled off the main thoroughfare and into the Seven Sisters Slums. "I mean it's not like they don't pull a half dozen bodies out of the Sisters every morning."

Tantei glanced away from the passing urban blight to her young partner. "He's supposedly some kind of street boss. Patrol's worried this might be the start of a turf war or power grab. They just want us to look around and weigh in."

"You know it's crazy," Talib said, shaking his head watching the slums roll past his window. "The city's prohibition of organized crime didn't get rid of organized crime. All it did was fracture it into smaller units that are more unstable and prone to violence against each other."

"Yeah, well, they may be smaller and more volatile," Tantei replied reluctantly, "but they're easier to deal with, even though you may have to intervene more often. Remember how tough it was uprooting Banavor once he got his organization established. I'll take dealing with punks any day of the cluster. They're a lot easier to figure out."

"They aren't the brightest of the lot," Talib conceded.

Tantei chuckled. "Lucky for us, most of them couldn't find their dicks if they were holding them to take a piss."

The image made Talib smile and the rest of the short ride went in silence until they saw the red quarantine rope ahead. They cordoned an area off around a Vurr Cleric's refuse cart parked at the end of the street. As usual, a small crowd of curious onlookers gathered, as well as two patrol guards.

"Hey Tay, have you noticed the boss has been in a much better mood lately?" Tantei asked, exiting the hackney.

"As a matter of fact, yes," Talib said, nodding in agreement, "for about a cluster or so. He still drinks like a fish though."

"Come to think of it, I don't ever think I've seen him sober," Tantei said, nodding to the guard and lifting the rope so they could pass under.

The two partners could not have been more different in appearance. Talib's short and heavy-set body came with a head full of curly black hair. Tantei had a slim, athletic frame with pretty features and a bald head.

Once inside the crime perimeter, all banter ceased and both detectives closely surveyed the area. The Vurr cart at the center of the crime scene, was one of the ones left out on the streets for people to place their trash in during the Kan. Practically every avenue in Zor had one.

The body rested in the road, beside the cart's open back end. He lay on his back, staring upward with a wide-eyed, surprised look and his head had been cleaved almost in two. A gruesome looking crimson trail led down the street from his prone position.

"His name is Sef de Sedam," The patrol guard said. "He ran this street."

"Any witnesses?" Talib asked hopefully.

The patrol guard chuckled. "Are you kidding? This *is* the Sisters. No one saw nothing."

Talib sighed. "Yeah, but I had to ask."

"So, who runs the street now?" Tantei asked, examining the trail of dried blood.

"Unknown," the patrolman replied sounding quite bored.

"Yeah, well, it sure looks like somebody took over," Tantei said, lifting the rope and following the crimson path.

The broad swath of blood ended twenty yards down the street, in front of a wide set of open doors. She could hear activity inside when she stepped up to the threshold.

The room easily measured a hundred feet square and was devoid of any furnishings. Four men, who looked like the typical inhabitance of the Sisters, labored cleaning the place, under the direction of a much better dressed Drugo.

"Well, if this isn't an industrious group, if ever I saw one," she said cheerfully, stepping into the room.

Work suddenly halted and all turned to face her. The workers' vacuous looks told her they obviously didn't understand the greeting. All eyes followed her, heading for the one who appeared to be in charge. Drugo eyed her suspiciously and then fixed his gaze on the Ukko placard, emblazoned with the winged sword and shield of the Zorian Guards, hanging by a lanyard around her neck.

"We're busy," Drugo said impatiently, "Who are you and what do you want?"

"Investigator Tantei, Zorian Guards," she said, still maintaining her friendly deportment. "And you are?"

"Busy," he answered hostilely.

Tantei stopped just in front of him, gave a sarcastic chuckle and shook her head.

"Just so you know," she began, her expression turning serious. "Not only will that shitty attitude not get you anywhere, you're already well on your way to pissing me off! And that's a shame, because so far, the morning has been going pretty well. Now, you can answer my questions, or I'll have your skinny little ass slapped in the stocks until you feel chattier. So, if you're through fucking around, let's start with your name!"

He stared obstinately at her penetrating gaze before glancing away.

"Drugo," he said begrudgingly.

The investigator's chipper attitude immediately returned. "There we go! That wasn't so bad, was it? So, Si. Drugo, you've got a dead body just down the street and a trail of blood that leads to these doors. You wouldn't happen to know anything about that, would you?"

"No, it was there when we arrived."

"I see, and you didn't think anything was strange about that?"

"You obviously don't live around here, do you?"

Tantei exhaled loudly. "See, there you go again with the smartass attitude."

Drugo scowled in defeat. "No, I didn't think it was strange."

"Did you know him?"

"No."

"Hmm," Tantei said, looking around at the group's progress. "See, that, in itself is odd, because he was the street boss and nothing happens on this street without his okay."

Drugo gave a defiant shrug. "So?"

"So, who did you clear this little project with?"

"Nobody, some lady showed up and paid me to get some locals together and clean this place up."

"You were paid?"

"Yeah, two gold pieces for me to supervise and a gold piece per worker."

"That's *pretty* generous," Tantei said, nodding her head appreciatively. "Any idea who she was?"

"Never saw her before."

Tantei's eyes narrowed. "So, this woman you've never seen before, just walked up to you and gave you money to clean this place."

"That's right."

"Did she give her name?"

"No."

"What did she look like?"

"Young, pretty, shoulder length brown hair."

"Did she say why she wanted this place cleaned up?"

"No."

Tantei knew he wasn't telling her everything, but short of bringing him in and working him over, she knew this would be all the cagey young man dared reveal.

"Okay," she said reluctantly. "Thank you for your time."

She stepped back out onto the street and found Talib kneeling over a large red spot at the blood trail's end, dislodging something stuck between the cobblestones with his pocketknife.

"What have you got?" she asked, kneeling beside him.

Talib held up his knife, revealing a small piece of grey fleshy material embedded on the tip.

"Unless I'm mistaken," he said, carefully examining it. "This is a chunk of brain matter. This is where our street boss was killed, for sure."

It would be easy to overlook Konesai de Lomen. An unassuming little man, slightly pudgy with light brown skin and cleanshaven features, fit in just about everywhere. A conservative dresser, he always managed to blend into the chaos that constituted the trading floor of the Zorian Commodities Exchange.

Given his mild deportment, upon first meeting, most thought him unsuited for the fast-paced aggressive career of a floor trader. However, in the din of those shouting around him, he always managed to calmly buy and sell at the proper moment, confounding even the most veteran of traders.

Unbeknownst to all, Konesai had a secret to his success, a singular advantage which, if found out, could cost him dearly. He, as well as his wife, two sons and several others, still served Pa-Waga. A potentially dangerous choice since the expulsion and dispersion of the faithful to Tannimore.

Lord Banavor chose him before ascending into the heavens, carried by great winged beings to dwell with Saint Stryder the Proffitt. He tasked him to be the eyes and ears of the faith in the land of the idolaters. Even though he longed to be with his kind, he knew his mission to be important and inwardly beamed with pride, having finally completed his most recent assignment.

In fact, he would be personally thanked and mentioned this evening, in the once-a-cluster inspirational message from Lord Wikk the First, Keeper of the Faith. Perhaps now, with his mission complete, he and his family would be called home. He knew Tannimore thrived as a city of unbridled potential without the restrictive laws and regulations standing in the way of progress and prosperity. Yes, perhaps *this* cluster's message would be the one that welcomed him back into the bosom of the Lord.

Trading had just ended for the cycle, punctuated by the Grand Turine in the Zorian harbor ringing five bells. Konesai counted his buy and sell tickets, making sure to note each in his trading log.

He could hardly contain his excitement when he turned in his paperwork and headed out the front doors along with the crowd of his associates. He wanted to get home quickly, the message would be broadcast at exactly seven bells and his fellow followers would all be in attendance.

During the hackney bus ride, he actually found himself fidgeting nervously, thinking about the recognition to his family and peers for a job well done. He almost didn't feel worthy. The task had been so simple, each cycle he bought ten Etheria notes and sent them to Tannimore.

He didn't know why and he didn't have to. The Lord worked in mysterious ways and he felt happy to be a small part of whatever plans happened to be afoot.

When he arrived at his spacious three-bedroom apartment in the Tuath Plat, several of his guests had already arrived. His wife, Fawna, met him warmly at the door and he greeted everyone while he put away his coat and made his way over to the table of food she had prepared.

He really cherished this once a cluster gathering of the faithful. Small house churches, like his, were now the backbone of the believers in Pa-Waga and his message of prosperity and plenty.

"Is Lord Wikk really going to mention you, daddy?" his son, Rokka, asked excitedly.

. "So, I've been told," Konesai said, smiling at the gangly fourteen-grand-old before popping a meatball into his mouth.

A deci before the broadcast, the small congregation of twelve men and women put away the food, removed their clothing and stood in a circle around their host.

"May Pa-Waga bless this gathering," Konesai said emphatically, his face raised to the ceiling.

He then picked up a small ceremonial dagger and slowly lanced his forefinger. When the blood pooled at the end of the digit, he marked an X and an I on his forehead. Then, stepping up to his wife, he made the same marks on her.

"May the prosperity of the Lord be upon you," he said reverently.

"And you," she replied.

His sons were next to receive the same markings, with call and response. Making his way around the circle, all received the mark and blessing. Fawna then brought out the Larimar screen and set it upright on a table so all could see.

At precisely seven bells from the Turine, the screen flickered with blue sparkles and the face of Wikk the First came into view. He appeared the same as always, with his penetrating blue eyes and intense expression.

"Greetings brethren," he began, "May the prosperity of the Lord be upon all of you…"

The front door crashed open, raucously interrupting the benedictional greeting. Twelve surprised and frightened faces watched the Zorian Guard's feared Red Division rush into the room with crossbows leveled. Several of the women cried out while the men peered about with panicked expressions. The elite city guards, with a reputation for ruthlessness, silently fanned out in the room, while several of the congregation modestly attempted to cover themselves. None bothered to appear outraged at the intrusion, all knew what it meant.

Once all the city guards were in position, the lone figure of Mukavar casually stepped out of the foggy street and into the room. He glanced around at the recorded message still playing without an audience and the bloody markings on their foreheads. Forlornly sighing, he rubbed his temple.

"You realize this is an illegal gathering," Mukavar said calmly and unnervingly.

No one spoke, but their terrorized faces betrayed the trepidation of being caught practicing a now forbidden religion.

"The High Council was merciful in allowing your kind to leave the city," the Calden mechanic said icily. "For some reason, you all have decided to stay. Just so you know, it was you, Konesai, who betrayed your group's existence. If you hadn't been suspiciously buying up those Etheria notes and sending them to Tannimore, we would have probably never found you."

Mukavar then strolled around the room casually examining the naked bodies. "And I would hate to think that your parts in your leaders' plan were all in vain. We know what's going on."

"I… I don't even know what's going on," Konesai said, his voice cracking. "They didn't tell me about any plan. I just did as I was ordered."

Mukavar looked thoughtfully downward while drawing his pistol. "Pity."

He then glanced over at one of the members of Red Division. "Make sure this is on the Vurr Cleric's route tomorrow morning."

The guard nodded. The ones responsible for disposing of the city's dead and waste would be notified. He then surveyed the group once more with a truly forlorn expression.

"You all seemed like genuinely nice people," he said cocking the weapon. "Please believe me when I tell you, I take no pleasure in this."

Chen found it amusing that procuring passage to the nearby Zer-Tal Twins Island group took twice as long as the voyage itself. From the starboard side railing of the empty transport ship, he watched the two large islands slowly pass. The dual isles were connected by the Umbilical Pass which never measured more than a few feet deep. You could literally walk from the big island of Zer-Tal to the smaller, wilder, Tal Island five miles to the west.

The ship's destination had been the capital city of Oramor, on Zer-Tal's southern shore. There, they were to pick up a load of salt and return it to the thriving culinary scene blossoming in Zor. The salt lakes of Zer-Tal happened to be the only location in the Annigan producing this rare and expensive commodity.

The salt barons overseeing salt harvesting and distribution were all handpicked by the Aramos patriarch and married off to Chen's aunts to ensure loyalty and honesty to the great human house. The same place where they had sent his siblings upon his mother's death.

Closing his eyes, he enjoyed the wind in his hair and the sea spray on his face. He chose a more modest set of robes to travel in, rather than the flashy blue academy garment. Zorian Swordsmen were often the target of random dualists trying to make a name for themselves. He decided early on, discretion and anonymity almost always were rewarded with uneventful travels. Still, it remained difficult disguising his red hilted sword, which immediately gave him away to anyone who knew what to look for.

The coastline of manicured fruit trees gave way to a small inlet and his destination, the busy port of Oramor. Walled to the sea, Oramor contained a heavy presence of Forsvara Guards. These Aramos soldiers not only protected against bandits attempting to steal the salt, but also marauding Tal-Hatesh, primitive, barbarian lizard people crossing the pass from Tal Island. The Tal-Hatesh attacked virtually anything that wasn't them and stole anything not nailed down.

The ship moored in the middle of the six industrial sized docks and, because he traveled light, Chen easily disembarked and moved along the wharf surrounded by busy dock workers loading wagons full of salt. Finding a line of wagons waiting to unload, he walked their length asking if anyone would be heading back to the Cypris Plantation.

He had made several inquiries with no results, when an old driver, hunched over the reins, spit on the ground and eyed him up and down.

"Old Man Cypris don't take to strangers," he said suspiciously. "Why in the name of the gods do you want to go *there*?"

"It's my aunt and uncle's plantation," Chen said jovially. "So, you see, I'm really not a stranger."

The old man spit again and scoffed loudly. "I wouldn't be too quick to admit that. Cypris Gatza's as mean as a snake. Not many people seek him out. Lots of rumors though. They say he…"

"I'll take you," a young man's voice interrupted. "Just let me unload and I'm headed directly back. Lord Cypris demands punctuality."

Chen looked over at the wagon next in line. A thin, bald indenture sat on the buckboard. Chen nodded at the old gossip who stared indifferently back at him.

"Many thanks," he said to the young man, tossing his travel bag onto the seat and climbing up.

He had to admit, the old man's warnings, in addition to the servant's comment about punctuality, gave him cause for concern. No matter, he had cast his lot, more than prepared to see it through.

"Who again is this person we are searching for?" Noorim asked, still staring out from the hackney's rear seat.

"His name is Larzz," Taleeka said, sitting beside her. "He's a half EEtah that my family's used in the past. We may need some muscle on this one."

"Granted, I've only been amongst you for a short time," the Amarenian said thoughtfully, "but I have never encountered nor even heard of such a racial combination."

"That's because it's bloody rare," Gidaria said over her shoulder from the driver's seat. "If the mother somehow lives through getting pregnant, she probably won't make it through the birth."

Noorim's pale face scrunched in revulsion. "What woman would put herself through that?"

"Rape and prostitution mostly," Taleeka replied.

"Can they not end the pregnancy?"

"If they're smart they will."

"Okay Tally, we're here," Gidaria announced.

She stopped the hackney in front of a wrought iron fence surrounding a playground and a dormitory style, two-story building. A placard reading, 'ARVA HOUSE," posted next to the wide single gate caught all their attention.

A solitary bell rang three times from inside the compound just before the front doors flew open and twenty human children of various ages rushed out and onto the playground, squealing in delight. A seven-foot-tall human/EEtah hybrid lumbered out trailing behind the raucous pack of youngsters.

In comparison with the children, the figure appeared immense. He had mostly unkempt human features with quickly shifting eyes and a bald head. Taleeka could make out his permanent shadow of facial hair framing a totally overwhelmed expression. He wore a thin, white, tank top tee-shirt, stretched tightly over an enormous pot belly and thick bluish white skin with random patches of hair poking out of the garment's edges.

Noorim glanced over at Taleeka with an amused expression. "An orphanage, seriously?"

"He drifts from job to job depending on what it pays," Taleeka said, watching him comically attempting to wrangle the rambunctious group of children. "My mom always paid more so he would drop whatever he was doing."

"He certainly does not look like much," Noorim said skeptically.

Taleeka gave a wry chuckle. "Yeah, but you sure don't want him to get his hands on you."

"He does appear quite strong," Noorim said, noting his broad chest and thickly muscled arms.

"Okay, we'll be back," Taleeka announced, opening the door.

"No rush," Gidaria said, grabbing the end of Brzo's leash. "I gotta take Brzo for his Ka-ka walk."

At the mention of the phrase, the lizard sat up excitedly and began a series of short enthusiastic hisses.

When Taleeka and Noorim passed through the gate, Larzz had just stopped a boy of fourteen from picking on a much smaller twelve-grand-old. The half EEtah held the petrified boy aloft by the back of his collar so he came up to eye level.

"Did that sentient give you permission to lay your grimy little hands on him?" Larzz asked through bared teeth.

The wide-eyed youth vigorously shook his head.

"You're not going to do it again, are you?"

Once again, the boy gave a fearful head shake.

Larzz's sneer suddenly turned into a smile and he set the boy down. "Good, now go play nice."

The rebuked young man darted off past Noorim and Taleeka, almost colliding with them.

They watched him run past, then Taleeka turned her attention to the hulking babysitter.

"Interesting career choice," she said with a broad grin.

"Eh, one of the older girls got raped a few clusters ago and they decided they needed security," he said, surveying the children running around noisily playing. "So, Tally, long time no see."

"Yeah, it's been a while."

"Four grands ago," he said after a brief reflection. "That load of stolen Valdurian weapons, with you and your folks, over on Moreen Island."

Taleeka grinned at the memory. "Yeah, as I recall, after that gig was over you spent the whole next cycle drinking with the locals."

"They were just showing their gratitude for killing that bandit chief. Boy, she was *ruthless* and not much older than you at the time."

Taleeka scoffed and rolled her eyes." As I remember, it took all of us to haul your drunk ass back to the *Haraka.*"

"Both enjoyed a laugh, then Larzz stared wistfully into space. "Good times. So, who's your pasty friend?"

Noorim's eyes narrowed and Taleeka smiled at his description.

"This is Noorim Sheed," Taleeka replied. "She's *my* security."

Larzz skeptically eyed the thin young woman. "If you say so."

"Don't be fooled, she's got skills."

"Oh yeah?" he said dubiously, before lunging at the Amarenian with both arms extended.

Noorim easily sidestepped the crude attack and allowed the much larger opponent to rush past her. Once behind him, she quickly kicked to the back of his knee. The combination of his momentum, as well as the kick, completely broke his balance. Noorim gave a simple shove to his back sending the half EEtah face first onto the ground.

He slowly regained his feet to the sound of the children's boisterous laughter.

"Yep, she's got skills," Larzz said good naturedly, dusting himself off. "Well, I'm willing to bet you didn't look me up just to reminisce?"

"You would be correct," Taleeka concurred. "I've got a job that just may call for your special talents."

"What's it pay?"

Reaching into a side pocket on her pack she pulled out a hundred secor gold note and handed it to him.

"In advance, as usual."

Larzz eyed the payment approvingly. "What's the job?"

"I'll let you know once we're in the air. Just be ready to go on a centi's notice."

Larzz grinned widely and held the note up. "For this kind of money, I'm yours ten-fifty."

Tor-Ga felt the cold breeze ruffle the orange fur on his face when a gust raced through the streets of Penaber. As station chief for the Order of Kaplan, his main duty mostly consisted of running the secret listening station in the remote northern city. He found it a mostly boring job, which suited the tired former military officer just fine.

He had led a small detachment of Singas on a mission in the Arborea Forest when the Do-Tarr over ran their cities and killed everyone within. This lucky circumstance had saved him, but not his family. He grew tired of fighting and welcomed the new philosophy of the remaining Tiikeri when they reformed as The Order of Kaplan.

That changed five cycles ago, when a lone Ash-Ta delivered a scented message for him. He had followed the orders, what else could he do? However, the seasoned veteran could feel trouble just around the corner. Thankfully, his role in whatever loomed ahead seemed small and almost over. He couldn't wait to get back to his warm comfortable office and his dull yet fulfilling job.

With the moon setting a short while ago, the central square of the city seemed almost vacant. He watched several Vidra laughing and joking around as they crossed the square and disappeared down one of the five wide boulevards intersecting at this central point in the city.

The happy-go-lucky humanoid otters were probably headed out for a night of revelry. The friendly, playful sentients were fun loving and, for the most part, peaceful in an urban setting such as this. However, in their rural homes among the thousands of lakes dotting the Narrow Lands, they had a more dangerous reputation. Over the grands, Vidra had played many a sentient to death, inadvertently drowning their victims in the cold lake waters to which the otter-men were impervious.

Once the happy chattering of the Vidra faded away, he surveyed the lights coming from the windows of the shops open late. The large three-story building housing city hall loomed quietly, with its business cycle done until the next moonrise. Off to the side of the massive structure sat the offices of the Calden Naval Bureau, the only area showing any signs of life as they always remained open.

He focused on the tall purple pillar dominating the center of the square. The Azurite Etheria column stood as a gateway to the Middle Realms. They found the magical edifice easier to navigate and infinitely safer than the large permanent Flavian Portal to the north in the Innaca Deep.

The Turine rang six bells in the Penaber harbor and Tor-Ga gave out a frustrated sigh. They were late and his stomach grumbled, eager for the evening meal. The irritating thought had no sooner tramped across his consciousness when a ring of blue sparks encircled the pillar's base. The azure shower ran up the monolith's sides until the light show covered its entire surface. Just above the base, a swirling vortex slowly formed and Tor-Ga watched four Mawls step out of the cyclone and onto the cobblestone street.

A Yagur in robes stepped out first. The humanoid jaguar peered curiously out from below a cowl pulled low over his head. A brown sterned faced mongrel came through next, followed by an orange Tiikeri. A white Tiikeri in blue silk robes, carrying an air of authority, exited last.

"I'm Tor-Ga, station chief for Penaber," he greeted warmly. "Welcome to our frozen part of the Annigan."

The white Tiikeri nodded but offered no introductions, nor did he offer his hand.

"It was your team which intercepted the message out of Tannimore?" the white Tiikeri finally asked officially.

"Uh, yes, sir," Tor-Ga replied nervously.

"You and your team did well," the Tiikeri praised in the same formal manner. "The humans are now indebted to us and suspect nothing."

"Thank you, sir," Tor-Ga said, unsure what the secretive mawl referred to.

"Did you secure our lodging?"

"Uh, yes, sir. The orders said something by, or on the water. I've rented a medium sized barge at the end of the far western docks."

"Very good," the Tiikeri said with a nod. "You have performed your duty well and will feature prominently in my report. You are now dismissed."

"Yes, sir, thank you, sir," Tor-Ga said, then turned to go.

"Oh, and Tor-Ga," the Tiikeri said with an even more serious tone.

The already rattled station chief peered nervously back over his shoulder.

"Yes, sir?"

"This meeting never happened."

Rafel knew better. In fact, he had made a promise to himself long ago not to be obsessive about his partner's daily comings and goings. It had ruined many a relationship in the past and he constantly fought the urge to snoop.

However, the spymaster in him would not be denied. There were things he just had to know, things his tight-lipped lover wasn't sharing. Perhaps it came from a deep-seated insecurity. He had pondered that topic on many occasions. The more likely explanation would be his base nature and the singular quality which made him an excellent espionage chief. No matter the reasoning, he had a rare bit of spare time this cycle and now found himself giving in to the temptation, tailing his newest love, Mukavar.

The trail wasn't difficult to pick up on. Mukavar currently worked on a case dealing with a mutinous Calden crew and a murdered captain. So, he started on the docks at pier twenty-three. Luckily, plenty of crates stacked about afforded him plenty of cover to take advantage of.

Sure enough, there he stood, interviewing the harbormaster in front of the besieged ship. Rafel noted the burn marks scorching around the broken windows to the bridge and concluded it must have been bad. Then again, any incident calling for a mechanic of Mukavar's status would have to be bad, indeed.

From there, Mukavar moved onto the ship itself, where he disappeared from Rafel's view. Suddenly, something else caught the spymaster's attention. A beautiful, bare chested young man dressed as a prostitute with sheer harem pants slit up the side and nothing underneath, slowly moved down the wharf, obviously searching for something or someone. He ignored the salacious calls from the dock workers, maintaining his watchful vigil. Rafel found himself transfixed by his youthful loveliness, with shoulder length dark hair, light brown skin and full sensuous lips. Rafel felt so enamored, he didn't notice Mukavar climbing out of the ships forward hatch onto the deck.

What he witnessed next paralyzed the seasoned, worldly master spy in shock. The moment Mukavar and the young man saw each other, they rushed over to each other.

They met at the base of the gangplank and hugged, obviously delighted to see one another. Rafel felt his stomach grow taut and his knees become unsteady when they kissed. The world around the two now became an opaque cloud and he watched them have a brief, intimate conversation before walking off together.

Summoning the will to move, the mortified head spy followed the two at a discrete distance. The short walk ended at a low-rent boarding house next to several taverns, known as a haven for prostitutes.

Rafel's head flooded with turbulent emotions. Chief of which; with their active sex life, what did he need a prostitute for? Or could it be love? They had never mentioned exclusivity in their relationship, but when they moved in together Rafel took it for granted. It would seem that his partner didn't.

The initial jolt of discovery passed. Soon another emotion rose within him, rage!

She knew the horse's name to be Silver and Barr-Ani considered the beast her favorite. The Bailian loved horses, choosing to spend most of her time outside of class volunteering at the stables just east of Zor. The High Holy City boasted the largest herd of equine, outside of her home in The Twilight Lands. Barr-Ani's family happened to be the leading horse brokers in the Annigan, with strong ties to the solitary horse breeders in the world, the On'Dara. That close relationship with the Horse Lords of the Taka-Vir made her family rich enough to send their daughter halfway around the world to go to school.

Enjoying the windy spring cycle, she sat mounted on the crest of a low rise, the rolling foothills of the Goyan Mountains stretching out before her. In the distance, she witnessed the smoke trailing upward from Mount Goya, caught by the breeze, and swept northward blending with the swiftly advancing clouds.

She squeezed her calves on Silver's sides, setting horse and rider moving through the waving grasslands. Barr-Ani loved this alone time away from the hustle of city and college life. As a sensitive, the ability to pick up on other's thoughts, intentions and moods eventually became overwhelming. She needed time away, and while she could sense the horse's mental state, the simple animal proved easy to deal with.

Humans and the other sentients of The Annigan bombarded her with their various temperaments and agendas causing her need for solitude.

This cycle, however, seemed slightly different than the others. A nagging uneasy sensation, so slight and almost undetectable, tugged at the recesses of her consciousness. Something felt amiss on a grand scale and it just now bubbled to the surface.

Stopping her mount on a hilltop, she scanned the horizon and then closed her eyes to take in any emanations no matter how slight. Now concentrating on it, the errant feeling seemed to come from the distant west.

She considered the Innaca Deep lay in that direction and could be more than capable of those types of psychic effluences. The giant Flavian Portal always gave off waves of psychic displacement, especially when in use.

No, that wasn't it. This felt much more subtle, for the time being. Barr-Ani gave a frustrated sigh. Her restorative ride had been ruined today and she decided to pack it in.

"Come on Silver, let's go home," she said, patting the horse's neck then turning her around.

The feeling followed her on the short ride back. Coming up on the stables, she saw Taleeka standing by the corral feeding a carrot to a spotted brown mare. Thirty-feet-away, just off the road, Gidaria stood beside her hackney, playing with Brzo. She couldn't help but think the excited lizard acted more like a dog, leaping and chasing after a stick the driver tossed about.

"Tally, what are you doing here?" she asked, riding up to her.

"I'm here to see you," Taleeka replied, feeding the horse the last of the carrot then giving it a pat.

"Oh?" she said questioningly, dismounting.

"I've got a thing going on over in Tannimore and I was wondering if you could tag along. I've got a feeling I'm going to need your special talents."

"I would think Noorim would be much better suited to help," she said, leading the horse into the stable.

"She's coming too," Taleeka said, falling in with her.

"Oh, okay, what's the job?"

Taleeka gave a coy side glance at her friend. "I'd rather tell everyone once we get in the air."

"Everyone?"

"Yeah," Taleeka said. "It's a party, you'll love it."

Barr-Ani knew that she didn't need to be a sensitive to realize Taleeka wasn't telling her everything. The Bailian considered revealing the strange sensations she had been experiencing, but ultimately decided to wait. Tannimore lay to the west and, while she didn't think the feeling originated there, she would be heading in the right general direction. Perhaps the sensation would become clearer the closer she got to the source.

The Cypris salt plantation appeared to Chen as an impressive, enormous compound, consisting of forty buildings set around a common plaza with a large manor house placed in the rear, overlooking Lake Cypris.

When they arrived, it became evident to Chen, by the fearful look on the driver's face and the commotion in the square, that things were amiss. A crowd had gathered and screaming could be heard above the commotion.

"Lord Cypris appears angry," the driver said, voice quivering.

"Is this a common occurrence?" Chen asked, grabbing his bag and hopping to the ground.

"Yes, Lord Cypris is an exacting man who does not tolerate disappointment."

"I see," Chen said, moving towards the uproar, making sure the tote bag covered the distinctive hilt of his sword. "Thanks for the ride."

The indentured driver merely nodded, then headed in the opposite direction of the disturbance.

The crowd consisted of mostly house and field slaves. A woman and two young men, who appeared to be twins, stood by the manor house. One of the men and the woman had horrified expressions on their faces, while the other appeared to be excited by the spectacle.

A man with shoulder length black hair, a large droopy moustache and an overall sinister appearance seemed to be the source of the ruckus. He hit and kicked a naked field slave with short brown hair and a scraggly beard. The unfortunate recipient of the beating knelt pleading, while the man administering the punishment continued cursing loudly.

Suddenly, a house slave came out the manor's front door, carrying two sheathed swords. He ran past the women, handed them to the man and cowered away.

"You dare speak of my wife in such a disrespectful, lurid manner!" he said indignantly. "In times past, I would have killed you on the spot! But now, now I give you a choice."

He tossed one of the swords in front of the kneeling slave.

"Pick it up!" he demanded with a scowl.

The terrified young man glanced down at the sheathed weapon in a panic, then back to his enraged master.

"I said pick it up, you insolent piece of shit!"

The servant now looked around with a pleadingly terrified expression.

The master dramatically drew his blade and sneered down at the slave. "You can fight me like a man or be cut down like a dog. The choice is yours!"

The slave openly wept and stared at the weapon laying before him. Suddenly a resigned look passed over the servant and, with trembling hands, he picked up the sword, drew it and came to his feet on wobbly legs.

"Now, strike me!" the master commanded.

The slave stood paralyzed in fear, crying and shaking his head. He held the weapon, a delicate rapier, clumsily in both badly trembling hands.

"I said strike me!"

A cry of frustration escaped from the slave's lips and he timidly poked at his master.

The man easily parried the clumsy halfhearted attack then promptly ran him through.

A shocked, painful look filled the slave's face, while the master's glowed with sadistic glee. When he pulled the blade out, the injured man looked at the open wound and the blood streaming down his nude body. Suddenly his eyes crossed and his head went back, he dropped his sword and followed it to the ground.

Chen scowled disapprovingly at the blatantly unfair fight. He considered this, however, none of his affair. It wasn't his place to chastise the lord of the manor.

"You two," the master said, pointing at two servants in the crowd. "Feed him to the swine and clean up this mess!"

Wiping his blade on the dead body, he sheathed it while walking over to the woman and the twins. The crowd quickly dispersed, so Chen chose this as an opportunity to approach.

"Hello," Chen greeted guardedly but friendly.

Everyone looked his way and Chen quickly made a mental assessment of the group. By his short terse movements and scowl, the master of the house still appeared angry. The woman's pleasant light brown features betrayed her distress at the recent event, as did one of the twins. Both of the young men were identical, with the meeker one sporting a short beard.

"Who the fuck are you," the man spat.

"Cypris!" the woman admonished brushing back a strand of her long brown hair. "Is that any way to talk to a stranger at our gate?"

She then turned her attention back to Chen and attempted a weak smile. "Hello."

"My name is Chen Arador," he said, addressing the woman, completely ignoring the rude man, "and unless I'm mistaken, you are my Aunt Leeza."

All distress at the unpleasantries vanished and a look of delighted surprise swept across her face. "Chen! By the Goddess, it's been ages!"

"It has," Chen confirmed.

"This is my husband Lord Cypris Gatza," she said, gracefully indicating the mustached man.

"Uncle," Chen greeted formally, extending his hand.

Cypris's handshake seemed weak and insincere. An expression of intrigued suspicion replaced the rage.

"And these are our twin boys, Roland and Tucker."

Chen shook both of the handsome young men's hands and noted the bearded Tucker seemed genuinely glad to see him, while Roland's expression mirrored his father's.

"So, nephew, what causes you to visit?" Cypris asked guardedly.

"I was hoping to visit with my baby brother, Goma," Chen replied looking around. "Is he about?"

Chen immediately realized something felt wrong. At the mention of his younger brother's name, his aunt and uncle traded nervous glances.

Leeza's face suddenly went somber. "Chen, I'm afraid Goma died eight grands ago. I'm sorry."

Chen frowned and sighed deeply.

"Yes, farm accident," Cypris quickly added. "I told the boy not to pull those horse's tails."

"I would very much like to hear about him," Chen said sadly, noticing Tucker turn away.

"Then you must stay for supper and we can put you up for the evening," Leeza offered causing Cypris to frown at his wife.

"Thanks Auntie, but I wouldn't want to be a bother," Chen said, noting his uncle's disapproving look.

"Nonsense," Leeza said matronly. "We have plenty of room and food. Besides, the Kan will be starting soon. And I know I'm eager to hear about what you've been up to all these grands."

Chen smiled sadly. "If you insist, Auntie."

"I do," Leeza said firmly. "Now, let's get you settled in."

"If I may make a request?" Chen asked humbly. "If he is interned around here, I would very much like to visit his grave."

Leeza returned the poignant smile. "Of course, he's buried in the family cemetery about a mile from here. I can take you there tomorrow."

"I'd like to go too," Tucker said passively.

"No!" Cypris snapped. "Some of us have work to do."

Both Leeza and Tucker bowed their heads and frowned, embarrassed at the Lord of the Manor's outburst.

Leeza quickly recovered and the placating smile returned. "Come, let's get you settled in."

Chen accompanied his aunt into the large two-story manor house, all the while silently pondering what he wasn't being told.

The tension in the warehouse felt as thick as the Kan fog outside. Thirty-six Zorian street bosses and their seconds-in-command congregated in loosely allied groupings, each dependent upon which bosses got along. Four bosses, however, chose not to attend and would be delt with later.

For now, the ones who decided to appear, nervously chatted in low tones, gazing around at the renovated structure. Everyone grew subdued when Mazie stepped onto a small low stage at the rear of the room and stood quietly waiting for calm.

She had purposefully considered every aspect of her demeanor and dress for the proper effect. Her hair, pulled back in a bun, symbolized professionalism and she radiated confidence. The flared riding pants, tucked into knee high riding boots, and white blouse with the top three buttons strategically undone, showed a wilder side not to be underestimated. On her belt, in the small of her back, nestled a specially designed holster for her weapon of choice, the cleaver, representing the consequences of crossing her.

"Firstly, I want to thank you all for coming," Mazie began amiably. "You certainly didn't have to. I think you just might be interested in what I have to propose. My name is Mazie, and I realize you don't know me, but I have a plan to make you all very rich and powerful men."

The statement caused a ripple of excited chatter.

"Yeah, how ya gonna do that?" a boss asked insolently.

Mazie met his gaze with a devious smile before continuing her address. "Quite simply, by working together with a common goal, instead of forty different entities all pulling in different directions."

This statement caused another round of uneasy chatter.

"In case you haven't heard," another spoke up. "The Zorian Guards aren't going to allow any kind of large gang."

"I realize that," Mazie countered. "What I'm proposing is… different. My plan is based on one that was instituted to rebuild the city of Makatooa ten grands ago.

"Gentlemen, we're not going to be gangsters, we're going to be pillars of the community, *our* community. My plan is nothing less than rebuilding the Sisters into a moneymaking district, with *us* in charge. Eventually, I see us becoming an almost autonomous region of the city."

"With you at the top, I suppose?" someone called out.

"I'll be fronting the money, so, yes. I also want a twenty percent cut of the profits. Each one of you would still be in charge of your own block. As block bosses, choose a representative from each of your seven plats to act as a ruling council to help settle disputes."

The murmurs grew contemplative and Mazie decided to drive her point. "All you need to do is look around you. This warehouse was refurbished in a matter of cycles. We've got a huge idle workforce out there and I've got the financing. What say we put the Sisters on a paying basis and get rich doing it."

"The High Council will never go for it!" someone yelled.

"Why not?" Mazie challenged. "More people making money in this city, means more people paying taxes, and I don't know any politician that would oppose that. And we're not going to descend on them like a pack of thugs. Next cycle, I'm securing a barrister to represent us and smooth the way. Someone who speaks their language. This *will* work if we *all* pull together!"

"What if we decide we don't want to go along," a boss asked, standing up front. "Is the same thing that happened to Sef, going to happen to us?"

"Nothing so dramatic I can assure you. When you see the areas around you start generating a lot of income, you'll be back, hat in hand. And, of course we'll welcome you, but the buy-in will cost a lot more then. So, I say, why not get in on the ground floor? There's nowhere to go but up."

Mazie saw the vast majority of the street bosses conferring and nodding their heads. A few scowled and appeared argumentative with their seconds-in-command.

"Well, I, for one, want nothing to do with it!" a defiant voice rang out, joined by several others. "All it's going to do is draw the Security Council's unwanted attention on us and that means, Rafel and Red Division!"

"No one is forcing you to do anything," Mazie said calmly. "Anyone who doesn't want to participate is free to leave. The rest can stay and I'll fill you in on the details."

Mazie watched six bosses and their underlings leave. It really didn't matter, though. By the lifting of the Kan, she would be dealing with their seconds-in-command anyways.

Mukavar sensed something wrong the moment he stepped in the front door. The lights were out and the dwelling felt unusually still. He heard the tell-tale crackling and saw the flames dancing in the fireplace. Then he caught the distinct smell of whiskey.

Cautiously moving into the living area, he caught the glint off the glass in Rafel's hand, reflecting the fire he sat silently staring into.

"Rafel?" Mukavar called out cautiously.

Rafel acknowledged the greeting by silently taking a sip of the amber liquid, never taking his eyes off the hearth.

"Rafel, what's wrong?" Mukavar asked, stepping over beside the brooding spymaster.

His mate once again refused to answer. The Calden Intelligencer now became genuinely worried and knelt down beside his unresponsive partner.

"Rafel, talk to me," he said tenderly, placing a hand on his leg.

He reacted by jerking the leg away and gulping down the last of the drink. A long tense silence lingered before Mukavar tried again.

"Rafel, I can't help you if you won't talk to me."

Slowly, the heartbroken spy chief peered over at Mukavar's distressed face.

"I'm sorry I wasn't enough for you," Rafel said finally, his voice straining on the edge of breaking down.

Mukavar's disposition quickly transformed from apprehensive, to befuddled. "Rafel, what in the name of the gods are you talking about?"

"I saw you today, down on the docks."

Mukavar shook his head in confusion. "Yeah, I was working a mutiny. If you were there, why didn't you drop by and say hello?"

"Oh, you looked *occupied*," Rafel said accusatorily.

Mukavar now appeared thoroughly baffled. "Yeah, that's what happens when I work. You still could have stopped by."

"I didn't want to interrupt you and your little *bitch boy!*" Rafel spat, tears welling up in his eyes.

"What?!" Mukavar said incredulously, standing.

"He's very pretty, I'll give you that."

"Rafel, you have got this all wrong!"

"Do I?"

"Yes, you do! And I just gotta say, I don't like what I'm being accused of!"

"And I don't like this entire thing," Rafel said defiantly with a sniffle, before coming to his feet. "I waited for you because I wanted to tell you face to face. I'm leaving!"

"You're what?!" Mukavar stammered.

He then noticed the two packed suitcases sitting in the open bedroom door, casting long shadows from the fire onto their bed.

"I can't believe it," Mukavar said, watching him walk over and grab his luggage. "You're not even interested in hearing what I have to say about it?"

"No."

"Is this some sort of bad joke?!" he asked, watching Rafel opening the door to the thick Kan fog. "There is an explanation you know!"

"Save it! And it looks like the joke was on me." Rafel said, before slamming the door behind him.

Mukavar stood staring at the door in stunned silence, a torrent of emotions coursing through him. Disbelief quickly turned to sorrow, then finally anger at being falsely accused.

"What the fuck just happened?!" he found himself asking the empty room.

The Calden agent, not normally a drinker, angrily spun and headed for the counter against the far wall, where Rafel's half empty whisky bottle beckoned.

With his Aunt Leeza driving the one-lizard carriage, Chen settled back and tried to enjoy the ride. The conversation seemed much the same as at dinner last Kan, with him answering many questions about what he had been up to the past thirteen grands.

He couldn't help but notice the answers becoming much vaguer when he inquired about life on the plantation and especially his brother's death. He could also feel a wave of underlying tension in the household between the pairings of Leeza and Tucker on one side versus Cypris and Roland on the other.

At one point, a lengthy pause allowed Chen to watch the rows of nut trees go by before he decided on a more direct approach.

"Auntie, what was my kid brother like?" Chen asked non-threateningly.

For a lengthy moment she silently stared at the road ahead before giving a forlorn sigh.

"He was a sensitive, gentle soul," she said thoughtfully. "Of course, we got him at age two, but the very next grand he started showing great aptitude in verbal skills. He was talking by the end of the grand and reading well by four. Much to your uncle's dismay, he showed no desire to participate in any of the activities boys liked to do, perfectly content to just sitting and reading."

"Did Uncle ever really accept him?"

This caused another protracted period of silence while Leeza framed her answer.

"Your uncle very much wanted someone who could help out around the plantation," she said cautiously. "And your little brother, while too young to really work, was not shaping up to be laborer material.

"I had to remind him that we needed trusted people to keep the books and records straight. He just didn't want to hear that everyone wasn't suited to outdoor work.

"Your Uncle Cypris just kept pushing him. It was starting to take its toll too. A full grand before the incident, he had grown sullen and distant. He even lost the desire to read."

Chen felt shocked but tempered his outrage at his hostess.

"Auntie, how could you allow this?!"

Leeza gave a somber, scoffing chuckle. "My husband is a very stubborn man, known for bouts of cruelty. He runs this plantation with an iron fist."

The small graveyard rested on the side of a low hill. Chen could see the headstones from quite a way off and he wondered how he would react to seeing his brother's marker. They had placed a simple placard over Goma's four-foot plot near the foot of the hill.

"He wasn't very big," Chen noted woefully.

"And so vulnerable," Leeza added. "He really couldn't protect himself. I mean Tucker would stick up for him, but he couldn't be around all the time."

"What about Roland?"

"Who do you think he was sticking up against?"

"Roland was cruel to him?" Chen asked sternly.

Leeza shrugged. "The usual, boys picking on each other."

"But you said Goma couldn't defend himself."

Leeza sullenly nodded, saying nothing.

They stood in silence, staring down at the simple memorial, until Leeza placed a gentle hand on Chen's shoulder.

"We should be getting back," she said softly. "Stay for another cycle. By the time we get there, the Kan will rise soon after. It will be too late to go anywhere. You can set off in the morning."

"I'm not so sure that will sit well with Uncle Cypris," Chen said, climbing back into the buggy. "He has made it very clear that I am not really welcome here."

A sardonic smile played at Leeza's lips, spurring the lizard onward. "He really doesn't have a choice."

"Oh?!"

"Life in the country is quite different than what you experienced in the big city. We have different rules out here, one of which is hospitality. To refuse hospitality to someone when the next place to get aid may be miles away could mean their death. So, you see, he's duty bound to give you shelter. Otherwise, it would reflect great discredit on him."

Chen peered over at his smirking aunt. "And something tells me you very much enjoy his predicament, Auntie."

Tantei set the report down on her desk and, without looking away from it, reached over to pull a hunk of Kell meat off the skewer to her right and smacked away at the epicurean delicacy.

"You know, if only these patrol guys could *write*... argh!" She shook her head in frustration, ripping off another bite of Kell. "Okay Tay, you were a patrol guy once. Were you're reports this shitty?"

"Nope," Talib answered somberly, "mine were pretty good. I imagine it's one of the things that got me into Investigation Division."

Talib's melancholy tone caused Tantei to glance over at her partner.

"You haven't touched your breakfast," she said, staring down at the meat stick on his desk, unwrapped, and untouched.

"Eh, I'm not hungry."

"You're kidding!" she protested. "I go through all the trouble to stop at your favorite food cart and you're not even going to touch it?!"

"Sorry."

"Alright, if you're not going to eat it, give it here."

"How do you stay so skinny eating like that?" Talib asked, handing her the culinary spear.

Tantei took it and placed it beside her partially eaten one.

"I try and maintain a strict regimen of fighting and fucking to keep my girlish figure," she said, biting off another chunk of meat.

Talib gave a weak smile, but continued silently staring at the paper in front of him.

"Come on!" she said, spinning to face him. "I don't even get a sympathy laugh?"

Without looking up, Talib managed another feeble grin.

"Sorry."

"Sorry, my ass!" Tantei gave an exasperated huff. "It's been two grands since your dad died, Tay, and you're still moping around, beating yourself up like it was your fault. Here's a clue for you, investigator, *it wasn't*. You have got to let that shit go before it eats you alive. Hey, I know what you need. You need to get laid!"

"Come on Tee, knock it off! I *don't* need to get laid."

Tantei blinked in astonishment. "Okay my friend, that's just crazy talk! Everybody needs to get laid. I know! I could be your sidekick!"

Talib's responded with a singular unamused glance.

"What?! Seriously, I'd be a great sidekick!"

Vanir poked his head inside their partially open door, preempting Talib's next reply. The investigators were immediately struck by the quarter inch thick braids in his long red hair, flanking each side of his face.

"My office," he said quickly, before disappearing back into the hall.

Both detectives remained seated, staring quizzically at each other.

"Did you see the…" Talib asked, motioning on either side of his face.

Tantei already rose to her feet. "I sure did!"

"This is going to be good!" Talib said enthusiastically, bounding up from his desk, all hint of melancholy gone.

Once in Vanir's office, both watched their captain already sipping on his morning whisky.

"So, Boss," Tantei said, closing the door behind her. "What's with the hair?"

Vanir set the glass down and threw her an annoyed, slightly embarrassed look. "I was indulging a friend."

"A female friend?" Tantei asked with a salacious grin.

"We can discuss my personal life later. Right now, you two have got a very busy cycle ahead of you."

Tantei immediately turned serious. "I'm pretty sure I don't like the sound of that."

"What's up, chief?" Talib asked cautiously.

"You two need to get down to the Sisters right away," Vanir said, reaching for his glass. "The reports started coming in about a deci ago. We got bodies turning up. Ten of them, to be exact."

"Don't tell me," Tantei said flippantly. "They're all street bosses."

Tantei's eyes went wide at Vanir's serious expression while taking another drink.

"Hey, wait a minute," Tantei said warily. "I was just being a smart ass. Really, all ten are street bosses?"

"Yep, all ten were killed on their own blocks, all across the Sisters."

"Well, that rules out turf wars," Talib said, staring thoughtfully into space. "Maybe some sort of power grab?"

"Speculate after you've had a look," Vanir said, before taking another sip.

"We're on it, Boss," Tantei said whirling towards the door. "Come on Tay. Time to do my second favorite morning thing, looking at dead bodies."

The *Vastus* dropped out of a swirling cloud bank, sweeping the area known as the Doldrums and settled into its eerily calm interior. Taleeka had only been here once before and always marveled at the fifty-mile diameter circle in the southwestern Ocean Deep where no currents of air or water moved. Neither she, nor her parents, had ever run into anyone who knew the origin of this dead calm area of Lumina, and she made a mental note to ask Nibira to research it.

The floating Free City of Tannimore jutted up from the glass smooth water ahead like a lone beacon. The city had grown substantially since she and her folks visited last. Most notable would be the addition of a massive flight deck and control tower jutting out over the water from the second level on the west side of the city.

A massive purple Etheria tower of Azurite stood next to the wide flat surface, acting as a gateway through the Middle Realms for those who dared use it. The edifice almost seemed to glow and pulse from the staccato rays of sunlight shooting out from behind it. Up above it, the moon shined brilliantly on its way to setting in the western sky.

"The parking lot looks a little crowded," Taleeka noted to Gidaria, in front of her in the pilot's seat.

Brzo occupied the navigator's seat beside the pilot. The exuberant lizard sat panting and looking out the windshield.

When Taleeka heard a loud thump and groan towards the center of the craft, she closed her eyes and sighed. She spun in her chair and saw Larzz flat on his back between the rows of seats. Noorim loomed over his hulking body and had her knee on his neck, while she held one arm aloft barred at the elbow, in what looked like an extremely painful position. The much smaller Amarenian's face contained a rare grin, while the half EEtah below her grimaced in agony.

"Will you two quit screwing around," Taleeka admonished. "We're almost there."

Noorim relinquished the hold and the two got to their feet sporting innocent looks.

"I'm just trying to keep the pasty lady on her toes," Larzz said innocuously, massaging his arm.

Taleeka gave an amused scoff. "Yeah, how's that going?"

"She's improving nicely."

Taleeka and Noorim shared an entertained smirk as the Kovos practitioner took her seat.

"Okay," Taleeka said, turning her attention to Barr-Ani, "I feel a little guilty bringing you here. This place is the pleasure city of Lumina, now run by the Pa-Waga people. It was already a wild place before they got exiled here. Ever since, they've done a real good job of expanding it and turning a hefty profit along the way. You could easily go into sensory overload here. Try to tune out the random debauchery and concentrate on what I need you to focus on."

"I don't know, Tally," the Bailian said meekly. "I feel what I feel."

"Try," Taleeka said seriously. "I don't want this little adventure to cause you to have to spend a cluster in a dark quiet room just to recoup."

Barr-Ani gave a weak smile and nodded.

"Stay with the ship," Taleeka ordered her pilot. "If you have to go out to get something to eat or whatever, leave Brzo here. This place is way too crowded and dangerous for him to go bounding around."

Taleeka reached into her pack hanging from the captain's chair and retrieved a one-hundred-secor Etheria Note. She handed the Ukko wafer to Gidaria.

"Top off the PSI battery," she said. "I guarantee they'll accept that form of payment."

"You got it, Captain," she said cheerfully, accepting the note without taking her eyes off the busy flight deck below. "Tannimore tower just designated a space for us."

"Okay, put her down," Taleeka ordered, before addressing her crew once more. "Alright kids, it's show time. Remember we're just here for some recon. You all know what to do, just keep a low profile. And for the sake of the Goddess, don't let yourself get distracted. This place literally has something for everyone and that means *you*. So, keep your wits about you. We'll meet back here at moonrise. That should give us plenty of time."

Everyone nodded they understood and Gidaria deftly slipped the *Vastus* into a slot among a row of airships parked along the edge of the flight deck, with their noses sticking out towards open water. When everyone stood, Brzo started fidgeting excitedly in his seat. Gidaria patted the reptile on the head sympathetically.

"No, baby," she cajoled in a sing-song tone. "Brzo's going to have to stay here with Mommy. Isn't that right? We'll play in the back, won't we?"

The lizard's attention spastically switched back and forth, torn between his master's attentive voice and everyone else piling out the side hatch.

*Father dead.*

*Lord Banavor missing.*

*Their God abandoning them.*

*The fearful faces of the estates staff looking to her for guidance and stability.*

*Calming them with reassuring words, "This is not the end. I will take care of you. You work for me, now."*

*Ascending the stairs to her father's bedroom.*

*Moving the floorboards by the head of the bed revealing three chests.*

*Just where he always said they would be.*

*All three packed with hundred secor commodity notes.*

*The building blocks for a new empire. Her empire.*

"Here he comes now, ma'am," Vozac said, drawing Mazie's attention to the handsome, clean-cut man in a white high collared shirt and black slacks, making his way across Judgement Square.

"It appears Si. Lushi is running a bit late this morning," she said, a touch irritated.

"Yes ma'am," Vozac replied, before getting out and opening her door.

"Stay with the vehicle," Mazie ordered. "It's Judgment Square, I'm probably safe here."

"Yes ma'am," Vozac dutifully responded, then took up his position by the driver's door, standing ominously.

Mazie caught up to Karta as he unlocked his office door.

"Si Lushi," she said with a broad smile. "Glad I could finally catch you."

Karta gazed at the beautiful woman in riding pants and boots with a white blouse open three buttons down on the top displaying her ample cleavage.

"Yeah," he said, turning the key. "I had court first thing this morning and it went a little over."

Mazie extended her hand, about to introduce herself, when a loud crack and cry of pain rang out from the stocks, immediately followed by a single, piercing scolding.

"Naughty!"

The rebuke had been uttered by a squat old lady, carrying a three-foot-long sturdy wooden paddle. She moved systematically down the rows of stocks, giving each of the naked prisoners a solid smack on their bare bottoms. Her single word rebuke came immediately after. Some begged her not to, to no avail. One large laborer didn't cry out and he got three more blows until he did. Mazie peered back at Karta with a curiously amused look.

"Old Lady Zartada," he said with a shake of his head. "She comes here once a cycle, every cycle, rain or shine, since before I became a barrister. Nobody knows why she does it. So, in addition to having insults and rotten fruit thrown at them, they get a daily spanking too."

"Very odd," Mazie said, entertained at the notion.

"Welcome to my world," Karta said, opening the door. "Please come in."

Mazie followed him into his large office lined with bookshelves. On one wall, hung his framed diploma from the University of Marassa School of Law.

"Please have a seat," he said, stepping behind his wide ornate desk and sitting down in an equally elaborate high-backed chair.

"Well," Karta began. "You obviously know who I am, but I find myself at a bit of a disadvantage."

Mazie smiled and shifted in her seat to afford Karta a better look at her partially exposed breasts. "My name is Mazie de Goya and quite simply I want to hire you for an extended period."

"You realize of course, that could get quite expensive?"

"I do, and I also know you are the best barrister in Zor and that means the whole Annigan. I assumed your fee was going to be substantial."

Karta sat back in his chair and held his arms out in a welcoming gesture. "Well, as long as money isn't an issue, how can I be of service?"

"My associates and I are about to embark on several large projects in the Seven Sisters and we would like you to smooth out any municipal entanglements we encounter."

Karta gave a sly smile. "Are these projects legal?"

"Mostly," Mazie said honestly, "but all are philanthropic in nature. However, I know things can go afoul with certain official organizations, and that is where you would come in."

"I see," Karta replied. "And by *official organizations*, you're talking about the High Council, Imperial Judges and the Zorian Guards?"

Mazie smiled coyly. "Well, you are after all, a lawyer."

"That I am," Karta said, sitting forward. "And how soon will you be requiring my services?"

"Almost immediately I would think," Mazie said, her face taking on a serious expression. "Within the next few cycles, I'm going to be opening a large soup kitchen in the Sister's Tasa Plat. Now I'm sure the residents are going to be thrilled, but as with any large endeavor, some bureaucrat somewhere is going to get into a snit about it."

"How is this soup kitchen going to be paid for?" Karta asked curiously.

"The burden will be borne by me," Mazie assured. "There will be no need for any extra taxes or fees."

"That's very generous!" Karta said appreciatively.

"I was born in the Sisters," Mazie said with a sad smile. "I just want to give something back."

"Well, I'm pretty confident I can defend a free soup kitchen that won't cost the council a single copper piece."

"Then, you'll take the job?"

"Sure!" Karta replied enthusiastically.

"Splendid!" Mazie said, standing and reaching into her pocket. She pulled out a five hundred secor gold note and placed it on Karta's desk. "I'll be in touch."

Karta stared at the large sum of money, and then back up to Mazie. "Five thousand gold pieces is quite the retainer."

"I'm only interested in the best. Please let me know if any more is required."

"You bet," Karta said, picking up the Ukko wafer and watching Mazie's shapely behind, in her custom fitted riding pants, walk out the door. *Beauty in this instance*, he silently mused, *offset by danger in the form of a holstered cleaver.*

A still suspicious Chen stepped over to his bedroom's second story window. Taking a moment away from packing, he watched the salt production on Lake Cypris winding down for the cycle. Aunt Leeza was right, by the time they made it back from the grave site, the cycle was almost over. She had also been right about Cypris having to accept him for one more Kan.

He found himself staring in fascination at the salt boats making the cycle's final run. Whether you approved of Lord Cypris' methods or not, he ran an efficient operation. The barges crisscrossed the lake, making methodical stops along the rows of pilons submerged in one of the few salty bodies of water in the Annigan. Chen could see the pillars caked with salt when they were winched out of the water and over the barge. There, several large slaves rapidly scraped off the salt with rounded dull machetes before resubmerging the column. Now, with the faintest hint of fog in the air, Chen watched the barges make their way towards the shore.

Moving away from the window, he resumed packing, when a soft knock at the door interrupted him.

"Come in," he said, while quickly noting the location of his sword.

To Chen's surprise, a hunched over Tucker slinked into the room, nervously looked around then quietly closed the door. Leaning back against it, he sighed deeply.

"Tucker, is everything alright?"

"I can't do this anymore," Tucker said forlornly, stepping away from the door.

"Tucker, can't do what anymore? What are you talking about?"

The anxious young man woefully shook his head. "This horrible lie I'm being forced to live with!"

Chen now found himself intrigued. He suspected something sinister bubbling just below the surface of Cypris family life.

"Cousin," Chen said patiently. "Is there anything I can do to help?"

Tucker shook his head. "No, but there is something you should know. I've got to get this off my chest."

"Rest assured, I can be discreet."

"No! It's time this ugly scandal be brought out from under the rock where it's been hiding."

"Very well, you have my attention."

70

Tucker paused and took a deep breath. "Your brother wasn't killed by a horse kicking him. He committed suicide. We made it look like an accident so mother wouldn't know. She feels bad enough thinking it was a mishap that could have been avoided."

The news struck Chen hard, but he still felt that this wasn't the whole story.

"Why would Goma commit suicide?" Chen probed.

"He couldn't live with the pain anymore," Tucker replied with his face turned sorrowfully downward. "Father had been raping him regularly for over a grand."

Now it all started to make sense. Aunt Leeza had mentioned the radical shift in his personality. Rape would be a good reason. Taking a deep breath, Chen felt his anger starting to build the more he pondered his brother's fate.

"And you *did* nothing?!"

"I didn't know until a little after he killed himself. At the time I just thought we were protecting mom's feelings. Roland knew about it all along. He joked about it afterwards. That's how I found out."

Chen finally felt like he had the complete truth. Staring off into space, he found his fists clenching and mouth growing taut. He realized, however, that unbridled fury would not be the answer. He would take the coming Kan to meditate on the matter. The morning would reveal his course of action.

When out in public, Rafel always sat at the corner table with his back to the wall. He practiced this precautionary measure even in establishments he frequented and knew well, such as the Demon's Gate Inn. Ever since he checked in last cycle, he had found himself constantly in the tavern area with a bottle as his companion.

Staring absentmindedly into the bottle of whiskey before him, gut wrenching loss and betrayal seemed to be all he could feel. His mood constantly fluctuated between deep sorrow and murderous rage. He gave himself, body and soul, to this man. He had shared his innermost longings to someone he thought understood his intimate connection between pain and pleasure. All of that vanished in one selfish, lustful act.

Working with him would be difficult too and unavoidable. He knew he would have to deal with that, perhaps as soon as the next cycle.

Rafel just didn't understand how Muuky could throw it all away for a brief romp with a pretty boy.

Compounding his grief; he had no real friends due to the nature of his profession. No shoulder to lean on, or someone to commiserate with.

When he felt the current wave of sorrow begin to subside, replaced by the building tsunami of agitation within, he instinctively reached again for his only friend at that moment, the bottle.

The mid-cycle's bells of Zor's Grand Turine peeled out over the city's skyline. The only thing moving quicker happened to be the savory odor of simmering stew which wafted through the streets of the Seven Sisters Slums. The soup kitchen celebrated its opening day and a modest crowd showed up the first morning meal of soup, sweetbread and tea. However, news about free food spread quickly through the impoverished neighborhoods and by the time of the next meal, the line to get in the soup kitchen stretched for blocks. The scruffy looking citizens, some naked, remained wary at first, but the rumors turned out to be true. Everyone ate their fill, with no questions asked and seconds never refused.

Mazie stood triumphantly on the riser in the rear of the room watching the feast. Alongside her, Drugo and Karta nodded appreciatively, while Vozac's hulking form loomed protectively behind her. She had transformed the once empty warehouse into a giant dining hall, with a dozen long tables filled with diners of all ages. Along the far side of the room, four large cauldrons simmered, filling the interior and the streets outside with their intoxicating aroma. They hired a handful of the locals as cooks and servers, meaning that, along with being fed, they actually earned money.

"Quite a success," Karta admitted, watching the poorest citizens of Zor receiving possibly the first decent meal of their lives. "I had to see this for myself."

"At this rate, we'll be serving all cycle," Mazie noted, her mind quickly calculating crowds and amounts. "Maybe we should open one of these in each of the Sister's seven plats. It'll cut down on the congestion."

A commotion by the doorway caused a break in the conversation. Mazie watched with rapidly growing resentment as two Zorian Guards, led by a patrol sergeant, burst into the room and antagonistically approached them.

"Who's in charge here?!" the sergeant demanded gruffly.

Mazie stepped forward and eyed him contemptuously. He stood a full head shorter than his two large patrolmen, with a long walrus moustache covering his lips and nervously darting eyes.

"That would be me," she said confidently. "What can I do for the Zorian Guards today? Perhaps you would like something to eat?"

"You can disperse this crowd," he insisted tersely. "This is an illegal gathering!"

Mazie stood staring at the indignant guard for a brief moment and Karta stepped up beside her.

"Uh, sergeant, what was your name?" Karta asked.

"I'm Patrol Sergeant Haserre!" he proclaimed proudly. "Who the fuck are you?!"

Karta gave a confident smile and leaned slightly forward.

"Well, Patrol Sergeant Haserre. My name is Karta Lushi, and I am this woman's barrister. Sergeant, I can assure you no laws are being broken here. But you are within your rights to challenge me. In fact, I can have us in front of an Imperial Judge within the deci. One thing you should keep in mind though, Patrol Sergeant Haserre. Judges hate to have their time wasted by frivolous harassment complaints. As I said, no laws are being broken."

The belligerent municipal employee sputtered in frustration while mentally attempting to rally from the smiling barrister's subtle but stinging rebuttal.

"The crowds outside are blocking traffic!" he said finally, with a bit less bravado.

"Sergeant, this matter can be settled quickly and easily," Mazie said diplomatically. "I will have my two associates here go outside and move the crowd into orderly lines, off the street. Will that be agreeable?"

"Well, I..." Haserre said, struggling to find a problem with the proposed compromise.

Mazie gently but persistently continued, intent on driving the point home. "This way traffic gets moving again and I get to feed these people without judges or hearings being needed. What do you say?"

Haserre glowered in defeat at Mazie and Karta. "Fine! Just be quick about it!"

Thank you, Sergeant," she said sweetly, before peering back at her two allies. "Drugo, Vozac."

The two men snapped into action, quickly moving out the door, past the line of patrons waiting to get inside.

"There we are, all taken care of," Mazie said, extending her arms in a placating gesture. "Sergeant, my previous invitation was genuine. You and your men are more than welcome to stay for a bit and get something to eat."

The two junior guards traded hopeful glances until their superior dashed any prospects of getting fed.

"We're on duty," he said brusquely, before addressing his men. "Come on, let's go."

The three left, with Haserre complaining about the good old days, before the lawyers. Mazie contentedly watched them leave. Today, she accomplished two important things. She fed the masses, gaining favor in their eyes, and she showed them she was not afraid to stand up to the authorities on their behalf.

Yes, things were progressing nicely. Soon she would have a large segment of the city's population beholden to her and eager to do her bidding.

And she had just gotten started.

At the lifting of the Kan, the Cypris Plantation already buzzed with activity. Leeza stood by the kitchen, conferring with the head house slave about organizing the morning meal when she saw Chen, travel bag over his shoulder marching down the stairs. He headed for the front door with a determined stride.

"Chen," she called out, breaking away from the conversation. "You aren't leaving without saying good-bye, are you?"

Chen abruptly stopped and came over. She didn't like the look of grim determination mixed with anger on his face.

"Chen, what's wrong?"

Her nephew gave a sad smile, then reached out and held both her shoulders.

"Auntie, I'm sorry to cause you this pain, but there is something I must do!"

He then abruptly headed for the front door. Leeza had a dire feeling about this and she warily followed her nephew outside. From the front porch, she witnessed Chen's determined pace walking over to where Cypris and her two sons conferred with three boat captains. Along the way, he tossed his travel bag onto the seat of the carriage prepared for him.

The group immediately stopped talking and stared inquisitively at Chen, who stopped in front of Cypris. Leeza cried out in surprise, raising both hands in front of her mouth when Chen lashed out with a savage backhand across his uncle's face. The unexpected blow rocked the Lord of the Manor and he bellowed in rage. The five others were too stunned to move and stood there with mouths agape.

"What is the meaning of this!"

"I challenge you to a duel, you child rapist!"

An evil leer crossed the older man's face, accentuated by a thin ribbon of blood running from the corner of his mouth.

"So, you found out," Cypris said defiantly, not relinquishing his maniacal smirk. "I imagine it was my pussy son over there who told you."

"A duel, you sick bastard!" Chen spat.

"You want a duel, *fine!*" he replied, and then turned to Roland. "Go fetch my blade."

Roland took off for the house and Cypris sneered at Tucker. "I'll take care of you later, *pussy!*"

Cypris spun back to face Chen. "The little pussy boy should have thanked me for finally finding a use for him.

Yeah, that was one tight asshole he had. He screamed at first, before he got used to it."

Leeza's mouth dropped open in shock, horrified that her husband could be capable of such vicious debauchery. With his public admission, she also now sided with Chen and needed to see him punished. No matter the outcome of the duel, life on this plantation would never be the same.

Roland came running out of the front door past her, carrying her husband's finest sword. All the while, Cypris continued to berate Chen, who silently glowered at him.

"Yeah, you may have attended some fancy ass sword school, but I learned to fight the hard way. I'll teach your prissy ass a thing or two."

"At least it will be a fairer fight than the one I witnessed upon my arrival, *coward*!"

By now Roland had reached his father, Chen noted that he too had armed himself. A wide-eyed Roland handed Cypris his sword, and then timidly backed away. Cypris dramatically unsheathed it with a shout and tossed the sheath to the ground.

Leeza watched through tear-filled eyes as Chen ceremoniously drew his weapon and reverently held the flat of the blade to his forehead reciting a brief prayer. His aunt's cry of alarm snapped him back into the moment, alerting him to Cypris' attempted ambush while mouthing his devotional.

Cypris charged yelling, with long hair and moustache flowing. Chen simply raised his blade over his head. The initial clash of steel connected with such a powerful blow, everyone watching cringed. He slid his blade downward and to the side, sending an off-balance Cypris plummeting forward. Taking advantage of his opponent's displacement, Chen swung the blade in an arc with an overhand strike. Cypris managed to raise his sword just in time to deflect it.

With both contestants now on a solid footing, they circled each other warily.

"See boy," Cypris gloated, spittle forming on his moustache. "I ain't no pushover. I'm gonna rape your corpse, and that pussy son of mine's, when this is all over!"

Chen remained silent. Cypris lashed out in a rapid motion with a crossed overhead strike and a subsequent lunge. Chen deflected both and, once again, sidestepped the lunge, sending the lord of the manor back into the dirt.

Seizing the opportunity, Chen vaulted over to him with blade raised. He stopped abruptly when greeted by a handful of sand thrown into his eyes. Sputtering, he staggered back, desperately attempting to clear his vision. This allowed Cypris time to regain his feet. Once standing, he launched a swift volley of strikes that Chen barely fended off.

By this time Cypris had become totally enraged and Leeza gasped at the ferocity her husband displayed. He screamed while repeatedly striking at his nephew's defensive position with powerful overhand attacks, driving him down onto one knee.

With anger clouding Cypris' judgement, Chen took advantage of the repetition. When the next strike came, Chen tilted his sword slightly upward sending the assaulting weapon sliding down the bastard sword's blade and into the pommel, breaking teeth by the guard.

Using both hands on the hilt, Chen twisted with all his strength and Cypris' sword snapped in two with a loud metallic clap. Two feet of broken steel flew off and landed on the ground ten feet away. Leeza clearly saw the stunned expression on her husband's face peering helplessly at his broken sword.

"Today, you die!" She heard Chen say, before lunging the tip of his blade at Cypris. The old man moved faster than Leeza anticipated and dodged the lunge. She saw Cypris retrieve a small hidden dagger from his boot and nimbly roll along the ground in a somersault, gripping the blade firmly in his right fist. Before momentum carried him back to his feet, Chen checked his uncle with his hip and threw him back down onto his face and knees, ass up.

In a single fluid move, Chen plunged the blade through his uncle's anus, piercing about a foot before stopping. Cypris screamed and howled with the cold metal violating his colon. Chen steadied himself, placing his left hand on his uncle's lower back, and slowly twisted the sword.

"Just try to get used to it," Chen taunted over his uncle's shrieks.

With that, he drove the blade up through Cypris' torso until the tip jutted out of his mouth, splitting lip, septum and nose, before piercing the ground beneath his face.

The Lord of the Manor quivered and spasmed, blood erupting from his bifurcated mouth and nose. Both Leeza and Roland cried out when Chen pulled the blade free in a stream of gory excrement and Cypris flopped lifelessly to the ground.

"You Bastard!" Roland screamed, charging and drawing his sword.

"Roland, No!" Leeza cried out, but the plea came too late.

Chen flicked the foul-smelling slime off his blade and it splattered across Roland's eyes. The boy gasped in disgust and swung blindly. Chen sidestepped the assaulting youth and, using the momentum of a backwards spin, sliced deeply across his lower back, severing the spinal cord. Roland's face mimicked Cypris' own shocked expression when he tumbled forward to the ground, not three feet from where his father lay.

"Now," Chen snarled at Roland writhing in a pool of blood, "you really *are* spineless and blind to your father's sins."

A blanket of silence descended on the plaza, punctuated by the soft, nervous murmurings of the crowd. Leeza slowly walked over to where her dead husband and son lay and stared down at their bodies oozing lifeblood onto the ground.

"I'm sorry it had to come to this, Auntie," Chen said, sheathing his weapon.

"I am too," she said mournfully, "but I ran out of tears for that man many grands ago. And now, finding out what he did. I never thought I'd ever say this about a member of my family, but I'm glad the son-of-a-bitch is dead."

"And Roland?"

"He was shaping up to be just like his father," Leeza said with a shake of her head. "Sooner or later, he would have become a monster too."

"I think this will be a much happier place without them," Chen said, watching Tucker approach looking anguished.

"A new beginning," Leeza said, picking up the hilted end of Cypris' broken blade. "I'm going to hang on to this as a reminder of what happened here today."

She smiled sadly at Tucker. "And I want to wipe the name Cypris from our moniker and legacy. From now on, this will be Broken Sword Lake and Plantation."

"It's a good name," Tucker said, unable to take his eyes off the broken weapon.

"I must go now," Chen said, glancing over at the wagon. "There's still the matter of finding my sister. I believe the Argos Plantation is further north on the main road?"

"Yes, I'll give you a ride," Tucker said, still shaken up. "I need to put a little distance between me and this place."

Chen reached out and hugged Leeza. "Good-bye Auntie, I hope our paths cross again someday."

"I do too," she said.

They climbed into the small wagon and, still standing by the grisly scene, she waved farewell, watching it roll out of the compound, knowing it probably carried her nephew from her life forever.

Gidaria knew Taleeka had told her to keep Brzo in *The Vastus*, but the four-foot lizard now acted like he needed to relieve himself, pacing back and forth in front of the hatch. She seriously doubted Taleeka wanted him to go inside her new prized birthday gift. Grabbing its leash sent the impatient reptile bounding at the side hatch.

"Does my baby have to ka-ka?" she asked, slipping the harness of the leash around the exuberant animal.

The lizard happily licked her face and she dropped the hatchway, turning it into a ramp. She immediately noted the heat. With no ocean breeze to cool things down, the sun in the far western sky beat down mercilessly on the flight deck.

"Okay Brzo let's go ka-ka!" she commanded.

The unusually strong pet began tugging her along. Of course, as always, the proper spot must be located and that involved checking out the nearby airships and any cargo deposited by each one, respectively. Gidaria sighed in acceptance as Brzo, tongue flicking wildly took in the strange new scents.

Gidaria started to grow impatient. They had traversed the length of one side of the air station and started up the other.

"Come on Brzo," she pleaded. "Ka-ka, ka-ka!"

She felt relieved when the fickle reptile discovered the perfect spot, near the edge of the deck, between two parked air taxis.

While the animal defecated, Gidaria boringly looked around. The place appeared busy, with all manner of airships arriving and departing, carrying passengers and cargo alike. It piqued her curiosity when her gaze swept across four identical small passenger ships sitting side by side. The four stony faced Piety Watch members guarding it greatly aroused her suspicion.

She checked on her pet, finding his business done and him happily resting his belly on the warm flight deck. His head remained in perpetual motion, observing the activity around him, while his tongue constantly flicked in the air. Kicking the six hard black pellets he had excreted over the side, she tugged at his leash.

"Come on Brzo, let's take a walk," she said, leading him towards the dubious aircraft.

The guards noticeably tensed up when she approached.

"Hey!" Gidaria called out happily, while appreciatively eyeing the ships. "Aren't those modified Wagoo Class? Those are real beauties!"

"This space is restricted," one said coldly.

"I just wanted to know about the ships," Gidaria said.

"Didn't you hear," another said, stepping forward antagonistically. "This area is off limits, so, you and that filthy animal get away from here."

Gidaria gave her best disappointed look, but she had already seen enough.

"Well, it was good talking with you," she said sarcastically, before walking calmly away with Brzo bounding happily beside her.

When she returned to *The Vastus*, she opened the hatch with her fob then went immediately to the pilot's seat. Brzo jumped excitedly into the seat next to her.

"No baby," she said scratching under the lizard's chin. "We're not going anywhere yet."

She then reached up and touched the Larimar disk in the overhead console.

"Hey Tally," she called out.

When Gidaria's voice filled Taleeka's head, she reached into her shirt collar and touched the Larimar necklace shaped like a teardrop.

"What's up?" Taleeka asked softly.

"I just got back from taking Brzo for a potty walk and saw something very interesting, okay, maybe not particularly interesting, just odd and…"

"Gidaria, what did you see?" Taleeka broke in, halting a potentially lengthy monologue.

"Well, it was on the far side of the flight deck. Four modified Wagoo Class scout ships with the passenger seats removed. They were being guarded by a bunch of no-nonsense Piety Watch goons."

"Interesting," Taleeka said, gazing around the large anteroom of the Pa-Waga temple/bank vault.

She surveyed the large steel door, and then over at four locking boxes stacked one atop the other.

"Because I'm looking at four chests just about that size. Are you back at the ship?"

"Yeah, can you believe it they called Brzo a filthy animal and…"

"Gidaria, this is not a good time! Just be ready to go in a centi's notice."

"Right, got it, Tally."

Taleeka heaved a sigh and put the bauble back under her shirt when two quick warning raps on the door came from Barr-Ani standing lookout in the hall.

"Hey, what are you doing here?" She overheard a gruff male voice ask. "You're not supposed to be here! How did you get in here?"

"Oh, I'm so sorry," she heard Barr-Ani's voice, turning on the charm. "I'm lost, I got all turned around."

"Yeah, but how did you get back here?" a second male voice asked.

"The doors weren't locked," she purred innocently. "I just wandered in here. Where am I?"

"Somewhere you're not supposed to be," the first voice answered. "Those doors were supposed to be locked."

Taleeka, realizing she had left the door unlocked, reached over and quietly latched it while listening to Barr-Ani being questioned.

"Where exactly were you headed?" the second voice asked suspiciously.

"I was just looking for a place to get something to eat. Look, I'm truly sorry, but I really am lost," Barr-Ani could be heard pleading. "You two work here. Can't you help me?"

"We do not *work* anywhere," the first said defensively. "We serve a mighty God."

"I'm so sorry. I didn't mean to offend."

A tense moment of silence passed before the first one spoke again. "Take her to the one next to the temple."

"Thank you," Barr-Ani said, sounding relieved.

Taleeka heard the two shuffling off down the hall. When the first guard tested the latch, her hand rested just above her shrouding stone, but he seemed satisfied and moved off. She reached for her Larimar necklace.

"Noorim, Larzz, what have you got?" Taleeka whispered.

Larzz's voice came through first. "This place is crawling with Piety Watch. Security is pretty tight."

"Yes, but they seem more interested in keeping an eye on their *guests* than internal security," Noorim added.

"Okay, lets rendezvous at the pub next to the bank. Barr-Ani's already there. I think I've got an idea."

The short, somber wagon ride to the Argos Plantation passed mostly in silence. Tucker kept his eyes straight ahead on the river road which appeared surprisingly busy. Chen watched the salt barges on the river to his right, heading to one of Zer-Tal's main ports for shipping. He couldn't help feeling a bit awkward being in Tucker's presence. After all, he had just killed his father and brother. Tucker, however, seemed to bear no ill will towards him.

Chen felt certain many in the past would have liked to kill the hated Cypris. Still, some sadness could be expected, not to mention uncertainty about the future. Tucker and his mother had to step up to run the plantation themselves.

The Argos Plantation measured roughly the same size as the Cypris operation. Approximately forty buildings were set in a semi-circle around a central plaza on the shore of Lake Argos. Much like the plantation he had just left, he saw a whirlwind of activity, minus the tension filled atmosphere.

They seemed to know Tucker, evident by the good-natured nods and greetings he received the moment he drove the wagon into the compound. Everyone, especially the women, seemed to be curious about the handsome stranger with the long blonde hair sitting beside him.

When they entered the central plaza, Chen got a good look at the salt harvesting on the lake. Despite the Argos barges looking a bit different, the methods used seemed exactly the same as the Cypris Plantation.

"Thanks for the ride," Chen said, when the wagon came to a stop. "I'm truly sorry for your loss."

"Thanks," Tucker said, extending his hand, "but I'm not sorry. My father was a bad man. As far as I'm concerned, he got off easy. And you're welcome for the ride. Now, I gotta go bury my father and brother."

Chen shook his hand, grabbed his travel bag and stepped down off the rig.

Much like his arrival, Chen's presence caused most to stare, if only in passing. A small group on the other side of the square, two men and a woman holding a newborn in her arms, caught Chen's attention. The woman's long blonde hair, stood out from the other dark-haired people and her brown skin appeared a touch lighter. One of the men looked older, short and heavy set with a receding hair line. His ruddy complexion, with short unkempt facial hair, adorned a jovial disposition. The other struck Chen as much younger, cleanshaven, with shoulder length, black hair parted in the middle. Both men happily doted on the tiny baby, ignoring their surroundings.

When the woman saw Chen, her mouth dropped open and she cried out. Quickly handing the infant to the young man, she rushed across the plaza colliding with her brother and exuberantly throwing her arms around him.

"Chen!" she squealed. "I thought I would never see you again!"

She then held him out at arm's length. "You have grown up nicely."

"And you look well and happy, Intia," Chen said, smiling broadly.

"I'm very happy," she replied. "Come, there's some people I want you to meet."

Taking him by the arm, she energetically led him to the people she stood with. Both had curious expressions, the young man eyed him with a touch of jealous suspicion.

Uncle, Senarra, this is my brother Chen, all the way from Zor," she announced proudly.

Chen couldn't help but note the look of relief on the young man's face at the introduction and he handed the baby back to Intia.

"Chen," she continued, settling the baby into her arms. "This is our uncle, Argos Zout, my husband, Senarra, and our baby boy, Bosley."

"I'm truly pleased to meet you all," Chen said with a nod. "Actually, I just came from the Cypris Plantation, but I do call Zor home."

Argus' face erupted in delight at the introductions and he threw his arms open.

"Welcome nephew!" he said, before capturing Chen in an enthusiastic bear hug which pinned his arms to his sides.

Chen looked over helplessly at Intia who merely smiled.

"So, you were just at the Cypris Plantation?" she asked when their uncle finally released him.

"Yes," Chen replied, his mood turning serious. "You, of course, know about Goma."

Intia nodded with a frown. "We heard. That was a while ago."

"Yes," Argos said sadly. "Terrible accident."

"Unfortunately, that was a story invented to save Aunt Leeza's feelings," Chen said grimly. "The truth is much more sinister."

The startled look on their faces caused Chen to downplay any potential drama. "Not to worry, the matter is resolved."

"Well then, enough of this sinister talk," Argos said, his jolly deportment returning. "Your aunt is going to be so happy to see you and you have yet to meet your cousins."

Throwing open the front door to the manor house, Argos led the way.

"Cleaire!" he bellowed into the interior. "Come see our nephew who's come to visit!"

Junior Lieutenant Muasi de Tugor knew his execution to be at hand, he just didn't know how. His friend and fellow officer, Senior Lieutenant Amotinat de Voria, first mate on the Calden frigate *Tamarud,* shared the same fate in the stocks beside him. It really came as no surprise. Mutiny carried the same sentence to the officers who incited it.

Death.

They jammed the rest of the crew who participated into the Zorian jail, awaiting transport to Lorovan prison in the far northern Goyodian Chain. There, they would most likely freeze or starve to death before completing their twenty-five grand sentences.

When just sixteen-grands-old, Muasi joined the navy to get away from the monotony of fishing village life and see the world. Athletic, a quick study and a natural seaman, Muasi rapidly rose through the ranks, attaining third in command of the Calden Frigate *Tamarud*.

Muasi loved the men under his command, some not much older than himself. Life and career looked good for the baby-faced officer just growing his first trace of whiskers. Until the fateful cycle Captain Kejem assumed command.

Kejem Yalta acquired his commission through his family's bespoke name and wealth. He proved totally inept as a naval officer but shined as a sly bureaucrat. He had managed to repeatedly postpone earning his Brightstar pin, required for all Calden naval captains. He also revealed himself to be incredibly cruel to the crew, a condition which only worsened as his command continued.

Everything came to a head one Kan on the bridge, when Captain Kejem ordered them to run the shallows between the islands of the Zer-Tal Twins known as the Umbilical Pass. This reckless act would have grounded the ship and caused numerous injuries. And now, they languished in Zor's infamous Judgement Square, awaiting to die in some manner or another.

When Muasi heard the jail door creak open and the sound of shambling men in irons, his throat went dry and he began to tremble. They were assembling the naked, mutinous crew to witness the executions.

The time had now arrived.

Once the prisoners were gathered, they released Amotinat from the stocks and muscled him over to a simple wooden frame. The guards bound his hands and feet, winching him up by his wrists so his feet barely touched the ground.

A long, tense silence passed, with everyone guessing at the method of the condemned men's fate. Their unspoken questions were answered when a shirtless Mukavar slowly paraded in front of the hanged man. Muasi couldn't help but notice his muscles rippling while wrapping his knuckles with cloth strips.

Mukavar stopped directly in front of Amotinat and stared coldly at the man dangling before him, while he finished wrapping his hands. The anger and frustration of Rafel's rejection boiled inside him demanding some sort of release. The two stared briefly at each other before the Calden mechanic suddenly, without warning, sent his fist crashing into his Amotinat's exposed balls. The former first mate screamed and lurched against his restraints, rocking about like a human punching bag. He then began dry heaving the nonexistent contents of his empty stomach.

Mukavar waited before delivering a series of savage blows to the abdomen. When he moved up to the ribs, roundhouse punches fell with a thud, followed by the cracking sound of bones breaking. With his lungs now punctured in numerous places, blood gushed out of Amotinat's mouth and nose, soaking his neatly trimmed beard and chest.

The horrified prisoners in attendance winced with every strike and some turned away. Tears streamed down Muasi's face and he trembled uncontrollably. So, this was to be his fate, he woefully mused to himself. Beaten to death with the executioner's bare hands.

With the next round of punches, breaking the collarbone and smashing the mouth, Muasi felt his bladder give way and felt the urine running down his legs, pooling at his bare feet.

Amotinat seemed to be all but unconscious when Mukavar methodically pounded his way around to his back. Punishing hook punches ruptured kidneys and cracked the ribs where they attached to the spine. By the time Mukavar leisurely made his way back around to the front of his victim, Amotinat was little more than a barely alive sack of meat.

With a sneer and a shout, Mukavar's fist launched outward, crushing Amotinat's throat. The killing blow seemed to have little effect on the unresponsive hostage.

When they dropped the corpse and removed it, a sweaty, panting Mukavar turned his attention to Muasi who stammered incoherently, paralyzed with fear. The Calden mechanic slowly flexed his hands now covered in bloody rags watching a stunned and cooperative Muasi being bound and suspended like his comrade.

Mukavar peered mercilessly into the youth's terrorized face then stepped up to within striking distance.

"I'm having a bit of a bad cluster," he said ominously, slightly out of breath. "The judge has thankfully given me you, as an outlet for my frustration. Don't worry, as skinny as you are, you probably won't feel anything after the first two or three punches."

It had been an eventful evening at the Argos Plantation. Aunt Cleaire made the kitchen staff prepare a feast and they gave Chen the royal treatment. His cousins were indeed all happy to meet him. The eldest son, Byden, shared his father's buoyant demeanor and strikingly similar features. Their three daughters, Dana, Hilde and Catori, all raven-haired beauties like their mother, fixated on Chen. At the dinner table, Chen felt almost unnerved at how they stared and whispered amongst themselves.

It also became evident, during the feast, how his sister seemed perfectly happy in her life here and had no intention of leaving. Seeing how everything seemed to be in place, Chen announced his intentions to return to Zor on the next cycle. Knowing his family was settled and he no longer had to worry about his siblings, he laid back in the bed his aunt had thoughtfully offered and drifted off to sleep.

At some unknown point during the Kan, the sensation of the bed sheets being pulled down and hands caressing his thighs and chest startled him awake. Quickly sitting up, he found himself automatically reaching for his sword until he saw the nature of the disturbance.

Two of his female cousins sat naked beside him on the bed. The third stood next to the bed loosening her nightgown. She let it slip to the floor with a seductive smile before joining her sisters. The flabbergasted swordsman peered around at three smiling faces and strikingly similar, gorgeous, slender brown bodies.

Chen lived at the academy since he was five grands old. Their stringent training regimen forbade him from engaging in sexual relationships. He lived his entire youth never knowing the touch of a lover. Although there were other students of both sexes he found attractive—and there were many nights where he dreamt about sex with them—the academy strictly enforced a no sex policy, extending all the way to banning masturbation. They expected students to conserve and channel their physical desires into the training. Rumors claimed the masters could feel any erotic shift of energies in their students. It may have been true, because they quickly discovered any who broke this rule and exiled them from the academy. So, at the overly ripe age of eighteen grands, Chen remained a virgin.

"Isn't he beautiful?" Hilde cooed, running her hands across his taut stomach.

"So beautiful," Dana replied, stroking his growing member.

"I told you he slept naked," Catori said, reaching out to him. "I just knew it!"

"Dana, Hilde, Catori!" Chen sputtered. "What are you doing in my bedchamber?"

The question caused a round of giggles to pass between the sisters.

"Why do you think, silly?" Dana said with a lustful smirk. "You're leaving tomorrow and we just had to have you."

"Yeah," Hilde chimed in. "The only men we really get a chance to see are the slaves and they're very unappealing."

"But…" Chen started to protest.

"It's okay," Catori said, stroking his cheek. "We share."

"Yeah, you can have any one of us," Hilde said.

"Or all of us," Dana added, continuing to stroke Chen's now full erection.

"That looks so good," Hilde said bringing her mouth down over the tip. Dana then joined her by cupping his balls and running her mouth up and down the shaft.

He could only enjoy the show momentarily because Catori gently pushed him back in bed and straddled his face.

Quite the sendoff, Chen thought as his cousin's thighs clamped around his head and his nostrils filled with her musky aroma. She pressed her wet sex against his mouth and, unsure of what to do, he began kissing and probing with his tongue.

It amused him when he realized this was the first time he had kissed a girl intimately. He wondered how different Catori's other lips felt.

The sensation of Dana and Hilde's combined mouths seemed to stimulate every nerve in his body until he lost himself in pleasure. He moaned in sync with Catori's muffled cries of satisfaction and involuntarily bucked his hips as he experienced a rapturous first climax.

Chen nearly passed out from the release, but much to his cousins' delight, his erection remained. Once he started cumming, Chen felt like he couldn't stop. He certainly didn't want to and the combination of his discipline and pent up desire facilitated it. Finally, just before the end of the Kan, the cousins begged him to stop. They found themselves completely exhausted and needed to rest.

They slipped out of his bed, walking gingerly, like they had been racing horses all cycle. Chen watched them dress and leave, then fell asleep the moment they closed the door behind them.

Talib's lungs felt on fire and he could swear his legs had lead weights attached to them.

*I gotta get in better shape*, he silently self-admonished while attempting to gulp in air.

His pace had slowed considerably since the chase began a short while ago. He and Tantei intended to question a street level informant named Dousnik, to see if he could shed any light on the ten dead street bosses. Dousnik, however, took off running the moment he saw the pair of investigators exit the hackney.

Talib rapidly gave up hope of catching the fleet target who already pulled at least sixty feet ahead of the portly detective, while navigating full speed around people and various obstacles on the narrow side street.

Suddenly an excited cry erupted just ahead, followed by a blur from the right when Tantei collided with Dousnik in a flying tackle, sending both tumbling to the ground. The Zorian martial arts instructor deftly rolled away and back to her feet. Dousnik lay still for a moment, groaning, before slowly sitting up.

Talib eventually caught up with the pair, huffing in a slow trot. He stopped several feet away and bent over, hands on his knees, fighting to catch his breath.

"You my friend, need to get in better shape," Tantei said glibly.

Talib slowly stood up straight. "The thought *did* occur to me."

"Why'd you run from us all of a sudden, Doosey?" Tantei asked mockingly. "You trying to hurt my feelings?"

"I'm just trying to stay alive," he answered defeatedly.

"By running from us? Boy, does that plan suck! Your sudden lack of cooperation wouldn't have anything to do with those ten dead street bosses, would it?"

Dousnik remained silent and stared straight ahead.

"Okay Doosey, have it your way." She reached down and grabbed him by the arm, wrenching him to his feet. "Maybe some time in the stocks will grease that tongue of yours. Get ready to be naked and cold for a while."

"Come on Dousnik," Talib pleaded. "You've done time in the stocks before. You know what it's like. Why don't you save us all some time and you a whole bunch of discomfort."

Dousnik searched both their faces before lowering his head and softly speaking directly to Talib. "There's a new boss in the Sisters. They've organized the street bosses. The ones they couldn't convince to get in line were killed."

"Who is this new boss?" Talib probed gently.

"Only the street bosses know," Dousnik answered, radiating fear from his cracking voice. "This... This is something new."

"New? New how?" Tantei pressed.

"I don't know, but from what I've been hearing, this new organization is set up different than other mobs."

"Different, how?" Talib followed up.

Dousnik nervously shook his head. "I don't know. I've told you everything I know. They'll kill me if they find out that I said anything!"

"Doosey," Tantei said, with a disappointed pout. "Discretion is my *middle name*, now beat it."

The two investigators watched Dousnik bolt down the street, disappearing into the Seven Sisters.

"Well, that tears it," Talib said resolutely. "Mobsters are trying to organize."

"Yep," Tantei concurred. "We need to get this latest bit of information in front of Vanir and Rafel."

Talib sighed. "And I'm sure at some point Captain Trenton and Red Division will be called in."

"Not our call," Tantei replied. "Our job's spotting them. Their job's swatting them."

Barr-Ani sat at a table in the Shinko Tavern, located on the second level of Tannimore, right beside the Pa-Waga Temple/Bank. She admired the large picture window overlooking the distant sun's reflection off the mirror-smooth waters of the Doldrums.

After the Picean server brought a glass of water to the table she positioned herself to watch the entrance. The Bailian diligently scrutinized the patrons arriving, searching for her friends. This turned out to be no small undertaking.

The place teemed with mostly human visitors, who, with the energy they gave off, seemed to be enjoying the many hedonistic services the city offered. Her Bailian extra senses, however, picked up on something else going on in the room. The sensation felt weak, but still present, nonetheless.

"Hey, Blue," Larzz's voice broke her out of the trance.

"What, how did you get in without me seeing you?!"

The half EEtah grinned and shrugged, sitting down next to her. "Beats me, I'm kinda hard to miss."

She noticed Noorim arriving moments later, her pale white complexion stood out from the dark-skinned humans around her. She sat next to Larzz and eyed the empty chair.

"I hope Taleeka is not encountering any trouble," the Amarenian said concernedly.

"Me too," Barr-Ani replied, peeking over at the door. "I was almost caught standing lookout for her. I managed to convince them I was merely lost and one of them personally escorted me here. I hated to leave her in the vault room, but I had no choice."

"She should be fine," Larzz said, signaling for a server. "I've seen her get in and out of some real tight spots."

"So," Noorim said curiously, "Taleeka mentioned that the two of you have worked together before."

"Yeah, mostly with her folks," Larzz answered. "She's a perfect blend of the two. She's got her mom's head for strategy and coolness under fire and her father's code of ethics and martial ability. Not to mention being a pretty accomplished thief. She picked up those skills young, when she lived on the streets."

Their conversation paused when the same Picean server stepped up to the table and looked around expectantly.

"Three ales," Larzz ordered, holding up as many fingers.

"I'm sorry Larzz," Barr-Ani said apologetically, but I do not drink alcohol."

"Nor I," Noorim agreed.

Larzz laughed and his potbelly shook underneath his thin white tank top. "Those are for me."

The two females shared an amusingly embarrassed look, just before Taleeka slipped into the remaining chair.

"So, what did I miss?" she asked, noting everyone's amused expressions.

"We were just discussing Larzz's intake of ale," Noorim replied coyly.

This caused Taleeka to give a scoffing laugh. "You don't want to get into a drinking contest with him. You'll die from alcohol poisoning long before he even begins to get drunk."

A laugh went around the table and three large tankards of ale were placed in front of a smiling Larzz.

"Okay," Taleeka said, nonchalantly sliding one of Larzz's tankards in front of her. "This place is locked up tighter than a virgin's thighs."

Noorim and Barr-Ani kept entertained watching Larzz's pouting, helpless expression when Taleeka took a sip from the tankard she commandeered.

"To make matters worse," Taleeka continued. "It looks like they've arranged for three identical airships as decoys."

"All four airships are decoys," came an unfamiliar female voice beside their table.

Everyone looked up to see a human female in her forties. She had bloodshot, tired eyes and long graying hair. Her blouse and slacks had an official air to them and everyone except Barr-Ani stared at her in stunned surprise. The Bailian sighed with relief knowing this to be the source of the underlying sensation she felt. The woman came across as a sensitive much like herself, but the alcohol she consumed muted her powers.

"They're going by boat," she continued, her breath reeking of whiskey.

Everyone's eyes shifted nervously around the table at each other, mortified someone had eavesdropped on them. Larzz acted first, scooting his chair to make room. He then reached over to the chair she occupied at the next table and slid it beside him.

"Somebody needs to buy this lady a drink," Larzz said, offering her the seat.

"Hello Sister," she said to Barr-Ani while sitting down. "I felt your presence when you entered and I've been keeping an eye on you all."

Taleeka watched Barr-Ani's reaction to the woman for any indication of trouble. Her premonition abilities had never failed in the past. So far, her friend showed no signs of distress, so she decided to roll with the situation.

"Alright," Taleeka said, waving the Picean server over. "Let's start with the basics. Who are you?"

"My name is Folsom and I do clerical work in the harbormaster's office."

"Well, that covers the who, what and where," Taleeka said guardedly. "Now, what about the why?"

A glass of whisky arrived and Folsom quickly downed it in one gulp. Setting the glass down she eyed the group with a determined look.

"I know how they got those bank notes," she said hauntingly. "They're the blood ransom paid in the return of the Zerian forest."

Folsom paused and her face fell in despair. "I was Storm Winds Clan, until they took the forest. I lost my entire family on that desert plane until your parents rescued us."

She looked at Taleeka. "I'll help any way I can."

Everyone now stared at Taleeka, who appeared just as shocked.

"You're a Zerian Ranger?" she whispered.

Folsom gave a solemn nod. "One other thing about those notes, you've got competition."

When the women departed Chen's bed in the wee hours, it left him only a few precious deci for sleep. At the breakfast table, Chen concentrated on his plate of food and Argos' work directions for the cycle, while the three female cousins shared satisfied smiles and knowing glances.

"So, do you have any plans once you return to Zor?" Argos asked, before popping a small biscuit into his mouth.

"Well, I've been offered a teaching position at the Zorian Sword Academy," Chen said, then sat back and sighed. "I don't know. I just spent thirteen grands of my life there. I may just wander around a bit and see all that I missed."

"You are always welcome to live here," Argos said with a welcoming smile. "I can use a good man."

"Oh, that would be lovely!" Intia ardently concurred.

The female cousins immediately offered their bubbly approval and Argos pointed towards the women. "See, we all want you to stay."

Chen gave a bashful smile to the females and shook his head. "I thank you for your kind offer, but salt harvesting is not my calling in life."

This caused Argos to laugh. "Oh, you wouldn't be harvesting salt. That's what slaves are for. I'd put you in charge of security."

The statement caused Chen to quizzically tilt his head. "Security?"

"Sure thing," Argos replied. "Remember the three lakes on this island continent are the only places in the Annigan that produce salt. It's a rare enough product to warrant its own commodity Note. Someone's always trying to steal it. Right now, it's all the boy and I can do to keep up with it. You'd be a great help."

"A most tempting offer, Uncle," Chen said, actually contemplating the arrangement.

Argos saw the hesitation and gave an understanding smile. "No matter what, you are always welcome."

"Your kindness and hospitality are greatly appreciated," Chen said, looking around the table. "All of you."

The last statement caused his female cousins to blush and look away.

"Give me a little time to stretch my legs in the world and I may just take you up on your offer." Chen said reassuringly.

"Splendid!" Argos thundered jovially. "We'll be glad to have you!"

"Yes, cousin," Dana said shyly. "Please feel free to visit anytime."

Argos motioned towards his son. "In the meantime, Byden's taking a load of salt to the port in Ustess. You can ride with him and catch a ship from there to wherever you're going."

"Ustess?" Chen asked. "I would have thought you would use Oramor, where I arrived."

Argos shook his head. "Nah, too far south. Ustess is just to the north of us."

"Very well, Ustess it is!" Chen agreed heartily.

After breakfast Byden went out to make sure he had loaded the wagon properly, while Chen retrieved his already packed bag and met everyone outside the front door.

"Well, I guess this is goodbye," Chen said with a touch of sorrow.

Argos slapped him on the shoulder. "I prefer, 'Till we meet again.'"

Chen smiled, nodded and accepted a bag from his aunt.

"I had the kitchen staff pack you something in case you get hungry," she said kindly, before hugging him.

"I've got a going away gift for you too," Argos said, handing him a small leather pouch sinched at the top.

"Thank you Uncle," Chen said, curiously eyeing the bag.

"It's salt," Argos said, pointing to it. "You never know when you'll need some food seasoned, or to sell it in case you're in need of gold."

"Thank you again, Uncle," Chen said, nodding appreciatively and placing it in his travel bag.

The female cousins were next. Each in turn gave him a passionate hug, whisperingly recounting their favorite amorous activity from the Kan before. Each one then gave him a clandestine squeeze of his butt cheek.

Intia and her husband were last. Resolvedly nodding, she threw her arms around him.

"Thank you for seeking me out, Brother. Please come back for at least a visit, but if you can't, just know that I'll never forget you." Stepping back, she wiped the tears from her eyes and gave a sad smile.

"May the gods watch over you," Senarra said, shaking his hand.

"I love you all and hope to return soon," Chen said, before climbing up on the buckboard beside Byden.

As they drove through the north gate of the Argos Plantation, Chen couldn't help but reflect on how completely different and preferable the parting from this plantation had been over the previous.

The procession of three mawls, with hoods covering their heads and faces turned downward, padded silently through the streets of Penaber. They arrived at a warehouse directly on the western wharf, not far from their barge.

The moon had recently risen and the Calden seaport long since came to life. A vast array of sentients passed on either side of the mawl line up. The crowd consisted predominately of humans, with a choice smattering of Yupik, Picean, EEtahs and myriad hybrids.

Ruu-Da, the seasoned older white Tiikeri, while struck with the various lifeforms the city supported, seemed more concerned about the two mawls with him. Both the young orange Tiikeri, Faa-Nar, and the Yagur, Geeorn, being relatively new members of the Order of Kaplan, had no experience with what they were about to encounter.

Ruu-Da had only experienced the Chanakans once before, over ten grands ago, in the now destroyed Tiikeri port city of Ka-Beer. He remembered the awe he felt watching their protective bubble rise from the Ocean Deep and float out just beyond the main dock.

Being early in his career as an officer in the Tiikeri Empire, he didn't interact directly. He thought it just as well though. Citizens of the Ocean Deep, Chanakans were ancient, natural water mages and radically different than any lifeform encountered on land. Now, he found himself forced to deal with one.

Ruu-Da stopped by the warehouse door and stared intensely at his charges. "Alright, here's a few things you'd do well to remember. You probably won't be able to get a good look at him, but just in case, *do not look him directly in the eye*. Don't stare at his tentacles. His voice is going to be in your head and he may try to speak to each of us privately. Be respectful but don't let him lure you into anything. And, for the sake of the gods, let me do all the talking."

Both Yagur and Tiikeri nodded they understood and traded anxious glances, tails swishing against their capes. Faa-Nar actually jumped when Ruu-Da banged on the door and winced at the overpowering fishy odor once the door opened. Two Gar'Kal, humanoid fish-men, greeted the mawls. Unlike the Picean's pleasant features, these Gar'Kal had an unattractive fish head with sharp teeth on a green, scaly, humanoid body with webbing between their sharp, pointed fingers and toes.

"We have an appointment with Lord Voronich," Ruu-Da announced confidently.

The lead Gar'Kal nodded, motioning for them to follow, and stepped into the dimly lit interior. Once inside, the rancorous odor made the mawls wince uncomfortably and Geeorn's eyes teared up. The single room warehouse seemed small in comparison to the other warehouses lining the docks. It extended out over the water with a winch hanging above a large, rectangular cargo loading hole in the floor at the far end of the room.

In the center of the room, flanked by two more Gar'Kal, loomed a twelve-foot mysterious bubble. It appeared to be filled with a thick, translucent liquid. They could make out an approximately seven-foot-tall, humanoid shape moving about in the murky fluid. Long spindly arms moved around its sides and a forest of three-foot tentacles undulated atop the Chanakan's head.

Ruu-Da found that he still felt the same reverent wonderment as the first time he saw them. His two comrades, however, practically quaked in fear at the deep one's presence.

A lone Yupik knelt before Lord Voronich, trembling and waving his arms frantically, while attempting to explain himself in his own guttural language. His wide eyes blinked in a panic and sweat poured off his tapered head. Just as Ruu-da warned, they couldn't hear the Chanakan, but the seemingly one-sided conversation gave the impression of a tense admonishment.

The Gar'Kal held out his arm indicating they should wait until their master had finished. It didn't take long until Voronich's hand lashed out and touched the inner wall of the bubble. The mawls could now clearly see suckers on the tips of his long scaly fingers. Swarms of tentacles churned the water green and pink flashes of phosphorescence striated the surface of the orb like liquid lightning.

Immediately the Yupik began to sputter and gasp. A cloud of steam rose from his body and he stared at the escaping vapors with a mystified look. The ice clansman cried out when the volume of steam started building. Wincing in pain, his body dried up and shriveled until its dehydrated husk dropped to the floor. One of the Gar'Kal picked up the withered remains and tossed it down through the hole in the floor.

The creature standing beside them then lowered his arm allowing them to pass. The three mawls stepped before the Chanakan's protective bubble with heads bowed.

*I see you have travelled all the way from Nocturn for an audience with me,* the deep voice reverberated through their heads. *Why?*

"Lord Voronich," Ruu-Da answered reverently, head still bowed. "We are in need of items that we are told you are the best one to provide."

*And exactly what items are my visitors from Nocturn interested in?*

"Etheria."

*Did you not come from the Land of Mists? Etheria is plentiful there, is it not?*

"Yes, Lord Voronich," Ruu-Da confirmed, "but we could not travel with the quantities we require."

They could make out the Chanakan accepting the explanation with a nod of his tentacled head.

"What Etheria do you need and in what quantities?"

Ruu-Da peered over at the Yagur and nodded. "Geeorn?"

Geeorn stepped forward, his tail thrashing wildly. "Uh, sir… Lord Voronich, we require two-foot square blocks of Amber, Aur-Quaz, Azurite, Diamond, Septarian, Trinilic and Vivante."

The Yagur shaman performed a quick, nervous bow and stepped back. The Chanakan grew silent for a moment.

*That is a sizeable order. What is it for?"*

"With all due respect Lord Voronich," Ruu-Da said humbly. "That is a sensitive, private matter."

*I thought it might be,"* Voronich said slyly. *It is also a very expensive order. Tell me, how do you intend to pay for it?*

"We have gold," Ruu-Da replied.

The answer caused the Chanakan to take on a more introspective tone. *If I were home, I would say that gold does not interest me. Unfortunately, the upkeep of this establishment requires gold, but that is not what I seek.*

"What else could we possibly have that you would want?"

*Not what you have, it's what you can provide.* Voronich moved close to the edge of the bubble and they all looked away before they could see his eyes. *My price is one hundred humans, alive and unharmed.*

I... I don't understand," Ruu-Da stammered.

*It's quite simple, bring me one hundred humans alive and unharmed. That is my price.*

"But, Lord Voronich, where are we going to get a hundred humans?"

*That is not my concern. You are in a position to walk amongst them. I am not. When you complete the payment, you shall have your Etheria before a single cycle has passed.*

"But, Lord Voronich, what do you want with that many humans?"

*Much like with you, that is a sensitive, private matter.*

It had been three cycles since he had left Mukavar and Rafel still found it hard to concentrate. It seemed like he had stared at the same report most of the morning and still couldn't decide whether recent activities in the Seven Sisters constituted gang activity. He knew he must remain watchful of his mood. In his current state, he found himself just as inclined to send Red Division in, have the offending parties killed and be done with it.

A gentle knock at his open door brought his attention up from the sheet of paper. Seeing Mukavar standing in the doorway made the spymaster's stomach knot. He definitely didn't want to discuss anything yet. The incident occurred too recently, his emotions were still too raw, so he chose to ignore the situation and return his attention back to the report. He knew this would be difficult when Mukavar stepped into the room and closed the door.

"I didn't say you could come in," Rafel said coldly, without looking up.

The Calden mechanic froze and stared uneasily at his still angry lover.

"Rafel, you've got to be reasonable about this. You haven't even given me a chance to explain!"

"I didn't want to hear it then and I still don't want to hear it now."

"Why? Because you might just hear something that will make you embarrassed about this little tantrum you're throwing."

"I don't throw tantrums," Rafel said, a bit of tension finding its way into his voice, "and I have work to do."

"You know, Rafel, sooner or later you're going to realize you're wrong and you're being a whiney little bitch. You just better hope I'm still around when you come to your senses."

Rafel felt a twinge of anger shoot through him at being called a 'whiney little bitch' but he chose not to take the bait.

"Please close the door on your way out."

Sbirro de Goya appeared ordinary looking in every way, average height and build with light brown skin, short dark hair and beard. He excelled at blending into most groups of people. This particular skill had served him well most of his adult life, eluding the authorities in whatever city he chose to ply his illicit trade of kidnapping.

Snatching people and ransoming them off to wealthy relatives came easily to the smooth-talking malfeasant.

Children of the privileged class were his favorite prey. They were simple to capture and the parents were more than willing to come up with the gold.

His latest endeavor in Penaber, however, proved to be the easiest, most lucrative to date. Normally, he would have to spend at least a cluster stalking his victims. Travelling routes and habits had to be noted and, of course, he had to have assurances the ransom could be paid.

A group of mawls hired him to grab random people and deliver them unharmed. The cat people paid a gold piece per person. No footwork, no ransom demands, just pure profit for very little effort. Sbirro had no idea what they wanted them for, and even though it wasn't his concern, he did find himself macabrely curious.

He moved his small wagon through the darkened streets of Penaber. Listening to the wheels clicking on the cobblestones, he almost regretted taking the job. The girl he nabbed this moonless turned out to be a high-ranking Calden naval officer's daughter. He estimated her worth at least several hundred gold pieces if he were allowed to ransom her, but he felt these mawl employers of his were not to be crossed. He would take his single gold piece and be happy with it. However, he did want to have his curiosity satisfied, one way or another.

Pulling up to the wide warehouse door, he rapped five times in the arranged pattern. A moment later, the door slid open and the mongrel nodded, indicating he could enter.

Once inside with the door closed, the mongrel and the orange Tiikeri uncovered the unconscious girl and brought her over to the opening in the floor. She appeared to be no more than thirteen grands old, with beautiful features and short blonde hair. With little finesse, they removed and discarded her clothing.

Normally he wouldn't even get down from the wagon, just accept his payment and leave, but this time, the white Tiikeri beckoned him over to where he stood supervising. By the time he had gotten down and secured the horse, the orange Tiikeri had also joined him. Sbirro, curious at the change of protocol, warily approached.

"I want to commend you on your living up to your end of our bargain," the white Tiikeri said authoritatively. "Sbirro is it?"

"Uh, yes sir," Sbirro replied nervously.

"Unfortunately, this is moving at much to slow a pace."

"Too slow, sir?"

"Yes, we have a deadline approaching and at the rate of one or two per cycle we're not going to make it."

"Deadline, sir?"

"Yes, we're going to have to step this up."

"I don't know how, sir, I'm working as fast as I can."

The Tiikeri gave an understanding nod. "It's not your labors that are in question. We have to think bigger."

"Bigger sir?"

"Yes, my colleague has devised a plan. There will be some peril involved. Are you interested?"

"I guess that all depends on the plan," Sbirro answered guardedly.

"It will be very profitable for you," the Tiikeri assured. "It requires a more active part by you in our little operation. Regrettably, I can't reveal any of the details until I know you're on board."

"Well, I was kinda curious," Sbirro replied, "and my previous occupation contained a fair amount of danger…"

"Is that a yes?"

"Sure, why not," Sbirro said with a nod.

Both Tiikeris smiled, then, the white one nodded over at the Yagur standing by the opening and body.

The humanoid jaguar picked up a lone piece of tubing and pushed one end through the opening in the floor down into the water. Placing his mouth over the other end he let out a caterwaul and then stepped back, returning the tubing to its place against the wall.

A long moment passed, then Sbirro saw the water below the wharf become agitated. He nervously licked his lips and looked over at the mawls for some sort of reassurance. They appeared calm, so he decided that, as unnerving as this appeared, he had agreed to whatever they planned. Now, he just wasn't so sure he wanted to know what that was.

He considered breaking and running when a large bubble broke the surface. The cat people seemed unphased, so, as unsettling as this seemed, Sbirro remained frozen in place. Inside the orb's murky liquid, he could make out long arms and legs as well as tentacles undulating about.

The young woman, now awake, acted groggy and incoherent. The mongrel lifted her to her feet and secured a grip on her arms. Sbirro wondered if this could be some sort of weird sacrifice to a sea monster. He dismissed that idea when he saw a second, smaller bubble forming from the side of the larger one.

By the time the second orb separated from its parent, the teenage girl became cognizant of her surroundings and started struggling. She just had time to cry out when they thrust her against the side of the smaller sphere. To Sbirro's amazement, she passed through the clear surface into the spheroid's interior.

The girl panicked for a moment, trying to hold her breath. When she finally gave in and gulped in the liquid, the initial apprehension slowly vanished with the realization she could actually breathe the fluid.

The large bubble boiled and elongated, slowly covering about a third of the smaller one. The water inside the larger bubble churned and clouds of ink, swirling inside like a dark maelstrom, dyed the liquid pitch black. Sbirro could make out something sickly green and pink swimming through the shadowy water. Two long gangly arms reached over and suction cupped fingertips locked onto the side where the two globes met.

Sbirro saw a humanoid shape behind the arms, lighter than the stained waters, lifting its lower torso, arching its back to thrust its pelvis toward her and opening wing like flaps on its crotch. Thick ink erupted from its groin area, massing together and forming viscous, undulating tentacles.

They moved in unison, growing in length until they penetrated the smaller bubble. Some of the ink leaked from them, trailing the tentacles and clouding the water behind them.

The slithering appendages stopped and spread out just inside the smaller bubble. Sbirro couldn't take his eyes off the young woman's terrified face as she gulped water, gasping the liquid in a panic while pushing back as far as possible against the bubble. The tentacles swelled, growing to about the width of a ship's rope and coiled back their tips likes snakes readying to strike. All at once they surged and grabbed her arms and legs, holding them open.

Sbirro heard her muffled screams when a tentacle penetrated her vaginally. Her cries rose when another found its way up her anus. A third silenced her, forcing its way down her throat. Together they ravaged her, plunging and thrusting her spontaneously orgasming body until they pulled free and released simultaneously. Each tentacle ejaculated a single, fleshy worm swimming in an inky mucus cloud. The girl, clearly alive and still seizing with orgasms, didn't try to resist as the worms wiggled back into her despoiled orifices.

The tentacles retracted and both bubbles began submerging. He watched the teen's pale body go rigid and slip into unconsciousness as they descended. When they finally disappeared below the surface, a wave of relief flooded over Sbirro. He let out a heavy sigh, realizing he had been holding his breath.

The white Tiikeri then handed him a leather pouch tied at the top. By the weight, he ascertained it held quite a few coins, much to his surprise and delight.

"Now, we need ninety-three more humans," the Tiikeri leader said. "As I said before, my colleague has a plan."

With the revelation from Folsom that the notes were to be transported by ship, Taleeka directed everyone to fan out across Tannimore's wharf. Larzz positioned himself between the commercial and passenger docks. He marveled at the sheer scope of the people and goods he watched pass by and wondered how they would ever discover anything.

"It sure would be nice to know what we're looking for," Larzz softly said into his talking stone.

"Focus on the commercial and freight docks," Taleeka's voice came through. "Outgoing only and with high security."

"Still, a most daunting task," Noorim's voice joined the conversation.

"Until we get more details from Folsom this is the best we can do," Taleeka replied. "Just keep your eyes open."

Taleeka sat back in her chair and glanced over at Barr-Ani next to her. The pair sat at an open-air café on the fourth level, overlooking the entire waterfront.

On the sixth level above them, a massive walkway connected the two man-o-war flagships renowned for being the first two vessels which formed the foundation of the city. All other ships wishing to join and be bolted together with them had to give up their name and autonomy. Naked and almost naked revelers lined up along the ornate walkway, waving and cheering at those arriving by ships below.

"So, you really think we can trust this Folsom person?" Taleeka asked, before taking a sip of tea from a sturdy mug.

"Yes, I detected no deception in her," the Bailian said, looking melancholy. "She struggles with her gift like I do. The feelings can be overwhelming at times. She drinks to quiet the voices in her head."

Taleeka set the cup down and stared at her friend. "I just hope she can get us the intel on that shipment or we're going to be shooting in the dark, like we are now."

Barr-Ani's brow suddenly furrowed and she peered over the railing at the docks. She scanned the rivers of people arriving and departing from the various ships until fixating upon a single person.

"I'm getting intense sensations of paranoia, caution and focused concentration coming from that individual," she said, indicating a nondescript, clean shaven, human in a dull green tunic.

Taleeka leaned nonchalantly forward and took in the suspicious character. He attempted to look busy, while eyeing several small transport ships being loaded.

"How can you lock in on that one guy among all those people down there?" she asked.

"In this case, easily," Barr-Ani replied. "There are only two main sensations from that crowd, having fun and servicing patrons. He may as well be carrying a torch."

"Good catch!" Taleeka said, warily watching. "I would have never spotted him unless you pointed him out."

Barr-Ani beamed at the compliment. "So, what now?"

"Larzz is close," Taleeka noted, reaching for her Larimar necklace she still hadn't tucked back under her shirt.

"Larzz," she said softly, touching the milky white, tear shaped bauble.

"I'm here, Tally."

Taleeka grinned. "I know, I can see you. There's a human male to your left, cleanshaven wearing a green tunic. This may be our guy. I want to have a chat and see if he is indeed our competition. Try to discreetly get him to my room."

"You got it, Tally."

"Okay, let's go wait for our suspect," Taleeka said, tucking the necklace back under her shirt, downing the last of her tea and standing.

Larzz, locked on to his target, decided approaching from behind him to be the best course of action. He started to move when a voice rang out behind him.

"Valued guest, a word?"

Larzz spun to see two members of the Piety Watch approaching him.

"Yeah?" Larzz asked innocently.

"A gentle reminder, in Tannimore, loitering is a serious offence. We observed you standing idly for quite a while."

Taleeka briefly closed her eyes and gave a frustrated sigh when they detained Larzz. Making matters worse, their person of interest was moving off and almost out of sight.

"It's always something," she said under her breath, while reaching for her Larimar necklace once more.

"Noorim!" she called out softly, while touching the Etheria talking stone.

"Yes, Taleeka?"

"Larzz is being detained by a couple of Piety Watch goons. His mark is headed your way. Cleanshaven, green tunic. It's up to you, get him to my room."

"I am on it."

When Noorim caught sight of her quarry, he had moved to another location on the commercial loading docks to observe the outgoing activity. She came up behind him, glided unobtrusively by his side and gently slid her hand inside his forearm, caressing it down to the wrist. She placed her other hand on his elbow, tenderly cupping it.

The man, thinking himself being solicited by a prostitute, offered no resistance. He smiled until he looked over at Noorim and his face fell. At that exact moment, the Amarenian pinched a pressure point on the inside of the elbow and he winced in agony.

"If you attempt to cry out or fight me, I will break your arm," she whispered.

"Who are you?" The man's face contained a mixture of pain and panic. "What do you want?"

"This is not a robbery," Noorim assured softly. "Who I am, is not important. What I want, is for us to take a stroll."

Barr-Ani sat on the bed in Taleeka's room and jumped at the knock on the door. Taleeka, who had been pacing, opened the door and acted immediately relieved. Noorim stood beside the distraught man, her arms still locked with his. Larzz's hulking frame filled the doorway behind them.

Once inside, Noorim released her hold and Larzz stood in front of the door, arms crossed defiantly.

"What in the name of the gods is going on here?!" he asked incredulously. "You kidnap me from a public..."

"Kidnapping is such an ugly word," Taleeka interrupted with a friendly smile, "and in this case, inaccurate. I just needed to get your attention for a private chat."

"You could have just asked," he said indignantly.

Taleeka shrugged and nodded. "Yeah, I could have. This way made sure you accepted my invitation."

The man, seeing assault or robbery unlikely, settled into a suspiciously indignant demeanor. "Alright, you got me here, so what do you want with me?!"

"So, you enjoying your little stay here in Tannimore?" Taleeka began, still keeping her gracious deportment.

The man said nothing, but Taleeka caught a little irritation into his attitude at the seemingly innocuous small talk.

"You know," Taleeka continued, "a little gambling, a little whoring…"

"What are you, the fucking chamber of commerce?" he asked heatedly.

"What do you know about a shipment of Etheria notes?" Taleeka kept smiling affably while her tone went serious.

The man's behavior suddenly turned nervous and he quickly shifted his eyes across the group.

"I don't know what those are," he said defensively, "and I don't know *anything* about *any* shipment."

Taleeka gave a quick glance at Barr-Ani who silently shook her head, sensing the lie. Taleeka nodded and then continued on as if she hadn't heard him.

"Yeah, those Etheria notes are pretty specialized. Not known by the general public. I can't help but wonder who would hire you to procure such a little-known currency?"

"I told you. I don't know what you're talking about!"

Taleeka once again glanced over at Barr-Ani who slightly nodded with a sly smile.

"Well," Taleeka said defeatedly. "If you don't know, you don't know. You're free to go."

Larzz stepped away from the door and the man looked around skeptically.

"What? That's it?"

Taleeka gave a helpless shrug. "Sure, what did you think, we would torture you or something?"

The man's attitude shifted from wary to quizzical. "What makes you think I won't report this to the authorities?"

"And tell them what?" Taleeka asked, amused. "We haven't broken any laws. You haven't been robbed or beaten. Which, by the way, *aren't* illegal here."

"So, why are you asking around about those… things?"

"We're from the Imperial Bank," Taleeka lied.

"And I'm just free to go?"

Taleeka extended her hand towards the door. The man peered around hesitantly before quickly leaving.

The door closed and Taleeka turned to Barr-Ani. "Well?"

"He was lying, that's for sure. When you mentioned procuring the notes, I saw he was part of a small team of thieves. They have no real plan. They're just trying to find the notes, much like we are. When you asked about who hired him, I clearly saw a vision of Tiikeri in a place called Penaber, which is where he was from."

"Well, what do you know," Taleeka said smugly. "The Tiikeri are trying to make a grab for the Etheria notes. They never change, even with a supposed new lease on life."

Rafel could smell him long before he looked up from the paperwork he had been studying. It came across as a musky lavender aroma, which the spymaster actually found quite enticing. When he looked up and saw the young prostitute standing in his office's doorway, he sat stunned in surprise with a flood of emotions crashing over him.

Much like before, Rafel couldn't help being entranced by his beauty. He now got a closer look at his flawless light brown complexion and perfectly symmetrical features. All crowned by a head full of wavy, dark shoulder length hair. This time, he appeared dressed much more modestly than before, in simple draw string pants and ruffled shirt.

Humiliation, hurt and anger coursed through Rafel. It rendered him speechless, unable to do anything but watch the brash young man step inside and close the door. When he turned, the two shared a tense moment, before he stepped forward with a stern expression and trembling hands.

"I'm here to tell you how unfair and hurtful you're being to Muuky," he said nervously.

Rafel felt himself rooted in place, unable to speak.

We aren't lovers," the youth added, "and he hasn't been my client since he started seeing you."

A tide of anger at the perceived lie finally gave Rafel his voice back. "Just like the other cycle, when he went with you back to your place?!"

A touch of defiance crossed the prostitute's face. "Yes, it's true he went there, but we didn't do anything sexual. He helped me. I literally didn't know where else to turn!"

Though still angry, this piqued Rafel's curiosity and the spymaster let him continue, waiting to catch him in a lie.

"The hoon of the house beats us on a regular basis," he confessed with a sad chuckle. "We're almost used to that, but when he raised his cut to eighty percent…"

His head shook and tears welled in his eyes. "You can't live on that! I'm the one getting my asshole pounded every cycle. I should be able to live off the fruits of my labors!"

Listening to him, Rafel felt his anger slowly giving way to sympathy.

"So," the youth continued, "I went and got the only person I knew that could stand up to him. If you would have stuck around awhile longer you would have seen the Clerria's carrying that hoon out."

Rafel had conducted more than enough interrogations in his career to know when he was being lied to. From the timbre of his voice, the story's believability and the young man's bravery in confronting him, his anger melted away, replaced by rising twinges of guilt.

"I guess that's all I've got to say," he said wearily. "You're hurting him badly. He hasn't been unfaithful, at least not with me." With tears still in his eyes and, without another word, he turned and slipped back through the door, leaving a remorseful spymaster berating himself for jumping to conclusions.

He would fix this. *He had to fix this!*

Chen Arador sipped slowly on his third ale when the Grand Turine in the Zorian Harbor rang out nine bells, indicating the Kan was well under way outside. He set the mug down and contemplated the whirlwind of events in the last cluster.

He felt a profound sense of loss at the death of his younger brother, Goma, on top of the guilt from not being there to prevent it. He smiled, happy for his sister and thankful for his uncle's offer of employment, but he just wasn't sure what to do. He needed a quiet little bar to drink and think.

The Bilge Rat Tavern on Zor's rough and tumble southern docks seemed like the perfect small, quiet retreat. The five drunken, rowdy Calden sailors, sitting at the table next to him, proved otherwise. Several times this evening he had been sprayed with ale from their antics. At first, they apologized, but as the drinks flowed, and they grew more unruly, the regrets seemed to vanish along with their civility.

Now, they just pissed him off. He wasn't the only one bothered by the raucous behavior. The bartender, a thin older man with a scarred face, nervously eyed them while wiping down the bar and pouring drinks for the other half-dozen patrons. The lone serving wench, a portly young lady with enormous breasts spilling out of her low-cut peasant dress, had received her fair share of lewd comments and groping. Several times during the evening, they grabbed her buttocks and breasts while she served their table.

One got up and stood behind her pulling her top down to her waist. Laughing uproariously, he reached around her with both arms and bounced her mammoth breasts in his hands. Another knelt before her trying to catch one of her nipples in his mouth. Their laughter and shouts drowned out her cries of protest and the bartender froze, wide-eyed with concern.

Chen stood with a frustrated sigh and stepped over to the overzealous sailors. He grabbed the wrist of the sailor manhandling the server's breasts and yanked a hand away. This broke the sailor's revelry and he glared angrily.

With a silent scolding pout, Chen shook his head. Both assaulting sailors completely forgot about the woman and glowered at the swordsman. The server took full advantage of the distraction. She ducked under Chen's arm and quickly moved away while pulling up her top.

Chen calmly returned to his seat and took a sip of ale. The two assaulting sailors assertively stepped over to his table. The sailor who mauled the woman's breasts sneered and leaned intimidatingly on the table. His breath stunk of whisky and rotting teeth.

"I don't know who the fuck you think you are," he growled, "but you just earned a beatdown you won't soon forget!"

No one noticed Chen's hands surreptitiously move to his lap, but they all saw the glistening blur of his dagger plunging through the back of his aggressor's hand and pinning it to the table.

The man screamed and grabbed at his wrist and Chen came to his feet, drawing the sword from the scabbard on his back. In one fluid motion, he brought the pummel of the handle down on the accompanying sailor's forehead, dropping him unconscious to the floor.

Chen allowed the blade to travel in its original arc until the tip pointed threateningly at the remaining three sailors aggressively rising to their feet. The stunned sailors raised their hands and shook their heads, but Chen still held the blade pointed at them.

"I believe I speak for everyone in saying, you have worn out your welcome here," Chen said calmly but seriously. "Best grab your friends and be on your merry way."

He yanked the dagger out of the table, through the wounded hand, and wiped it on the man's sleeve before he could withdraw his damaged appendage. Two of the others dragged off their unconscious mate, while the last helped wrap the bleeding hand while heading for the door.

Chen shook his head and sat back down. The serving wench immediately appeared with a fresh tankard of ale and a cloth.

"Thanks," she said, wiping the blood from the table. "I couldn't take any more of that. This one's on the house."

"You're quite welcome," Chen replied, with a reassuring smile. "I hope the rest of the Kan is more placid."

"Me too," she said, stepping away. "Thanks again."

When the server returned to her duties, a young man with short brown hair and wild eyes got up from his table across the room and walked over to Chen.

"Hello," he said, meeting Chen's questioning gaze with a broad grin. "My name is Drugo. I would also like to buy you a drink. May I please sit down?"

Now that the two psychics had met and Barr-Ani knew what to look for, keeping watch on Folsom became relatively easy. She knew Folsom drank to quiet the voices and visions storming across her mind, but there seemed something else. Some pervasive darkness tortured her inner most self for which she sought solace in a whisky bottle.

Barr-Ani sat cross legged on the bed in their room and followed her human counterpart, through her eyes, as she went about her morning routine. Folsom's routine remained virtually the same for the last two cycles, as Barr-Ani surmised it did much the same every cycle.

She lived alone on the fifth level of the floating city, in a small two-bedroom apartment. Each cycle, she rose before the moon with a pained look on her face. After stumbling over to a small basin, she fondled her breasts and squeezed the nipples until white liquid squirted out into the receptacle. A look of relief would slowly descend on her face with each jettison of fluid. She heaved a sigh of relief when finished and leaned on the counter.

Once she collected herself, she dressed and made a cup of tea. While the tea brewed, she would visit the second bedroom, where she remained until the teapot's whistle cut through the morning stillness.

The simply appointed nursery with crib and bassinet appeared to have been vacant for quite a while. The Bailian sensitive could feel the waves of grief and sorrow exuding from Folsom, who ran her hands lovingly across the pristine surfaces while tears welled up in her eyes.

Barr-Ani gasped and placed a hand across her mouth. "A child!"

"What was that?" Taleeka asked, from the other side of the room.

"Folsom recently lost a child," Barr-Ani said sorrowfully.

"You mean in addition to losing her family when the Zerian Forest was snatched?"

Barr-Ani merely nodded, eyes wide in shock and sadness.

"Well, there's a reason to drink if ever I heard one," Taleeka replied, shaking her head.

"She's on the move," Barr-Ani said abruptly, settling back into her seated position and closing her eyes.

A hush settled across the room. From the corner of her eye, Taleeka saw Larzz and Noorim standing beside each other by the door, equally entranced by the Bailian psychic. Without warning, the much larger half EEtah suddenly reached out and grabbed the Amarenian's shoulder.

Without looking away, Noorim reached across and placed her hand over his, trapping it. She then broke his grip at the thumb, painfully twisting the wrist and driving him down on one knee with a muffled grunt. When Taleeka shot them an irritated glance, both looked with guilty expressions over at her. Larzz's pursed his lips tightly together, trying not to cry out in pain and break Barr-Ani's concentration.

"She's heading for the Harbormaster's Office," Barr-Ani reported suddenly, her eyelids fluttering.

Taleeka's attention finally returned to the clairvoyant. Larzz rose to his feet and rubbed his sore wrist. Noorim, not changing expressions or stances, calmly watched the Bailian sitting on the bed as if nothing happened.

"She's there," Barr-Ani reported after a few lengthy moments of silence. "It's hard for her to be around people. I'm sensing she hasn't had any time to grieve her loss."

"Doesn't surprise me," Taleeka said sarcastically, "considering the whole productivity thing these Pa-Waga people obsess over."

"She is updating today's logs," Barr-Ani continued. "Wait, she's paused on one."

The Bailian hesitated and looked towards the ceiling with Folsom's voice resonating in her head. *Unregistered Vidette Boat with no manifest or destination plotted. Moored in Slip 8b, under guard. It leaves tomorrow, mid-luna.*

"That's gotta be it," Taleeka said confidently, after Barr-Ani reported what she had detected. "Now, all we have to do is make sure we're in position to intercept it before it reaches Immor-Onn."

Chen had briefly experienced luxury before, as a child in the Aramos ancestral palace in Aris, before being indentured to the Zorian Sword Academy at an early age. He had to admit, the Banavor estate rivaled everything he remembered from his privileged childhood. Standing in the mansion's library, the high ceilings, dark wood paneling and the smell of luxurious leather furniture took him back in time. He could see just a small portion of the well-manicured grounds through the Kan fog outside the tall windows.

The swordsman felt cautiously optimistic about his situation. So far, everything Drugo promised last Kan had come to pass. A private hackney picked him up and the driver offered him a drink from the small bar in the back seat. It turned out the glass of fortified wine lasted the entire lengthy trip far to the east of town. Drugo and a house slave met him when he arrived and he found himself once again offered refreshments while being led through the palatial interior. Now, he awaited meeting the mistress of the estate, and perhaps a lucrative offer.

He was studying a painting depicting an intricate pastoral scene, when the large double doors to the library opened and Mazie, along with Drugo, swept into the room.

Chen and Mazie immediately locked eyes and grinned beguilingly. He paused, truly taken back by her beauty. A head full of luxurious, black, shoulder length hair framed her light brown skin, sensuous lips and hypnotic eyes perfectly. The blue form fitting, floor length dress accentuated her attributes, complimented by a slit up the side to her waist and a high collar.

"You said he was good with a blade, Drugo. You didn't tell me he was beautiful!" Mazie said, stepping up to Chen and offering her hand with an alluring look.

"Madame, please allow me to present, swordsman extraordinaire, Chen Arador. Si. Arador, it is my pleasure to introduce Mz. Mazie de Goya, mistress of the manor."

"The pleasure is mine," Chen said, taking her hand and raising it to his lips. "And may I say I was not informed of your beauty either."

Mazie smiled coyly and gave a shy tilt of her head.

"So, Arador?" she said, still holding his gaze. "Doesn't that mean you have Aramos and Eldorian parents?! Talk about the best of both worlds!"

"You would think so," Chen said, slightly embarrassed. "I mean, my mother was King Shom Eldor's older sister and my father... Well, he might have been pretty far down the house order of succession, but he was Head of the Quartermasters Guild. In spite of all of that, they sold me into indentureship shortly after I turned five grands old."

"What in the name of the gods?!" Mazie balked. "Why would they do that?"

"My mother, Durri Eldor, left for the Twilight Lands and never returned. So, my father, Stryder Aramos..."

"*The,* Stryder Aramos?" she asked incredulously. "Betrayer of the realm, Stryder Aramos?"

"One and the same," Chen admitted, now regretting the admission. "Evidently, he was a jerk back then, too. After my mom's death, he abandoned us to House Aramos. For some reason, they just wanted to sweep us under the rug, so they sent my little brother and sister off to the backwoods of the Zer-Tal Twins and indentured me to the Zorian Sword Academy."

"Did you escape?"

"No," he answered, shaking his head, "this year marked the end of my contract. So, here I am."

"So, you're the King's nephew?" she said breathlessly, taking him by the arm and guiding him towards a couch. "Fascinating! My story's almost the opposite but strangely parallel to yours."

They sat side by side on the sofa and Chen's gaze lingered on Mazie's shapely legs peeking out from the slit in the dress. He sensed her assessing him as well.

"Well, I wasn't born to a noble house," Mazie began, smiling bitterly, "or even to any house, for that matter. We lived in shelters and begged on the streets. I never knew my mother. I think she left shortly after my birth. Dad never talked about her. He tried to keep me safe like a good father and provide the best he could, but that all changed when he went to work for Lord Banavor…"

"*The,* Lord Banavor?" Chen teased, with a sly grin. "Betrayer of the realm, Lord Banavor?"

They both laughed and took a sip from their drinks. Chen found her smile infectious and he stared, unable to look away.

"Yeah," she answered, locking eyes with him, "he's the prick of my story. Banavor separated us and put me to work in the kitchens. I never saw my father alive again. When Lord Banavor disappeared, I was forced to step in and take over things. As you can imagine running an estate of this size is a formidable undertaking."

"I can imagine," Chen replied, feeling her knee touch his. "Drugo, I think I can handle this from here," she said, keeping her flirtatious gaze on Chen. "You're excused."

"Yes ma'am, thank you ma'am," the young man said, promptly exiting.

Now alone, Mazie snuggled a little closer to Chen with their knees still touching. Sighing demurely, she looked away for a brief moment to collect her thoughts before returning her adoring stare.

"And, now that I have things running smoothly here at home," she said, "I find myself restless and in need of undertaking a large endeavor."

Chen still wasn't sure where this was going, but her captivating beauty and lyrical voice amused him, so he nodded sympathetically.

"I've decided to clean up the Seven Sisters," she continued, "to raise them out of poverty."

"A daunting goal most assuredly," Chen said, taken by surprise. "How do you plan on doing that?"

"I've already started," she said, inching closer. "I rallied the local street bosses behind me and, with their help, I opened the first soup kitchen four cycles ago. Hungry people make a poor workforce."

"It sounds like you're off to a good start." Chen said, with an impressed nod. "How do I play into all of this?"

Mazie's expression suddenly took on a pleading quality and she placed her hands on his thighs. "Chen, I find myself in need of a bodyguard. People with a vision often find themselves in the position of ruffling feathers. I've found that the larger the endeavor, the more small-minded people will oppose it."

"Who in the name of the gods would oppose the cleaning up of the most dangerous section of the city?" Chen asked, brow furrowed.

"You would be surprised," she said with a pouty smile. "Please say you'll do it!"

Chen placed his hands gently on hers still resting on his leg. "At the risk 'of sounding boorish, what does it pay?"

Mazie tittered at the question. "Practical questions aren't boorish. In fact, if you *hadn't* asked, I would have become suspicious. The job pays one hundred secors per cluster."

"That's a lot of money," Chen admitted.

"And there are other benefits too," she said, softly stroking his cheek.

"Oh?"

"Uh huh," she purred, "because I'll need constant protection, you'll move in here. Your bedroom is attached to mine. Subsequently, you'll get your meals here, too."

Chen nodded approvingly. "A large sum of money regularly, *with* room and board, Quite the offer."

"Then you'll take it?" she asked softly, moving her face within inches of his.

"Something tells me you're not the kind of woman who takes 'no' for an answer."

"Smart boy," she said rapturously, before leaning in and passionately kissing him.

"You didn't mention the pleasurable working conditions in this interview." Chen said, when she finally broke away.

Smiling sensuously, she stood and took his hand. "Come, let me show you to your room."

"The one attached to yours?" Chen confirmed, following.

"That's right, you'll be on call ten/fifty. I want you prepared," she said, pausing when they reached the top landing of the stairs. "So that part of the interview is over."

"How'd I do?"

Mazie slipped her hand around his waist and pulled him close. "I'm happy to say you passed with flying colors."

She then grabbed his hand once more and started leading him down the hall to her bedroom.

"Now, let's test your stamina."

The deceptively calm waters surrounding the Free City of Tannimore are some of the most treacherous in all of Lumina. There is no danger from strong currents because none exist in the fifty-mile patch of Ocean Deep called the Doldrums. The peril lies in the multitude of apex predator sea creatures congregating around the floating metropolis, feeding off the constant dumping of the city's refuse, including bodies of all sorts.

The moon dipped below the western horizon some time ago and the debauched community above hummed with activity. Larzz swam half-naked just under the surface, armed with a short sword. He entered the central canal running through the city which served as their wharf.

The murky water made visibility all but impossible and because he had never been here before, he had no scent profile to follow. Further complicating things, the weak orange rays of the sun in the western sky made visibility even more of a challenge. The reed snorkel also complicated his task, because if spotted, it would instantly reveal his presence. Being only half EEtah and minus a tail, his swimming abilities didn't match up to his full-blooded relatives nor could he breathe underwater.

He reached out and touched sterns of ships as he passed them, carefully counting the number of occupied slips to his target ship in correspondence with his reconnaissance earlier that cycle. Once confident he had reached slip, 8b, he silently surfaced, poking his head above the water behind the boat.

Treading water, he listened to guards softly talking on the dock and knew he had reached the right spot. He swam under the Vedette boat's Ukko rudder, which served as both the craft's steering and propulsion, now pulled up out of the water. Reaching into the pocket of his pants, he pulled out the female end of an amber Etheria tracker. Examining the stern, he found a small horizontal cavity where the rudder's hinge met the ship's stern and he nestled the crystal tracker safely in place, out of view.

Putting the reed back into his mouth, the half EEtah slipped silently below the surface for the return trip. He had made it to where the end of the docks met open ocean, when he sensed a large presence in front of him and heard the muffled sound of raucous laughter. Popping his head quickly above the water, he had just enough time to dive back down, narrowly avoiding an incoming transport yacht full of the city's newest arrivals.

He heaved a sigh of relief watching the well-lit ship pull up to the docks and then submerged once more. Just outside the wharf proper, he knew the shrouded *Vastus* hovered just above the glass smooth waters, awaiting his return.

Swimming clear of the docks and within reach of his ship, Larzz complimented himself on another successful mission. He drew his next breath through the thin reed when something slimy wrapped around his leg and violently yanked him down into the deep. He could feel suckers with tiny teeth gnawing at his pant leg, but the need for air dominated his thoughts.

He fought for the surface when another tentacle attempted to latch on to his other leg. In a desperate move, he lashed out with his free foot only to discover this maneuver merely aided the creature in entrapping him. Now, with both legs entangled, he felt himself being pulled deeper under the water towards the maw of whatever lurked beneath.

Twenty feet down, he saw a dark shape in front of him. His lungs burned with the need for air and he instinctively reached for the short sword he had tucked into his belt. Once close enough he got a good look at his attacker. It appeared to be a large octopus with a body about twelve feet in length sporting a single large eye and unusually long tentacles, two of which had him.

When another one of its appendages undulated up from the deep and wrapped around his bare chest, he knew his thick hide wouldn't withstand the onslaught of the suckers. The tentacle's pressure constricted his chest, making holding his breath almost impossible.

Larzz lunged the tip of the blade forward and punctured its eye, sending a cloud of grey and red fluid out into the sea. He heard a high-pitched squeal from its beak somewhere below. The beast immediately released him and jetted off into the darkness with a large cloud of ink trailing it.

Not wasting any time, he quickly broke the surface with frenzied gasps, gulping in much needed oxygen. He looked around and saw the rendezvous point only a short swim away, but in his condition it seemed torturous. When he finally rapped on the invisible hull, the side hatch dropped and he slowly climbed in.

"You had us worried there for a moment. We expected you sooner," Taleeka said with a relieved smile.

She nodded towards the Larimar screen on the console with the male half of the Etheria tracker plugged into its frame. "The tracker's working great."

Larzz dropped exhaustedly into a seat and rested his elbows on his knees, still breathing heavily.

"Yeah, sorry I'm a bit late," he said through labored breaths. "I got a bit tied up back there."

"Alright, they're on the move," Taleeka said, watching the red blip move across the map projected on the milk white Etheria screen. "Everybody stay sharp. Gidaria, give me a cross reference on their position. I don't want to lose them."

"Okay Tally," the pilot replied, before looking over at the lizard in the seat beside her. "Blink blink, Brzo, blink blink."

The reptile sat up excitedly. Its long tongue snaked out and licked her on the cheek. He then butted his snout against the Etheria button of the croquis in front of him and the blue phantasmal globe projected upward from the dashboard.

The scene displayed their current position at the southernmost location in the Goyan Islands. From their vantage point, floating among the jagged peaks of Dal Island in the lower Tellasian Chain, they commanded unobstructed access to the Southern Ocean Deep all the way to the Wild Lands at the South Pole.

The six-hundred-mile-wide passage happened to be the only clear route to the Twilight Lands and Taleeka expected that once they cleared the Goyan Islands, they would probably adopt an east northeasterly course to avoid the Banok Atoll and its giant Flavian Portal. For the time being, they would be waiting and watching.

"Wow, they're really moving fast," Gidaria said, watching the dot on the screen move quickly away from the Doldrums.

"Yeah, Vedette Boats are fast," Taleeka replied. "The driver has probably got his rudder buried deep in the water."

"Wait!" Taleeka sat forward in the captain's chair. "Why in the name of the Goddess are they heading northeast?!"

"Can you not get to the Twilight Lands in that direction?" Noorim asked.

"Sure, if you want to go a thousand miles out of your way and navigate a lot more treacherous waters," Taleeka replied, clearly perplexed. "Unless…"

"Unless what?" Gidaria asked, keeping her eye on the dot moving rapidly across the globe.

"Unless they're not going to Immor-Onn," Taleeka said, reaching up and touching the Larimar disk in the overhead console between the pilot and navigator's stations.

"Nibira, are you there?"

"Sure, Tally," the librarian's voice filled her head. "What's up?"

"Other than Immor-Onn, where else could you cash in Etheria notes?"

"Any place that has an Imperial Bank," Nibira said. "The Full Faith and Credit Clause in the Zorian Monetary Compact of 3850 P.A. states that Imperial Notes can be redeemed at any Imperial Bank location. The Bailian government backs the notes, but you don't have to be in Immor-Onn to redeem them."

Taleeka sat back in her chair, eyes shifting from side to side while her mind raced.

"Tally?" Nibira broke the moment of silence.

"Yeah, I'm here. Okay, thanks, dinner when I get back?"

"You bet, hope that helped."

"It sure did and in the nick of time," Taleeka said firmly, touching the talking stone once more, breaking the connection.

"They're heading to Zor!" Taleeka announced anxiously. "We're in the wrong spot and they've got a head start on us!"

Jambor hated not wearing his uniform, but for his current mission, he knew it to be unavoidable. In the six grands since he had taken his vows, shaved his head and received his new, holy name, he only removed the garments for sleep. For him, the red blouse and black high collard cape of the Piety Watch displayed a symbol of pride, respect and fear.

He loved enforcing the Lord's will over the grands. His cane had thrashed many a slothful and impoverished individual whose very lifestyle was deemed wicked in the eyes of the mighty God he served.

Now, his God called on him to perform a vital mission in Zor, the very city he and the rest of his fellow adherents of Pa-Waga were banished from. The Imperial Bank there must redeem the three chests of Etheria notes nestled in the center of their Vedette Boat.

Feeling the cool sea spray on his face, he peered over at his three comrades hunkered down on either side of the crates, with crossbows slung across their backs. All traded relieved looks when the boat driver announced they had exited Ocean Deep and were now in the Shallow Sea.

The mountain peaks of the outer bodies of the Goyan Islands could be seen in the distance. This comforted Jambor, for he felt this boat to be entirely too small to traverse the open ocean. He understood however, speed would be critical on this mission and the only watercraft faster than a Vedette Boat happened to be a Quartermaster's Interceptor. Speed would also prove essential once they reached the High Holy City, where the enemies of the Lord were everywhere.

He allowed himself a smile of satisfaction when Narian Bay and the Zorean waterfront came into view. His mission almost complete, he allowed himself to relax a bit.

Everyone in the boat concentrated so intently on their destination they didn't notice the *Vastus* dropping its shrouding and appearing thirty feet behind them. They didn't see the tip of a Trinilic rod beneath the airship's hull begin glowing before spitting out a small burning orb.

All felt scorching hot water when the apple sized fireball plunged into the sea just behind the craft striking the Ukko Wood rudder and setting it ablaze. With its propulsion and navigation device destroyed, the Vedette Boat slowly came to a halt, dead in the water.

The driver screamed and pitched forward, unconscious, onto the chests, his back already blistering from the scalding seawater. The explosion jolted Jambor and the rest of the Piety Watch, and they spun around to see the rudder burning under the waves. They looked around frantically for the source of the attack, but the *Vastus* resumed shrouding immediately after firing.

The Piety Watch pulled their crossbows from their backs, and held them at the ready, but could see no enemy. They looked up in unnerved confusion when they heard the winching sounds of a large hatch being opened just above their heads. They could still see nothing as the invisible airship lowered itself over the boat.

Keeping his crossbow pointed forward, Jambor gasped in disbelief when the interior of an immense hangar revealed itself while the airship slowly swallowed the crippled

Vedette boat. Once completely engulfed, the bay doors closed beneath them, breaking off the burning rudder.

"Toss the cases on the deck and we'll return you and your boat to the water," Larzz ordered, walking their way.

Fearing Mistress Ve-Qua's punishment for failure more than a fight, Jambor fired at the half EEtah. If he had to die, let it be in combat, not by torture. The crossbow bolt struck Larzz in the upper shoulder, but it didn't deter his advance. He looked down at the projectile lodged in his tough skin and gave a bored expression, before yanking it out.

"Ouch," he said calmly, tossing the bolt to the floor.

Despite what they had just witnessed, the rest of the Piety Watch began firing, peppering his chest with arrows.

"You're just pissing me off boys!" Larzz growled, not bothering to remove the lodged missiles.

The Piety Watch now entered a full-blown panic, looking around for an escape route when they felt the airship rising. They heard the rear cargo door open behind them and the wind began whipping all around.

"I tried to be nice about this," Larzz said, moving up on them, "but you weren't having any of it. I sure hope you boys can swim."

Nadila de Kim knew something seemed wrong, she just couldn't put her finger on it. The auburn-haired waitress always had a keen sense of direction, a trait she had picked up from her father back in the farming hamlet of Kimadorn, where she had been born. As a naked serving wench on the Tannimore/Zor shuttle, she had little chance to put that skill to use until now. She had made dozens of runs taking partiers out to Tannimore, then returning the broke revelers back to their everyday lives in the capital city. The route had always remained the same. The large luxury yacht traveled east, past the island of Zer with its enchanted forest, out of the Goyan Islands. Once they cleared the Goyan Rise and were in Ocean Deep, they set a southeasterly course for the Doldrums and their destination, the Free City of Tannimore. She could always tell when they entered deep water by the temperature dropping and the sea color. That happened a while ago and yet they still maintained an easterly course.

She also noted that their speed seemed faster than normal and the temperature continued to drop. Nadila considered herself no expert in geography, but she felt certain they weren't headed for Tannimore.

"Hey there sweet cheeks," an obnoxious male voice pulled her attention back to her job. "Why don't you scare us up another round of drinks. And what's with the cold weather?"

She peered over at a group of four men seated at a table on deck. Two of them had naked women in their laps who appeared to be shivering.

"I mean don't get me wrong," the lecherous man continued, playing with the woman's extremely erect nipples. "I like the effect on my companion, I'm just afraid that the way her teeth are chattering she's gonna bite down on my dick instead of sucking it!"

The lewd comment sent the four men into peals of laughter while their female companions continued looking uncomfortable. Nadila ignored the remark and headed off to the bar to fill their order. She had long since gotten used to the off-color remarks and being groped.

Technically, the boat servers were not supposed to have sex with the patrons. That fell to the prostitutes in Tannimore. However, every now and then, with a nice customer, an extra couple gold pieces would get a quick, discreet hand-job from her.

Radeen, another one of her naked co-workers, joined Nadila while waiting for the bartender to fill their orders. With a sway of her wide hips and enormous breasts, Radeen swished her long black hair out of the way. She smiled at Nadila and her pleasant dark brown features lit up her face.

"Hey hon," Radeen said, snuggling up against the bar. "What's with the weather? I'm freezing out here with nothing on."

"We're still headed east," Nadila said anxiously. "I don't think we're going to Tannimore."

"Maybe they're taking us another way," Radeen offered. "I mean it wouldn't be the first time they changed things up without letting us folks on the bottom know."

"Maybe," Nadila conceded reluctantly. "But why such an uncomfortable route? I mean the weather and those swells are really getting big. I don't think this ship was designed for these kinds of seas."

"I don't know hon. Hey, why are we stopping?"

Nadila felt it too. The craft slowed to a complete stop and bobbed about in the heavy swells. Forgetting about her drinks, she stepped out onto the deck and surveyed the area. Customers now had problems steadying themselves and started to loudly complain. Even more disturbing; twenty miles off the bow of the ship, the tops of the low mountain range of the Narrow Lands could be seen above the horizon.

Staring suspiciously at the barren peaks, curiosity got the better of her and she bolted to a nearby stairwell leading to the bridge. When she made it up to the smaller third deck, she found the hatch to the wheelhouse unusually closed.

Rushing up to it, she peered through the porthole, gasped and quickly ducked down in horror. There were five sentients crowded in the limited space. The captain, first mate and two men holding them at gunpoint. And a creature she had never seen before stood behind the men holding a pistol crossbow, a humanoid tiger who appeared in charge.

Summoning her courage once more, she peeked again in time to see one of the men firing into the ship's controls, rendering them useless. They then began moving their prisoners towards the hatch.

Nadila rushed over to a narrow solitary ladder to her left and quickly shimmied up it just before the hijackers and ship's officers exited the bridge beneath her. The ladder led to a contained crow's nest recently made obsolete by the modern Etheria navigational devices. Now, it served only as a love nest used by the captain to take the working girls up for a quickie.

Thankfully, the hatch had been left unlocked. She quickly slipped inside, closed and locked the door behind her. The circular room spanned only ten feet in diameter. It had no furnishings and reeked of the musky odor of sex.

A narrow storm window encircled the room at eye level with a sliding cover allowing visual access to the outside. She cracked it and peered out the bird's eye view of the entire ship below and the turbulent surrounding ocean. The hijackers had all seventy passengers and twenty-five crew on the deck, making them disrobe. At first Nadila thought the motive was robbery but dismissed that idea when they cast the clothing and valuables haphazardly onto the deck.

Her heart pounded furiously witnessing the spectacle below and she jumped when she heard someone try the hatch. She sighed in relief when a voice on the other side of the door said, "It's locked."

With her eyes off the horizon, the relentless rocking of the waves twisted her stomach with sea sickness. Nadila swallowed back vomit and resisted the urge to look out at the skyline to stop the nausea. Suddenly the ship ceased rocking, the winds died and the seas stilled. With trembling hands, she quietly slid the cover back and peered out through the narrow lookout gap.

For a hundred yards around the ship the ocean appeared calm, while just outside the invisible barrier, waves crashed, cresting at over five feet. The air stilled, seemingly growing thinner, and her lungs labored to catch her breath. Even without the wind, the temperature continued to plummet. The naked captives on deck huddled together, crossing their arms, shivering from cold and fear.

A nervous gasp came up from the crowd when, twenty feet off the port side, a large bubble emerged from the water. Nadila could make out a tall figure with long spindly limbs and a swirling knot of tentacles rising from the top of its head within the murky water inside the sphere. Every now and then, phosphorescent flashes of green and pink lit up the bubble's interior. The swirling and hypnotic lights morbidly entranced her and she found herself incapable of moving, except for her trembling limbs and fluttering stomach.

The bubble completely rose above the waters and levitated off the port side. The shadowy being within raised his hands and spread its legs out to bubble's edge. A mass of oily black tentacles unfurled from beneath its lower torso and erupted out of the sphere to shrieks of terror from the crowd.

The tentacles swelled and coiled, seemingly multiplying into the hundreds, until they surrounded all the captives and herded them towards the center of the deck. Moving in slithering unison, the tentacles reared back and struck at once, penetrating every available orifice of the ninety-five passengers and crew members. Muffled gagging replaced the screams, until all resistance melted into a pit of orgasmic writhing.

Nadila recognized Radeen's body rolling to the top of the massive knot of slimy flesh and tentacles. Snakelike phalluses pumped in and out of her every orifice. She surrendered completely to the ravishing and her eyes rolled back in her head with sexual abandon.

The abominable mass rutting continued until, one by one, the tentacles ejaculated torrents of a thick, inky mucus filling and overflowing every violated hole. When Nadila saw the fleshy worms burrowing into the victims' greased openings, she could no longer hold back her revulsion and vomited. She desperately covered her mouth with shaking hands for fear of drawing attention. When she finally stopped retching, she dared look back down to the deck.

The tentacles were withdrawing back into the floating bubble, while smaller spheres rose to the surface and surrounded the ship. Tears streamed down Nadila's face and she started to quake when the somnambulistic bodies on deck opened their milky white eyes and slowly untangled from the pile. They crawled directly to the nearest edge and fell overboard, each into their own floating bubble. As they passed through, the thin membranes of the empty spheres sealed behind them and they silently descended under the calm seas.

Once the deck was clear except for the hijackers, the large sphere floated over to the side of the ship. The two men holstered their arms and joined the humanoid tiger climbing inside with the strange being.

The walls of the sphere undulated and it followed the smaller spheres below the still surface waters. As soon as it disappeared from sight, the winds rose and the sea returned to its tumultuous rolling.

Nadila couldn't stop weeping while her simple mind struggled to make sense of what she had just seen. Spinning, she slid down the wall into a fetal position. The waitress hugged her bent knees tightly, staring vacantly, sobbing and quaking uncontrollably.

*There is always one.*

*The one who stands in the way,*
*Resistant to the inevitable.*
*Banavor's old head house slave, Aurkari, with her short greying hair and permanent scowl, defying her at every turn.*
*Until the day she went too far, rallying the domestics against her!*
*The first true challenge of her authority.*
*Order must be maintained.*
*How can she rule an empire, but not her own home?*
*A change was needed.*
*A public show of force.*
*Regrettable but necessary.*
*Lining up the domestic staff out front of the mansion.*
*Vozac seizing Aurkari from the line.*
*Her cleaver, severing the tongue from her head.*
*The screaming, the blood…*
*Contract terminated.*

"Ma'am, they're here."

Vozac's voice broke her vigil at the window overlooking the very spot she took the traitorous bitches' tongue.

"Show them into the library," Mazie ordered, "and get Chen,"

"Yes ma'am," Vozac said, scowling.

Mazie sighed wearily. "I know you resent Chen, but for the hundredth time, Vozac, he's not here to replace you! It's imperative that you two are able to work together."

"Yes ma'am," he said begrudgingly. "But there's something else…"

"What is it?"

"It's only an old woman with a shoulder bag," Vozac said, confused.

Mazie cocked her head in bewilderment. "Does she appear armed?"

"No ma'am, apparently not."

"Some sort of sorcery?"

"It wouldn't get past the ward on the door."

"Very well, show her in. I don't think we'll need Chen."

"Yes ma'am," Vozac said, relief in his voice that Chen would not be present.

When Mazie made it to the library, she found her driver, with a rare smile, engaging in a heartwarming conversation with someone that could easily have been his grandmother. The slightly hunched over woman's head of short grey hair barely came up to his chest. A strap stretched across the shoulders of her plain brown dress and her shoulder bag, as reported, rested on her left thigh.

"Oh, hello dear," she greeted kindly. "You must be Mz. Mazie."

"I'm Mazie," she said, still confused. "Who are you?"

"Oh my, Dearie," she said amusingly. "Who I am just isn't that important. I do have an important delivery for you though. May I?"

Mazie now felt consumed with curiosity and she gestured for her to proceed. The old lady unslung her bag then patted Vozac on the arm.

"I'm sorry dear," she said apologetically, with a sad face. "This is for your boss only."

"Yes ma'am," he said, before looking over at Mazie, who nodded confirmation.

"Oh, young man," she said, when he reached the door. "You take care of that sore throat before it gets worse. Peppermint and honey should do the trick."

"Yes ma'am, thank you ma'am," he said, before leaving and closing the door.

"Now, where were we?" she said absentmindedly. "Oh yes!"

Reaching into her bag, she pulled out three thin wire stands and placed them in a shallow semicircle on the library table. She next retrieved three six-by-nine-inch Larimar Etheria tablets. With great care, her wrinkled hands placed the milk white talking stones on the stands and then carefully inspected her work.

When satisfied she had secured the crystalline rectangles, she produced three inch-long, iridescent and golden brown Etheria nodules, each with a small nipple in the middle. With meticulous care, she inserted each nodule into the top edge of the Larimar tablets. Once finished, she stood back, placed her hands on her hips and gave a contented sigh.

"Well Dear," she said, her voice beaming with satisfaction and pride, "it looks like you are all set up. I've got to leave you now. You are a beautiful young lady. You and your man seem like wonderful people and I am so glad I got to meet you."

Pulling a small vile from her bag, she uncorked it and gave Mazie a wide grin. "It was a pleasure dear, good-bye."

Before Mazie could say anything, the sweet old lady with no name, downed the contents of the container.

"Wait, what…? Mazie asked concernedly.

The woman smiled contentedly at Mazie for a short moment, her body shook with ecstatic convulsions and she toppled to the floor, dead. Mazie reeled in stunned surprise.

"Vozac!" she screamed.

Immediately the door flew open and Vozac bounded into the room just as the three screens flickered to life.

"What happened?! What's going on?!" Mazie found herself on the verge of hysterics. "Why… Why did she do that?!"

"I can assure you she felt no pain," a friendly voice proclaimed from one of the screens. "In fact, it was quite pleasurable and it was by her uncoerced choice."

Mazie looked over at the screen and saw the face of a hammerhead EEtah and then back at the old lady on the floor staring lifelessly upward with a veil of total bliss on her face. Vozac knelt over the woman's body and, with a sorrowful expression, he closed her eyes."

"Lord Hanara what is this?!" Mazie asked, still shaken.

"She was a Legate," Hanara said patiently. "A little-known service offered by the slavers at House Whitmar,

142

used almost exclusively by the Silent Partner and Society of Whispers. No witnesses, you understand. They consist of mostly the elderly or terminally ill, who indenture themselves as suicide messengers. In payment, their family is taken care of. It's really quite popular. One last loving gesture for the family as it were."

The explanation seemed to satisfy Mazie, but her mind still reeled from the shock.

"Well," came a male voice from the middle tablet, "I certainly hope we didn't waste too much money on that one for this meeting,"

Mazie peered in at a thin, stern-faced, middle-aged man, with greying black hair and a uniformed unshaved stubble.

"We'll try not to waste your time, Papi Soden," she cajoled, knowing the crime lord's mercurial nature.

"I, for one, am very curious," a bald man with a short greying beard said from the next tablet over.

"I appreciate your willingness to hear us out, Papi Ardung. In fact, I wish to thank all of you…"

"Yes, yes, get on with it!" Soden snapped.

"Emil, where are your manners," Hanara admonished gingerly, "or is this how etiquette has declined in the Tellasian Chain?"

Soden scowled at the rebuke but seemed to calm.

"I'll get right to the point," Mazie said confidently. "I have a plan, already in motion, organizing here in Zor. As the Papi's of the Silent Partner Cabals, you control the island chains east of the Goyan continent. Seeing how we're going to be neighbors, I thought I'd reach out and offer my hand in cooperation and friendship."

"As long as you're still alive," Soden said sardonically, with a look of disbelief. "Are you fucking kidding me? Red Division will be crawling up your ass so fast, you won't have time to blink!"

Mazie ignored the warning and concentrated on the two mobsters flanking him. Tai Ardung quietly assessed her statement and Lord Hanara seemed genuinely interested.

"What exactly is your plan, young lady?" Hanara asked.

"Well, I must admit, it's a plan inspired by your approach in Makatooa, which I hear is running smoothly."

"It's taken awhile," Hanara said, appreciating the flattery, "but the populace finally got used to living amongst Cul-Ta and I'm finally seeing a return on my investment."

Mazie aimed her next comment directly at Soden. "And it's because of the legal structure of my organization that I hope to avoid any municipal entanglements. This is why I keep a crack barrister on retainer. I think you'll find that in modern-day Zor, Red Division is not the feared entity it used to be. There are now laws in place that render brute squad tactics all but obsolete."

"So, what is it you wish from us?" Ardung asked cautiously.

"Absolutely nothing," Mazie said, shaking her head. "If anything, once I've a foothold in Zor, it'll be about what I can do for *you*. With the High Holy City finally open to the Silent Partner, I can see massive profits from our cooperation."

"It'll never work!" Soden said bleakly.

"Emil, you heard her," Hanara said, "her plan costs us nothing. If she fails, it's business as usual for us. If she succeeds, we will grow richer. I for one like this. You are a bold, forward thinker, Mazie. I wish you good fortune."

"I have no problem with this arrangement," Ardung said thoughtfully.

All eyes turned to the scowling Emil Soden, who, seeing himself outnumbered, softened his gaze. "Yeah, I guess it's okay. It's your neck, Princess! Are we done here?"

"I am," Mazie confirmed.

"Good!" he said curtly, before his tablet went blank.

Once the image faded, the nodule at the top of the tablet sparked several times and the Etheria rectangle shattered into a pile of small shards, accumulating around the metal stand.

"I wish you luck," Ardung said to Mazie, with a nod. "Hanara, good to see you as always."

Ardung's screen went blank and suffered the same pyrotechnic destruction. Mazie stared into the last tablet at the face of the Papi of the Nallor Cabal and head of the powerful Spice Islands Trading Company.

"Now that we have some privacy, young lady," he said, with an attentive nod of his head. "I am very much interested in the details of this intriguing operation of yours."

Ebba Tate considered herself a practical woman and a loyal subject of Amarenian queen, Omaris Atona. The third oldest daughter in the low ranked Tate Banja of Amoso Dor, she had managed to build a successful small construction business, which now served both Amoso and neighboring Taia Dor with over twenty indentures under her.

She preferred indentures to punishment slaves because they tended to be less trouble and needed no security. She also preferred men in that capacity, because of their upper body strength. That, however, is where her appreciation for the male of the species ended.

Ebba especially despised the queen's new laws concerning the inclusion of men in Amarenian society. She scowled in protest, confronting her personal feelings about that very subject, because she found herself in the employ of Alto and Maluria Konrad.

She had, in fact, little to say on the matter. When the queen bequeathed the abandoned farmhouse and modest estate to Maluria sixteen grand lunas ago, she personally chose Ebba's company to renovate the estate, even though she claimed no one would be living there.

Yet, when Valorous Sister Maluria recently retired, she *did* take up residence here, and brought along her dag husband. The queen even granted him full citizenship, along with the title of Valorous Citizen. Yet another slap in the face of tradition.

When the couple contacted her a short while ago about adding two additional rooms to their home, she felt like she had little choice but to accept the job. She placed her five best indentures on it in hopes they would finish quickly and she could be done with the offensive pair.

In reality, she viewed her limited contact with the Konrads a blessing from the Goddess. As with any job, she would check on their work at the end of the luna when she came to pick her indentures up. This particular luna marked the last pick-up at Konrad House East. With the job now complete, they were to pay her the final installment and she could be done with it.

Ebba paused at the entry road to the estate, stood on the buckboard of her carriage and surveyed the job from a distance. At five-foot-seven, with petite features and small upturned breasts, she hardly looked like the owner of a construction crew. Yet, her short whitish blonde hair and piercing hazel eyes demanded even the burliest workers think twice about challenging her.

She smiled in satisfaction, nodding her approval. The job looked good from where she stood. They attached the two new circular rooms to the south side of the large circular main house and built two independent living structures just to the north of the primary residence. All that remained now would be the final inspection.

She sat back down and spurred the single horse up the road towards the newly renovated domicile. Drawing closer, she continued her visual assessment, admittedly pleased with the work. However, the next thing she saw sent her blood boiling.

Her indentured workers sat around the new patio, with drinks in their hands, laughing and talking with Alto Konrad.

"What is the meaning of this?!" she said incredulously, leaping off the carriage.

The workers looked up in wide eyed panic and quickly rose to their feet, heads meekly bowed.

Alto merely smiled, watching her storm their way.

"Why aren't you working?!" she demanded tersely.

"They finished early and it *is* a warm cycle," Alto answered, the serene smile never leaving his face. "They worked hard, so I provided refreshments."

Ebba shot Alto an irritated glare. She loathed the thought of being in this dag's presence. Even his manner of dress insulted her. Now bestowed full Amarenian citizenship, he had adopted the bare-chested look and wore the native brown cropped pants.

"I wasn't talking to *you!*" she spat.

"It was unclear who you were speaking to," Alto said, completely unphased by the outburst, "so I took the liberty of answering."

Ebba caught herself before vocalizing her next toxic thought. Realizing it was probably not a good idea to anger a Valorous citizen and friend of the queen. Instead, she turned back to her men.

"Get in the wagon," she ordered bluntly, before addressing Alto again. "Where is the mistress of the house? She is supposed to have my final payment."

"My wife has gone to Taia, in order to procure some domestic help. She has left me with the task of paying you."

This was yet another cultural slap in the face. A man handling money seemed nothing short of preposterous.

"How very *modern* of her," Ebba said sarcastically.

"I will go and get it directly," Alto said, before disappearing inside.

With Alto gone, Ebba did a quick close-up inspection. As usual, her men did an excellent job, but they would still have to be punished for their impertinence.

Alto returned with a small pouch sinched at the top and handed it to her.

"Please count it," Alto said pleasantly.

Ebba eyed him suspiciously when opening the pouch. A quick glance inside accounted for all of the gold pieces agreed upon.

"I cannot help but notice your agitated demeanor," Alto said congenially. "If I have done anything to offend, I most humbly apologize."

"Your very presence here offends," Ebba answered icily. "The queen has decreed new laws and I must accept them. I don't have to like it."

"Change is the only constant in the multiverse," Alto said thoughtfully. "I feel your life would be more harmonious if you embraced the change instead of combatting it."

Ebba's eyes flashed with anger at the swordmaster. She spun and climbed back up on the buckboard.

"There was a time, not very long ago that I would have killed any dag who dared speak to me so disrespectfully." She hurled each of the words like verbal daggers at the master of the house.

"Ah yes," Alto countered sarcastically. "The good old days, no doubt. And by the way, that's *Valorous dag* to you, if you please."

Ebba gave Alto a last contemptuous sneer before snapping the reins and heading off.

The fact spring was well under way across the better part of Lumina made little impact on the weather in the Narrow Lands. With their wind-swept tundra and remote fjords, the return of birds and blooms remained a foreign concept to the far northern strip of real estate. Despite its inhospitable climate, the hearty Yupik ice clansmen thrived and even the humans of House Calden made a permanent presence there.

The City of Penaber, on the continent's northwest coast, proved a shining example of human will and determination. The small city counted itself a thriving metropolis, dealing mostly in the export of Yupik textiles and crafts. A seaport in its own rite, it also hosted a Calden naval base standing watch over the shipping for hundreds of square miles of the world's northern Ocean Deep. With the coming of cities, however, crime and skullduggery became an unwanted but inevitable byproduct of congregated sentients.

Admiral Metauri de Voria, Commander of the Calden Naval Constabulary stationed in Penaber, sat behind her desk and watched the last of the snow melting through her barred windows and sighed. At thirty-five, she had risen as the youngest constabulary commander in history with her first command. They chose Penaber specifically for the junior admiral to cut her teeth on because of its remote locale and relatively low crime rate.

Lately, however, things seemed anything but calm. Several people mysteriously went missing, much in the same manner, one of which happened to be the daughter of a prominent naval officer. This would be her first real test and she had no intention of failing.

A soft knock on her partially open door brought her out of the gloomy mulling she found herself in. Her attention focused on the slender canine head of her spymaster poking inside her door.

"Excuse me, Admiral," he said in a refined baritone. "Might I have a word?"

"Sure, Casus, come on in," she said smiling, thankful for the interruption.

The four-foot-tall Akina nodded his thanks, entered and closed the door. The rust brown, humanoid fox, originally from the Barrens, always appeared impeccably dressed and cultured. She inherited him from the last commander and, even though she had been unaccustomed to having civilians under her, so far, she had taken a liking to him. He proved to be sly and resourceful, but by far his biggest asset turned out to be his considerable knowledge of the city.

"Admiral, much like the others, there've been no ransom demands, so far," he said somberly.

Metauri exhaled loudly and nodded at the disappointing news.

"And I suppose just like the others, there are no leads?" she said, running a hand over her bald head.

"I'm afraid the trail has gone as cold as the wind blowing outside your window, Admiral."

Metauri scoffed loudly. "I don't see how you all put up with this weather as a constant. I mean, I've only been here a quinte and I'm already sick of it."

"Actually, Admiral," the Akina said, grinning, "where I hail from, this would be considered balmy."

The admiral shook her head in frustration. "We've gotta be missing something!"

"Perhaps we are dealing with some form of illicit underground slave operation. We might wish to get House Whitmar involved?"

"Maybe," she conceded, still sounding unconvinced. "But for right now it's a Calden problem. You are right about one thing though."

"How so, ma'am?"

"We're probably gonna need help on this one. Contact the embassy in Zor. Have them assign us a mechanic. We've got to get a handle on this before it gets too far out of control."

Rafel's heart pounded and he fought back waves of panic rushing out the doors to the Zorian Guards' headquarters. He had gone to Mukavar's office with hat in hand to apologize and beg for forgiveness, only to find it empty. They told him that the Calden Mechanic left mere centis before on an assignment and, if he hurried, he might be able to catch him.

The anxious spymaster raced across Judgment Square, hailed a hackney and set out for the air station. He nervously drummed his fingers on the seat beside him, desperately formulating what he would say, while the vehicle plodded through the congested Zorian traffic.

He just *had* to catch him.

Mukavar, well known for taking potentially dangerous missions, could very well disappear and not come back. If anything should happen to him while away on assignment, Rafel would never be able to forgive himself.

After the cab dropped him off in front of Air Station Three, he found himself running to the flight decks, his mind consumed with apprehension. When the EEtah guard at the entrance of the military hangar stopped him, he fumbled for his identification while franticly peering around the man-shark's massive frame, searching the departing airships.

When finally allowed to pass, Rafel bolted for the first flight gate. He pulled aside one of the ground crew, a young woman with short brown hair in a green jump-suit, and frantically searched her face while taking in gulps of air.

"You're a departing ground crewmember?" he asked through labored breaths.

"Yes sir."

"Did you see a Calden naval officer, tall, handsome with salt and pepper hair and beard?"

"Yes sir, I just put his sea bag in that ship," she said, pointing to a Resistance Class Cruiser waiting for the air boss' go order.

He quickly thanked her, before sprinting over to the ship. Approaching the Air Boss, he retrieved his identification and held it up for inspection.

"I need you to hold that ship!" the spymaster ordered.

The older, balding man briefly studied Rafel's credentials and then touched a Larimar shard on the upper sleeve of his jumpsuit. "Uh, we've got a Zorian captain that needs access before takeoff."

Rafel couldn't hear the response in the Air boss' head, but the side hatch of the craft slowly lowered. Without waiting for the entry way to fully extend, he sprinted to the waiting ship and up the ramp.

Inside, the captain, pilot and navigator sat in command chairs staring quizzically at him, as did the six Calden Marines seated along the hull. Peering back at the puzzled faces, Rafel's heart sank. Mukavar wasn't on board.

"Is there something we can help you with, Captain?" the ship's captain asked cautiously.

"It's… it's nothing, a mistake," a dejected Rafel said on the verge of tears. "Sorry to delay your flight."

He turned to leave, shaking his lowered head mournfully.

"Oh, you weren't holding up the flight," the captain replied. "We're waiting on one more passenger. They already delivered his gear. Believe me, if his orders didn't come from the top, we would have left his ass!"

Rafel immediately brightened at the news. When he looked back up, he saw Mukavar standing at the bottom of the ramp staring up at him.

The walk down the ramp felt like slow motion and Rafel noted the hopeful look on Mukavar's face. All of the remorseful soliloquies the spymaster had rehearsed evaporated the moment he stood before him.

"I'm so sorry, I know the truth now. Please forgive me," the remorseful spymaster stammered.

"I've been miserable this last cluster," Mukavar said, his voice cracking slightly.

"I know," Rafel said, tears welling up in his eyes. "I'm so sorry! I love you! Can you forgive me for being a suspicious little shit?"

"You *were* a little shit," Mukavar remarked with a touch of relief.

Tears now streamed down Rafel's face and he nodded while sniffling. "I know. I'm so sorry."

Mukavar reached out, put his arms around his sobbing lover and pulled him close.

"Apology accepted," he whispered in Rafel's ear, "and you are forgiven."

Mukavar paused and eyes lit up mischievously. "You do realize there's going to be a suitable punishment for you when I get back?"

An overjoyed Rafel peered up into Mukavar's face as he leaned down and kissed him hard. Then suddenly breaking, he pushed the spymaster back.

"I've got a flight to catch!" he said, stepping toward the ramp.

"You're moving back in, right?"

"As soon as I leave here," Rafel said, still sniffling.

"We'll talk more once I get back, I gotta go!"

"Where are you going?" Rafel asked, finding his voice.

"To investigate an abandoned party barge off the coast of the Narrow Lands. Then, I'm heading over to Penaber to deal with disappearing locals," the Calden Mechanic said, before heading up the ramp and disappearing into the airship.

Pierce Calden excitedly rushed through the crowded halls of the Zorian Forum. After a relatively dull morning, he received news of Taleeka Konrad's return and her request for an audience. Rounding the corner leading to the conference rooms, he spied Joc' Valdur coming down the hallway from the opposite direction. He too, carried the same effervescent expression. They met in front of the double doors of Meeting Room C, where a Zorian Guard, standing sentry, saluted them.

"What do you think?" Pierce asked eagerly.

"I think we're about to find out," Joc' replied, reaching for the door handle.

The pair found Taleeka casually seated with her feet propped up on the long conference table. Noorim sat rigidly next to her, staring uncertainly around the room. Larzz stood by the wall at the far end of the table with three medium sized chests at his feet.

"Oh, hey guys!" Taleeka greeted robustly. "We're back!"

"Did you get them?!" Pierce blurted.

"What, no hello?" Taleeka teased. "How ya doing, Tally? Is everybody okay, Tally?"

With a broad grin, Taleeka gracefully took her feet off the table and sat up straight.

"You know, for a couple of diplomats, you guys really need some work in the diplomatic department."

Two unamused stares met her quip.

Rolling her eyes in resignation, she glanced over at the half EEtah. "Larzz?"

A smile broke out on Larzz's face as he reached down and opened the chests. All three were full of one-hundred-Secor Etheria notes. Pierce whistled in appreciation and both men walked over to the chests.

"Well, you did it," Joc' said reverently, picking up three of the oblong wafers. "We knew it was a long shot, but..."

"That's why you had *us* do it," Taleeka said smugly.

Joc' nodded in agreement and, with a satisfied smile, handed a note to both Larzz and Noorim, who accepted them with looks of pleasant surprise.

"They've already been paid," Taleeka said, getting to her feet, "but if you want to tip them, go right ahead."

When Joc' tried to hand one to Taleeka, she raised her hand and shook her head.

"Thanks," she said, the smile never leaving her face, "but like I said when I took this job, 'I don't want your money.'"

Pierce's grin turned sly. "You want a favor."

"Well, *yeah!*" Taleeka admitted gleefully, "and believe me, it'll be a *big* one. I just don't need one right now."

"I guess we'll just add this to the growing list of favors we owe you," Joc' said admiringly.

"Just the way I like it."

"So, did you run into any difficulties?" Pierce inquired, his mood changing from happy to serious.

"So, now he asks!" Taleeka threw her hands in the air in fake exasperation.

Pierce recoiled at the statement, clearly taken aback.

"Relax," Taleeka said, her jovial demeanor returning. "Kidding! And yeah, we hit a few snags, but we took care of them. That's why we get the big bucks! I'll tell you one thing, your Tiikeri buddies are not to be trusted. One of those snags I was referring to? The Tiikeri had their own people there making a play for the notes."

Joc' and Pierce traded concerned glances while Taleeka continued. "You can't expect a tiger to change its stripes. They've had their eye on the Etheria for quite a while now."

"Yes, we went to war over it, as I recall," Joc' said grimly.

"We interrogated one of their guys," Taleeka recounted. "He said they worked out of Penaber. Why? I don't know.

"Hey, on second thought... I *will* take that note. It's for Barr-Ani, the one who actually extracted the information. She couldn't be here."

"Sure," Joc' replied handing her the Ukko wafer.

"This is the third time Penaber has come to my attention in a very short period of time," Pierce said, furrowing his brow, "and not in a good way. In fact, we just dispatched a mechanic there."

"Who?" Taleeka asked, reaching for her backpack in the seat beside her.

"Mukavar," Pierce replied solemnly.

"Wow," Taleeka said with a raised eyebrow. "If you've sent Muuky, it must be serious."

"It is," the Calden ambassador confirmed.

"This whole Tiikeri thing certainly piqued my curiosity," Taleeka said, slipping the note in her pack and slinging it over her shoulder. "I think a little trip to Penaber might just be the thing to satisfy my nosiness."

The moon set over the Free City of Tannimore and Wikk Roncel, better known to his subjects as Wikk the First, stood by the railing watching the moon intersect with the sun, causing what the locals called "the evening flare." Watching the orb slip below the horizon, he suddenly realized he inadvertently held onto the railing with a death grip.

It had only been three lunas since his Etheria notes had been stolen and he found himself so incensed that clear thinking seemed almost impossible. They ran a thorough sweep of the city and rounded up the five thieves.

They, along with two of the surviving guards which allowed the theft to happen, were handed over to his Minister of Justice, Mistress Ve-Qua. The tenth level Kinjuto Master wasted no time in extracting information from them and now she had news.

"Brother Wikk," came a familiar voice on his left. "Is it true? She has information?"

Harper Aramos joined his fellow acolyte of Pa-Waga at the railing, and they stared out at the mistress' infamous barge on the edge of the floating city. The two men could not have looked more different. Both stood just under six feet, but Harper's close-cropped hair and beard accented a basically jovial demeanor. On the other hand, Wikk's light golden skin and cleanshaven face radiated cruelty.

"That's what she says," Wikk replied tersely.

"Well, we may as well get this over with," Harper suggested reluctantly.

He started off for the barge, but briefly paused halfway up the ramp, allowing Wikk to catch up.

"I don't like this place," Harper admitted quietly when Wikk fell in beside him. "It's one thing to indulge her at council meetings, but I find her abode... *unsettling* and her methods... *extreme*."

Wikk said nothing, still lost in his own melancholy. It was true, the torture mage's methods *were* extreme, but she got results and that suited him just fine. When they stepped off the entrance ramp onto her barge, Wikk noticed Harper wincing at the moans and agonized cries coming from within the large open hatchway.

"Best steel yourself for this," he advised when they reached the stairway leading down into the Atrium of Pain. "It won't be pretty."

Harper swallowed hard and the two descended into the morose gloom. To keep Harper from becoming too skittish, Wikk directed him rapidly down the steps to the third level and into her private dungeon, avoiding the unpleasantries on the first two floors.

Unfortunately, the mistress kept her private chambers in the rear of the level and Harper found himself forced to endure passing through a host of people painfully affixed to numerous blood-stained contraptions. By the time they made it through the beaded curtain and into Ve-Qua's lair, Harper appeared pale and sweated profusely. What the mild-mannered, former banker witnessed upon entering caused him to heave. He closed his eyes, lest he lose the contents of his stomach.

Five corpses hung by their wrists in a row with their feet barely touching the floor. She completely flayed their skin off of them and they lay in wet, gruesome piles at their feet.

A naked Ve-Qua stood by the line of death with her head thrown back in ecstasy. Two nude, low-level students attended to her. One, down on all fours to her side, licked her blood-stained feet with enthusiastic abandon. The other knelt before her with Ve-Qua's hand gripping the back of his head, grinding his face into her open vaginal lips. Her bolted breasts heaved and swayed with every relentless thrust.

A naked Amarenian, holding a thin-bladed skinning knife, stood on the other end of the row of corpses. Crimson streaked her alabaster skin and she kept her face lowered while her mistress heaped morbid praise upon her through gasps of pleasure.

Wikk stepped up to the macabre scene and, out of the corner of his eye, saw Harper staring down at the floor. Wanting to get his comrade out of there as soon as possible, he loudly cleared his throat.

The unexpected noise caused everyone to stop and gaze over at the two priests of Pa-Waga. A head of wild black hair framed the Amarenian's pale baby face. Like her mistress, ominous black circles formed under her eyes and a merciless scowl twisted her mouth.

Ve-Qua grinned broadly, immediately abandoning her hedonistic revelry.

"Hello dearies," she greeted huskily. "So good of you to visit!"

"You said you had something?" Wikk asked in a monotone.

"I do!" she bubbled.

The Kinjuto mistress gave a refreshed sigh and shoved the man with his face buried in her vulva to the floor. She then kicked the one licking her feet in the nose. He fell beside the other, blood flowing from both nostrils.

"Right this way," she said playfully, stepping past the two on the floor and walking up to the Amarenian.

"This is my top student, Qasia," she said, leading the group over to the line of five dangling corpses. "I had her perfecting flaying techniques this luna. She did very well."

Ve-Qua suddenly stopped and gave Harper's staring at the floor an amused look.

"Oh Harpy," she cajoled, stroking his cheek. "I would have thought you had gotten over the whole squeamish thing by now."

Harper recoiled at her touch, causing the Mistress of Pain to giggle.

"Okay," she said, addressing Wikk once more, "that's your five thieves. Only one really saw anything. The rest were just practice for Qasia. They were hired by a Tiikeri over in Penaber. They, however, were beaten to the treasure by another group."

Wikk once again found his fists clenched in rage. "Who?"

"He saw four of them; a Bailian female, an Amarenian female, a seven-foot-tall human hybrid of some sort and what he assumed was their leader, a young Goyan female in her late teens."

"Anything else?"

"Yes, he also said the Amarenian was able to tie him up with her hands, as he put it. That's how they captured him."

"Kovos," Qasia said.

"Kovos?" Wikk inquired cautiously.

"An Amarenian martial art. It uses circular movements, throws and joint locks. They've got a Kovos practitioner on their team."

When Wikk nodded that he understood, Ve-Qua continued, "They claim a huge, invisible airship rendered them dead in the water and then the ship swallowed them up, Vedette boat and all. The surviving guards all said the same thing about the human hybrid. He basically took their crates and threw the men out into the ocean."

"We're never going to get those notes back," Harper lamented, shaking his head sorrowfully.

"Maybe not," Wikk said sneering, "but we can make them pay dearly for them."

Wikk then cast his enraged gaze on the blood streaked Amarenian. "You know something about these people. You will be the hand of vengeance for the Lord. I command you to hunt down the ones responsible for this blasphemy and kill them, slowly. Take two Piety Watch with you to assist."

"I am honored, Lord Wikk," she said, bowing her head. "Shall I bring you their skins, my Lord?"

"Yes, afterwards you can present them to your mistress to add to her collection."

This caused Ve-Qua to titter sensually. "It's talk like this that never fails to get my pussy wet!"

# ACT TWO

## Suspicious Gatherings

*T*hey don't call it the sea of storms for nothing, Mukavar noted to himself, peering down at the turbulent waters of Lumina's northeast Ocean Deep through the rain pelting the windshield. Their airship rapidly approached the Narrow Lands, which meant the Innaca Deep lay just to the north, adding waves of Flavian displacement to the tempest around them.

Looking back into the cabin from behind the command chairs, he checked on his Calden Maritime Legion charges. The detachment of six sat facing each other, staring out with bored expressions. Two actually had their chins on their chests, snoozing away.

Mukavar chose to move up to the ship's forward area not for the view, but for the distraction. In spite of the importance of the dual mission at hand, his mind kept drifting back to returning home and an extended session of make-up sex with Rafel.

The craft violently lurched one final time before exiting the squall line and the Calden agent had to grab onto the back of the captain's chair to avoid being tossed to the deck. The rain abruptly ceased, but not the wind and the large swells below spoke to the difficulty of the mission.

"There she is," the navigator said, pointing out the windshield.

Everyone peered where the wiry young woman with short blonde hair pointed and Mukavar exhaled loudly. The shallow hulled, abandoned pleasure yacht tossed about in the frigid waters below like a bath toy.

"I'm surprised she's still afloat," Mukavar said, intently surveying the situation. "That boat wasn't designed for these waters."

He called back over his shoulder, "Sergeant!"

Immediately, a rugged looking young marine got up and made his way over, carefully watching his balance with every step.

"Yes Lieutenant?"

Mukavar nodded towards the battered vessel. "That's what we're dealing with. Those have got to be twelve-foot swells. Who's the pilot on your team?"

"I am, sir."

"Can you get that ship back to Zor?"

"Can do, sir!"

"Alright, Captain, take us to right over the foredeck and hold while we secure that craft. I'll be reboarding as soon as we're finished."

"You heard the lieutenant, Helmsman," the captain said. "Take us in and hold."

"Yes sir."

The deck of the yacht bobbed amongst the giant waves, swaying and tilting, with water violently crashing over the sides. With guided precision, the Valdurian air ship positioned itself seven feet over the bow of the undulating craft and lowered the cargo bay doors underneath the rear of the ship.

Standing by the open hatchway, a frigid blast of air and sea spray struck Mukavar. He glanced behind him checking on his men. All six marines wore blue Calden cold weather outfits. Much like the Valdurian Ghost Suits, these thermal, rubberized jumpsuits had plenty of pockets and attachments, as well as Ukko threads woven throughout. Non-skid boots and gloves covered their hands and feet, insuring traction on slick surfaces. Each armed themselves with Firehammer Carbines and four additional magazines.

Mukavar nodded to the sergeant, they appeared ready.

"Alright legionnaires," he said, "watch that deck it's swaying pretty good. Once we land, perform a standard sweep of the ship.

"Sergeant, you and I make our way to the bridge and get this vessel under some sort of control. Got it?!"

"Yes sir!"

"And... go!" Mukavar yelled, then jumped through the large opening in the floor.

The Calden mechanic landed in a crouch. He rose laboring to stay on his feet when a wave crashed across the bow, pummeling him with a rush of icy sea water. Moving off to his right, he unholstered his Mark Seven pistol and waited for the others.

One by one, the marines leapt onto the undulating deck, unstrapping their carbines from their backs upon landing.

The last one misjudged the timing of the lurching craft and slipped. Water surging across the deck swept him against the railing and he teetered precariously trying to gain a foothold. Two of his comrades quickly grabbed him by the arms, keeping him from being swept overboard.

Once everyone safely boarded, Mukavar signaled and the marines spread out, performing their well-rehearsed roles. Mukavar and the sergeant identified the wide windows of the wheelhouse and made for the nearest stairwell. Once inside, the bridge felt relatively comfortable, it still felt cold, but at least they were out of the freezing winds.

"Even though someone shot into this panel, there's nothing wrong with these controls, sir," the sergeant reported after examining the control panel. "The Ukko rudders are working fine and I can have us under way as soon as you give the order."

"Very good, Sergeant. Once we have the all clear from your team."

The door to the bridge suddenly opened and a chilly blast of air followed a corporal inside.

"Sir, we swept the ship. There's no one on board. Nothing's been touched. It looks like they just up and disappeared without a trace... and without their clothes. There's a pile of clothing and valuables on the deck."

Mukavar nodded in acknowledgment. "Alright then, Sergeant, prepare to get underway and..."

Mukavar abruptly paused and cocked his head. "Did you hear that?"

All went quiet on the bridge and they could hear the faint, but distinct sound of rapping.

"It's coming from above us," the sergeant said, peering up at the ceiling.

Mukavar stepped out of the wheelhouse and noticed the narrow ladder leading upward to the crow's nest.

"Okay," he said, starting up the rungs. "This is where it gets interesting. Corporal, you're with me. Sergeant, cover us from down here."

The rapping grew increasingly louder the higher they climbed and didn't cease when they stopped outside the door to the abandoned crow's nest.

Mukavar readied his pistol and nodded to the corporal who hefted his carbine and nodded back. Stepping off to the side, he blasted the handle and flung the door open. When no attack came, he leapt inside, weapon pointed.

"By the gods!" he gasped, lowering the pistol.

A beautiful naked woman with coffee brown skin and bright red hair crouched on the far side of the tiny round room. The rapping they had heard was her trembling knee, knocking against the hull. The moment she saw them she recoiled in fear and began pleading.

"Take it easy ma'am," Mukavar said reassuringly. "I'm Lieutenant Mukavar, Calden Navy, we're here to help."

Relief flooded across the woman's face and she broke down in tears, while still violently trembling.

"Corporal, find this woman a blanket and perhaps some warm clothes." Mukavar ordered, holstering his pistol.

"Okay ma'am," he said, stepping into the small room. "We're gonna get you warm and safe. What's your name?"

"Nadila, Nadila de Kim," she replied through chattering teeth.

"So, Nadila," he said soothingly, kneeling beside her. "You're from Kimadorn? That's a long way from here."

"W… waitress…" she stammered.

"What were you doing up here?"

"Hiding."

"Here you are, sir," the corporal said, returning with a thick woolen blanket. "All the clothes we found were for warm weather."

Mukavar gently draped the covering over her and gave her a sympathetic look.

"Who were you hiding from?" Mukavar asked softly. "Can you tell me what happened?"

"Hijacked," she said, pulling the blanket tighter. "As soon as we cleared the Goyan Islands."

"You hid up here. Did you see them?"

She nodded; her face filled with dread. "At least five men, led by… I don't know, I've never seen one before. It was a tiger man."

Mukavar's eyes narrowed. A Tiikeri had to be the last thing he expected to hear about.

"What happened then?"

"They brought us here," she said, gazing uneasily at the Calden agent. "They got everyone on deck and then the sea went calm."

"You're talking about that sea out there?" Mukavar clarified.

Nadila nodded once again. "Then, this giant bubble surfaced and… the thing inside…Th… Those tentacles. So many tentacles... They couldn't escape. All those people…"

She wept as the memory traumatized her again, gasping and blubbering, snot and tears streamed down her face. Grasping the wool blanket with her fists, she pressed it over her mouth and steadied her breathing to calm herself.

"What happened to the people?" Mukavar asked quietly.

"After the tentacles…" She fought to say the words aloud. "After the tentacles… had their way with them..." Her body shook as she sobbed back the hysteria from the memory. "Afterwards, everyone just crawled overboard. Bubbles swallowed them all up. And, just like that, they were gone… into the deep."

"Everyone?"

Tears poured from her eyes and she nodded.

"What about the hijackers?"

"They got into the bigger bubble with that… that tentacled creature."

*Tiikeri and Chanakans*, Mukavar thought. *The forces of Nocturn at it again, but what are they up to?*

"Alright Nadila, we're going to get you someplace safe and warm. You could probably use a meal too." Mukavar then gazed down the ladder. "Sergeant, she's coming with me to Penaber. The constabulary there will take a more detailed statement. I need you and your team to get this ship safely back to Zor."

"Yes sir, we won't let you down!"

Criada loved working for the Konrad's. Mistress Konrad had struck him as boisterous, but kind and her husband Mora Alto quiet and disciplined.

At twenty-one, he had been in their service as a domestic for the past five grands, ever since the Amarenian monarch gave him as a gift to them. Mistress Konrad couldn't very well refuse a gift from her friend the queen, but she immediately freed him, stating definitively that she had never owned a slave and had no intention in starting now.

He had been free to leave, but where would he go? He considered this life the only one he had ever known. Rayth raiders had taken Criada at only five, along with his parents.

Stepping from the heat of the kitchen into the common room, he wiped the sweat from his bald head and delicate brown features and tried to recall, but couldn't really remember, his mother and father. Of late, he couldn't even see their faces in his mind. They were separated and snatched from his life forever as soon as they hit the slave market in Mostas.

The young man didn't even really remember the pain of his total castration in the Najuka Ceremony. The wound, however, constantly reminded him of it, every time he urinated. The hideous scar and barely functioning urethral hole left in the middle of his crotch continued to be a constant reminder of his lowly place in Amarenian society.

He did remember his time in the royal kitchens, the cooking, serving, cleaning, and regular beatings. The queen's head domestic slave turned out to be a cruel one and Criada's copious scars on his back and buttocks proved it.

Now, as a free man, he could enjoy a life of productivity where he could earn his living. Yes, there still remained rampant prejudice amongst the fair-skinned inhabitants of the continent. However, now the darker-skinned people from the Goyan Islands were an everyday sight in the big cities and he no longer stood out.

Mistress Konrad even insisted he wear clothes, which he found a very unusual sensation at first. Garments, he soon discovered, further enabled him to blend in with the other free men.

Criada considered his wages the best part, by far. He had never had money of his own before and the earnings paid by Mistress Konrad were considered generous. At five Volas a luna, he could afford some of the luxuries in life previously denied him, especially seeing how she also paid for a modest room in Taia for him.

Yes, for Criada, life now had become very good.

"Shall I clear the table, mistress?" Criada asked, surveying the empty plates littering the table.

"Sure thing, Criada," Mal said, sitting back from the table and placing both hands on her belly. "As usual, another out-fucking-standing dinner!"

"Thank you, Mistress," he said, collecting the three main dinner plates. Normally the two dined alone, but this moonless he also cooked for their neighbor and Mora Alto's Kovos instructor, Kennari Napp.

Throughout the evening, he caught snippets of the conversation while performing his duties. His ears perked up when he heard Mora complaining that he still had been referred to as a dag and it wore on him.

Criada knew all too well what that name meant. He had endured that hateful word his entire life. It now no longer just meant slave, it had evolved into a general derogatory term for any male, especially the dark-skinned ones.

The High Amarenians, the ones with the porcelain white skin, used it the most. Kennari counted herself as one of those, but she seemed different. She had befriended Mora two grands ago and they really bonded when they were put on trial together. The trial fascinated him and he remembered the turmoil it caused in the household.

He overheard Mal asking about Kennari's youngest two daughters, the ones who brought the charges. He felt sad but understood when Kennari said she had forgiven them because they honestly thought they did the right thing. She exiled them from the plantation, however. They had violated her trust and *that* she couldn't forget.

When Criada made his way out of the kitchen to finish cleaning the table, the conversation, thankfully, had worked its way around to Alto's training.

"You know you're progressing nicely," Kennari said.

"Thank you, Geta," Alto replied humbly. "That means a great deal to me."

"I feel it's time for you to receive your first Vardee."

Criada paused at the door to the kitchen with the remainder of the dirty dishes in his hands, curious at Alto's response. He knew the Vardee, wide floor length divided pants resembling a skirt, served as the official Kovos uniform, only worn by serious practitioners and only with the master's approval.

Surprisingly, Mora paused at the offer. "Geta, are you sure? I feel that I am already under a fair amount of prejudicial scrutiny by my mere presence. Do you not feel this will open me up to more scorn? After all, I would be the first male to wear it, would I not?"

Kennari smiled and Criada sighed in relief, happy she took no offence at Mora's hesitation and questioning of her judgement, but then, he knew the master of the house to be a master in his own right.

"It's true you will be the first," Kennari said patiently, "but there must be a first time for everything. Do not let small-minded people dictate how you live your life. Right now, you are better than most Kovos instructors I know. And I know that because I trained a lot of them.

"If anyone is qualified to wear the Vardee, it's you. Mora, we have the law and rights on our side. The naysayer's mean nothing. Next cycle I will come to pick you up. I know two tailors in Taia specializing in the Vardee. Tomorrow, we'll get you fitted."

The *Vastus* streaked westward out of the Goyan Islands and over Lumina's Ocean Deep. Taleeka leaned forward in the captain's chair and stared at the blueish globe being projected from the console. Brzo sat directly in front of it staring at it. Several times the lizard's long tongue snaked out, only to pass through it. The reptile would quizzically turn its head side to side and look over at Gidaria in the pilot's seat.

In the overhead console between them, the Larimar disk glowed milk white and the voice of Nibira filled the cabin.

"How's the weather?" the librarian asked.

"Pretty clear," Taleeka replied, confused by the question. "We're picking up some turbulence though."

It's a giant Flavian Portal, literally a hole in the ocean. The waters around it are called the Sea of Storms. I was kinda surprised when you said it was clear."

"We've got the area up on the croquis and it looks like there's a Valdurian air station over it," Taleeka explained. "It's just to the north of Penaber."

"That's right, about a couple of hundred feet over it," Nibira said, "but it's more than an air traffic control station. It says here that the Valdurians recently upgraded it. They installed Blue Opal Etheria panels to power defensive wards on the portal. I guess they don't want anything nasty popping in from the Middle Realms. The wards are so powerful they are displacing waves of psychic energy."

"Yes," Barr-Ani called out from her seat. "I can feel it building the closer we get."

"Well, keeping your PSI batteries fully charged shouldn't be a problem in Penaber." Nibira paused, while she continued reading.

"So, tell me about Penaber." Taleeka asked, thankful she had the resources of the greatest library in the world and a friend who knew how to access it.

"It started out as a Calden naval outpost for training Brightstar sailors. It grew quickly. First, by industries designed to part military folks from their money, like gambling, prostitution and such. Others eventually followed.

"The city's not nearly as big as Zor but because of its proximity to the Innaca Deep it's one of the most magical places in Lumina. Very cosmopolitan too, thanks to the portal. Supposedly, it's a haven for magic users of all kinds."

Taleeka sat back and gently stroked her chin. "So, let's see, we've got Tiikeri, secretly operating out of a highly magical city, trying to score a bunch of Etheria. That doesn't sound suspicious at all!"

Noorim frowned. "Taleeka, what are you saying? That sounds *very* suspicious!"

Taleeka, Gidaria and Barr-Ani, could not suppress their smiles, while Noorim peered around innocently.

"Uh, Noorim," Nibira's amused voice came through. "I'm pretty sure Tally was using irony."

"Oh," the Amarenian said, still a bit confused. "Irony, I see."

Gidaria scrunched up her face, shook her head and mouthed, "I don't think so," at Taleeka, before returning to the controls.

The pilot had no sooner taken the wheel, when a massive, extended wave of psychic discharge rocked the airship, causing all to sway in their seats.

"Looks like we're getting close," Gidaria said, examining the croquis.

"I don't need a map to tell me that," Taleeka said, as several more minor bursts of energy bumped her around in her seat.

Suddenly the Larimar disk began pulsing and a strange male voice reverberated in all their heads. "Uh, Resistance Class Cruiser, this is Innaca Station. Please identify yourself and destination."

Gidaria reached up and touched the talking stone. "Roger that, Innaca Station. This is the *Vastus* and we're bound for beautiful sunny Penaber."

"Roger that," the amused voice replied. "You've got a clear shot, with light air traffic. Penaber control will pick you up shortly and guide you in. Enjoy the weather while it lasts."

"Thanks, Innaca Station, we're out."

"Okay, you're getting ready to land," Nibira's voice came through once again. "I'm gonna get off the frequency. Let me know if you need any more information."

"Thanks, and you can count on it," Taleeka said, before swiveling her chair to face Barr-Ani. "Well, my sensitive friend, just like in Tannimore, I'm going to be relying on you to give me the heads up on any psychic activity that may try and befall us. I've got a feeling you're going to be busy."

True to her word, Kennari arrived shortly after moonrise and, following a morning meal prepared by Criada, they were off to town, leaving Mal to attend to some much-anticipated gardening.

"This is exciting," Kennari said, popping the reins and spurring the lone horse onward. "I remember being fitted for my first Vardee. Each one is made exclusively for the one commissioning it. No two are exactly alike. You are going to need three."

"Three?"

Kenari smiled and kept her eyes straight ahead. "Yes, two black ones for everyday wear and a white formal one."

"Everyday wear?" Alto said quizzically. "I was under the impression they were for training."

"They are, but they can be worn as part of your normal wardrobe. Not many can wear the Vardee. It marks your status in society as an instructor in Kovos. Be proud of your Vardee. Wear it as you wish."

"But you only wear yours during training," Alto noted curiously.

"At the risk of sounding boastful Alto, I don't need to wear it in public. Everyone knows who I am, especially in this Dor."

"And you say this tailor specializes in the crafting of these garments?" Alto asked, watching the agricultural fields of Taia Dor go by from the Napp's two seated carriage.

"Yes, she makes other clothes of course, but she is one of two in Taia that is qualified and approved to make the Vardee. Oh, she doesn't actually make them herself anymore, she supervises. Potoloa Samryn is the largest garment maker in Taia. She has quite the operation, a dozen seamstresses, two loom workers and so on."

"Samryn, I have heard that name before," Alto said, searching his memory. "Only in passing though."

"Her Banja is two levels above mine. As far as political influence, she outranks me. My title of Geta sort of evens out our status. The political hierarchy under the queen can be very complex. All the Banjas of each Dor are constantly seeking to elevate their status. Some can be quite unscrupulous."

"Each one vying for the number one status within their Dor?"

"Yes, but for Banjas on the bottom like mine, it's very unlikely. We generally shift around a few notches, but the number one status is the Dor's Lideri. You would call them a regional governess. A thankless job, I, for one, don't want any part of."

Slowly the agricultural fields gave way to small circular clusters of individual dwellings, grouped closer together. The Amarenians passing them on the street nodded at Kennari, but eyed Alto suspiciously.

Alto shook his head disappointedly. "I have been living amongst them for two grands now. You would think they would be used to me by this time."

"The old ways are always the hardest to change. Give it time. You are already conforming to the manner of dress here by going shirtless. I imagine bare chested males are not an everyday sight where you are from?"

"Only common laborers and street people."

"Once you get your Vardee, between that and your bare chest you should cut quite the striking figure. All will immediately recognize your status."

"Which brings me back to my original concern. Surely there will be some practitioners that will take offence that I wear the Vardee."

"Perhaps."

"Taking offence often leads to duels."

"Perhaps," Kennari said, before a long pause.

She nodded resolutely and finally took her eyes off the road to look at Alto.

"Mora, I have full confidence in your abilities."

Gradually, the clusters of dwellings grew more congested and arranged in concentric circles, all connected by roads cutting through the rings of buildings like living spokes. Eventually, the circles became smaller and smaller, with the Lideri's palace at the center.

The carriage's progress slowed significantly. Mostly lighter-skinned, bare-chested women congested the streets. Occasionally a darker-skinned Goyan would be amongst the crowd. The predominant darker-skinned people however, remained naked slaves, most carrying the Whitmar brand on their backs.

They found Potoloan's tailor shop situated near the edge of town, in spite of its large size, indicating Potoloan's Banja's status at ninth. Kennari parked her cart in the rear of the circular single-story structure, hitched up her horse and led Alto through the beaded front door.

Once inside, the scope of the operation astounded Alto. Just as Kennari said, a dozen seamstresses fed cloth under the piercing needles of large box-like sewing machines lining the outer wall. Naked, muscular slaves turned circular cranks on the sides of the machines, powering the needles. The seamstresses' commands governed their speed.

Two looms and a massive cutting table stood in the center of the room. In all, Alto counted sixteen Amarenians, and as many slaves, all dutifully tarrying away.

"There she is," Kennari said, indicating a small-boned woman of medium height. Her pale white face appeared thin as her frame, as did her lips, white hair and the squint of her piercing blue eyes. She conferred with one of the cutters over a large bolt of red fabric.

Making their way across the floor, Alto's presence became a gradually building point of interest. Work ceased in his wake and everyone began staring. Eventually, Potoloan noticed the silence of the labor stoppage and gave Alto an irritated glance.

"Get back to work!" she bellowed.

By the time the pair made it over to her, the hum of work fully resumed.

"Geta," Potoloan greeted, totally ignoring Alto.

"Sister," Kennari returned the salutation. "This is Mora Alto Konrad, my student, who is now in need of his very own Vardee."

Potoloan managed a weak smile at Kennari, and then shot Alto another disdainful look.

"Yes, I heard something about you teaching a dag," she said with a sneer. "I prayed to the Goddess it wasn't true, but here you are."

Kennari's eyes bore into the tailor. "Need I remind you, Sister, he is a Valorous Citizen as decreed by the queen herself? He is no dag and is due all the respect of his title!"

"As you say," Potoloan begrudgingly acknowledged with a scowl. "I'm afraid I'm not going to be able to help you. I'm simply too backed up with work. At the rate I'm behind, it would be several grands before I could deliver your garment. Perhaps one of the other tailors in the city may be agreeable."

"Agreeable?" Kennari said suspiciously. "This reluctance on your part wouldn't have anything to do with your membership in Era Zaharrak?"

"There are many of us who still feel the old ways are the best and the queen needs to be constantly reminded of that."

Kennari sighed in frustration. "Belonging to a political party that advocates moving our society backwards will not gain you any favors in the eyes of the queen."

"Nevertheless," Potoloan said dismissively. "I don't have the time to stand here and debate politics. As I said, I have work to do and we're backed up. So, have a pleasant luna, and good-bye."

The moment Qasia stepped off the boat onto the Zorian waterfront, she knew her mission would not be an easy one. Unlike Tannimore, with its mostly human population, the sheer diversity of life here guaranteed her search for the thieves would prove much more difficult than expected.

"There are human hybrids of all sorts here," Brother Hardee of the Piety Watch said futilely. "How are we supposed to find the right one?"

"Have faith in the Lord, His vengeance shall be realized," Qasia said, more to convince herself than anyone. "The ones we seek are thieves. We should start in the poorer section of the city."

After a few inquiries, the trio found themselves amidst the noise and smells of the industrial Southern Docks, looking up the hill into the abject squalor of the Seven Sisters Slums.

"I remember this accursed place," Brother Hardee said, contemptuously. "The sloth, the poverty. It's disgusting."

"Yes," Brother Telek, the other Piety Watch agreed. "I conducted daily beatings here until I thought my arm was going to fall off. These people just never learn that the only path to prosperity is productivity."

"Don't let the city guards hear you," Qasia warned ominously. "They threw you out once. I don't think they will be as lenient this time."

They walked cautiously through the hardpacked streets. Ramshackle wooden structures, some no more than large boxes stacked precariously atop one another, formed towering canyons of despair all around them. On either side of the street, filthy, partially clad and totally naked humans suspiciously eyed them from open doorways and windows. In the distance, they could hear the distinct sounds of hammering and sawing.

"I recognize that one," Telek said, indicating a man talking with a group of six standing at a street corner. "The short one is a street boss who goes by the name of Luusoe."

"Well, if you recognize him, he'll probably remember you," Qasia said, singling out Luusoe. "Especially if you were the one beating on him. Better hang back, Brother Hardee, let me see what these retches know."

The men stopped talking when the two approached and confidently assessed the strangers. Luusoe stood a little under six feet tall, with shoulder length black hair and an unshaved stubble on the bottom half of his thin angular face. A large golden earring dangled from his left earlobe and his eyes appeared naturally sleepy with dangerous undertones.

Stepping up to the mobster, she noticed the others fanning out, effectively surrounding them.

"You are Luusoe?" Qasia asked fearlessly.

The Amarenian's ghastly appearance gave the shocked mobster pause. "Who wants to know?"

"Someone who's interested in locating an individual that can provide intimidating protection, and perhaps some muscle if needed."

Luusoe grinned evilly and glanced around at his men. "For the right money, any one of my boys fits the bill."

With a confident grin, Qasia scanned around at the circle of thugs, then shook her head. "I said intimidating."

Luusoe's smile evaporated and quickly reverted to a sneer. "What do you say we just kill you and take your shit? How's that for intimidating?!"

"My friend over there with the pistol might have something to say about that," Qasia said, indicating Brother Hardee standing ten feet away.

Luusoe's face fell and Qasia quickly seized the moment.

"My friend, I'd much rather pay you than fight you," she said, nodding to Brother Hardee.

The Piety Watch parted his cloak, making sure all could see the pistol tucked in his belt then retrieved a ten-secor Commodity Note and handed it to Qasia.

"A hundred gold pieces just to talk to me," she said, offering him the Ukko rectangle. "In fact, I think I can narrow the field down a bit. I'm looking for someone specific I've heard about. Maybe you know of him. He's a EEtah hybrid, seven feet tall, bald with sharp teeth and a cleft in his chin."

"That sounds like Larzz," he said, taking the money. "He freelances with Tally Konrad's crew. In between jobs for her, he takes random security gigs, mostly as a bouncer."

"Tally Konrad?"

"Yeah, you haven't heard of the Konrad's?"

"I'm new to the city."

Luusoe scoffed. "The whole family are serious players, Heroes of the Realm. I mean, they don't hand out Bespoke names for having a nice smile."

"Do you know where I might find him?"

"I heard he's working one of the bars on Meridian Street."

Qasia reached out her hand out to Brother Hardee and he handed her another ten-secor note.

"And this is for keeping this conversation… *private*," she said, handing him the additional money.

Mukavar had never even seen an Akina before, much less worked with one. The four-foot-tall humanoid fox spoke the common tongue better than he did and appeared impeccably dressed in a green silk shirt, sleeves rolled up, and vest. Most impressive proved to be his knowledge of the way the streets worked in Penaber.

"So, you're from the Barrens over in the Twilight Lands?" Mukavar asked, from the passenger side of the private police hackney.

"Indeed," Casus replied, from his specially designed booster seat behind the wheel. "Now, *there*, my good fellow, is a most inhospitable place."

"So I've heard," Mukavar said. "Immor-Onn is as far east as I've ever been."

"A beautiful city, to be sure. My family briefly settled there," Casus said, turning the steering wheel and keeping his eye on the traffic flowing around them.

"So, why did you leave the Barrens?"

"Much too dangerous, between the Onay hordes and the Ghorn necromancers, the everyday peril grew simply too much for my mother. When my younger brother was carried off by the Onay, she decided it was time to leave."

"What about your father?"

"Akina males do not raise their offspring, that is left to the females."

"So, how'd you end up here, working for House Calden?"

"In Immor-Onn, I grew quite enamored with the Calden Navy, but my mother enrolled me in the Bailian Institute of Arts and Letters where I excelled. However, I spent any spare time on the waterfront watching ships.

"Once I graduated, I made quite a few naval friends," the Akina said, laughing. "They considered me a young mascot. I said my good-byes to mother and hopped on the next outgoing Calden naval vessel. Penaber was their destination and, as fortune would have it, I adapted quickly to the street life here. Because of my experience with the Calden Navy and my language skills, the constabulary snatched me up.

"Admiral Metauri, the constabulary commander you met upon arrival, was transferred from the Spice Islands. She was formally in charge of wharf security there. She's only been here a quinte and hates it. What about you?"

"Not much to tell," Mukavar recounted, shrugging. "I made Senior Lieutenant, and then the Society came calling a few grands after I got my Brightstar Pin.

"Hey, who is this guy were looking for?"

"His name is Sbirro," Casus answered. "He's a known snatch slaver, we just haven't been able to catch him in the act. He was our initial suspect, but we lacked sufficient evidence to bring him before a naval magistrate. That's why we sent for you. If he didn't kidnap the girl, I'm betting he knows who did. He spends quite a bit of his spare time in a scurrilous drinking establishment called the Opasno Social Club. That's our destination."

Mukavar gave a wry chuckle. "That's quite a mouthful."

"Indeed," the Akina replied. "And we're here."

Casus parked the hackney down the street from the entrance to the building, part of a long row of non-descript free standing businesses separated by narrow alleys.

"I'll go in first," Casus said, reaching for the door handle. "No point in letting them know we're together. Just hang back in case of trouble. I should be able to keep the situation in hand."

"Okee dokie," Mukavar said with an amused grin.

The Calden Intelligencer waited by the door for as long as his curiosity held out, before entering and looking around.

The dimly illuminated room smelled of savory cooking. People ate and gambled at a dozen tables gathered around a bar in the back hosting a handful of boisterous drinkers.

Casus had approached a table where four men played cards. Mukavar walked past the table to the bar and stood within earshot while ordering an ale.

"Sbirro!" Casus greeted exuberantly. "I thought I might find you here."

The game stopped and they peered antagonistically at the humanoid fox whose head barely reached above the table.

"Yeah?" a man with short dark hair and beard grumbled, sneering. "Who the fuck are you?"

"My name is Casus," the Akina said, showing his Ukko ID card, "with the Calden Maritime Constabulary. I would very much appreciate a moment of your time in private."

Sbirro scowled, returning his attention to his cards.

"Beat it! I'm busy."

"Oh dear," Casus said apologetically. "I'm afraid I wasn't very clear. You are obviously laboring under the pretense my directive was a request. It was not. Now, what say, a word?"

Mukavar quietly sipped his ale, watching the much larger Sbirro rise to his feet and glower menacingly down at the very composed sentient.

"*What say* I just kick your furry ass out into the street?!"

Casus sighed and gave a forlorn look. "That would be unfortunate. I can assure you, conversing with me will be much less painful."

Mukavar smiled, enthralled by the confrontation. The man had the Akina by two full feet in height and outweighed him by well over a hundred pounds. Casus wasn't stupid, he must have something up his sleeve. The answer of what, came a brief moment later when Sbirro lunged.

With inhuman speed and agility, the humanoid fox darted out of the way and the enraged human rushed past his target, almost falling. Bellowing, he turned and tried again with the same results.

*The little guy's fast*, Mukavar conceded to himself.

Abandoning his failed strategy, Sbirro just swung at his elusive objective. Each time, Casus simply wasn't there when the blow arrived.

When Sbirro tried to kick him, the agile Akina went down on all fours and darted under the kick. Now behind his attacker, Casus bounded to his feet and delivered a punishing roundhouse kick to the knee of the supporting leg. He heard the cracking sound of bones breaking and Sbirro screaming.

The human dropped to the floor, held his wounded joint and moaned in agony. Casus stepped over to the prone mobster while quickly pulling a length of metal wire from his back pocket.

"Well, you certainly can't say I didn't warn you," Casus said, attempting to bind the uncooperative Sbirro's hands with the wire.

"Oh, by the gods!" the Akina let out a frustrated cry.

He reached out and pinched the flailing human's neck. Sbirro immediately went unconscious, slumping into a heap on the floor.

The other men at the table now came to their feet scowling, which prompted Mukavar to pull his pistol.

"Ah, ah, ahh," he said, waving the barrel at them. "Let's not do anything stupid."

When Sbirro awoke, his head darted from side to side taking in his surroundings. He found himself strapped naked to a board in a windowless room, with stone walls and floor. The place smelled moldy, his teeth chattered from the cold and his knee radiated pain up and down his leg. The Akina stood by his head and Mukavar stood at his feet dispassionately assessing him.

"You're an extremely rude individual, aren't you?" Mukavar said smugly.

Sbirro stared contemptuously at the Calden agent, saying nothing.

"I'm talking to you!" Mukavar growled, lashing out and punching the man's wounded knee.

Sbirro screamed and thrashed futilely against his bonds. When the pain of the blow began to subside, he watched Mukavar withdraw a five-inch-long thick needle with a ring at one end.

"You know,' he said, running the tip against the exposed sole of Sbirro's foot. "My boyfriend is a lot better at this than I am. However, I have managed to pick up a few tricks from him. Now, my friend over there is going to ask you some questions and we're going to see how long it takes you to answer. But rest assured, you *will* answer them."

Mal admittedly could not call herself an expert on Amarenian law, but she damn well knew when the queen's direct edict had been challenged.

"I think this would be better served by letting the incident pass," Alto said, while trying to assess the exact level of Mal's irritation.

The pair crossed the last ring of structures surrounding the Lideri's palace in central Taia. Both dressed in traditional Amarenian garb, Mal wore the formal court dress, extending to floor length, cinched tight at the waist with breasts exposed, and Alto also went bare chested, proudly wearing the white, formal, Kovos Vardee—which received more than a few stares.

"It seems like such a trifling matter," Alto protested. "In the end, I got my Vardee. If you must press the matter, surely that is something the local traveling judge, their name escapes me, could have heard."

"They're called Sudac, and I sure as fuck don't have the time to wait on that roving dog and pony show getting around to us. This was a direct command from the queen herself, so we're going to bypass the bureaucratic bullshit!"

Alto well knew, when Mal made up her mind there would be little chance of changing it, so the swordmaster sighed and followed along.

The Mahaila city guard next to the beaded door saluted them both before pulling the lever on the side and parting the beads. The interior of the regional capital, like all Amarenian architecture, was circular with minor governmental offices against the outer wall. Each of the three concentric rings escalated in stature until one reached the center chamber of the regional governess herself. Hallways intersected these rings like the spokes on a wheel and the pair made their way directly to the receiving chamber of Lideri Saudari Atona, sister of the queen.

After identifying themselves to the Mahilia guard outside the door, they were promptly admitted. Brightly colored tapestries adorned the walls of the forty-foot diameter round room. Lideri's throne sat on the opposing wall to the main entrance between two smaller beaded doors on either side. A royal scribe sat at a small desk right beside the throne. She appeared short and squat, with two enormous breasts pushed up and out of her blue traditional court dress.

Lideri Saudari's white dress with red piping accentuated her alabaster skin as she gracefully lounged on the overstuffed chair. She smiled warmly when they entered, lifting a hand in welcome. Mal always felt astounded how much she favored her sister, with beautiful delicate features and a perfectly symmetrical face.

"Valorous citizens!" she called formally. "Come forth and be heard."

The duo approached and gave a brief nod out of respect, even though their status did not require it. The title of 'Valorous,' much like 'Heroes of the Realm' in the Goyan Islands, meant never having to bow to anyone.

"Thank you for such a prompt audience, Astute," Mal said appreciatively.

"Not at all," Saudari said, with a wave of her hand. "One of the benefits of your title is moving to the front of the line. Now, what can the Administration of Taia-Dor do for you?"

"Well, to be frank, I don't think there is anything that *can* be done," Mal said calmly, which surprised and amused Alto. "We're just here to inform you, that the queen's direct orders are being openly opposed."

"Oh?" The smile faded from the Lideri's face, and she sat forward on her throne. "You personally witnessed this?"

"No, but my mate did," Mal said, transferring the governess' attention onto the swordmaster.

Alto relayed the incident in the tailor shop on the last luna. Saudari listened intently and gave a deep forlorn sigh when he finished. For a moment silence enveloped the room, punctuated only by the sounds of the scribe's pen scratching across the paper.

"I apologize for your treatment by some of our fellow citizens. Unfortunately, we can make all the laws we want, but for some, the old ways are not easy to shake off. Further complicating the matter, Potoloa Samryn is Crone of the Samryn Banja. Crones have voting rights even against the queen. If enough of them band together, they can challenge any law, Lideri or the queen herself."

Alto nodded that he understood. "Is this perhaps the reason she chose to align herself with this, Era Zaharrak?"

"Ah yes," Saudari replied with a shake of her head. "The Old Ways Party. Yes, it's a small assemblage of likeminded crones and their followers. Fortunately, most of the Banja are doing well since establishing trade with the Goyan houses. The vast majority of crones do not favor kicking the Goyans off Amarenia to return to piracy and violence. Era Zaharrak is a small, but vocal group and there is nothing by law that can be done about it. Now, if their voices turn to violence, you are always free to defend yourself. Another benefit of the title, you get the benefit of the doubt when the Mahaila show up."

"That's good to know Astute," Mal said assuredly, "because if someone wants to get violent, our side of the story is the *only one* the Mahaila are going to get to hear."

Valdurian Corporal Alnaaqil de Atar always felt safe when the marines were around. The twenty-two grand old transport pilot wasn't especially brave, or martially trained. In fact, he had never been exposed to any large military conflict at all. The cleanshaven, gangly poet with a shaved head only joined the Valdurian Air Service to placate his father who insisted the service would toughen him up.

Now, he transported mostly machine parts and food stuff to the various Valdurian Airbases across Lumina. The few times they tasked him to deliver sensitive or dangerous materials, they assigned a marine detachment, like now.

For the past cluster, he and his marine protection detail had changed out the Landagar Mark Five pistols for the newer Mark Sixes. He felt a little more at ease on the final leg, with three crates of Mark Fives bound for the Valdurian Armory just outside the capital city of Dryden.

"Dryden control, this is military transport 663," Alnaaqil said into the Larimar disk in the overhead control panel. "We'll be doing a fly over to our final destination."

"Roger that, 663," the control tower responded.

By using the sixty-six prefix, the tower recognized his sensitive mission should not be delayed and bypassing the air station would not raise any alarms.

"Last run of the cycle," a thick-necked marine, who went by the name Parak, said, from the seat behind the pilot. "That first ale is gonna taste awful good!"

Molan, the marine seated next to him, chuckled in agreement. Alnaaqil had spent the better part of the last cluster with the two, and despite their brash attitudes and bravado, both were basically decent guys. Parak claimed to be a certified bachelor, who spent his off-duty time drinking and whoring. Molan, an average looking guy with short brown hair, turned out to be totally devoted to his family of a wife and two little girls. As for Alnaaqil, after his evening meal, he wanted to curl up with a glass of wine and try to get a few verses of poetry written.

"We're starting our descent guys," Alnaaqil said over his shoulder. "You're a little closer to that ale, Parak."

"Now you're talking! Parak announced boisterously. "Hey Al, why don't you come along? I'll get you drunk and laid. What do ya say?"

The pilot smiled at the invitation, the same which had been issued at the end of every run. "That's okay, I prefer my evenings a little less… *busy*."

"Eh, you and Molan," Parak said, shaking his head. "No sense of adventure."

The Valdurian Armory, a windowless, single-story building surrounded by an eight-foot-tall spiked wrought iron fence, sat on the outskirts of the city. A sentry stood at the gate and another at the armory's large roll-up door.

Alnaaqil could see several people in green jumpsuits walking away from a parked hackney box truck just to the right of the door. Settling the airship twenty feet away from the parked truck, the pilot noticed a lone driver at the wheel doing paperwork. Looking up, the man smiled and waved, prompting Alnaaqil to do the same.

"Alright guys, let's drop this load and be done with it, at least for this cycle," Alnaaqil said.

He watched the marines get to their feet and ready their carbines. Dropping the side hatch, he got up and followed them out of the ship.

"Okay," the pilot said. "I'm going to find me a cart. There're only three crates, but I've been toting and lifting all cycle. I want to make this in one trip."

Both marines smiled and nodded. They felt for the kid. Because they worked security, they were required to keep weapons ready and had been unable to help him with the actual loading and unloading.

Alnaaqil faced the armory's front door and heard doors suddenly opening on the hackney beside them. The pilot and both marines looked over to see the side and driver's doors of the box truck already open. Inside, an attractive brunette woman and four men pointed Firehammer carbines at them. The driver, who dropped his paperwork and got out, also produced a carbine and aimed it at the door guard.

Without hesitation, they all opened fire.

All three airship personnel went down in a hail of two-inch-long Na-Kab carbon bolts. Before any could react, their bodies lay riddled and bleeding beside the craft. The driver of the hackney fired at the door guard as he raised his weapon. The projectiles propelled him against the building, following most of the interior of his chest cavity which oozed down the walls, trailing him to the ground.

The driver then quickly turned to the sentry at the front gate who became alerted when the shooting started. He had just turned around when the driver caught him in the side of the head, vaporizing it into a fine red mist which painted the black wrought iron.

The driver next shot the gate's latch, blasted it open, leaving the gate swinging wildly. Mazie and the four henchmen jumped out of the truck, while the driver kept them covered.

Amazingly, Alnaaqil didn't die in the initial volley. glancing shots blew his left arm, left leg and right hip away, but he was spared a direct hit. He realized however, that at his current rate of blood loss, the end would be soon. He only wished he possessed the state of mind to compose a couplet befitting his death.

Groaning an agony, he watched the four men removing the cases containing the pistols, placing them in the hackney. The beautiful woman walked confidently over to him and looked down dispassionately.

"You look like you're in a lot of pain," she said, removing a meat cleaver from her belt. "Let me help."

"I swear to the gods, I've seen latrine tenders that lead more exciting lives than this guy," Mukavar said, lowering the spyglass.

Casus chuckled and joined him at the window of the small one room lodging they had rented. Out in the Penaber harbor several blocks away, the Turine rang out its warning that the moon would soon be setting. The view from the solitary window looked down on the single-story building housing the Kaplan listening post.

The name he had gotten from Sbirro three lunas ago turned out to be none other than Kaplan Station Chief for

Penaber, Tor-Ga. The resulting surveillance had proved to be mind-numbingly tedious. The older orange Tiikeri kept to himself, went to work, purchased any meals from a few local food vendors, then took it home and ate alone.

"Think Sbirro gave us a bad name before he died?" Casus asked, watching the street life break from their workday.

"Maybe," Mukavar admitted, raising the glass to his eye once more. "Like I said, I'm not as good as my boyfriend."

"You could have fooled me. The way you worked that needle between his toes sure seemed professional enough."

"Yeah well, finesse only counts if you get good intel. Hello, what's this?!"

"What?" Casus asked, peering in the direction Mukavar's spyglass pointed.

"Taleeka Konrad, interesting."

"Who?"

Tally Konrad, she's a freelancer out of Zor. Looks like she's sniffing around the same trail as us. I wonder why?"

"She appears to be alone?" Casus noted.

"That doesn't mean anything. She usually works with a small crew. I'm sure they're around somewhere.

Taleeka stepped off the busy street into a recessed doorway and pulled her talking stone necklace from under her shirt. She touched the teardrop shaped Larimar and envisioned her two friends.

"Barr-Ani, Noorim, you there?" she asked softly.

The Bailian's voice immediately filled her head. "We're almost to the end of the entire wharf. I must say, with all the unsavory characters we've encountered, I'm glad Noorim is here with me."

"There was really no danger," Noorim broke in, calmly correcting her companion.

"Barr-Ani, are you getting anything?"

"Only the normal background noise," the sensitive reported. "No big spikes like before."

"Okay, stay at it. I'm still watching the Tiikeri station chief. That guy needs a life!"

Taleeka concentrated so hard on making sure no one could see her talking, she failed to notice the shimmering directly to her right when Mukavar turned off his shrouding stone. Once she realized someone had appeared, she reflexively threw an elbow at the perceived threat.

"Woah, hold it there Tiger," Mukavar said, easily deflecting the strike. "Kinda jumpy, aren't we?"

Taleeka gave a sigh of relief, then shot the Calden mechanic an irritated glance for startling her.

"Muuky! You scared the crap out of me! What in the name of the Goddess are you doing here?"

Mukavar chuckled at her reaction.

"I was going to ask you the same question."

Taleeka rolled her eyes. "Yeah, well I asked first."

"A Calden naval officer's daughter, along with a few other people, got snatched in the same manner six lunas ago. The locals requested an assist because local legal obstructions hindered them. I got the name of the Tiikeri section chief from a reluctant informant. What about you?"

"I was pulling a job for the society in Tannimore when this rival crew tried to sabotage the operation. Upon questioning one of them, he revealed they were hired by, and I quote, 'A bunch of cat people in Penaber.' So, I decided to check it out. Tor-Ga is the station chief, so I figured he'd lead me to them. Turns out, watching him is like watching paint dry."

Mukavar gave a quick chortle at the reference. "First, I've heard of that. I mean, he's got a handful of mongrels he commands. But I didn't know anything about a group of Tiikeri. You sure the intel's good?"

Taleeka nodded her head. "Yeah, my sensitive pulled it out of his head. He wasn't lying."

"Well, I haven't seen or heard of any other Tiikeri in the city."

"If they are here, and I believe they are, it's a safe bet they're laying low somewhere. I've got my people searching the waterfront. I'm also betting Tor-Ga can lead us to them. It's pretty obvious he's not going to do that on his own. He just needs the right incentive."

Mukavar nodded with a sly grin. "I think I can give him a reason."

The cool air felt good on Qasia's skin and the reduced illumination allowed her eyes to relax a bit. The Amarenian continued to have a hard time adjusting to the Goyan Island's constant barrage of intense sunlight. The refreshing change from the heat and light above, however, didn't diminish the stench of the Zorian sewers.

Raising the gem high above her head, she peered down the tunnel as far as the illumination would allow. A shallow stream of wastewater ran the length of the ten-foot-wide shaft, complete with assorted floating bits of unidentifiable matter. She saw an intersection just ahead and knew they had to take a right.

"This way," she said over her shoulder to the two Piety Watch members following her.

Brother Hardee responded with a labored grunt over the muffled cries of the bound and gagged man they forced along. Their unfortunate captive, nothing more than a naked beggar, would definitely serve her purposes.

She finally found Larzz. The half EEtah worked security at the door of a dive bar in the Orta Plat of the Seven Sisters Slums and she had to admit being intimidated by his massive size. His ferocity could also prove troubling. She had watched him single handedly break up a ten-man brawl and knew that she and her Piety Watch would be no match.

It had become time to ply her abilities so attentively nurtured by Mistress Ve-Qua. For that however, she would need power and quite a bit of it. The psionic charge she received from the five that she flayed back in Tannimore waned. This would have to be a lengthy, drawn-out session, because she only had one subject to render from, but she found just the thing to aide her.

After turning the corner, another hundred feet of tunnel opened into a large juncture room, thirty feet square, with a fifteen-foot ceiling and multiple sewer lines leading off in all directions. In the far corner, loomed a ten-foot square opening in the floor. Leading them to the pit, she slipped off her dress revealing her nude, pale white body, while the Piety Watch held the captive over the lip of the opening and took off his gag.

"No, please," the man pleaded. "Don't do this!"

Qasia smiled demurely and stepped up close.

"Don't do what?" she purred sensuously. "You don't even know what I'm going to do to you, but don't you worry, I'm going to tell you."

She held the gem over the hole and tilted her head, directing his attention to the now well-lit opening.

"Look what I have for you," she said giddily.

Trembling, the man gazed down into the recesses. Bones lay scattered along the floor of the twenty-foot-deep pit.

Most disturbingly, the sheer black walls moved and undulated with rapid clicking sounds.

"Those are Mansa Beetles," she explained. "They eat flesh. They're going to eat you... alive. Isn't that exciting?"

"Please no, no!" he said, with tear filled eyes.

Qasia found the man's mental torment nothing short of an intoxicating ambrosia and the perfect way to begin. With every plea, every tear and quake of terror, the student torture mage could feel the power trickling into her body, causing her nipples to stiffen.

"It'll take quite a while too," she said, caressing his grimy tear-stained cheek. "You're going to be in a lot of pain for a long time and who knows how many times I'm going to cum. It's going to be *wonderful!*"

She embellished her last word with a rapturous rolling of her eyes. Still keeping her coy smile, she placed the gem on the floor then straddled it. The lone source of light cast deep shadows upwards over her body. She reached out gently and touched his chest, looking into his terrorized eyes.

"Pain is beautiful," she whispered. "Pain is nourishing. Pain is power!"

With the last shouted declaration, she shoved him backwards into the darkness. They heard the beggar cry out, more in surprise than pain, and then the thud of him hitting bottom, accompanied by the crack of a leg breaking. Screams of agony rapidly followed as thousands of beetles swarmed over his body.

Qasia raised her arms, threw back her head and trembled violently, receiving wave after wave of psionic energy radiating up from the recess in the floor. The screaming below continued for a full deci while a pulsing blue aura surrounded Qasia.

By the time the shrieking finally ceased, she had orgasmed at least a half dozen times. She dropped down on one knee to compose herself, physically drained from her multiple releases, but now at full psionic power.

Retrieving her dress from the floor, she slipped it on and stared at two badly trembling Piety Watch members, who had never witnessed anything of the kind before.

"The vengeance of the Lord is at hand!" she asserted, strolling past the two startled henchmen and out into the tunnel. "Are you coming or not?"

Tor-Ga had to admit, there were times he felt lonely. Being the station chief for the Order of Kaplan in Penaber thankfully kept him busy. It also provided him a welcome routine, but every now and then his mind would drift back to his former life as a commander for the Tiikeri Empire.

He became especially nostalgic preparing for work at moonrise. Back then, his mate would always have his uniform ready for him and he would say goodbye to her and his son. They died, along with so many others, eight grands and a lifetime ago when the Do-Tarr overran his home in the capital city of Hai-Darr.

He was away on assignment when the end came to his beloved empire and family. Upon word of his people's destruction, he rallied with the other stunned survivors in the only safe location left, the Unaligned City of Shun-Dra.

There, the five hundred remaining Tiikeri, and those in their charge, became the Order of Kaplan. The newly reformed group vowed two things; to never again follow the ways of the empire and to operate in the shadows facilitating the utter destruction of the Pa-Waga religion.

Now, that seemed like an eternity ago he thought, leaving his small two room apartment. Halfway on the short walk to work, he stopped at his usual food stall.

"Looks like it's going to be another beautiful luna," beamed the owner, a short bald, potbellied human named Yepel, while handing him a meat stick.

When they first met, the good-natured entrepreneur actually suggested giving him his skewers raw when he saw the Tiikeri's initial look of revulsion at the smell of roasting meat. Now, he had grown used to the stench. This adaptability proved to be a good thing, because one found food stalls everywhere in the cities of the Goyan Islands.

"Eh, we'll see about that, Yepel," he replied dropping two copper pieces on the counter and taking his breakfast wrapped in butcher's paper.

"Enjoy your luna!" Yepel called out cheerfully.

The old Tiikeri tucked his breakfast under his arm and merely waved his response while walking away.

He arrived at the listening post just as the mongrels working the moonless shift got off and he nodded to them as they left. Thankfully, the shift foreman had nothing dire to bring to his attention and he looked forward to reading his report while eating breakfast at his desk.

The luna's shift were already at their Larimar stations along the walls and, much like the departing moonless crew, he greeted them with silent nods. Unlocking the door to his office, he caught the smell of a human the moment the door cracked open.

Tor-Ga paused and his tail nervously swished back and forth. He took a deep breath and opened the door to find a smiling Mukavar seated on the edge of his desk with his arms crossed.

A stunned Tor-Ga stood motionless in the open doorway staring. This seemed impossible! The room had been locked, there were no windows, and the listening post's main room, from which he would have had to pass through, had been constantly occupied.

"Who are you?!" Tor-Ga sputtered incredulously. "How did you get in here?!"

"My name is Mukavar," he said, sliding off the edge of the desk onto his feet. "I'm working with the Calden Naval Constabulary. I just wanted to have a little chat."

"I have no time to *chat* and you are in a highly restricted area! I'm going to have to ask you to leave."

"Come in and close the door," Mukavar said, his smile replaced by a more serious expression. "I'll be out of your hair soon enough."

The Tiikeri chief cautiously did as requested and the Calden Intelligencer got straight to the point. "I'm investigating reports of a small party of your people that are operating within the city. I was wondering if you knew anything about that?"

Tor-Ga froze, remembering the mawl's arrival seventeen lunas ago.

"I have no idea what you're referring to," Tor-Ga lied, remembering the white Tiikeri's admonishment to forget the meeting. "As far as I know I am the only Tiikeri in this city."

"I just figured, as Kaplan station chief, you'd be the one to know."

"Sorry I can't help you. Tell me, if they *were* in town, what's your interest?"

"A young girl, a Calden naval officer's daughter, has gone missing and I wanted to see what they knew about it."

Tor-Ga recoiled in shock at the statement. "Surely you don't suspect the Order of Kaplan to be involved in such scurrilous matters?!"

"I don't know. That's why I'm investigating. One thing's for sure. If they *are* involved, it's not going to go well for them or *anyone* assisting them."

"Well, as I said before. I'm sorry I can't be of any help."

Mukavar nodded and headed for the door. "I trust if you discover anything, you'll contact me immediately?"

"Of course."

"Thank you for your cooperation. You can get word to me through the constabulary headquarters."

Mukavar stepped out onto the crowded Penaber streets and shivered inside his jacket. *Well*, he thought, *the trap is set. Let's see if he takes the bait.*

Taleeka stood in a crowded line of customers at a street vendor's cart and watched a flustered Tor-Ga hurriedly leave work in the middle of his shift.

"Hey Muuky," she reported into her talking stone, "your boy is on the move. I don't know what you said to him, but it just might have worked."

"I'm not going to be able to get there in time," Mukavar's voice came through. "We've got eyes on him from above, but on the ground would be nice."

"I'm on it."

"Thanks, I owe you one."

"I know."

She pulled the collar of her jacket up, kept her head lowered and took off behind the determined Tiikeri on the opposite side of the street. At various points in time along his route, the humanoid tiger would pause and look nervously around to make sure he wasn't being followed. Taleeka did her utmost to remain well ensconced within the diverse crowd plodding along the side of the street while a steady stream of hackneys and lizard drawn carts flowed in both directions on the road proper.

She wasn't surprised when he took a right at the intersection heading for the waterfront. Once on the docks, he turned left and headed to the far north end of the wharf. At this point, the thinner crowds forced her to hang farther back, blending into the mixture of dock workers and travelers milling about.

At the very end of the docks Tor-Ga entered a small barge that appeared to be permanently moored. He stayed there only a few moments before reemerging and heading back her way. Seeing him approaching, Taleeka quickly got in line to board a passenger ship and looked away from him.

The Tiikeri marched past within ten feet of her but failed to notice the subtle scrutiny he had fallen under. A hundred feet down the docks, he stopped in front of a warehouse extending partially out over the water. From the waterlines on the pilings, it looked like whoever built it had measured the tides precisely, because the high tidal markings came up to the floor of the extended room.

Peering cautiously both ways, he entered the large sliding door without knocking.

*Interesting*, Taleeka thought. *That's a lot of space. I wonder what they're up to. I think a little visit after moonfall is in order.*

Queen Omaris Atona of Amarenia felt determined to lead her people into the future, even if it meant dragging some of them kicking and screaming. For well over a thousand grands, Amarenians had led an isolated, larcenous existence that treated men as chattel. With the advent of air travel and exposure to the rest of the Annigan, this old way of life had proven untenable and detrimental to society as a whole.

She knew well there would be pushbacks to some of the new laws she had enacted, however the vast majority of the seventy-seven Banjas saw a direct and almost immediate increase in their wealth. Trading with the Goyans seemed lucrative enough for the crones of the noble families to modify their overall feelings of animosity towards men.

Still, fierce resistance persisted. Only eleven Banjas had joined the Era Zaharrak, or the Old Ways Party, not nearly enough to challenge her new, progressive laws. They were, however, a distraction and an annoyance. There were even whispers of veiled threats. So, with an abundance of caution, she increased her Mahaila protection detail and added a personal guard from the Queen's Envoy Service.

She formed the Envoy Service seven grands ago as an official Amarenian intelligence agency to work in concert with the Goyan Society of Whispers. She recruited them out of the Mahaila City Guards before formerly sending them to Zor for specialized training.

The woman sitting next to her, in the backseat of her royal hackney making its way across Mostas, could be counted as just such an envoy. Tajna Cabeli stood nearly six-feet-tall with long blond hair kept up in a bun on the back of her head. Her skin, while pale in comparison to the Goyans, did not have the alabaster hue of the High Amarenians. People often described her pleasant features and full lips as dour because of her constant serious demeanor. She wore red crop pants and a luroh sash crossed between her bare breasts like the rest of the Mahailas. Unlike regular Mahaila's lurohs, she replaced the metal balls at either end with holsters containing Landagar Mark Four pistol crossbows.

"Oh Siji," the queen called out to the driver, looking out the side window. "Those tomatoes look absolutely beautiful. Pull over, I want to get some for the kitchen."

"Yes, ma'am," the young Amarenian replied, before pulling the hackney off to the side of the road.

"Your Majesty, do you think that wise?" Tajna asked, gazing out at the tent covered fruit stand situated in a small clearing between buildings.

"Envoy, I hardly think buying fruit is dangerous," the queen said flippantly.

Five Mahalia guards exited the hackney behind them and formed a perimeter around the very startled fruit vendor. The plump, older Amarenian watched wide-eyed when Siji opened the passenger door and Tajna, followed by the queen, stepped from the vehicle.

The woman did a quick nervous bow when they approached.

"Your Majesty, I'm honored!"

The queen smiled sweetly, her beautiful face lighting up. "Such beautiful produce! It's I who am honored. I simply must have some of those tomatoes."

While the woman filled a bag with the fruit and exchanged pleasantries with Queen Omaris, Tajna cautiously began a full visual sweep around the area. Before she could complete it, she heard a stream of rapid clicks and the queen screaming before they were showered in a warm liquid.

Lunging to her left, she tackled the Amarenian sovereign to the ground. On the way down, she saw the fruit vendor toppling over with a surprised look on her face and most of her chest missing. She also caught sight of several dead Mahailas killed before they even detached their luroh bolos.

She heard several more rapid-fire clicks shattering glass from the hackneys. Then, sudden silence. Tajna rolled off her sovereign and drew her pistols.

She quickly popped her head over the chewed-up fruit stand and saw two attackers, a tall, older, bald woman and a short younger one with wild black hair and dark rings under her eyes in the fashion of the Rayth pirates.

Both clearly untrained, they clumsily attempted to reload. Each fumbled with the magazine when attempting to place it in the magazine port. Tajna raised both pistols and fired simultaneously. The two assassins' chests exploded and the blasts catapulted them onto their backs.

The Envoy then dashed over to the queen. "Are you alright my queen?"

Omaris Atona nodded, her eyes wide in shock. Other than out of breath and showered in the vendor's blood, the monarch seemed shaken up but unharmed.

"Yes, yes, I'm fine," she said, attempting to get back to her feet. "They tried to *kill* me!"

Tajna helped her up while pressing the Larimar stone set in her luroh where the bands crossed between her breasts.

"Emergency, code thirteen, repeat code thirteen!" Tajna repeated, before giving their location.

Keeping her pistols drawn, she surveyed the grisly scene. Along with the two assassins, all five of the Mahailas, the fruit merchant and Siji, the driver, were dead. The attack shredded the tent, as well as the wooden produce stand itself.

She wondered grimly how this could have happened so fast. Within moments, city guards swarmed the area and Tajna ordered them to get the queen to safety while she examined her two attackers.

Both were High Amarenians with porcelain white skin, but she didn't recognize either of them. Their weapons raised the envoy's curiosity. They shot rapid fire without needing to pull the bolt back. These were next generation weaponry from even what she carried.

Kneeling down, she pried the pistol from the grip of the younger assassin. It resembled her Mark Four, but obviously more advanced. It looked smaller and lighter, with an optical sighting device on the top of a greatly miniaturized vertical bow. She checked inside the breach and discovered a firing mechanism totally different than the one in her weapon. An examination of an unloaded magazine, lying on the ground next to the body, revealed different ammunition as well.

*How, in the name of the Goddess, did the likes of these two get their hands on these?* She silently asked herself while looking through the weapon's sights. *How could they possibly have missed using these sights?*

A particularly fragrant low tide almost always punctuated Moonfall on the Penaber wharf. Taleeka wiggled her nose, wincing at the noxious fishy bouquet all around her.

The underside of the docks felt slimy, and with the copious outcroppings of barnacles, more than a little treacherous. Carefully making sure she had a grip with both her hands and feet inside the boards above her, she pulled herself along the underside of the dock, all the while physically holding herself horizontally aloft.

The reconnaissance route she had chosen seemed her only option since there were no windows in the warehouse and she didn't want to tip off the Tiikeri with a forced entry on the front door. Because a full half of the structure had been built out over the water, she guessed there must be access from below. She felt relief at being correct.

Pausing at the lip of the thirty-foot hole in the floor, she listened for any signs of activity within. Hearing none, she examined the hole for traps and or alarms. The cautious burglar smiled when she saw a twinkle of reflected light at the end of an exposed beam and she shimmied over to it.

The milky blue gem set into the wood, looked to be an Etheria Blue Opal, making the warded opening dangerous and probably alarmed too. Holding on with one hand, she reached back into her pack and slipped her dagger out of its holster. Burrowing the tip of the fine Eldorian steel into the damp wood just below the gem she pushed down on the handle. The leverage forced the blue bauble to pop from its lodging and drop into the water with a small plop.

Detecting nothing further, she gripped the hole's lip and pulled herself up into the warehouse. The single room measured sixty-feet-square with a tall ceiling. Near the center of the room, a ten-foot tarp covered the only thing occupying the entire space.

She warily made her way across the room, lifted a corner of the covering and peered underneath. Tilting her head curiously, she gazed upon a contraption of some sort, constructed almost exclusively of various sized blocks of Etheria, around a crude seat and a small Etheria engine in the back of the bench.

*It's obviously a vehicle of some sort*, Taleeka silently pondered. *But that engine doesn't look very powerful. Wherever this has to go, it won't get very far or very fast.*

Taleeka placed her hands on her hips and shook her head. *So, this is why the Tiikeri wanted those Etheria notes*, she contemplated, *but what is it and where are they getting the Etheria from?*

Taleeka needed more information. Apparently, they were still in the process of building whatever it happened to be, so she needed eyes on the inside. Reaching into her pack, she located a two-inch square Etheria composite chip, composed of a milky white Larimar communication stone flanked by a strip of pale blue aquamarine for revealing and a diamond strip on the other side for transferring. Scaling up the wall nearest the tarp, she nestled the video transmitter on a narrow lip near the ceiling.

She had returned to the floor and made her way back over to the hole, when she heard Defari's low growl coming from the other holster in her pack. Reaching back, she grabbed the cudgel and lifted it free. The moment her hand touched the handle, the canine spirit within endowed her with its heightened senses. She smelled a distinct fishy odor, separate from the foul-smelling waterfront, and heard the flapping sound of fins on wood.

She made it to the hole in the floor just in time to see two Gar-Kal heads pop up through the opening. The humanoid fish-men hissed malevolently when they noticed her. She instinctively lashed out at one, smacking it with the Ukko club and knocking it unconscious mid hiss. Its head propelled back against the rim of the hole, neck breaking with a loud crack. The body plummeted down into the water with a muted splash.

The attack gave the other Gar-Kal the chance to leap up onto the floor in front of Taleeka. The scaley creature stood four-feet-tall at the peak of its mostly fish head. Sharp teeth filled a wide mouth and short, hooked claws extended from its webbed hands and feet.

It lashed out quickly and its claws raked across the front of Taleeka's Ghost Suit. Ukko fibers threaded through the material prevented a cut, but the force of the blow knocked her to the ground and sent Defari clattering across the floor and through the hole. Taleeka's heart sunk when she heard the splash of it hitting the water below.

Taking advantage of its downed opponent, the fish creature lunged on top of her, snapping its jaws. She could smell rotted fish on its breath with each gnash of its teeth. Taleeka managed to duck her head out of the way of the first two lunges, but the creature's superior speed and strength quickly overcame her.

It pinned her shoulders to the ground to hold her steady and she felt the searing pain of its claws slowly digging in through her protective suit. She knew Ukko only repelled fast moving objects and the deliberate nature of its attack rendered this particular protective quality of the suit useless.

Taleeka quickly moved her head to the side, barely avoiding the next lunge and realized she needed to do something fast. She felt fatigue setting in, but the Gar-Kal seemed to still retain its original vigor.

With Defari out of sight, and possibly out of earshot underwater, she didn't know if would work, but she screamed at the top of her lungs, "Defari come!"

The Gar-Kal lunged in again and Taleeka turned away from the attack, but it bit down on her left shoulder. Its teeth shredded the flesh of her neck not covered by the fabric of the suit. It readjusted and turned toward her throat. Her right hand pressed against its slimy forehead, frantically holding it back.

She knew she could not resist it much longer when her eyes caught the sight of a dripping wet Defari hovering over the hole in the floor.

She rotated her left arm at the elbow and pointed at the monster's head.

"Defari, attack!"

The Ukko projectile launched across the room and struck the Gar-Kal's forehead with a loud pop. The impact knocked the attacker completely off Taleeka and into a heap five feet away.

Taleeka slowly sat up and flexed her bleeding neck and shoulders. She knew her wounds needed to be quickly attended to. Who knew what kind of diseases they carried?

Getting to her feet she called for Defari and the club flew into her hand. She stared at it in awe, amazed at the depth and range of their connection.

"*Good* girl," she said, sliding Defari back in its holster.

Walking over to the prone Gar-Kal, she saw that Defari's impact caved its skull in. She grabbed one of its arms, dragged it to the hole and pushed it over the edge. When she saw the splash below, she followed it out the egress and, despite the pain, left in the same manner she had arrived.

Taleeka wasn't sure what The Order of Kaplan had planned. They certainly seemed benign enough. She hoped the little voyeuristic device she had planted would yield some answers.

One thing Taleeka felt certain of, whether their mysterious project proved harmless or not, she didn't trust the Tiikeri. They had proven time and again how treacherous and self-serving they were by nature. No re-branding or shift in dogma would change that. She must let Mukavar and the others know what she had found and maybe they could shed some light on it.

Zekoff looked up from the papers he had been grading at Vanir sitting across from him. He watched him take a long slow swig off his flask, sigh heavily, and then continue his thousand-yard stare.

The former Commander of the City Guards turned college professor had grown used to these frequent visits to his office on campus from his protégé. This visit, however, seemed different and carried a distinct melancholy note.

"You know," the redheaded lead investigator finally said. "I can't help but feel like an utter failure."

"Oh, how so?" Zekoff asked, setting his pen down and reaching for his pipe.

"Under your command, you completely wiped -out organized crime in this city and kept it away. I take over, and, during my first stretch in charge, I allow a gang to form." Vanir sorrowfully shook his head and hit the flask one more time. "I just don't know."

The old colonel lit the pipe and sat back, allowing a column of evergreen smoke to trail upward.

"I wouldn't beat yourself up too bad about that," Zekoff said, feeling genuinely sorry for the man he and his late wife raised from a young boy. "It was easier back then. Now, you've got all kinds of rules you have to follow and laws which can be debilitating at times. Back in my time, if I got wind that someone was trying to organize, I'd send in a brute squad to break up things. If it really got bad, Red Division did a lot of the dirty work."

"I don't even know who's at the head of this snake," Vanir said, sounding devoid of hope. "You mentioned all the new laws and rules. Whoever is in charge has hired the best barrister in the city to make sure those laws work for them."

"That would be Karta Lushi."

"The same."

"He's good," Zekoff said appreciatively.

"So far he's been keeping my hands tied."

"Alright, barristers aside," Zekoff said, sitting forward and setting his pipe down. "You've got to get back to basics. Granted you don't know who's in charge, and even if you did you still would have to make a case, but you do know the street bosses. Lean on them, sooner or later they'll lead you to the one at the top."

"I guess."

Zekoff gave a sympathetic smile. "Take what you learned from dismantling Banavor's little empire. Sooner or later this group is going to get their fingers into a bunch of other things and multiple agencies are going to get involved. Work together, just like before and you'll get it done."

Vanir returned the smile, took another swig off the flask, then put it away. These talks with his former mentor always made him feel better.

"Alrighty then," Vanir said, coming to his feet. "Thanks for listening. I've got some street bosses to lean on."

With a quick knock, Mukavar swung open the door to Admiral Metauri de Voria's office, then quickly entered with Taleeka right behind him. The commander of the Calden Naval Constabulary, seated behind her desk talked casually with Casus, her spymaster.

"Admiral, Casus, this is Taleeka Konrad." Mukavar said excitedly. "She has something for us."

Both constables rose to greet them.

"I had the pleasure of working with your mom quite a while back," the admiral said.

"Yes," Casus added, "I've been hearing quite a bit about you since your mother's retirement."

"I've got something you all are going to want to see," Taleeka said, shaking their hands.

"Mukavar said it was urgent," the admiral said, sitting back down.

"Right," Taleeka said, removing her backpack and opening it. "The other cycle, when Mukavar rattled Tor-Ga's cage, I followed him to a barge on the far northern dock, where I believe our mawl friends are living. Then to a warehouse not far from there, also on the northern docks."

Taleeka removed her Larimar Etheria Tablet and plugged an inch long Obsidian nodule into a slot along the top edge.

"So, I went back during the moonless and left a little snooping device," she explained as the screen came to life. "It caught this about a deci ago when the tide rose."

The interior of the warehouse became plainly visible. A Yagur, with the hood of his cape pulled back, uncovered and tinkered with the mysterious Etheria device. The orange and white Tiikeri stood beside him, supervising.

"What is that thing they're working on?" Metauri asked, squinting at the screen.

"I'm not sure," Taleeka replied. "At first glance it appears to be some sort of vehicle, but not anything I'd ride in or on. I can't tell. The good part's coming up."

They continued staring at the milk white screen and saw the water begin to churn through the hole. A translucent membrane boiled through the hole and formed into an elongating orb. Phosphorescent flashes of green and pink striated the surface of the orb, revealing a swarm of tentacles writhing in the murky fluid. When a few of the tentacles touched the side of the sphere two smaller bubbles slowly extended from the surface of the swirling orb.

"What in the name of the Goddess is going on?" Admiral Metauri gasped.

Mukavar whistled softly. "So, the Chanakans really are working with the Order of Kaplan!"

"To what end?!" Casus asked incredulously.

"You were there when we debriefed the only survivor of that pleasure yacht. Those spheres featured prominently," Mukavar said, shrugging. "Whatever it is, it can't be good."

"An unusual pairing," Metauri noted, her gaze transfixed.

While the Tiikeri seemed to be having a conversation with the tentacled figure in the large bubble, the mongrel suddenly came into view, walking over to the two smaller spheres. Sticking the top half of its body through the walls of the orbs, he began removing Etheria blocks of all different shapes and sizes.

"Well, now we know where the Tiikeri are getting their Etheria from," Taleeka said.

"Yes," Casus said quizzically. "But the question still remains, why?"

"I don't think it really matters," Metauri said, turning her attention to her comrades. "I don't see them breaking any laws."

"Snatching a hundred plus people off the high seas sure is," Mukavar replied. "I've never known those two parties to have an agenda that wasn't harmful to every living thing in Lumina. If that's the rendezvous point for mawl and Chanakan, it looks like I'm going for a swim."

The somber mood in Queen Omaris' private chambers hung like a wet sheet. Mal's attention shifted from the confused, angry face of the Amarenian ruler to the grimly determined expression of her envoy, Tajna.

"I can't believe people are angry enough to want me dead," Omaris said, sorrowfully shaking her head. "There has never been an attempt on a queen's life in the history of our peoples."

"I gotta say that's one fucking disturbing precedent someone set."

"Whoever it is, they must greatly fear that you challenge their way of life," Alto said, standing next to Mal with his hands clasped behind his back.

"We all know Era Zaharrak is behind it," Tajna said disdainfully, her upper lip contorting in a sneer. "We identified the two assassins, Cike Skelos and Vrah Wiert of Durik-Dor. They discreetly followed the Queen's entourage in a lizard pulled merchant's wagon and blended in with the other merchants. By the time the guards noticed them drawing their weapons, the assassins had already gotten the drop on them and the sheer firepower of the weapons outgunned the guards.

"Durik-Dor is still in chaos from the Rayth purge almost twenty grands ago, a ripe breeding ground for assassins and insurgents. The Crones of those Banjas have now become powerful Sardors…"

She noticed the confused look on Mal's face.

"Warlords," she clarified. "These crones are very influential in Era Zaharrak and, even though they no longer wield any official political power, they still have sympathizers."

"I don't fucking get it," Mal said, rubbing the back of her neck. "If this 'Old Ways' group is causing so much trouble, why don't you just arrest them, or kill them, or whatever?"

"I'm afraid it's not that simple," the queen responded with a sad, patient smile. "Crones carry the title of Astute Sister and hold considerable power. They are the only ones who can openly speak out against a law, even though they and their Banjas must obey it. If a majority of the seventy-seven Crones oppose a law, they can challenge it."

"Okay your majesty, so how do we play into this?" Mal asked. "I mean, we were summoned."

"Valorous, I charge the three of you to find those responsible for this assassination attempt and bring them to justice. You may use whatever means you deem necessary."

"Anointed," Mal said ominously. "With orders like that, you do realize things are probably going to get broken along the way? What about pushback?"

"Tajna will take care of any Mahaila issues you may encounter. Although, with two valorous citizens and a Queen's Envoy on a royal mission, there will be few with the authority to confront you."

Mal exhaled loudly. "Fair enough, but things are going to get bumpy, fairly quick."

"I say we pay a visit to the Skelos and Wiert plantations," Tajna said aggressively.

"Eventually," Mal replied calculatingly. "Durik-Dor may be where the assassins came from, but I've got the feeling the orders came from somewhere close to the seat of power and I know just the place to start."

Of late, Drugo had made it a habit to have breakfast at the Daraka Eatery before starting his cycle. The popular twelve table diner on Zor's Southern Docks, chosen for its short walk to Mazie's soup kitchen, served a mean stack of pancakes, which were his favorite.

The mobster had just poured a drizzle of syrup on a warm heap of the delectable cakes when a brash female voice cut through his peaceful morning routine. "Keep eating those pancakes every cycle and you're gonna get fat."

Drugo looked up at Tantei, dressed in a button up shirt, slacks and a loose-fitting jacket. The Goyan Islands were well into Spring and it got warmer by the cycle, which meant she wore the coat strictly for concealing her weapon.

The brazen investigator smiled broadly, pulled out a chair across the table and sat down.

"Did I invite you to join me?" Drugo asked, before popping a fork full of pancakes into his mouth.

"Nah," Tantei said good naturedly, "but you're a friendly guy. So, I figured why not."

He swallowed his mouthful and scoffed loudly, "You figured wrong. Get lost. I'm trying to eat my breakfast in peace."

"Aw, come on Drugo, I just wanna talk. We can do it here, while you leisurely eat your breakfast, or I can drag your ass down to Judgement Square and put you in some really uncomfortable contraption while we chat."

Drugo paused a moment and then glared over the table at the detective. "Alright, so talk."

"There's a reasonable fellow! So, Drugo, there's a new guy on your corner. What, you get a promotion or something?"

"I don't know what the fuck you're talking about."

"Of course you don't! Look pecker breath, you're not going to score any points by insulting my intelligence. First, your street boss is killed and you end up taking his place. I would naturally assume you gave him a permanent early retirement, until a bunch of street bosses turned up dead."

Tantei sat back and chuckled. "Now, there's somebody on *your* corner replacing you, but you're still alive. Word on the street says that a new player in town is trying to organize the low life population in the Sisters. So, we circle back around to my original question, did you get a promotion?"

"I don't do street stuff anymore. Too dangerous. I'm a pillanthrofist now."

An amused smirk played at the corners of the investigator's mouth. "A philanthropist, huh? You're a real pillar of the community. So, what's your game now?"

"None of your fucking business. It ain't illegal so get off my ass!"

Tantei rolled her eyes. "Drugo, if I was on your ass, it would be a lot more unpleasant than watching you eat."

"Yeah, well, because of you my cakes are cold. Thanks a lot, asshole," he said, standing with an angry scowl. "You ruined them. You get the bill. And leave me the fuck alone!"

Tantei smiled and shook her head watching him leave. The moment he stepped out the door, she reached into her coat pocket and touched her Larimar talking stone.

"You got eyes on him Tay?" she asked softly.

"Big as life," Talib's voice came through in her head. "He's heading into the Sisters."

"Stay on him," she said, sliding the plate of partially eaten pancakes in front of her and raising her hand for the serving wench. "Can I get another fork over here?"

Just under a deci after moonset, Mukavar crouched behind a stack of crates on the Penaber wharf and waited for the last of the workers to finally leave. The Calden agent silently arranged his equipment on the wooden dock and considered how much he preferred being on top of the waves instead of below them.

*Damn that water looks cold*, he thought, slipping on his swim fins.

Training as an elite Brightstar sailor qualified him to pilot ships under the most extreme conditions the sea offered and his time as a mechanic for the Calden Intelligencer Service taught him to endure and triumph under the most challenging of circumstances, like now. Mukavar wasn't even sure what waited for him down there, if anything, but if the Chanakans accessed the warehouse from under these docks, he needed to have a look.

He examined the Garrett Aquatic Mask, his last new piece of gear, fresh from the Etheria laboratory of the Landagar Group. This would be his first time using it and he looked forward to putting it through its paces. The mask covered the entire face with a rubber head band and gasket around the edges. The lab treated the glass of the face shield with Etheria, much like the airship's windshields. Blue Aquamarine, for revealing, which could shift to Orange Trinilic, for seeing heat sources if the water grew too dark or murky. They also set a small clear strip of Calcite in the upper right corner on the inside, easily visible to the wearer, to aid in navigation.

However, Mukavar considered the contoured, blue green breathing device the most important feature. They attached a custom-formed crystal, infused with water magic, to the bottom of the face covering, which fit snugly around the nose and mouth. The Etheria mask within a mask allowed the user to breathe while submerged.

After making sure to secure everything on his Ghost Suit, he stepped off the edge of the dock and slipped almost soundlessly into the dark ocean. Mukavar gasped slightly at the bracingly cold sea, but adjusted quickly and took in his surroundings. He found himself in roughly twenty feet of water and he marveled at the natural flow of air the Etheria mask provided. His face shield already shifted to pale orange and he could plainly see the aquatic life swimming around him. Even the massive pilons of the dock above glowed with the living barnacles coating them.

He kept an eye on the navigational shard to make sure it still blinked green, indicating he was headed in the right direction. Feeling confident his equipment worked properly, he slowly swam north, paralleling the docks. The closer he got to his destination, the slower the rate of strobing until it went solid green. He slipped under the dock and warehouse, gazing upward through the hole in the floor, but there appeared to be no activity inside. Circling the area, he saw nothing except aquatic sea life and debris littering the bottom under the hole.

He scowled in frustration and, sensing there had to be more, began systematically widening his search. The closer he got to the end of the northern docks the more intrigued he grew. Just ahead, directly under the stationery barge, there appeared multiple heat signatures. The closer he swam, the more he realized the mammoth scope of the glow.

Mukavar's eyes widened in shock when he finally got a look at a field of the translucent orbs covering the entire bottom of the barge. Unlike the ones he had seen on Taleeka's screen, these housed an individual body, whose heat signatures made the area glitter like a city at night.

A sinking feeling came over him as he cautiously approached the first bubble. The person inside appeared unconscious in a murky fluid. He knew the unfortunate victim wasn't dead because he still gave off heat. Something didn't appear quite right and Mukavar studied the nude man. He discovered slits in the side of his neck resembling gills and webbing formed between the fingers and toes.

The next globe revealed a nude woman with the same gill slits and webbing. Checking several more, he discovered the rest similarly afflicted. Like a blow to the stomach, a horrific realization swept across the Calden agent.

*These were the people taken from that pleasure yacht.*

Mukavar's mind reeled. *What happened to them? What were the Chanakans up to?*

Suddenly, a disturbing thought came to mind and he quickly swam to the orbs on the other end of the barge. His heart sank when he arrived at the first in line. There he found what remained of Nyara de Eltos, the young girl he had been called in to locate. She stared out at him with lidless, black eyes devoid of any emotion. Her entire body seemed to be in the final stages of transformation into a Gar-Kal, a humanoid fish creature. The few blonde tufts of hair on the back of her fish head remained her only facade of humanity.

While pondering his next course of action, Mukavar caught motion out of the corner of his eye on the left. He spun to face two Gar-Kal aggressively swimming his way.

Without hesitation, the Calden mechanic pulled his Mark Seven pistol and fired. Although the drag of the water hampered the bolt's velocity, it still possessed a sufficient level of lethality and punched a hole in the fish creature's chest, lodging in its body. The Gar-Kal spun stomach up towards the surface and clouds of black blood rushed from the wound.

The second one immediately dove, barely dodging the next round and swiftly closed the distance. It grabbed Mukavar's gun hand by the wrist and attempted to wrestle the weapon away, all the while lunging at the agent with snapping jaws.

Mukavar had been so caught up in the conflict he failed to notice the Chanakan's large bubble emerging from out of the gloom. By the time he caught sight of it, the globe had advanced to less than twenty feet away. The human agent desperately tried to figure out what to do, when a high-pitched squeal emitted from the Chanakan.

Mukavar recoiled in agony, as a tornado stormed across his brain and he fell unconscious. He dropped the pistol and it sunk to the bottom. The Gar-Kal moved Mukavar's body to a smaller orb, forming from the Chanakan's bubble. When the globe completely formed, but remained attached to its parent, the fish creature shoved Mukavar through the permeable walls, into the murky, liquid filled interior.

The Chanakan's spindly arm reached through the membrane and removed Mukavar's mask, letting it drift to the bottom of the bubble. Surges of phosphorescence strobed, lighting the murky waters and revealing the black viscous tentacles surrounding his face. The inky appendages lingered inside Mukavar's prison, before simultaneously entering his mouth, nostrils and ear cavities. The tendril thrusting into his mouth pushed past his tongue while the others held his head still. It pulsed and swelled when it ejaculated a small worm down Mukavar's throat. Once it inseminated the parasite, the ink tentacles withdrew from the agent's body and dissipated in the water.

When the two orbs separated, the Gar-Kal guided Mukavar to the underside of the barge and added his bubble to the many others dangling in neat lines.

The moonless felt cool and slightly damp for spring. Thick broken bands of dark, rain laden clouds raced westward across the Amarenian sky. From her position in a stand of trees on a small hill overlooking the Samryn Plantation, Mal could smell the distinct perfume of jasmine traveling on the wind. She wished she could enjoy it from the patio of her home. After all, wasn't she supposed to be retired and not working yet another potentially dangerous job? Still, when the queen calls you to duty, the luxury of refusal blows away much like the clouds overhead.

Down below, the lights twinkled in the plantation house and there appeared to be plenty of activity between the main house and the various satellite structures. The main road into the plantation complex ran through a shallow valley at the bottom of the hill.

Alto positioned himself laying in the tall grass on the hill directly opposite her. The Queen's Envoy, Tajna, who followed Potoloa Samryn home from her tailor shop, now crouched beside the former spice rat.

"You know, we were completely outgunned," Tajna reflected softly, not taking her eyes off the plantation.

"What?" Mal asked, surprised by the sudden enigmatic revelation.

"The assassination attempt on the queen, we were totally outgunned. It was pure dumb luck the queen got out of it without a scratch."

Uncertain of what to say, Mal remained silent.

"You said those were Mark Fives, right?" Tajna asked.

Mal nodded.

"It's not that we don't appreciate trade and help from the Goyans," Tajna continued, finally looking her way, "but we need better equipment. Like the hardware you're carrying."

Mal gave a wry chuckle. "Not too many people are carrying what I have. This is a Mark Seven. Most city guards, at least in the big cities, carry Mark Sixes."

A sad smile crossed Tajna's face. "Valorous, you make my point for me. We're carrying Mark fours. The assassins had Mark Fives. We need better equipment! Now, we're supposed to be allies. Either you trust us, or you don't!"

"Why fucking tell me? Isn't this a conversation you should be having with your trade representative?"

"I know you have a tight relationship with House Valdur. I was maybe hoping you could put in a word."

"I don't have near the pull I used to. My main contact, Joc' Valdur is about to be voted Sovereign, by the Council of Air Lords, so he'll be gone."

"I would think knowing the king would be even better."

Mal smiled, about to acquiesce, when a startled look crossed the envoy's face.

"Valorous, look!"

It appeared as a glint in the western sky to Tajna, but Mal clearly saw a Resistance Class Cruiser rapidly approaching the plantation with her Trinilic spectacles. Both made sure they were well camouflaged from the air, while maintaining visual contact.

The airship circled the area, while a door to a barn opened and a wagon, pulled by two slaves, rolled out into the main plaza in front of the manor house. The airship settled gently down twenty feet from the wagon. Several Amarenians exited the house to stand by the wagons, watching the craft's side and rear hatch open.

Mal didn't recognize Mazie or Chen when they exited the side hatch. She had never officially seen Potoloa Samryn, who went up to greet the two newcomers. The Amarenian to Potoloan's right proved to be a different matter altogether.

"Well, just fuck me!"

"Do you see what I see my love?" Alto's voice came through in Mal's head.

She grasped her Larimar talking stone necklace. "Are you fucking kidding me, it's Tengah Napp?! It fucking figures she'd be involved with Era Zaharrak."

"She might even be one of the leaders," Alto offered.

"You can bet if Tengah is here, Sorgina can't be far behind."

"It would appear this is where the Napp sisters now reside."

"Makes sense, they sure as fuck can't stay with their mother."

They watched as Mazie and Tengah embraced, while Chen stood respectfully back. The two shared a brief conversation, then Tengah directed two of the other Amarenians into the rear of the ship. They hauled three crates out of the cargo bay and placed them in the back of the wagon.

After briefly speaking again, Mazie retrieved a meat cleaver from a rear holster. Everyone smiled, so Mal didn't expect an altercation. She silently congratulated herself on being correct when the female mobster used the back of the cleaver's blade to pry open one of the crates.

Mazie pulled out a Mark Five Pistol and handed it to Tengah. The Amarenian eyed the weapon lovingly and held it up for inspection.

"What the fuck!" Mal gasped in astonishment. "That's a Mark Five. Who the fuck is that woman?!"

"I do not know, my love. I have never seen her before, but the man with her, who I assume is her bodyguard, is a Zorian swordsman."

Mazie then opened another crate and handed Tengah a magazine and a Na-Kab Carbon bolt. Tengah nodded in satisfaction and Potoloa handed Mazie a fat envelope.

Tengah and Mazie embraced once more, before she and Chen got back in the airship. Once the hatches were closed, it rapidly rose and sped away back in the direction it had come from.

Tengah hefted the pistol, inserted the magazine and then tucked it into the waistband of her crop pants. The other two Amarenians pushed the wagon back into the barn, locked the door and one remained standing guard. Everyone else returned to the manor house, as the plantation seemed to be settling down for the moonless.

"Whoever that is, she's arming Era Zaharrak," Tajna said direly. "That's sedition!"

"Obviously," Mal responded, "the Mark Fives the assassins used were just a taste of the candy. Looks like they liked the taste because they just bought out the whole fucking store! I think we found the responsible parties."

"We can't let them have those weapons," Tajna asserted, shaking her head. "We've got to call for help."

They'll be just as outgunned as before," Mal replied. "Besides, I'm supposed to be retired. I think a mechanic is what's called for here."

Mal reached back into her shirt and touched her Larimar once more. "Shurta, you in earshot?"

"Hey Mal," Shurta's jovial voice resonated in her head. "Long time no see. How's retirement?"

Mal scoffed. "What retirement? Hey, are you guys by any chance missing some Mark Fives?"

A lengthy pause hung on the other end. "As a matter of fact, yes. A shipment of them got stolen on their way to the armory in Dryden. Why?"

"Because I know where they are."

Meridian Street is the longest continual roadway in The High Holy City of Zor. The broad thoroughfare stretches north and south, connecting the northern docks, Shimol and Tuath Plats. During the cycle, the congested boulevard serves as a major conduit, bringing passengers into and out of the main mercantile areas of the city. During the Kan, the activity does not abate, but rather takes on a more festive nature, with pubs and eateries conducting most of the business.

Larzz stood just outside the door of the Fog City Lounge and watched the traffic on Meridian course back and forth in front of the less than reputable drinking establishment. So far, it had been a slow Kan, with no altercations or belligerent drunks. That generally meant one thing, Larzz had grown bored. Eight cycles passed since he had returned from Tannimore and he found himself still slightly jacked up from the experience, not to mention a lot richer. In fact, he really didn't need this job, but he figured he'd better keep his hand in it in case the work with Tally dried up. Which he doubted. It seemed like that kid could always find something to get into, and just like her parents, she paid well.

The half EEtah bouncer had just about given up on anything exciting when a woman's scream from the side of the building caught his attention. Peering around the corner, he saw two men in capes and hoods playing tug of war with an unusually pale woman almost out of sight in the thick fog. Each held an arm, desperately trying to claim her, while she looked less than eager for either's companionship.

"Hey, knock it off!" he ordered tersely, while heading their way.

The woman stared at him with a pleading look, while the men ignored his command.

"I said let her go!"

When Larzz made it ten feet away, one of the men dropped her arm and took off running. She continued struggling when the other pulled her into his arms. He laughed and tightly held onto her squirming frame.

"It's gonna be hard to use that pecker of yours from an infirmary bed! Let her go now!"

As he approached the tussling couple, he got a better look at them. More than just pale, her alabaster skin revealed her as an Amarenian, but the dark circles under her eyes gave her a rather unnerving and sinister appearance.

The hulking half EEtah chuckled when the man transferred the woman to one arm and pulled a dagger.

"Congratulations asshole," Larzz said, stepping up to them. "You just graduated from the Clerria House infirmary to the Vurr Pyres."

Larzz wasn't prepared for what happened next. The man quickly reversed the dagger and stabbed himself in the upper leg, wincing in pain. The woman, no longer struggling, seemingly became enraptured by the man's torment. She swept her hand in front of Larzz's face and blew a shower of blue sparks from her fingertips, engulfing his entire head.

A mysterious light show overtook Larzz's field of vision right before everything went black. The bouncer teetered and dropped to the street.

Qasia peered down at the unconscious Larzz dispassionately. "Soon you will feel the vengeance of the Lord, as will your friends."

Brother Hardee quickly tied a bandage around his shallow wound while Brother Telek came back around the building driving a lizard drawn cart.

"Quickly, get him in the cart," she said, stepping out of the way.

"I don't see why we don't just kill him outright and be done with it." Hardee said, attempting to move Larzz's three hundred pounds of dead weight.

"I promised Lord Wikk it would be done slowly. Then my mistress wants their skins," Qasia said with a pout. "What are you trying to do, spoil all my fun?"

The alley behind the soup kitchen stunk of urine, vomit and stale booze. Talib listened to the Grand Turine in the Zorian Harbor ring ten bells and knew it was going to be a long Kan. The tattered rags he wore itched and he desperately needed a bath. Directly across the alley, Tantei, dressed similarly, curled herself up in the fetal position by a pile of rubbish, pretending to sleep.

They had been at this stake-out now for three Kans and so far, they had seen nothing but the city's homeless population wandering in for a free meal.

*Become an investigator*, Talib silently lamented. *It'll be glamourous and exciting. Solve mysteries and catch bad guys.*

He scoffed at the line of hungry street people forming around the building, waiting to get fed. Sighing with acceptance, he resigned himself into settling into a misery laden watch when the lights of a private hackney cut through the fog and pulled into the alley.

Talib suspiciously eyed the luxury six-seater with a sizable trunk as it silently glided up to the kitchen's back door and cut the engine. The front doors opened immediately upon stopping and two men got out.

Talib couldn't ID the driver, a bull of a man with a thick neck and bald head, but a panic swept across him when he recognized Drugo and he ducked his head. The street boss could identify both him and his partner from their run-in earlier this cycle. Across the alley, he noticed Tantei also shielded her face.

Drugo stepped up to the back door and knocked. A few moments later, someone he couldn't see answered the door. They held a brief conversation then the door closed, leaving the street boss waiting.

Moments later, a beautiful dark-haired woman in riding pants and boots joined him. Followed by a man a full head taller than her with light copper skin, long blonde hair and goatee, obviously her bodyguard. The handle wrapping on the long sword strapped to his back identified him as an instructor for the Zorian Sword Academy.

"So, what have you got?" he overheard Mazie ask.

"I really think you're gonna like this ma'am," Drugo replied respectfully, before leading them over to the trunk of the hackney and opening it.

Talib couldn't see what the trunk contained, but the delighted look on Mazie's face told her it was something that greatly pleased her.

"Excellent work," she praised. "Drugo, you've got street bosses to check up on. Chen, Vozac, we've got a delivery to make."

"Yes ma'am," Drugo said, before walking off down the alley in the other direction.

Chen opened the door for Mazie and he climbed after her into the back of the hackney. Vozac settled into the driver's seat and the vehicle drifted off past the two investigators, lethargically pulling into traffic. Once gone, the detectives rose to their feet and met in the middle of the alley.

"I guess my first question would be, what does the manager of a soup kitchen need with a bodyguard?" Talib wondered.

"I'd be willing to bet next cluster's pay that she's the one in charge. Everyone seemed to be acquiescing to her. Did you get a look at that meat cleaver on her belt."

Nah, I was too busy staring at her tits. She keeps those buttons undone pretty low."

Tantei sighed, shook her head and closed her eyes.

"What?" Talib asked innocently.

Tantei went back to the spot where she had been laying and pulled her shoulder bag from behind the pile of debris.

"Come on," she said, "let's not lose them. I want to see exactly what this 'delivery' is."

Chen found himself questioning his new employer's motives. He sat next to her, in the back seat of her private hackney, constantly checking on her out of the corner of his eye. Vozac's hulking frame hunched over the wheel in the driver's seat, jealously brooding about his presence while navigating the Zorian streets.

Chen had to admit Mazie's beauty could not be questioned. She smelled intoxicating, performed like an absolute demon in bed and she paid well.

It was the man bound in the trunk that gave the swordsman pause.

"I don't quite understand," Chen said, watching the building outlines of the Tuath Plat go by through the thick Kan fog. "Pa-Waga is a religion forbidden in Zor. Why didn't you merely turn him over to the city guards?"

Mazie peered over at him with a calculating look.

"Believe it or not," she answered, "I've discovered some sentients who hate that religion more than I do. I want to form an alliance with them and our friend in the trunk is going to be my little welcome gift."

A sly smile suddenly crossed Mazie's face. "You ask a lot of questions for a bodyguard."

Chen gave a small, flippant nod of the head. "If I'm going to be able to adequately protect you, I have to know what you are getting us into. Besides, by the way you have been defiling me every Kan since my hiring, I thought my status somewhat more elevated than a mere bodyguard."

Chen made the last statement solely for Vozac's benefit and he grinned watching the driver's fists tighten on the steering wheel. The sentients she mentioned intrigued him. He knew she blamed the religion for her father's death. Imagining someone harboring even greater animosity seemed almost inconceivable.

Mazie reached over and patted him on his thigh condescendingly. "It's a good thing you're pretty."

They rode the rest of the short ride in silence. Vozac navigated the vehicle off the main thoroughfare onto a deserted side street. Pulling up in front of a hackney garage, Mazie touched one of her Larimar earrings. The simple, small white bulb, easily confused as a pearl, became an effective use of the Etheria talking stone.

"We're here," she said.

A hooded figure slid open the wide grimy door. Light streamed out from the opening, bathing the section of street in its glow. Vozac guided the hackney inside and the door closed behind them.

Chen cocked his head, completely taken by surprise. He had never seen a Tiikeri before and now there were two of the orange tiger-men standing together by a workbench against the wall.

They wore cloaks with the hoods pulled back and one measured a full head taller than the other. Three similarly dressed mongrel mawls surrounded them. The one who had opened the door joined them and pulled his hood back revealing him to be a mongrel too.

"Never seen Tiikeri before?" Mazie asked, not taking her eyes off the humanoid tigers."

Chen shook his head. "You?"

"Only from afar," she replied nervously. "They're called The Order of Kaplan and wiping out all traces of Pa-Waga is in their charter. These are going to be good allies to have. Alright, smiles everyone. Let's make some friends."

Vozac got out first and opened Chen's door before his employer's. The swordsman kept a stoic expression but knew this must be just maddening for Vozac. Chen accompanied the resentful servant to Mazie's door, standing guard while he opened it and she gracefully slid out.

Mazie led the procession across the garage to the Tiikeri. Vozac remained behind, standing imposingly by the hackney's door, his pistol close at hand.

"Hello," Mazie said, keeping her initial deportment friendly yet business-like. "Thank you for meeting with me. My name is Mazie and I think we can be of benefit to one another. You represent The Order of Kaplan, no?"

"How is it you knew where to find us, let alone know about us at all?" the larger one asked guardedly.

Mazie smiled confidently. "I pay a lot of money for eyes all over town, especially in the Sisters. The moment I found out about your charter, I sought you out, knowing we shared a mutual interest."

"And what might that be?"

Mazie's smile turned sinister. "The utter and complete destruction of the Pa-Waga cult."

The Tiikeri paused, then glanced briefly at one another, before relaxing slightly.

"I am Sor-Narr," the larger one said. "And this is De-Mat. Yes, we represent The Order of Kaplan here in Zor. What is your complaint against Pa-Waga?"

Mazie's smile vanished. "They murdered my father."

"They almost caused our entire race to be wiped out," Sor-Narr said unemotionally.

"I know, and until a little while ago I didn't think anyone hated Pa-Waga more than me. Then I found out about you and your charter. I gotta hand it to you, building their destruction into your very founding document sure has my squabble with them beat."

"We are always pleased to meet our enemy's enemy, but why are we here?"

The sly smile returned to Mazie's face. "Well, like I said before, I think we can be of benefit to one another. I propose we form an alliance."

The curious look on the Tiikeri told Mazie she had his interest.

"Benefit how? What sort of alliance are you suggesting?"

"You have a presence in the Narrow Lands and The Land of Mists. I'm seeking to expand my operations and those areas could be of interest to me."

"What would you need from us, and what do you have to offer?"

"What I need, and offer is the same, information. I think we can be a useful part of each other's intelligence network."

The Tiikeri glanced intriguingly at each other once more.

"What information could you possibly have for us?" De-Mat finally spoke up.

"Unfortunately, where you have to stay in the shadows, my people can move through the city unnoticed. All adherents of the cult will either be turned over to you personally or their location will be provided."

Both Tiikeris weighed the deal before Sor-Narr's tail began to twitch. "And what do you want from us?"

"Right now, nothing," Mazie replied raising her hand, signaling Vozac. "In fact, I have something for you. Think of it as a goodwill gesture, a little something to get this alliance off on the right foot."

The burley driver left his post, went around behind the hackney and muscled a bound, gagged and nude middle-aged man out of the trunk. He carried him on his shoulder and threw him on the ground in front of the mawls.

The dark brown skinned man with short black hair looked thin and frail. Fear radiated in his eyes, darting wildly back and forth over his gag.

"A gift," Mazie said sincerely. "He has the mark."

She saw the hesitation on their faces.

"Show them," she ordered Vozac.

Vozac gruffly turned the terrified man until his back faced the cat-men. The Tiikeri nodded in approval when they saw the X and I, carved on either side of the base of his spine.

"Very well!" Sor-Narr agreed, motioning for his companions to take charge of their prisoner. "We accept your gift and The Order of Kaplan thanks you. You claim you can provide more?"

"My people are constantly on the lookout for any that might have chosen to stay and go underground. They can be hard to locate, but when we do, we'll turn them over to you."

"And you say you want nothing from us?" De-Mat squinted cautiously.

"That's right," Mazie assured. "I'm just laying the groundwork for future endeavors westward."

Tantei rushed over to the garage's front door and pulled a tubed Etheria listening device from her messenger bag. The two-foot-long apparatus contained large and small suction cones at either end. Etheria Crystals lined the rim of each cup. She set the bag down, placed the larger end against the door and the smaller one against her ear while Talib stood watch, pistol drawn.

"She's meeting with Tiikeri!" Tantei said in a startled whisper.

Talib's eyes enlarged in surprise, but he kept his silent visual on the fog shrouded streets.

"She's proposing an alliance between them."

"What kind of alliance?"

Tantei raised her hand for silence while she furrowed her brow in concentration.

"The delivery she was talking about is a gift for them.'" Tantei's face hardened. "It's a person! It's a follower of Pa-Waga they captured."

Another brief few moments of intense eavesdropping passed before Tantei hurriedly pulled the listening device away from her ear. "Okay, the meetings breaking up. I've heard enough."

On the hackney ride back to headquarters, Talib glanced over quizzically at his partner. "So, I don't get it. Tiikeri are forbidden in Zor. Why didn't we arrest them?"

"A hunch," she replied simply.

"Oh?"

"The Tiikeri's now call themselves The Order of Kaplan and it sounds like something much bigger is going on. I'm gonna have the boss put a fifty/ten surveillance on this place. Once we find out, then we stick it to them, hard."

Barr-Ani awoke with a start and bolted up in bed. Her heart pounded, a rushing sound flooded her ears and her breath grew ragged. She peered around her shared room and found everything quiet and normal. Taleeka slept silently in the bed next to her with Defari by her side gently snoring. Noorim, who had been sitting cross-legged in front of the door meditating, bounded to her feet and over to her bedside.

"Are you alright?" Noorim asked quietly, gently touching Barr-Ani's upper arm.

"The dream!" she swallowed hard, clearly rattled.

"A nightmare?"

Barr-Ani nodded her head. "A large explosion you could see from everywhere, then lots of little ones. There was fire and death, so much death. Tens of thousands, gone in an instant. In the air… it was raining crystal shards."

Her expression suddenly turned hopeless.

Shaking her head, and on the verge of tears, she spoke in a dire whisper, "The Annigan… changed forever."

"Did you see the nature of this large explosion?"

The psychic shook her head. "I heard some sort of loud crash just before, but I didn't see it."

"Do you know when, and if it can be stopped?"

"No," Barr-Ani said, head shaking and eyes misting over.

Were this a regular dreamer having a nightmare, the Amarenian would have comforted them, to help them back to sleep. She knew the Bailian sensitive, however, was no ordinary slumberer.

It now became time to wake Taleeka.

Larzz still saw sparkles in front of his face when he finally opened his eyes. He peered around the small stone room and shook his head to clear it. He had been bound naked, spread eagle on a vertical, thick wooden board.

Qasia and the two Piety Watch stood directly in front of him staring malevolently. The woman, with her pale white skin and dark circles under her eyes looked especially ominous. She stood next to a small oblong table. Two rows of menacing looking blades, saws and pincers were neatly arranged on its surface.

"You have stolen from the Lord and have been sentenced to a slow, painful death," Qasia said with righteous indignation.

She held up a long thin spike and allowed the room's crystal glow to glint off its surface, while she examined its length. "I have been chosen to be the vengeance of our mighty god. If you have any last words or prayers to offer, now is the time. Once I begin, all you will be able to do is scream."

"If ya let me go now, you get to live," The half EEtah said with a snarl.

"Are you sure you want *those* to be your last words?"

Larzz remained silent, darkly glaring at her.

Qasia shrugged. "So be it."

She slowly held the spike aloft for all to see, then brought it down to the front of his thigh and pushed on it. Larzz didn't stare at the intimidating weapon, but kept his eyes locked on his tormenter's. When the sharpened tip did not immediately puncture Larzz's tough skin, a wave of confusion swept across the torture mage's face and she pressed harder.

When it finally penetrated, Larzz flinched slightly and then a maniacal smile danced across his face. The deeper she drove the spike into his flesh, the more rapidly Larzz breathed, but he didn't cry out.

Qasia stared at the long quill buried in his leg and nodded appreciatively. "Impressive, but rest assured, before I am finished with you, I shall savor your anguished cries."

"You've never dealt with my people before, have you?" Larzz growled, watching her reach for another needle. "Pain doesn't scare us. It doesn't make us weak. Pain makes us *angry!*"

Larzz bellowed loudly and strained at his bonds. The Pa-Waga cultists looked on in shocked disbelief when the metal brackets restraining the behemoth began to move, slowly being pulled free.

Qasia lunged the needle forward into her captive's abdomen in a wide-eyed panic. The tip barely pierced the skin and hung limply when Larzz pulled his hands free. She rapidly backed up, her face etched in terror while brothers Hardee and Telek scrambled for the locked door.

Hardee reached for the bolt first before being violently propelled into the door. Larzz's escape had straightened out one of the restraining brackets and the man-shark threw the metal with such force it completely impaled Hardee's upper back, pinning his torso to both the edge of the door and jamb. A sheet of crimson descended down to the floor.

With their only avenue of escape blocked, the Pa-Waga adherents spun in a panic in time to see Larzz pop his feet free. He stepped onto the floor with fists clenched and lather forming on the sides of his snarling mouth. The seven-foot tall EEtah hybrid growled and lunged savagely at them.

Rafel, beside himself with concern, had tried to no avail to get ahold of Mukavar most of the morning. He scowled and drummed his fingers on his desk until he noticed a rather animated Vanir stepping into his doorway.

"Got a centi?" asked the red headed lead investigator.

Rafel sighed and glanced nervously at his Larimar stone before nodding.

"So," Vanir said, stepping inside and closing the door. "What do you know about an organization called 'The Order of Kaplan?'"

Rafel momentarily froze, forgetting about Mukavar.

"Where did you hear that name?" he asked cautiously.

"One of my investigators, surveilling some Tiikeri operating clandestinely in Zor, said the name came up."

Rafel sat back and exhaled loudly. "Vanir, I'm afraid at this point in time I really can't talk about that."

Vanir's face fell. "Oh…"

Rafel sat forward. "And I'm afraid I need your people to back off from that particular investigation."

"That could be tough."

"How so?"

Vanir tugged nervously on his beard. "The Tiikeri's are just the newest addition to an already complex case."

Rafel's eyes narrowed questioningly.

"We've got an attempt to organize in the Sisters. My people were following our prime suspect as the leader when they encountered The Order of Kaplan last Kan. Looks like she's trying to fold them into her burgeoning empire."

"Okay," Rafel placated. "Let me run this by the security council and see how they want this played out. As for now 'The Order of Kaplan,' is strictly hush-hush. So, get word to your people, no talking."

Vanir nodded and headed for the door. "Got ya, do that meeting soon. This situation has become very fluid."

"I'm meeting with them later this cycle."

Vanir replied by silently waving as he stepped out into the hall, leaving the spymaster to his worried brooding. Once alone, Rafel immediately reached for his Larimar talking stone. It lay conveniently in front of him, fresh from the twelve times he had used it just before Vanir's visit.

Gripping the three-inch-long milk white shard he envisioned Mukavar's face. "Muuky, are you there?"

Much like previous attempts, the silence caused Rafel to slump down in his chair and sigh. His eyes shot wide open and he bolted up when static suddenly broke through his consciousness.

"Muuky, can you hear me?!"

The static slowly gave way to the sound of water flowing, punctuated by gurgling.

"Muuky, if you can hear me give me a signal!"

The gurgling soon became the prominent sound over the rushing water and Rafel's face became a mixture of hopefulness combined with anxiety.

"Muuky, talk to me!"

Slowly the gurgling began to become labored words.

"Wwaatter…"

*He said water*! Rafel excitedly thought.

"Unner watter…"

*Underwater, he's in trouble*! "Muuky, keep your stone activated and this channel open. We're coming for you."

Immediately Rafel pictured the Akina, Casus, in his mind.

"Casus, you there? This is an emergency!"

"Why, Rafel," came the refined voice of the Penaber spymaster. "How good of you to reach out. Whatever can I do for you?"

"I've got a whisperer down in your city," Rafel said urgently. "I'm going to be headed your way. What assets can you loan me?"

"I'm sorry to hear about your personnel. Unfortunately, most of my assets are involved in an ongoing investigation. They're already in the field."

"What can you spare?"

"Perhaps five or maybe ten harbor patrol agents," Casus replied weakly.

"Toss in as many Picean divers and you got a deal. I'm bringing some of my own people."

"Very well, Rafel. Any assistance I can render forth shall be done."

"Okay, thanks Casus," Rafel said, breaking the connection.

The Zorian spymaster's next calls were to request two enforcers from Red Division and a pilot that could 'skirt the upwinds' to meet him immediately at the Air Station.

"Okay, hold up, I think we've got something here," Taleeka said, studying the Larimar screen.

Casus, fresh from his conversation with Rafel, joined her vigil with a twitch of his whiskers and swish of his tail. "What seems to be taking place?"

Taleeka nodded at the interior view of the warehouse on the Penaber wharf. One large and several smaller bubbles rose through the hole in the floor. The Chanakan could be seen through the murky fluid of the large orb, with tentacles undulating furiously on the top of its head. Much like before, the burly mongrel and orange Tiikeri unloaded Etheria from the smaller bubbles, while the white Tiikeri consulted with the Chanakan.

Taleeka tilted her head and scrunched up her face in bewilderment when she saw the manner in which they delivered the shipment. The Etheria came in the form of four individually encased four-foot-long rods. The loaders did their utmost to ensure the individual rods never came in contact with one another.

Taleeka had witnessed scenes like this play out over the grands on her adventures with her parents. Only one type of Etheria Crystal needed to be afforded such care in storage and transport.

"Trinilic!" Taleeka gasped in recognition.

"I beg your pardon," the Akina said, squinting at the screen.

Taleeka pointed at the tubes being unloaded. "That's Trinilic. It's only used for one thing, fire magic."

"How can you be so sure?" Casus asked with a tilt of his head.

"They're encased separately," Taleeka said, definitively. "That's how I know. Trinilic is very unstable. You can't let the rods touch."

The human teen peered ominously over at the humanoid fox. Forming a ball with both hands she pulled them apart, extending her fingers while mouthing the word, *"Boom!"*

Rafel had only skirted the upwinds twice before, both times under duress. The idea of launching yourself to the edges of the atmosphere to get to a remote location quickly, while sounding good, turned out to be quite unnerving. By the looks on the faces of the three Red Division enforcers seated across from him, they felt the same way.

"You're missing one heck of a view, Captain," The pilot called back jovially to Rafel.

The Zorian spymaster glanced over at the pilot just in time to see the curvature of the planet sweep across the windshield as the ship began its descent.

"That's alright captain," Rafel said, looking away from the continents of Lumina growing larger through the glass. "So, why did you call this 'pulling a Demetrius?'"

"There's only a handful of us pilots that can do this. We named it after the pilot that invented it, Demetrius de Vana. He died in the Etheria War."

Rafel nodded at the explanation. He had only met Demetrius once. The late pilot for The Society of Whispers usually got his orders through House Valdur.

"Okay sir," the pilot called back once more. "The Penaber wharf is coming up. Prepare to deploy."

Dalgic looked over at his four fish-men comrades of the Eighth Picean School and the five human Harbor Patrol agents, wondering what this sudden assignment could possibly be about. All they were told had been to report to Penaber's Northern Docks and be prepared to dive. They were to rendezvous with a Goyan team, and they were to take orders from their leader.

Late morning had finally arrived and the moon rapidly rose in the west. Dalgic lifted his face, taking in the weak radiant heat from the sun in the eastern sky. He nodded when he saw the airship approaching from the direction of the Goyan Islands. Soon they would find out what this was all about. The airship circled the area and put down beside a large permanently moored barge.

All suddenly turned when a private hackney pulled by an energetic lizard sped to a sudden stop. A human, a very pale Amarenian and a Bailian woman got out. These women were followed by a large truck hackney which lurched to a stop, beside the private one, in front of a warehouse next to them. The back doors flew open and ten heavily armed members of the Calden Naval Constabulary piled out with Casus trailing them into the street.

Although naturally curious, Dalgic kept his attention on the airship. This constituted the nature of their orders.

"Looks like you got a real party going on down there," the pilot said, surveying the wharf below.

Rafel quickly joined him at the controls and stared out the windshield.

"The warehouse is involved, so is that barge," Rafel said, pointing at the two objects. "It looks like they've got the warehouse covered. That must be where Casus needed his men. Put us down by the barge."

"Yes sir," the pilot said, pushing the wheel forward, initiating a rapid descent.

Taleeka had made up her mind to let the city guards do the heavy lifting in this operation. She would just make their job a little easier. While Casus and his men pooled around her, she reached into her backpack and pulled out her Mark Seven pistol. Aiming it at the latch on the wide, sliding door, she pulled the trigger. The wooden lock proved no match for the sub-sonic Na-Kab Carbon bolt. The door exploded in half and fell off the jamb, rattling noisily in the street. The sudden explosion caused the small crowd of onlookers to gasp and back up. With Firehammer Carbines at the ready, the Calden city guards charged through the now ragged open doorway, followed by Casus and Taleeka's group.

Just as he thought, Dalgic watched the airship bank to their left and settle on the dock in front of the barge. When the side hatch opened, three heavily armed men in Ghost Suits, along with an unarmed man in black robes emerged.

Sensing this to be the leader he needed to report to, Dalgic led the Penaber procession over to the newcomers.

"This is the dive team?" Rafel asked, eyeing the group.

"Yes sir," Dalgic replied, sensing both urgency and the specter of imminent havoc in his voice.

The Zorian spymaster reached inside his robes and pulled out a three by five-inch clear Etheria card and a milk white nodule. Gripping the inch long Larimar node, he envisioned

Mukavar in his mind then snapped it into a groove on the side of the Etheria card.

"One of our men is missing," he said, handing the card to Dalgic. "We believe him to be in these waters. This will lead you to him. Have your team sweep the waters around the docks. Pay special attention to this barge and that warehouse. If you find him, retrieve him and report."

"Yes sir," Dalgic said, before leading his team of Piceans over the side.

Rafel then addressed the Red Division sergeant. "Secure that barge."

"Yes sir," he said, then motioned for the two others to the hatch thirty feet away.

Rafel knew he didn't need to give any further instructions. Red Division's reputation of kill first and ask questions later went without saying.

"Everybody freeze! You are all under arrest!"

Taleeka could hear the squad commander barking orders at the head of the breaching team. She could also hear the indignant protests of the mawls inside.

"I said, freeze!" the commanding officer repeated.

Once inside, Taleeka could see the orange Tiikeri pushing the now completed Etheria device they had been building towards the hole in the floor. They attached the Trinilic rods underneath and fashioned a seat with a crude Ukkonite steering device. The mongrel in the chair tightly gripped the steering device and peered anxiously back at the humans bursting through the door.

The lead city guard raised his carbine and fired at the noncomplying Tiikeri. The bolt struck the mawl in the center of his back, completely blowing out his chest cavity onto the seated mongrel. The gore saturated mongrel cried out in alarm as his Etheria craft plunged into the water and quickly submerged. The body of the orange Tiikeri followed, dropping lifelessly through the opening.

The white Tiikeri and Yagur raised their hands in surrender and turned to face the rapidly advancing city guards with satisfied smiles.

Dalgic's Etheria card began blinking green the moment he entered the water. Shock and horror replaced any relief he felt over the device actually working when he saw the rows of bubbles attached to the barge's bottom. He peered over at his team and saw they were just as stunned.

Dalgic recovered quickly and pointed southward.

"You three follow the wharf and search for anything unusual. You, come with me," he squeaked out in their native language.

All four Piceans nodded and three swam off. The remaining two Piceans swam just below the field of occupied orbs, following the blinking card. Its pulses grew more rapid the closer they got to their objective.

"What is this?" the second Picean asked, staring intently at the hanging anomalies.

"I don't know," Dalgic replied, "but the missing agent is just ahead."

Dalgic's Etheria card strobed furiously when they reached the orb containing Mukavar. The Picean leader knew they had found the right one when the card stopped flashing and turned solid green. They strained to look through the murky fluid and could see the bearded agent, who appeared unconscious.

"Let's get this unattached," Dalgic directed, reaching for the knife sheathed to his ankle. "We'll worry about getting him out once we get him topside."

His partner nodded and Dalgic placed his blade where the orb's teardrop tip attached to the barnacle encrusted surface. When his knife sliced easily through the membrane the bubble came loose and the Piceans were surprised to find it light and quite buoyant.

Okay, let's get this to the surface," Dalgic said, just before a high-pitched alarm reverberated through the water.

"I'm placing both of you under arrest," Casus said, as the city guards surrounded the two mawls.

"We have broken no laws!" the white Tiikeri bellowed in protest, his tail twitching violently behind him.

"You are in possession of highly volatile and explosive materials," Casus replied firmly. "That makes you a danger to the community."

Taleeka gave a wry chuckle putting away her pistol.

"Yeah," she said, "and I'm sure that once these folks get through searching this place, they'll be able to come up with a few more charges."

"I demand to be seen by a judge or magistrate!"

The Akina's whiskers twitched in annoyance as he stepped up close to the much larger man-tiger. "*You*, are not in a position to demand anything!"

Taleeka shook her head and slung her pack onto her back.

"What I want to know," she asked, "is what was that thing you dumped in the water?"

Slowly, the Tiikeri's face changed from outrage to a cruel smile. "Final justice, long denied."

Taleeka looked over at Barr-Ani who nodded, indicating he told the truth. Casus turned, about to reply, when the guard just outside the front door poked his head inside.

"Uh, sir, we've got a problem."

"Secure them!" Casus ordered.

He and Taleeka rushed to the door with the patrol sergeant close behind when, fifty yards down the wharf, they saw the Tiikeri's barge under siege. The bubble containing Mukavar's body floated aimlessly beside the vessel it had once been tethered to.

Taleeka and Casus looked on in horror at Rafel and three members of Red Division staring down a small army of Gar-Kal fish creatures climbing from the water and screeching loudly. The four humans stood with their backs to each other in the center of the wide flat surface. The three Red Division held drawn pistols, while Rafel aimed his weapon at the nearest charging Gar-Kal.

Twenty feet away from the barge, a large orb broke the surface of the bay.

Rafel's first bolt took out three of the humanoid fish. The first Gar-Kal completely disintegrated. The bolt blew massive holes through the chests of the other two standing right behind it, spraying blackish blood and body parts onto the marauding mob.

It took only moments for the conflict to embroil the barge's entire deck. Hissing and screaming Gar-Kal frantically climbed over each other to get at the humans.

Rafel rapid fired his Mark Seven, fanning the trigger and blowing through the first wave of attackers. The spray of greasy, brackish blood blinded the following wave. The Red Division men took advantage of the momentary blindness and blew off their heads with deadly precision. Together they managed to pile up twenty Gar-Kal bodies around them, but numbers were on the side of the fish-men.

Suddenly, veins of phosphorescent light flashed along the surface of the membrane of the large bubble, silhouetting the outline of the tentacled creature thrashing inside. A high-pitched wail emanated from within and all four humans doubled over in pain, dropped their weapons and held the sides of their heads.

In an instant, the horde descended upon them.

The bulk of the city guards raced down the docks towards the fight. When Taleeka heard the high-pitch wail and witnessed Rafel and his people going down, she ran back inside the warehouse to the three constabularies left to guard the mawls.

"Hey, let me borrow that, will ya?" Taleeka asked.

She pointed at the carbine a guard held on their captives. The guard, a red headed young man with a slightly crooked mouth, gave her a confused look.

"I think the other two can more than handle things if the mawls try something stupid," she explained. "My pistol doesn't have the range. Now, I'm kinda in a hurry."

Reluctantly the guard surrendered his weapon and Taleeka bolted for the door. Once back out onto the docks, she could see the pile of Gar-Kal writhing on top of, and completely obscuring, the men below them. She knew Rafel must still be alive at the bottom of the heap, because when a new fish creature piled on and attempted to reach down for him, she saw their back erupt with a bolt blasting through their body.

She quickly raised the carbine and fired off a shot at the large floating orb. The bolt easily plowed through the permeable surface, and out the other side. Taleeka knew the shot hit its mark when she saw the liquid inside of the bubble turning black with the Chanakan's blood. With the Chanakan's death the noise immediately stopped and the bubble began sinking, leaving the smaller bubble containing Mukavar bobbing about in the waves.

The city guards reached the barge shouting and firing into the leaderless mob of fish creatures now in full retreat.

Barr-Ani, Noorim, and the guard Taleeka had borrowed the rifle from, joined her on the docks watching the Chanakan's orb slip beneath the surface.

"I sensed no life in that bubble," Barr-Anis explained, "but the person in the smaller bubble is definitely alive, but something's different. I can't tell from here."

"Thanks." Taleeka said, handing the guard his carbine.

She returned her attention to the guards removing the dead Gar-Kal from the pile. From the looks of things, the three Red Division enforcers were dead, but she saw a scratched up Rafel sitting up with assistance.

"He's in pain, but not seriously harmed," the Bailian reported.

"The bodies obviously shielded him," Noorim said. "Not to mention he had a more superior weapon than they did."

Taleeka heaved a sigh of relief. "Let's not count out pure dumb luck. Either way, I bet it's going to be awhile before he eats fish again."

Top Sergeant Kaṭhina de Atar of the Valdurian Marines had always been known as a hard woman. Standing only five foot four, her stark angular features and wiry muscled torso left little doubt as to her potency. She distinguished herself in the Unification War and got involved in just about every altercation House Valdur fought. She displayed a no-nonsense demeanor, courage under fire and love for those under her command.

At that moment, she felt a twinge of concern for her charges while watching the burley half Amarenian redhead in a Ghost Suit confer with the pilot.

Three cycles ago they gave her command of a ten member, all-female, volunteer squad gathered for a secret mission. She wasn't sure of the operation and had never worked with a mechanic before, but one look at this woman and she knew things were going to get hot.

The airship rocked once and the mechanic nodded at the pilot before stepping back into the cabin. She peered down the two rows of anxious faces staring back at her.

"All-right listen up," Shurta began. "We just entered Amarenian air space. We are almost at our destination, so I'm now going to brief you on our mission.

"Six cycles ago, three crates of Mark Five Pistols and ammunition were stolen on their way to the armory in Dryden. The pistols were traced here and quite simply we're going to get them back.

"This is going to be a joint Valdurian and Amarenian operation, which explains in part why there are no males in this detail. We are heading to a rendezvous with my Amarenian counterpart and a force of their Mahaila.

"The weapons are at a plantation in the region of Taia-Dor and are being held by a rebel faction. We must secure them before they can be distributed. One of them has already been used in an assassination attempt on their queen."

Shurta then focused on Kaṭhina. "Sergeant, get your people ready."

"Alright, you heard the woman," Kathina said, feeling the craft begin its descent. "Make sure you're locked and loaded with your gear stowed. Prepare to deploy!"

Mal watched the airship sailing in just above the treetops and wondered what kind of reinforcements they brought. Just behind her, twenty Mahaila, under the command of Tajna Cabeli, crouched in the same stand of trees as before.

According to Tajna, they kept the plantation under constant surveillance since the weapons arrived. The wagon containing them remained locked and guarded in the barn.

When the airship settled to the ground a short distance away from them, it pleased Mal to see Shurta leading the detachment of female marines, all armed with Firehammer carbines and side arms.

"Hey Shurta," Mal greeted softly. "I didn't expect you to be leading this group."

"What, and miss this party, no way."

"I see you put together an all-female unit, pretty fucking smart."

"Yeah, that's why it took me three cycles to get here. I figured if we were going to be kicking ass on foreign soil, it would be best if we somewhat fit in."

"Shurta, this is your Amarenian counterpart, Tajna Cabeli," Mal said, indicating the Queen's Envoy.

The two clasped their forearms and nodded to one another.

"Okay, what have we got here?" Shurta asked seriously.

"Well, the pistols arrived in a Resistance Class Cruiser when I called you three cycles ago," Mal said. "A woman wearing riding pants and sporting a meat cleaver sold them to the Amarenians. She had a bodyguard that looked prettier than most women I know."

Alto smiled at the description. "The wrappings on his sword's hilt identified him as a Zorian Swordsman."

"They loaded the crates into a wagon and it's been sitting in that barn," Tajna said, pointing out the structure. "I have no idea what they're waiting for, I'm just glad they did. Otherwise, the three of us would have had to take them on. Those weapons cannot fall into the hands of the rebels."

"How many are we dealing with down there?" Shurta asked.

"Maybe twenty potential combatants," Tajna replied. "Lots of slaves, but they're not going to put up a fight."

"Speaking of putting up a fight," Mal said, stepping up beside Alto. "This is where we bow out and head for home. We're gonna let the pros handle it from here."

Shurta reeled in surprise. "*Really*?!"

"Absofuckinglutely! I delivered on my promise to the queen to bring these dipshits to justice and right there they are, all in one place. The only thing more I could do would be tie a bow on them as a gift. Besides, we're retired from doing dangerous shit."

"Alright, suit yourself, but personally, I think we could use you," Shurta said, hefting her carbine and turning to address the marines. "We'll go in first in case they've got heavy hardware at the ready. I imagine you've got big plans for the traitors?"

"Oh yes!" Tajna said definitively.

"And by the way, I've been authorized to leave the pistols and ammo with you."

Tajna's face brightened. "Thank you... how?"

"Beats me, I let the politicians worry about that stuff. Now, let's go kick some ass!"

Tajna Cabeli studied the Amarenian guard in front of the barn from her newly acquired vantage point across the central plaza of the Samryn Plantation. She could see the young woman dressed in traditional Amarenian field garb was armed primarily with a long polearm.

The Queen's Envoy couldn't help but note the pistol crossbow on her hip. From her vantage point she guessed it to be an old Mark Three. These single-action bolt throwers were loud and clunky, but still quite deadly. If she got a shot off, it would awaken the entire area. Her fate, as well as her comrades, would be dependent on her upcoming actions.

The compound had settled down for the moonless and she waited for the Mahaila to get into position. They would make sure no one escaped and make arrests once the marines secured the plantation.

Tajna couldn't fathom treason against the crown. Not just because the Cabeli Banja had always sided with the queen, but ever since Amarenia formerly joined with the Goyans, Amarenians have experienced unprecedented peace and interconnectivity. She really didn't understand what could prompt people to assassinate a beloved leader and take up arms. Did they really hate the Goyans that much? Were these new ways really that repugnant to them?

Suddenly, from around the manor house came a clicking sound similar to a cricket. It became picked up by another, then another. The Mahaila were in place.

"Okay Shurta, it's a go!" she said, grasping the Larimar Talking Stone in her pocket.

Tajna had never witnessed a Valdurian airborne assault and she gasped when she saw the airship streak into the plaza and come to an abrupt halt just inches above the ground.

The guard in front of the barn stood frozen in place, staring at the bizarre spectacle. When the side hatches flew open and marines poured out, she reached for her sidearm.

Tajna, already prepared, fired before the guard's pistol cleared her holster. The bolt vaporized her upper torso, spraying the door behind her a gruesome shade of red. The projectile continued onward, smashing a large hole in the beaded door. The guard's weapons clattered to the ground followed by her teetering abdomen and legs.

Six of the ten marines breached the main house's front door and began the process of clearing the building. The four remaining marines systematically entered the satellite structures and herded the occupants into the plaza. Tajna could hear shouts and loud reports of Mark Three pistols going off inside the two-story manor house, while sporadic flashes lit up the windows.

She reached the broken entrance of the barn and found it unguarded. Inside, the round barn stretched forty feet across and the air hung heavy with the smell of livestock. A dozen closed horse pens arched along the far wall. The occupants whinnied in protest at the disturbance and shuffled around nervously in their confines.

In the center of the room, amongst bales of hay and farming implements, stood the lone wagon. She rushed over to it, excitedly pulled back the tarp and heaved a sigh of relief. All three crates were there.

By the time Tajna returned to the courtyard, she found it full of mostly naked Amarenians, kneeling with their hands on their heads. The Mahailas stood guard, with Shurta overseeing, carbine cradled in her arms. Tajna joined Shurta at the same time as Sergeant Kaṭhina.

"That's all of them from the main house," the sergeant reported triumphantly. "The Mahailas are rounding up any strays."

"Casualties?" Shurta inquired, staring at the prisoners.

"We lost two, they lost six. One of ours is slightly wounded," came the grim reply. "We're loading them on the ship now."

Shurta nodded her acknowledgement and then peered over at Tajna. "Well, they're all yours now. I'd like to stick around to see how you deal with them, but they keep me busy fixing broken things, like this."

"Thanks for helping us out on this one," Tajna said with a smirk, "and thanks for the weaponry."

"It's what we do," Shurta answered, before turning her attention to the armed women in green jumpsuits. "Alright marines, saddle up!"

While the marines piled back in the airship, Tajna surveyed her prisoners. She noted Potoloa Samryn, as well as Tengah and Sorgina Napp, in the front row leering at her with hate filled stares.

"Alright!" Tajna announced authoritatively. "All slaves may return to their quarters. Everyone else, remain where you are. Consider yourself under arrest until cleared!"

It was a beautiful day in the Free City of Tannimore, but then, most days were. The moon had risen to its usual mid-morning position in the east and, with the addition of the sun in the west, cast bright gentle light into a cloudless sky. The dead zone known as the Doldrums, kept most inclement meteorological events safely away from the floating metropolis known for its decadence and debauchery.

Wikk the First, Defender of the Realm and Keeper of the Faith stood on the balcony overlooking the wharf which divided his city in half and smiled with satisfaction. Another pleasure transport yacht had just docked and unloaded its passengers, eager to part with their money in one of the many games and services forbidden in every other city in Lumina.

While it was true, they had suffered some setbacks, most recently their cache of Etheria notes being stolen, their coffers steadily grew with the money spent by people he watched excitedly entering his city. The thefts would be avenged, he had seen to that and he felt confident in his faith in the God which had bestowed on him so much, Pa-Waga.

"Lord Wikk," a male voice interrupted gently, "there has been a delivery for you on Dock Six."

Wikk glanced cautiously over at the young Piety watch. He had expected no personal delivery. "What is it?"

"Lord, it is addressed for your eyes only."

"Very well," Wikk said with a sigh. "Bring it to me."

"Uh, Lord Wikk, it is quite sizeable."

Rolling his eyes, Wikk sighed again. "Very well, take me to it."

"It arrived shortly after moonrise on a transport from the Goyan Islands, more specifically Zor," the young man said, on their trek to the lower numbered industrial docks. "There is no indication as to who sent it."

Dock Six seemed as busy as usual, with various transport ships unloading the provisions and equipment necessary to keep the isolated municipality operating. The five-foot square wooden crate sat just where the winch operator had left it, with several human dock workers standing beside it awaiting instructions and a crowd of laborers and carts flowing around it.

Wikk first inspected the address. Sure enough, it had been addressed to him in Aramos-Ya with explicit instructions for his eyes and it contained no indication of a sender. He then walked around the crate and, with the exception of a strange odor he couldn't quite place, everything seemed normal.

"Alright, open it up," he ordered, taking a few steps back.

Crowbars were produced and when the workers removed the face of the box everyone gasped in shock and horror. There, piled in a heap, lay the mauled, partially eaten bodies of Qasia, Brother Hardee and Brother Telek. By the looks of terror frozen on their faces and the mutilated condition of their nude bodies, they had met a ghastly fate.

Carved into Quasia's pale chest were two words also in Aramos-Ya,

*"Nice try."*

Spring storm clouds hung low in the Amarenian sky, making the air thick and humid. Outside the Citadel of Truth, in central Mostas, gallows had been constructed and this morning the executioner had a full docket.

Mal and Alto, dressed in formal Amarenian garb, sat on a covered riser in the rear of the plaza facing the instrument of judgement. The Valorous Sister looked over at the queen, seated two chairs away, with Tajna standing dutifully on guard behind her. The regent appeared sad but resolute. Mal then peered into the forlorn face of Kennari Napp, seated next to her. The former Spice Rat macabrely pondered what her neighbor must be feeling watching her daughters die in such an undignified public manner. It wasn't just the Napp sisters that had a date with the noose. Potoloa Samryn and the nine other rebellious Crones, making up the leadership of the Era Zaharrak Party, all shared similar fates.

Their Banjas were also to be punished, demoted to last place in their respective Dor's ranking, with the Napp Banja elevated to the Samryn's old position at ninth.

The crowd excitedly murmured when they led the twelve condemned sisters into the courtyard with a Mahaila on each arm. They paraded them single file in front of Queen Omaris, where they halted and turned to face her with defiant expressions showing no signs of fear. The queen slowly surveyed the group before gracefully rising.

"I wish for you to know, I feel truly sorry it has come to this," she said mournfully, before her tone turned scolding, "but treason against the sisterhood, especially in such a reckless and brutal manner must be dealt with in the harshest manner. I thereby sentence you all to death, to be carried out immediately. Do any of you have any last words?"

"I, for one," Potoloa Samryn answered, sneering condescendingly at the monarch, "am glad I will not be around to see my people slip further into these new ways of weakness and attrition to the Dags of the West. You can have your land of cock lovers. I go to a better place!"

Marateen Scrim, the Crone from Durik-Dor who sent the assassin, scrunched her pale ruddy face and spat in the queen's direction. All others stood stone faced while the Napp sisters leered hatefully at their mother.

The queen waited a lengthy moment staring at the silent line of women.

"Nothing more?"

Defiant silence once again greeted the monarch.

"Very well, you four, will be last." She said, indicating Potoloa, Marateen and the Napp sisters.

Mal saw the initial drops of rain falling when they led the first of the condemned up the gallows stairs. It picked up by the time they made it to the landing. Mal sat frozen in place, seemingly outside of her body, fixated on the drops of water steadily falling from the noose before the executioner placed it around the first of the condemned necks.

Almost on cue, the rain began heavily falling the moment the trap door opened with a clatter, sending the woman to the bottom of the rope and her immediate death.

The crowd stood unmoving in the pouring rain, entranced watching the body being taken down and the rope winched up for the next.

Mal knew they would stay for the whole thing, no matter what the conditions.

*It's the same everywhere,* Mal cynically thought. *Coronations and executions, everyone loves a show.*

Rafel's eyes suddenly opened and he awoke with a start. Although his entire body ached and he could feel each one of the multiple lacerations across his nude torso, it surprised him he felt no real pain. The last thing he remembered was being pulled out from under the pile of dead fish creatures.

The spymaster attempted moving his stiff limbs. He slowly looked around and found himself on a narrow bed in an unadorned room at some sort of medical facility. Mukavar lay unconscious on an identical bed next to him.

"Well, someone's awake," came a cheerful male voice just out of visual range. "How are you feeling?"

"Sore," Rafel answered hoarsely.

"I'll bet," the man said, stepping up to the side of the bed. "You were pretty banged up when they brought you in."

The young man stood average height and build, wearing a Calden medical officer's uniform. His clean-shaven angular face contained a warm friendly smile.

Rafel nodded, wincing when he moved. "How long?"

"Have you been here?"

Rafel nodded once more.

"You've been unconscious now for three cycles. You're still in Penaber, at the Calden Naval Infirmary. I'm Junior Lieutenant Lekar, one of the doctors on duty. I was here when they brought you in."

Rafel groaned when he sat up. "What about my friend?"

Lekar glanced over at a comatose Mukavar, with a sheet draped over him so only his head was visible.

"Your friend is a different matter altogether," he said emotionlessly. "He was submerged in that strange fluid for some time. He also had some sort of small creature inside him. We got him to expel it when we used Xenoti on him. It's in that jar over there and it's still alive."

"Xenoti?" Rafel asked, attempting to get out of bed.

"You might want to take it easy." Lekar advised, when Rafel's knees buckled and he caught him by the arm. "Xenoti is an Etheria Crystal used to remove parasites and poisons. Even though that little guy wasn't a parasite, it sure drove it out. It's been banging around in that container trying to get back into your friend."

Rafel felt his stomach tighten and his attention kept shifting from Mukavar to the animated creature in the jar.

"Is he going to be alright?!"

"We really won't know that until he comes around. I can tell you one thing though. That creature was changing him."

"Changing him, how?"

"You okay to walk?" he asked, still holding Rafel's arm.

The spymaster nodded and Lekar guided him to Mukavar's bedside.

"This," the doctor said, pulling back the sheet.

The nude figure of Mukavar, for the most part, looked the same as always. Lekar pointed to several small vertical slits on both sides of his neck.

"Those are gills," he said grimly.

He then pointed to his hands and feet which now contained webbing between his fingers and toes.

Next, he indicated down to Mukavar's groin. The Calden mechanic's penis that Rafel loved was gone, replaced by a small nodule poking out from a vertical slit.

"We're not sure what's going on there," the doctor reported, with a shake of his head.

Rafel's eyes widened in shock and he let out a small gasp.

"That's just what we can see," Lekar continued. "We don't know what it changed inside him. It appears that little creature was slowly turning your friend into one of those fish-men. And he's not the only one."

Rafel's eyes narrowed quizzically at the doctor.

"The whole underside of that barge was covered in those bubbles. There were over a hundred of them, each one with a human in various stages of conversion. The oldest ones retained virtually no human features. Luckily, your friend hadn't been in there very long."

"Over a hundred you say?"

Lekar nodded. "Yep, our Picean divers brought them up. They're on top of the barge right now under guard. Their sending a team from the University of Marassa, due here any cycle now, to study them."

Rafel's concerned gaze never left his lover while he settled into a chair next to the bed.

"Thank you doctor. If you could get me something to wear and my things. I'm going to stay here with him." Rafel then pointed to the tiny creature pounding its body against the glass barrier. "You also might want to get that thing out of here and into a little more secure container."

"Captain," the doctor pleaded. "We don't know when, or even *if* he's going to wake up. We can't make you comfortable here."

"Thank you for your concern doctor," Rafel said solemnly, "but I'm not going anywhere."

If Chen had any second thoughts about his employer's behavior, her actions today were not helping the matter. He felt certain the errant street boss she had just finished publicly berating would probably agree.

"You disapprove of my methods?" Mazie queried glibly when she saw him silently sulking next to her in the rear seat.

"You didn't have to threaten his family."

Mazie gave an evil chortle. "It's called incentive."

"As if your cleaver next to his balls wasn't enough 'incentive!'"

"I bet he won't be late with my money again. Besides, you know how horny that kind of thing makes me. I know you don't mind that."

Chen remained silent and Mazie slipped her hand first onto his thigh, then onto his crotch.

"Fact is, the thought of my cleaver glinting next to those naked balls has really got me going," Mazie purred, while sliding up next to him and rubbing the beginnings of a bulge.

She bit him hard on the neck. "I don't think I can wait!"

She then slid to the other end of the bench seat and began unbuttoning her pants. "I definitely can't wait. My pussy needs some immediate attention."

Mazie pulled her riding pants down past her ankles. Flipping over onto her hands and knees, she presented Chen with an unobstructed view of her shapely ass and glistening pussy lips. Sliding her index finger through the folds caused her to moan lustfully at Chen.

Chen did a quick glance into the driver's seat and a glowering Vozac with his jealous death grip on the steering wheel. Audience or not, Mazie remained insistent.

"Well, get down there. It's not going to lick itself!"

"I really don't think this is the appropriate time or place," Chen said hesitantly.

Mazie scoffed loudly and looked back at him over her shoulder. "I don't pay you to think. I pay you to fight and fuck. Eating my pussy falls under your fucking duties. So, get to it!"

Chen reluctantly slipped down to the floorboard of the back seat so that his face aligned with her damp vulva. The closer he got, the more he could smell the traces of her last bowel movement she had not fully cleaned away and he paused, revolted by the smell.

Mazie's public form of humiliation and dominance over everyone started to really bother the swordsman. Her order proved two-fold, compelling him into a lewd public spectacle and forcing her driver to witness it, knowing about the jealousy Vozac felt towards him.

The hesitation caused Mazie to reach back, grab the top of Chen's head and shove his face between her legs. "

I said *get in there!*" she demanded. *"Get that tongue to work!"*

Chen tried in vain to hold his breath, however his senses of taste and smell were assaulted at the same time. The musky saltiness of her vagina filled his mouth and the fecal residue assaulted his nose angled perfectly to be buried into her overly pungent anal pucker.

The jarring sounds of hammering and sawing filled the large empty room, echoing off the bare walls. Drugo walked beside Mazie, giving her a tour of their progress, while a sullen Chen followed respectfully behind.

"How soon before we're operational?" Mazie asked, peering around at the once unemployed citizens of the Seven Sisters hard at work building her second soup kitchen.

"Well, construction should be finished up before cluster's end," Drugo said, wincing slightly at having to deliver bad news to his boss. "The problem is the blacksmith at the foundry which makes the stoves says he's backed up several quintes because of all the eatery's opening."

Mazie halted and stared over at her right-hand man with narrowing eyes and a sneer. "Are you telling me that my plans are being held up by an obstinate blacksmith?!"

"Um, well, yeah, I guess so."

Mazie's mood immediately shifted from anger to calculating. "It looks like we're just going to have to give him some incentive to move us to the top of the list. Take a few of the boys and pay this guy a visit. Start with financial incentive, tell him there's an extra hundred secors for him to give us priority each time we need him. Let him know we're going to be his best customer. If that doesn't work, ask him how he plans to ply his trade with two broken arms."

Drugo nodded and spun to leave when the front doors flew open and Talib and Tantei, along with five uniformed Zorian Guards armed with carbines, rushed in from the street.

"Mazie de Zor, you are under arrest!" Tantei announced loudly.

The sounds of construction trailed off and the guards swarmed over to the mob boss.

Mazie stood defiantly facing her impending incarceration. "Exactly what am I being accused of?!"

"Criminal conspiracy," Tantei said, pulling both of Mazie's hands behind her back and securing them.

"That's outrageous!" Mazie sputtered. "I'm cleaning up the Sisters. They should be giving me a medal, not arresting me!"

"Don't worry, you'll be allowed to tell your story to an Imperial Judge," Tantei said, pulling her along by the arm.

"Are you just going to stand there?!" Mazie said, scowling at Chen.

"And what would you have me do?" Chen asked calmly.

Mazie sneered at her bodyguard, knowing he could do nothing. She remained calm and glanced at Drugo while being led past him.

"Get Karta," came her only order before being led out the doors with a host of confused workers staring in disbelief.

Although their operation in Penaber did not technically constitute a suicide mission, Ruu-Da knew it would be perilous. Now under arrest and awaiting to be seen by a Calden military tribunal, the white Tiikeri considered the cost for this final act of vengeance.

Already one of his charges, Faa-Nar, the orange Tiikeri, had paid the ultimate price, as did the mongrel, Teeko. He and the Yagur shaman, Geeorn, were the only two remaining and they had been separated once they were placed in the stockade.

They secured him in a small, bare stone room with thick iron bars on the door and single window. To be sure the humanoid jaguar could not cast any spells, they held him in a windowless iron box, completely cut off from the natural forces from which he derived his power. His only hope now rested with Teeko's success in getting to the rendezvous point in time. If not, all of this would have been a waste of time, effort and lives.

When he felt the ground rumbling and heard what sounded like distant rolling thunder, he excitedly bound to his feet and rushed over to the barred window. The ground now shook violently and the southeastern sky lit up in a massive distant explosion.

Ruu-Da smiled in satisfaction and pride, watching a thick column of flame shoot aloft into the clouds. He knew The Order of Kaplan had finally honored their charter.

*Success*, he thought, closing his eyes and sighing wearily.

The Valdurian's Landagar Station is arguably one of the most secure locations in the Annigan. The floating city is set high in the Atarian Mountains on Atar Island, in the upper Goyodian Chain of the greater Goyan Islands and can only be accessed by air. Its isolation makes it the perfect location for top secret Etheria development, airship repair and intelligence gathering.

The large room dedicated to information collection and dissemination is still referred to as "The Squawk Box," from the days when gulls were the primary means of message delivery and the area was always host to a cacophony of the birds' squawks and cries. Nowadays, with the wide spread of Larimar Etheria, the space appeared considerably smaller, quieter and more efficient.

All sixteen Valdurian agents in the Squawk Box heard the rumbling in the distance but they didn't feel the tremors due to the station's suspension in mid-air.

"Sir, I just lost contact with Tannimore," a young female communications officer said, looking up from her Larimar station.

A concerned look crossed Commander Srota de Atar's face and he stepped over to his subordinate.

"Is it malfunctioning?" he asked, stroking the three days' worth of growth on his youthful face.

"No sir, I just ran a test," she replied. "I was receiving a report from one of our operatives there just before all that thunder, then it went dead."

"Perhaps the operative had to break off contact... or maybe weather conditions?"

"No sir, Tannimore really doesn't have any weather to speak of. It's just not there."

"Sir," another listener called out from across the room. "I'm getting reports of a massive explosion to the southwest."

"Same here," another called out.

"Let's see if we can get a peek," Srota said, reaching up and activating the large Larimar screen above the young woman's listening station.

The screen flickered to life and all in the room gasped. On the southwestern horizon a giant orange dome of Etheria fire slowly subsided, replaced by a huge mushroom cloud poking through the glow, heading for the upper atmosphere.

The earthquake hit Zor just as Peshk served lunch. Once Taleeka and her friends returned from Penaber after being away several cycles, they couldn't wait to get a taste of home. The Picean cook, housekeeper and Konrad family seneschal didn't disappoint, making sure all were fed and well taken care of. Nibira even took time away from her librarian duties at the university to join her comrades in a mid-cycle meal.

The quake began with what sounded like prolonged thunder from the southwest. When the ground started shaking, they knew it wasn't the weather. Long time residents of the High Holy City had experienced earthquakes before but they were infrequent.

The quaking subsided within moments, upon which Barr-Ani broke down in hysterical sobs.

"Barr-Ani, what's wrong?" Nibira asked, placing a calming hand on her shoulder.

"My dream," she choked out, looking around the table with wide terror filled eyes and tears streaming down her face. "They're dead, *all dead!*"

"Who's dead?" the librarian probed, while Taleeka and Noorim shared fearful knowing glances.

Nibira started to ask again, when the sound of screams and frightened cries from the street interrupted her. Taleeka jumped up from the table and rushed to the window.

A startled "uh oh!" escaped Taleeka's lips when she saw the mushroom cloud in the southwestern sky rising up to join with the white billows already present. Taleeka's cry brought all the friends to her side.

"That looks like it's out over the middle of the ocean," Taleeka noted solemnly.

Barr-Ani's sobbing intensified when she saw the aftermath of the explosion coursing upward.

*"Dead, they're all dead!"*

"Barr-Ani, who's dead?" Nibira pleaded. "What happened?"

"I *don't know* what happened," the Bailian lamented. "Thousands just died."

She remained morbidly transfixed on the giant plume in the distance. "The rain will start soon."

In a small one room cabin in the Os-Tor Forest just outside Immor-Onn, Zau Berin sat at the single two-person table and adjusted the five Tanem Charts in front of her. Furrowing her brow at the pattern, the female Singa manipulated the sheets of paper one more time and gasped at the results.

Zau rose and opened a chest at the foot of her single bed and pulled out what appeared to be a large walnut shell with a delicate hinge on one side, before returning to her chair. Checking her charts one more time, she opened the walnut shell revealing her false eye and took it out.

She lifted her eyepatch and placed the milky white eye in the empty socket. Immediately, a pale blue phantasmal globe projected from the eye, hovering just above the table. Across the clearly defined continents of the Annigan, lights flickered with Flavian Portals opening and closing. One unmoving point of light made her gasp again and refer to her charts one more time.

Konaleeta, Island of the Lost, had somehow returned home to the Doldrums. What of the people currently occupying that particular patch of ocean? The Doldrums were no more. What had become of Tannimore and the tens of thousands that called it home?

# ACT THREE

## Return of the Etherions

It had been a full three cycles since the mysterious huge explosion in the southern Ocean Deep rocked the better part of the light side of the world. Shortly after, a fine dirty mist from the fallout settled in over the Goyan Islands and most of western Lumina.

The Zorian High Council called an emergency meeting on cycle two and they cancelled all leaves, called up all personnel, and put all armed forces in the Goyan Islands and beyond on high alert. By the morning of the third cycle, the Valdurian Air Service ordered a scout craft into the air to get a look to see exactly what they were dealing with.

Lieutenant Nygift de Tonck, of the Valdurian Air Scouts, had every intention of being on his honeymoon with his new bride, Kiny, but the giant explosion immediately following their wedding vows squashed that. When the High Council gave the order for the recon mission, he drew the short straw on the fly-by. He really didn't mind. If he couldn't be with Kiny, he sure didn't want to just sit around waiting for word.

Staring into the sparkling light grey mist just outside his windshield, his mind drifted to his wife's beautiful face, with her creamy brown complexion and striking blue eyes. He just knew that with the combination of his smooth baby-faced features and her radiant beauty, their children were bound to be striking.

Checking the compass on the controls, he smiled at his recent change of heart about having children and a family.

The Air Service had been his entire life, until he laid eyes on her. Now she seemed to be all he thought about and he found himself trying out children's names in his head.

The blue Aquamarine Etheria lenses on his goggles cut through most of the mist and he watched the ocean streaking a thousand feet below him. According to his controls, he was approaching the estimated area of the explosion and he wasn't sure what he would find. It was, after all, open ocean. Perhaps he would find a giant fish kill. What happened to the floating city of Tannimore?

Reaching up to his overhead console he touched the Larimar disk embedded there.

"Control, this is Scout Twenty-Four."

"Got ya loud and clear Twenty-Four," a youthful male voice resonated in Nygift's head. "Hey Ny, bet you wish you were doing something else right about now."

Nygift chuckled sarcastically. "Whatever makes you say that Roart?"

Roart joined him in laughing. "Just a hunch."

"Alright control, I'm getting pretty close to the estimated blast area. I'm turning on my Larimar camera array now and activating their blue shields so you can actually see something through this soup."

He pushed seven Larimar buttons on the dash controls, activating the Etheria shards located fore and aft, port and starboard, the two mounted on the underside of the craft and the one on top.

"Okay Twenty-Four, we've got a visual here."

"Roger that, Control, you'll see something when I do."

Nygift had been circling the coordinates given to him for almost half the cycle with each circumambulation growing tighter and he saw nothing but open ocean devoid of ships.

"I don't know about you," Roart said sounding bored, "but I'm starting to nod off over here."

"If only I could," Nygift concurred. "Okay, I've reached the central point of the area. There's nothing going on here. I'm going to swing north and see how Tannimore fared,"

"Roger that."

The straight-line trip to the floating city took comparatively no time at all and Nygift squinted at the strange skyline. Gone were the nautical ship's spires, replaced instead by block shaped obelisks. The closer the scout craft got to the foreign architecture the stranger the scene became.

"Are you seeing this?!" Nygift asked excitedly.

"Where's Tannimore?!" Roart asked in confusion.

"It's gone!" Nygift noted in disbelief. "There's an island there now!"

"I'm patching this feed to Landagar," Roart said. "They're gonna want to see this."

"I hope you're recording this," Nygift said, banking over the northern coast. "It looks to be about fifty miles across."

"Yes, I'm recording," Roart answered. "People only think I'm an idiot. You know, that's exactly the same amount of area the Doldrums took up."

"I'm gonna go in for a closer look at those structures. I don't see any movement down there."

"Careful, Twenty-Four."

"Careful's my middle name," Nygift replied absentmindedly, pushing forward on the steering wheel, sending the craft into a shallow dive.

"I see no vegetation at all." Nygift reported, circling the tops of a grouping of wide columns. "It looks like the entire island is made out of crystal."

"Looks like it," Roart agreed, "and I see no life either."

Suddenly, off to his left, Nygift caught a flash when several arcs of blue lightning began connecting between two of the monoliths.

"Wow, did you see that?!" Nygift asked, veering the airship towards the activity. "I'm going in for a closer look."

Nygift deftly maneuvered the ship in a tight circle and slowly descended over the two lightning connected towers. He halted the craft, hovering it just above the light show.

"This is amazing! I've never seen anything like thi…!"

One of the arcs of lightning rapidly bowed upward, catching the airship in the middle of the bolt's circuit. The moment the craft became entrapped all the Etheria equipment in the cockpit began sparking just before exploding, filling the cabin with deadly flying shards of Etheria shrapnel, instantly killing Nygift. Next went the Etheria engines and all of the magical crystals lining the exterior, catching the Ukko wood tail of the ship on fire.

Scout Twenty-Four's burning hull remained caught between the tendrils of lightning until the bolts receded back into their respective structures. With nothing to hold it aloft, the smoldering airship plummeted to the hard crystalline surface below.

The Na-Kab Queen stands almost seven feet tall, towering well over her subjects. Like her people, her four insectoid legs could move with incredible speed and platelets covered her mantis thorax. The orange glow of their molten bowels could be plainly seen in the gaps between them. Unlike her hive, however, she did not possess a stinger tail and six teats full of her fiery nectar adorned her humanoid torso.

The Na-Kab, much like their less fiery cousins, the Do-Tarr possess a hive mind. The queen sees everything her brood does. Likewise, the tenor of the hive directly reflects the queen's mood. Right now, the Na-Kab Queen felt distressed.

Moving rapidly along the side wall of the busy tunnel, the mantis regent maintained visual contact through the eyes of the first arrivers. The maggot pit had been destroyed, along with fifty newborns and she witnessed this disaster firsthand.

When she personally arrived in the chamber, she found Lord Julius, the Avion Harbinger of Balance already present. He, along with several of her workers, stared intently at a huge column of blue crystal jutting from the pit where their young matured. A place which normally meant safety and nourishment to grow, became a tomb. Julius' wings twitched, sending small downy feathers into the air. He walked in circles, cradling invisible babies in his hands and simultaneously cooing and crying at the ghost infants.

"When did this happen?" she demanded, eying the twelve-foot-tall monolith.

"We came across this just after the fog cycle lifted, oh Queen," one of the workers replied. "We believe it has something to do with the earthquake three cycles ago."

"Lord Julius," the queen asked, "how do all of these events affect the Black Mural?"

"The same as how the Black Mural affects this event," he said dismissively, in the mantis creature's own language of clicks and whistles, not looking away from his inspection. "Or, for that matter, one could ask, what doesn't affect the Black Mural? No one is asking if there is a White Mural. Why so monochromatic? Why not a Paisley Wheel?"

He eventually sensed the queen's confusion leading to impatience and an annoyed stare. He fought to quiet the voices in his head and snapped his attention to her directly. "Oh, yes, sorry, Queen Bee, the one big event canceled the other out. Konaleeta returned after bouncing around the Middle Realms for thousands of grands and reinstated its own counterbalance."

The Avion held both hands in front of him palms up then dipped one side. "On the other hand, sixteen thousand humans perished. Hardly ever a bad thing."

He brought his hands level once more. "One cancels out the other. I tell you what though, I wouldn't want to be the Judge of the Dead right now. Not that anyone was asking me to be. I mean, I probably would take the job, but I wouldn't like it. I'm not saying old Boran is doing a bad job... I mean, there isn't anyone complaining. If they were, they would be dead wrong." Julius stopped and laughed at the wording. "*Dead* wrong but they're *dying* to tell Boran off. Oh, that's rich because he's Judge of the Dead. Whoo! I kill me."

The queen ignored the mad Avion's ramble and called over one of her brood.

"Go to the surface, to the city called Zor," she ordered. "Take a glamour stone so that you can walk amongst the fleshy ones. Find out what happened and if any are responsible, punish them."

The Na-Kab worker nodded then scampered off down the hall and out of sight.

"Well now," Julius said, placing his hands on his hips and looking at the crystal up and down. "It's crystal clear what we have to do about this monstrosity, isn't it? Oh man, I wish Dak was here, I'm on fire."

The queen nodded to the three remaining Na-Kab and then indicated the invading crystal pillar.

"You might want to stand back," she warned Julius.

The Avion stepped away just in time to avoid three streams of fire erupting from the mantis' mandible jaws. The blue edifice quickly melted under the intense heat, replaced by whiffs of smoke trailing up from the pit.

"Speaking about on fire!" Julius said, still laughing. "Careful not to burn out, boys."

With spring well under way, warmer weather and the inevitable showers accompanying it commonly occurred in and around the High Holy City of Zor. The dirty gray mist of the Tannimore winter hung in the air and one could barely see across the plaza.

Mazie and Karta smiled as they stepped out onto the rain-soaked cobblestones of Judgment Square, free from the Imperial Judges chambers. An equally jubilant Drugo and a stone-faced Chen waited for them at Mazie's private hackney. Vozac stood beside the driver's door, also smiling at his employer's release.

A grim Talib and Tantei exited just behind them, following them into the square.

"I hope there's no hard feelings investigators?" Mazie said sweetly. "I do hope to see more of you in the future."

Tantei stopped and turned to face the mob boss with a sinister grin. "Count on it, *bitch*."

Mazie ignored the taunt and led her small entourage to the waiting hackney. Vozac and Chen traded barbed stares while the bullnecked driver opened the door and Mazie said goodbye to Karta, complimenting him on a job well done.

Once settled in the moving vehicle, Mazie turned her attention to Drugo in the front seat beside Vozac.

"So, it was Maluria Konrad who ratted me out," she said with a calculating sneer. "That witness affidavit she supplied the local authorities with, almost sent me to the gallows."

"What happened in there, boss?" Drugo asked, peering back over the seat.

"The Konrad woman must have been spying on us when we sold those pistols to the Amarenians. Karta convinced the judge that the court had no proof that I stole the weapons and killed the guards. He maintained that I unwittingly purchased them and was trying to make a quick sale."

"It obviously worked," Drugo noted.

Mazie gave an appreciative chuckle. "Boy did it. That barrister is one smooth talker. I'm sure glad he's on our side."

"What now boss? You wanna send a hit team after the Konrad woman?'

Mazie stared out the window, a plan hatching in her head, before returning her attention to her second in command.

"No," she said. "She's too well entrenched down in Amarenia. Anything we do there could spark an international incident and direct way too much attention on us. Her daughter, however, is a player here in Zor. I think it's time we met and had a little chat.

"Bring her to me, will you Drugo?"

"Yes ma'am."

"Oh, and Drugo, I want her unharmed."

It just happened to be Saat-Sarr's first time in Zor and the thin, young Bailian courier fidgeted with nervous excitement. He had heard so much about the largest metropolis in the Annigan, he couldn't wait to take it all in. He especially wanted to see an EEtah. The giant man-sharks captured his imagination ever since he heard about them from his main clients in the Balian Government.

A sealed communication from his government now rested in his messenger bag. Even though it had been dispatched from Sira'Har, a low-level bureaucrat, it had to be important. They added a navigational chip on the document. The tiny

Etheria shard led him to a human by the name of Taleeka Konrad and would demand the sentient's signature.

Adjusting the sunglasses he had been issued, he peered out the side window of the small airship at the rooftops of the city below, now barely visible through the pervasive dirty grey mist. It would take some getting used to the constant bright sunlight directly overhead, especially the way it illuminated and refracted off the dirty water vapor in the air. He wondered how this would affect the Kan fog he had heard so much about.

He gripped his bag tightly and directed his attention out the front windshield when the gaping maw of Air Station Three loomed ahead. It wasn't quite as big as Air Station East in Immor-Onn, but they had used this facility as the template for his air station back home.

The courier had company, Tam'Eez, the Bailian spymaster, sat beside him. He took over with Kai's death in the Etheria War and now, headed for the University of Marassa to take a course in investigation taught by a human named Zekoff.

"First time in Zor?" Tam'Eez asked, noticing the young Bailian's exuberant surveying of his surroundings.

Saat-Sarr found himself surprised by the sudden question. The red headed Bailian/human hybrid had remained tight lipped for almost the whole trip.

"Yes, I've heard so much about it," Saat-Sarr bubbled excitedly.

"Well, if you've got some spare time after you make your delivery it's worth a look around. Just be careful during the Kan. That's when the nasties come out to play. Although with this damn Spring mist everywhere I'd keep my eyes open all the time."

"Thanks, I'll remember that," Saat-Sarr said, then quickly looked around when they entered the massive main hangar.

"And keep those glasses handy," Tam'Eez advised. "Your eyes aren't used to this much light. You'll even need them inside if the building has a lot of windows."

"You don't need them?"

"No, I'm half human."

The answer satisfied Saat-Sarr and he watched the airship settle into a slip beside several others.

"Alright, we're here," the Bailian pilot called back over her shoulder.

Tam'Eez gathered his things and looked over at Saat-Sarr. "I wish you success in your mission."

Saat-Sarr nodded his thanks and then followed the spymaster onto the tarmac, watching him heading for the front entrance and a line of waiting hackneys. He could now concentrate on finding his contact. To his surprise, the navigation chip began going off in his head the moment he stepped onto the flight deck. She should be close.

It took a few tries, heading in different directions with the alarm fading and rising. Soon enough, he found a tall, thin, attractive woman with honey brown skin talking with a very pale, shirtless, Amarenian female, with short black hair, outside the open side hatch to a resistance Class airship.

"Taleeka Konrad?" he asked, stepping up to the duo.

Taleeka eyed him suspiciously. "Maybe."

"Well, if you are, I have a special delivery letter for you."

"I guess that's me then," she said, prompting him to pull a large envelope from his messenger bag.

"That's good," he said, pressing the round Etheria medallion in the envelopes upper corner, "because this proximity alarm was just about to drive me crazy."

When Taleeka saw the Imperial Bailian seal on the envelope she grew excited.

"You're going to have to sign for it…"

"Tally Konrad!" a cheerful, booming male voice interrupted. "I've been looking for you."

Everyone watched Drugo quickly approaching with four disheveled homeless people stuffed into better clothing.

"My friends are the only ones that get to call me Tally," Taleeka said defiantly. "And I'm pretty sure none of you are my friends."

"Maybe not, *Tally*, but we represent someone who is very interested in meeting you," Drugo said, maintaining his pleasant demeanor.

Taleeka furrowed her brow and gave a sardonic chuckle. "What, are you trying to piss me off right from the get-go?"

"Not at all, Tally, but my boss wants to see you, *now*."

Taleeka scoffed, shaking her head in disbelief. "Well, as my mom would say, 'you're doing a real fucking good job of getting on my nerves.' Tell your boss to make an appointment just like everyone else. Right now, I'm busy."

Drugo continued smiling, unphased. "That's quite a mouth you've got on you."

"Yeah, you should meet my mom."

"Yes, well, I'm afraid my boss is the type of person that doesn't take 'no' for an answer."

Taleeka gave an amused smirk. "Yes, well, *I'm* afraid your boss is just going to have to learn to live with the disappointment."

Saat-Sarr grew more uncomfortable with each verbal volley and began cautiously backing away from the potential confrontation when Noorim stepped up beside her friend.

"Now, you've wasted enough of my time," Taleeka said firmly. "Have your boss make an appointment."

"I'm afraid that just won't do," Drugo said, directing his men forward.

Reaching over, Taleeka shoved the retreating Saat-Sarr away from the conflict, while retrieving Defari from the side holster on her backpack. The canine spirit gave out a loud angry howl when she launched the club at the first attacker's knee. The Ukko wood cudgel smashed into his kneecap with a loud crunch followed by the man's screams of pain. The force of the wood's repellent properties knocked the man's legs violently backward and out from under him. He went down face first wailing in agony while the growling club, returned to Taleeka's hand with a tug on the lanyard.

The second attacker reached out to grab Taleeka's arm. Noorim jammed her hip into him, throwing him off balance and tossed him to the ground several feet away. The two remaining thugs froze, unsure of what to do.

Drugo produced a pistol from the small of his back and pointed it at Taleeka. "I was really hoping it wouldn't come to this."

Taleeka gave an amused scoff and stepped directly in front of the weapon.

"So, what are you going to do, shoot me?" she asked. "I sure hope your boss can talk to the dead. Nah, I don't think so. Not after you went to all this trouble. I really don't think shooting me was part of your orders."

Drugo's eyes fearfully transfixed on the growling cudgel when Taleeka used it to gently push the pistol away from being trained on her.

"Now, why don't you put the pistol away, go back to your boss and tell them to make a damn appointment."

Drugo buckled under Taleeka's intense stare and the menacing club. He slowly holstered his pistol and backed away with a defeated look.

The man Noorim had thrown got back to his feet, nursing his shoulder. Drugo motioned toward the whimpering man with the shattered knee. The three remaining henchmen lifted their wounded comrade and Drugo led them off with an indignant look at Taleeka.

Saat-Sarr watched the mobsters leave, peeking around the nose of the airship. Taleeka gazed over at the rattled courier and attempted a smile.

"Now, you've got something for me?"

The Bailian glanced around nervously then stepped in front of the craft.

"Yes," he said, producing the envelope with trembling hands, "and you'll need to sign for it. *Please hurry*, before anything else happens."

He handed her a small ledger book and pen. Taleeka quickly scrawled her name where he indicated and he handed her the packet.

"Now, I'm going to get out of this crazy dangerous place," he said, moving off. "I planned to stay for a while and take in the sights. but this place is *way too dangerous*."

"Suit yourself," Taleeka said, watching the frightened messenger rapidly head for the ticket counter.

"Alright," Taleeka said, breaking the seal and tearing it open. "Let's see what's so all fired important that they had to send it by royal courier."

Taleeka could barely contain herself as she began reading. "It's from my boyfriend, Sira'Har," she said excitedly, studying the introduction. "I thought it might be!"

Noorim watched her friend reading the single sheet of paper, her face falling with each line read. When Taleeka finished, her hands dropped to her sides and she gave a dejected sigh. Noorim said nothing but her face betrayed a burning curiosity.

"The perfect way to set off an already crappy cycle," Taleeka said defeatedly. "I've officially been dumped!"

Anak Bramoul did not necessarily consider himself a cruel man. Most thought of him as ruthless in his business practices and in his acquisition of the rare items which gave him the moniker, The Antiquary. Every cycle, he wandered the grounds of his sprawling estate on the outskirts of Zor and reveled in the exotic plants, animals and statuary collected from across the Annigan.

He now worried about how they would fare in the damp grey mist which seemed to be everywhere. In his specially lit Nocturn greenhouse, flora from the dark side of the world flourished in their natural element. Nothing gave The Antiquary more joy than perusing through his extensive private museum. There you could find priceless, one of-a-kind items, from the very small, to entire rib sections of carved whale bones. By far the prize of his collection, given to him several grands ago by Taleeka Konrad, had to be the mawl God of greed and desire, Pa-Waga.

The black virtually featureless statue with blue binary runes covering its body always stood stoically in his specially designed Etheria cage, never speaking or moving. Anak made it a habit that every cycle after dinner he would stand in front of the cage and attempt a dialogue with the deity. After all, to get a god's perspective on just about anything would be coveted insight. For all his persistence The Antiquary had been constantly met with silence.

Three cycles ago, on the day of the earthquake, Anak made his usual rounds after dinner and, to his surprise, witnessed Pa-Waga seated in a rear corner of the cage, hugging his knees with his head bowed. Soon after, the reports of Tannimore's destruction reached him and he realized what happened to his prize possession.

Now, he stood outside the deity's cell and found himself staring curiously for quite a while at the motionless figure. Knowing their time to be potentially short, Anak knelt on his haunches and issued what could very well be his final taunt.

"I know you're dying," he said softly. "Tannimore was destroyed, with most of your followers. Gods die when there is no one left to believe in them. Sooner or later they'll all be gone and you will be an empty vessel."

Anak then stood and gazed down mercilessly at the weakened deity.

"It really doesn't matter to me. You've hardly been a sterling conversationalist. There is something you should consider before you die. How you will be remembered in the future by all who gaze upon you. Will you be standing, strong and defiant, or weak and sniveling on the floor? That will be up to you, and it may very well be your last decision, make it a good one."

Anak walked away knowing Pa-Waga had been listening and feeling a bit relieved that the deity's essence wouldn't be around to cause any potential mischief in the future. His effigy would have to be good enough.

The glamoured human form surrounding him felt strangely good. Even though his would be a mission of vengeance and death, he couldn't shake the sense that being amongst the fleshy ones of the world above would be enjoyable. He had always been curious about the world beyond the hive. There were so many things he wanted to try and experience but he realized he needed to stay focused. Above all, the ones responsible for disturbing the hive and killing their children would pay.

He caught a glimpse of his glamoured reflection walking past a storefront window. The Howlite Etheria Crystal worked perfectly and instead of seeing a fire mantis Na-Kab, he appeared as a tall handsome human male, cleanshaven with short black hair.

The queen informed him that he would have allies amongst the humans and his first task would be seeking them out. This strange world of sights and sounds delighted his senses but seemed very much beyond his experience. He would need some guidance and assistance.

Making his way from the Shimol Plat to the Zorian Northern Docks, he marveled at the massive forum set into the side of the mountain. All around him the streets hummed with life. Beings he had never seen before passed him at every turn and he marveled at their diversity. The large shark men especially fascinated him and he longed to question one of them. Snapping out of his momentary daydream, he admonished himself to stay focused.

The unmistakable sound of the rush of fire just ahead caught his attention and he followed the familiar noise over to the corner of a large plaza, where a small crowd had gathered. Drawing closer, he heard the whooshing again and over the spectators' heads he saw a long tongue of flame reach upward into the sky.

"Come, worship with us!" a priest called out to the crowd. "Show your gratitude for the abundance and fertility the Na-Kab have given our world! It was they who took over when the Avatar left us. It was they who saved us. Let us rejoice and praise them."

Another column of flame shot into the air and the priest moved to the front of the gathering. He could now clearly see the revelers. There were seven of them, four males and three females, all were nude with ominous looking burn scars covering most of their bronze-colored bodies. They stood around a twenty-foot-long bed of glowing red coals. The male addressing the crowd appeared completely covered with the self-administered scarring. He punctuated every plea to the onlookers by placing the end of a flaming stick in his mouth and belching out a tendril of fire.

"Behold Ayrel," he said, gesturing towards a hairless badly scarred young woman at the other end of the glowing path. "She is ready to take the final step toward full discipleship. Come my child. Enter into the full embrace of our saviors."

Blasting one more pillar of flame into the air for emphasis, the priest opened his arms invitingly and the woman fearlessly stepped onto the glowing coals. The crowd gasped and muttered amongst themselves watching the woman leisurely walk across the embers, showing no discomfort, all the while keeping her eyes straight ahead to the man and his open arms. When she reached the end, she stood with head bowed and arms at her side while the man tenderly embraced her and the crowd applauded.

*This is amusing, they actually worship us*, he thought watching the flattering ceremony play out in front of him. *These must be the allies I was told about.*

The completely scarred priest then held Ayrel out at arm's length and gave a broad smile. "Are you ready?"

She looked up at him, smiled back, then nodded her head. He spun her around and displayed the back of her left calf to the attendance, the only unscarred place on her whole body. The priest reached down and retrieved a stick whose tip had been resting in the coals. Placing the burning end inside his mouth, he let loose a smaller lick of fire which enveloped the lower half of her leg. The woman screamed but the Na-Kab could not discern if it be out of pleasure, pain, or a combination of the two.

He marveled at their discipline, for Ayrel displayed only joy, despite the pain she must be in. He knew the fleshy ones had no tolerance for burning. He smiled at the revelation, burning a small area at a time showed determination and sincerity with each section marked.

"Come, join us in showing your love and appreciation for those who…"

A shrill whistle broke the celebratory mood and the crowd scattered when two Zorian patrol guards walked up.

"Do you have a permit to hold a religious ceremony in public?!" the older guard of the two asked tersely.

"We freely give our thanks to the Na-Kab, as should you," the priest replied defiantly.

The guard scoffed loudly. "I don't care who you worship. I don't care if you want to have a damn orgy in the middle of the street. You gotta get a permit! Now, I'm giving you a deci to get all this shit cleared away. I want it all gone by the time we get back here."

The congregation looked dejected when the patrolmen walked away. The glamoured Na-Kab approached the priest.

"A most impressive display," he said, smiling at the defeated leader.

"Would you like to join us?" the priest asked with a touch of hope. "I could give you your first mark and initiate you long before they return."

"Yes, yes, join us," the others chanted, circling him.

"I do not need to join you, fleshy ones," he said.

He stepped onto the glowing coals and, for a brief moment, dropped the glamour spell, so they could see his true form. The cleric and small congregation gasped in surprise, dropping to their knees. The Na-Kab then quickly returned to his human form and peered around at the fawning group and the staring passersby.

"Rise to your feet, fleshy ones, you call attention to us!"

The kneeling humans looked around guiltily at one another and quickly stood.

"I have been sent on a mission by the very queen herself. The Fire Hive has been violated and I seek those responsible. You will assist me."

The priest agreeably bobbed his head. "It would be an honor to aid you in your quest. I am Kahin. Tell us great Na-Kab, what shall we call you?"

The question puzzled him because the Na-Kab's hive mind needed no names. Still, he could see the usefulness in his present situation.

"You may call me Krak."

*In ghostly Serma the Saytas sleep,*
*waiting to be called.*
*The bidding of the gods of death,*
*across the Annigan's hallowed halls.*
*Run if you can, to lands Afar,*
*and the lonely mountain top.*
*For if the Saytas are hunting you,*
*know they will never stop.*

The rite of Sayta had been invoked.

Kai's eyes opened in time to see a swirling blue vortex in front of her. In her mind only one thought dwelled, death. Death to the ones that transgressed against her God, Orad. This would be her first assignment since offering her essence for the return of her beloved Drucilla. She would not fail no matter how long it took.

The Order of Kaplan's days were indeed numbered.

The wrath of the gods can come in many forms, none of them pleasant. The various deities of death worshiped across the Annigan are especially feared, for good reason. The mawls of The Order of Kaplan in their celebratory glee were blissfully unaware of the grievous trespass they perpetrated.

While true, their "Operation Final Judgement" had been a rousing success, it now carried with it a heavy price. Orad showed Kai how they transported the Trinilic bomb through the portal in the Innaca Deep and detonated it at the precise moment to blast Konaleeta out of its Flavian Loop. This forced the Island of the Lost to return to its former place in Lumina from where it disappeared five thousand grands ago, the area now known as The Doldrums.

The Doldrums eventually became home to the floating, Free City of Tannimore. The return of the island thoroughly destroyed that metropolis, killing approximately fifteen thousand inhabitants, most adherents of the god Pa-Waga.

Retribution upon Pa-Waga's followers was the ultimate goal of The Order of Kaplan and one built into their very charter but avenging the destruction of the Tiikeri race carried other consequences. The mawls' plan did not consider that Tannimore was also the home to the Temple of Orad, the Air Goddess of Death.

Amongst the many lives claimed that day, one hundred were clerics of the Goddess of Death and some of the best assassins in the world. With no more assassins left to retaliate, other, more extreme measures were necessary.

Kai passed through the portal and stepped out into a windy, litter strewn alley in Penaber. Up above, the stars of the moonless vainly attempted to pierce the mist concealing the spring sky. This city, the one where the transgression originated, is where she would pick up the trail. Hearing a splashing sound, she saw a man taking a piss on the alley wall. The flash of the portal startled him and he looked over in a panic. Straining his eyes, he struggled to get a good look in the low light.

The small one-armed figure appeared to be female with pallid and ghastly features. Dark rings circled her eyes giving her a cold maniacal look. Waves of malevolence radiated from her and she smelled like a corpse. She passed through a cast shadow and disappeared briefly. When she stepped back into view, she had transformed into a beautiful nude blonde woman with thin swaying hips and pendulous breasts bouncing with each step.

He remained frozen in shock when she started for him. With penis still in hand and urine flowing, he began to back away not taking his eyes off the approaching woman. He found himself forced to a halt backed against another wall.

She smiled at him and with his bladder now empty, he felt the twinge of an erection starting. It faded when the breeze shifted back in his direction and he caught a whiff of her pungent aroma.

"I am not here for you," she whispered seductively, stepping up close. "I'm sorry, but I cannot have you witness my arrival."

Slowly, with a sad smile, she brushed his cheek with the back of her hand. He gasped at her icy touch, immediately followed by an intense burning sensation throughout his entire body. He silently slid down the wall convulsing as his blood literally boiled in his veins.

Kai stared down at the body for a moment before heading towards the main street twenty feet away.

The hunt was on.

Taleeka watched the morning traffic plodding their way through the grey mist from a window table in the Mengjes Inn. Noorim sat across from her, eating her breakfast, all the while keeping an eye on the several patrons scattered around the eatery, as well as the various doors leading in and out.

"I wonder how long this damn mist is going to last?" Taleeka asked out loud, not really expecting an answer.

Noorim paused and peered up from her bowl of stew at her friend and now employer. "I am sure the farmers are wondering the same thing. This obscuring of the sun must be having an effect on their crops."

Taleeka considered responding when she saw Noorim tense and narrow her eyes at something behind her.

"What?" Taleeka asked quietly, setting her spoon down.

"Perhaps nothing," Noorim replied, keeping her attention focused. "Four suspicious looking men just entered and appear to be surveilling the establishment."

A brief moment passed and Taleeka witnessed her friends face go from cautious to concerned.

"Now they appear to be evicting the other diners," she said, coming casually but quickly to her feet.

She stepped behind Taleeka, her body coiled and at the ready. Taleeka nonchalantly resumed eating.

"One is now giving the all-clear sign to someone outside," Noorim reported.

Noorim watched the men position themselves strategically around the room, allowing Mazie and Chen to enter and head their way.

"It would appear we are about to have company," Noorim announced softly.

"Taleeka Konrad," Mazie said robustly, sitting down next to her with Chen standing directly behind her. "My name is Mazie de Zor. You're a hard woman to get ahold of."

Taleeka quickly shot her an annoyed side glance. "Did I say you could sit down?"

Mazie glibly shrugged and looked around. "No, I didn't ask. Let's just consider this our appointment."

"Let's just consider you letting me eat in peace," Taleeka snapped, not looking up from her plate. "My breakfast is going to get cold and if my breakfast gets cold I'm going to get cranky."

"I'm not stopping you from eating," Mazie replied. "I hear you eat here all the time. You must like the food."

"Normally, yes, but I find irritating conversations bad for the digestion." Taleeka said, pushing her plate away and staring defiantly.

Mazie smiled, sat back in her chair and nodded at one of her men standing near the kitchen door. He knocked on it and another stepped out of the kitchen holding a knife to the throat of Rakeem, the owner of Mengjes Inn.

"What do you want?" Taleeka asked icily.

"I know all about you, Taleeka Konrad," Mazie explained patronizingly. "I know you like to help the helpless. Like how you helped ole Rakeem here, and saved his restaurant from a Piety Watch ban a few grands back. And I hear he didn't have to pay you a damn thing. You must really like his cooking."

"I imagine this rambling has a point, I suggest you get to it," Taleeka demanded.

"Oh, I also know about that violent streak of yours, just like your famous mom. So, if you don't drop the aggression, my man, Gino, over there, is going to slice Wakeel a second mouth."

"You might be able to kill him first," Taleeka said, lifting her hand slowly and putting it on the table in front of her, "but I promise you, you and your men won't leave this room alive if you do."

"My goodness, that arrogance must run in the blood," Mazie said judgmentally. "Oh, wait... you're not really a Konrad though, are you? You're just a little street trash orphan they took pity on and adopted, isn't that right?"

"You don't know me, slum queen," Taleeka said, looking Mazie in the eye, "and you sure as hell don't want to know the Konrads."

"If only that were true," Mazie replied. "I've had more than my fill of Konrads."

"Okay," Taleeka said, with a cold smile, "so, let me ask it like my mom would ask, 'what the fuck do you want?'"

Mazie paused for an awkward moment staring at Taleeka. "You're going to do a job for me."

"I don't hire out."

"I'm not hiring you. You're doing it for free."

Taleeka laughed out loud. "You don't look helpless to me, stupid maybe, but not helpless."

Mazie's face turned grim. "Your mother cost me a small fortune down in Amarenia and destroyed any contacts I may have made there. On top of that, her testimony almost got me executed. So, the way I figure it, the Konrads owe me a debt and you're the nearest Konrad."

Taleeka smiled and shook her head. "You know what? I'm out. I don't even want to know about your little job. If your beef is with my mom, take it up with her, and good luck with that, by the way.

"It's like you said, I 'help the helpless,' not some ghetto mob boss wannabe."

Noorim and Chen, who stared ominously at each other, shared a brief smile in appreciation of Taleeka's brashness.

'I'm sorry you feel that way," Mazie said icily, rising to her feet.

She took several steps away and then looked over at Chen. "Kill her."

The swordsman blinked in disbelief. "What?!"

"I said, kill her!"

Chen gave his boss an incredulous look. "Kill her, your damn self. You hired me as a bodyguard not an assassin!"

Mazie's expression went stern. "If I'm paying you, you'll do as I say!"

"Really?"

"Really!"

Chen sighed and shook his head. "Then, you can consider this my resignation."

His arm moved in a blur and a dagger slipped from his fingers. It struck her man holding the knife on Rakeem in the right eye, piercing his brain instantly. The thug dropped to the floor and Wakeel dodged back into the kitchen.

"Very well," Mazie agreed furiously.

Without another word, she spun and headed for the front door. Opening it, she looked around at her four remaining henchmen.

"Kill them all," she ordered calmly, before stepping out into the mist shrouded streets.

A brief, pregnant pause hung in the air after Mazie closed the door. Time seemed to stand still before the room descended into pandemonium.

All four of Mazie's thugs reached into their tunics while Chen grabbed the chair his former employer had been sitting in and hurled it at the men tasked to kill him. This maneuver, though hardly a decisive blow, served its purpose. The oversized projectile crashed into three of the attackers, causing them to recoil violently. The diversion proved just enough for the swordsman and Noorim to charge, while Taleeka drew Defari.

The club howled loudly exiting the holster and Taleeka flung it at the thug the chair missed. The living missile struck the man squarely in the middle of his face with the sound of snarling, snapping jaws. A loud crack of bones shattering and the resulting shower of blood disrupted him in mid-draw. The combatant flew backward onto the floor and his Mark Five pistol clattered harmlessly to the ground.

The ones struck by the chair recovered in just enough time before Chen and Noorim descended upon them. Chen drew his sword from the scabbard on his back and sent the blade slashing downward on the thug to his left. The man screamed and, in a completely futile gesture, raised his arm in the bastard sword's path. The blade sliced cleanly through the limb severing the forearm just below the elbow. It cut cleanly through to the skull where it lodged at eye level.

Noorim reached her man just as he raised his pistol at Chen. She grabbed his wrist and drove her other arm forcefully upward, snapping the elbow with a loud crunch. The pistol clattered to the floor, followed by a scream of pain, but the Kovos artist wasn't finished yet. Grabbing the now limp appendage, she spun the screaming man into his comrade who now took aim at Taleeka.

The two collided, but not before he got a shot off. The force of the body slamming into him made the shot go wild left, striking a nearby table. The missile struck with such velocity it exploded the table, reducing it to kindling and showering the room with splinters.

Taleeka drew her pistol and fired it at the only remaining threat. The expanding round punched a large hole through his torso and showered the glass front doors behind him with gore.

With ragged breaths, Taleeka slowly lowered her weapon and looked around at the scene of devastation. Only then did she notice the searing pain in her right arm and leg where she discovered half a dozen shards of wood shrapnel protruding from her limbs.

She winced pulling them out, watching Chen casually walk over to the man with the broken arm, rolling around in his companion's blood. The swordsman looked down dispassionately at his adversary writhing in agony and plunged the blade into his chest. The man immediately went limp and Noorim threw him a disapproving look.

"He was no longer a threat," she said judgmentally.

"This one will not be returning to fight another day," Chen replied, sheathing his blade.

"Everyone okay?" Taleeka asked, listening to the whistles of the Zorian Guards drawing closer.

"Yes, but you appear to be bleeding," Noorim said.

"I'm okay," Taleeka replied, putting her pistol back into her backpack.

"You're pretty handy with sharp pointy things," Taleeka said, slinging the pack onto her back and stepping over to Chen, "but if you're going to be operating in this city, I'd grab one of those pistols. Those clowns don't need them anymore and I think you'll live longer relying on a more ranged weapon."

Chen nodded in agreement. "I'll take two, they're small."

Taleeka chuckled and watched the swordsman pick up two pistols off the floor and stick them in his belt.

"Do you hire out?" she asked.

"I do," Chen said, stepping over the bodies littering the floor. "All of a sudden I find myself out of a job."

"I might be able to use you," Taleeka said smirking. "Let's keep in touch."

"I will," Chen replied, "but aren't you concerned about the city guards? They'll be here any time now."

"Nah," Taleeka said, shaking her head. "You can leave if you want, but I'll stick around to give a statement. I'm a bespoke citizen and Hero of the Realm. I'm pretty sure they'll believe me. Besides, all I was doing was eating breakfast, they started it."

Taleeka then looked over at Wakeel the owner and his serving wench Tonii, peering out the kitchen door with terrified looks on their faces.

"Those are the ones I care about," Taleeka said, unslinging her pack once more.

Walking over to the frightened pair, she pulled out a hundred secor gold note and handed it to the owner.

"Rakeem, I am truly sorry about all this," she said, handing him the money. "That should more than cover the clean-up and any lost business."

Rakeem accepted the Ukko wafer staring around at the destruction, his demeanor quickly shifting from terrified to angry. Taleeka spun away from the indignant restauranteur to face the city guards entering the blood-spattered front doors.

"Great!" she said in frustration. "Yet another establishment I can't come back to!"

The sounds of hammering and sawing echoed down the streets of the Kaya Plat of the Seven Sisters Slums. The once abandoned warehouse doors were thrown open and a steady stream of locals poured in and out. They carried wood and supplies to the busy workers inside, giving this neglected structure a much-needed facelift.

Mazie, with the hulking Vozac in tow, wandered through the construction zone inspecting the progress on her second soup kitchen. Before the end of the grand, she planned to open one in all seven of the Seven Sister's plats. Once the people were fed, she would begin rebuilding the squalid living conditions.

Vozac instinctively tensed when one of the workers, a burly, thickly muscled young man with a short dark beard approached. His smile and friendly deportment caused the mobster queen to raise her hand, stopping Vozac from intercepting him.

"Mz. Mazie," he greeted, keeping his head lowered. "I just want to thank you for giving me this job. I finally was able to buy my first pair of shoes with my last two cycles' payment."

"That's wonderful!" Mazie said cheerfully, patting him on the arm. "Keep up the good work."

"Yes, Mz. Mazie. May the gods bless you, Mz. Mazie," he said gratefully, before returning to work.

The worker's gratitude made her feel better, having just come from that dreadful incident with the Konrad woman and her now ex-bodyguard. It felt good to see her plan really working. These locals were now employed and becoming vested in their neighborhood. Even more important, they were falling into her debt. She fed and employed them. It wouldn't be long before they were completely beholden and reliant on her. Yes, soon the Sisters would be hers.

She halted her inspection when she saw Drugo enter, his normally intense gaze seemed even more penetrating.

"Is it done?" she asked softly.

Drugo scowled and shook his head. "No. All dead and Chen got ahold of two of our Mark Fives."

Mazie gave a frustrated sigh. "The pistols and people we can replace. As far as Chen and the Konrad woman are concerned, I want them dead. I don't care if you have to hire independents, I want them gone."

"Right, boss! Uh, one more thing…"

He winced slightly under Mazie's 'what now?' look. "That investigator is back. Actually, he never really left and he's sticking pretty close to you."

"Get rid of him too," she growled. "We start our new operation next cycle and I don't need a tail."

Ditord de Nier just knew this new job would eventually cost him his girlfriend. It seemed bad enough when he walked a beat as a patrolman with the Zorian Guards. Since then, he had graduated at the top of Zekoff's policing course at the university and Vanir's investigation division immediately snatched him up.

Once an investigator, any spare time he could devote to a relationship rapidly evaporated. As the new guy, they assigned him all the time-consuming shit jobs, sifting through mounds of reports, following up on endless leads resulting in dead ends, and then, there were the stakeouts at all hours, like now.

The Kan fog combined with the effects of the Tannimore Winter made the front gate of the old Banavor Mansion, just down the street, appear as a ghostly outline in the gloomy haze. He felt sure Mazie and her henchmen were locked away safely within its confines and this would prove to be another colossal waste of time. The other mansions in Zor's upscale Dhsni Plat with their spacious well-tended lawns and gardens were invisible, giving the young investigator a profound feeling of isolation.

Running a hand across his clean-cut youthful features, he looked over at the wrapped meat stick he purchased on his way here laying in the seat beside him and decided now to be as good a time as any to grab a quick bite. Giving in to the urge, he grabbed the delicious street fare and began to unwrap it.

He had the packaging half-way off when he caught movement to his left out of the corner of his eye. Quickly jerking his head to the side, he saw a male torso materialize out of the fog. He couldn't see the man's face, but he certainly saw the pistol trained on him.

The glass of the side window shattering made Ditord jump in surprise just before his head exploded, painting the entire front seat and passenger door of the hackney with most of his brains and a copious amount of blood.

"It's done," the assassin said into a Larimar shard, before disappearing back into the fog.

The dead investigator didn't hear him and he didn't see Mazie's private airship lifting off from the mansion's roof. At least he no longer had to fear losing his girlfriend.

Folsom de Onnal felt extremely lucky to be alive. Almost two clusters had passed since Taleeka and her crew rescued her from a life of drunkenness and degradation in Tannimore. Now, with the floating city's destruction she felt doubly lucky. Her life in the High Holy City certainly changed for the better. Taleeka secured her a job with the Harbor master's office and a small apartment.

Her friendship with Barr-Ani blossomed as well. The Bailian psychic showed her how her abilities were a gift, not a curse. She now no longer needed to drown herself in alcohol to mask the visions and premonitions. Barr-Ani also stressed the time necessary to shut out the world.

Once a cluster, she retreated to the Otick's Temple of the Golden Avatar, in the caves by the Zorian waterfront. There she found refuge in one of the crab people's giant oyster shells. In her isolation, cut off from the light, sounds and sensations of the Annigan, she could naturally recharge and calm herself.

Yes, for the first time in a long time, Folsom felt her life finally on the right track.

The Grand Turine in the Zorian harbor rang five bells, snapping her out of her elated musings. The Kan would start in a deci and, with the greyish mist already in the air, the Kan had become almost impossible to navigate through.

She straightened her desk and actually found herself humming. Rising to her feet with a satisfied smile, she headed across the small office and looked out its large picture window facing the wharf. She saw Skele, the Kan Harbormaster, peering through his spyglass at several late arriving transport ships attempting to dock.

"See you in the morning," she said, opening the door. "Try and stay awake."

Skele huffed and lowered the glass.

"Yeah," he said, smiling until his clean-cut features crinkled, "there's not much to do since the damn mist shut down Kan travel. You got plans?"

"Food cart and then home in front of a warm fire."

"Enjoy, see you in the morning."

Folsom smiled and nodded, stepping out onto the damp cobblestones. The smell of the wharf mixed with the stale odor of the mist made her nostrils flare. She certainly hoped this Tannimore Winter, as they called it, would dissipate soon. She sensed the people's anxiety and it felt palpable.

By the time she made it to the Shimol Plat with her dinner in hand, the Kan fog reached up to her knees, completely obscuring the street below her feet. She really wanted to make it home before the entire area became socked in and decided to take a short cut through a nearby side street.

The road appeared empty, but once turning the corner she heard the distinct sound of a woman sobbing. Folsom found it strange that she didn't feel the usual waves of sorrow wash over her, in fact she didn't feel anything.

"Hello," she said cautiously, moving closer to the sound of the lamentations.

There was no response. She searched the mist filled street until she saw a figure seated on a stoop in front of a five-story building.

"Are you alright?" she asked, moving closer and finding it odd she still did not receive any feelings at all.

Sensing no deception or treachery, she stepped up to the woman whose face remained buried in her hands, weeping uncontrollably, her body quivering with each sob. Folsom noticed the woman appeared tall and well dressed in slacks and a white blouse, with brown hair piled on top of her head. She couldn't get a look at her face.

"Can I help?" Folsom asked gently, kneeling down so that she would be at eye level with the woman.

Folsom cried out in alarm when the woman suddenly lashed out and grabbed her. The powerful grip felt cold and hard as stone. When she saw the woman's face, the pleasant features appeared completely unemotional. The woman then rose to her feet, effortlessly lifting Folsom as she stood.

After the initial shock, the psychic screamed and kicked. Her blows easily found their target, but the body was hard and dense, much the same as striking a wall.

The freakishly strong woman stared at the flailing and screaming sensitive in a curious manner before releasing one hand from her shoulder and bringing it up to her throat. Folsom's screams quickly became gurgled cries when the vice-like grip began to tighten. The shrill sound of a Zorian Guard's alarm whistle from the street entrance suddenly cut through the fog shrouded evening.

"Unhand her!" a young male's voice filled the empty boulevard, echoing off the surrounding buildings.

The assaulting woman paid no attention to the command, easily lifting Folsom over her head with one hand.

The young guard ran towards the altercation, unslinging his carbine and blowing his whistle. He halted twenty feet from the battling couple and raised his rifle. Carefully aiming so as not to affect the victim, he fired a single shot at the assailant's body.

The round penetrated her back with a loud unnatural crash, along with the sound of several small items clattering to the cobblestones. The woman stopped and released Folsom, who toppled to the ground clutching her throat and sputtering. The assailant froze and lowered her hand while the air around her began to shimmer. Folsom, who attempted to crawl away, gasped in surprise when the glamour spell faded and she could see her attacker for what it really was.

The creature stood well over six feet tall, constructed from a patchwork of different shaped crystals mimicking a humanoid form. The bolt blew a large hole in the creature's upper torso, but it showed no signs of distress. It looked about calmly with two illuminated blue gem eyes.

The young patrol guard stood stunned, paralyzed at the sight of the myriad gems shifting around the hole, rearranging themselves to fill in the void. From her vantage point close to the ground, Folsom could see the crystals blown onto the street, lining up and moving across the road, returning to the being from whom they originated.

The creature reformed quickly and turned towards the guard who shot it. Showing no signs of fear or anger, it ignored Folsom and started for the only person who could possibly do it harm.

The guard suddenly snapped out of his terrorized trance and fired again, striking the creature in the abdomen. The Na-Kab Carbon bolt punched a six-inch diameter hole in the being's lower torso, showering the cobblestones behind it with mostly black crystal shards.

This shot yielded a decidedly different result. The creature immediately froze in place and the light in its eyes went out. An eerie silence now shrouded the street and the guard ran over to check on Folsom.

"Are you alright, ma'am?" he asked, helping her up.

"I think so," she replied hoarsely. "What was that thing?"

"I have no idea," the young guard said, watching several more patrol guards finally arrive on the scene. "This is just my second cycle on the job. You hang tight. I'm going to get an investigator out here and see if they can make sense of it. They'll want to get your statement."

Folsom sighed deeply. *So much for my relaxing evening by the fire.*

Talib yawned and scratched his head.

"It's a statue," he said, bending over and peering through the gaping cavern in its abdomen, "with a hole in it."

"Yeah, a little while ago that statue tried to kill our victim over there," the young patrolman said, indicating Folsom while she gave her statement to Tantei. "It came after me when I shot it the first time. I don't know why the second one stopped it."

"I only see one wound," Talib noted.

"The first one was dead center of its chest. It quickly healed over."

Talib exhaled loudly and looked around at the surreal spectacle of the afflicted section of street. Large orange gems glowed through the Kan fog, appearing even thicker through the mist of the Tannimore Winter. Red rope cordoned off the area all around the crime scene. City guards moved through the illuminated haze, examining the vicinity and making Larimar renderings. The lateness of the cycle reduced the normal gawking crowd to a few denizens of the Kan, making their way home from the pubs.

"She's still in shock," Tantei said, coming up on the pair. "The thing was glamoured to appear as a woman in distress. The victim's a sensitive and claims she couldn't get a reading on it so she got too close."

"What are those black shards all over the road?" Talib asked, pointing behind the Etheria Gollum.

"Beats me," Tantei answered, "but they were blown out of it. Vanir's got a call out to Tally Konrad. He thinks she may have had some experience with this sort of thing."

"Speaking of which," Talib said, noticing Taleeka's private hackney pulled by a bridled lizard zipping vertically along the side of the building's wall.

An excited Gidaria glowed with enthusiasm behind the wheel. Talib could see her dark black features and her head of close-cropped hair with patterns carved into the stubble. She banked the craft downward on the wall and brought it smoothly to the ground outside of the cordoning rope. She then got out and opened the rear door. Once Taleeka and Noorim stepped onto the street, she closed the door and offered her lizard a treat from her pocket.

Both investigators were surprised when Taleeka and Folsom embraced. Taleeka could plainly be seen asking if she had been harmed. Folsom managed a weak nod and Taleeka gave her a comforting smile before sauntering past the red ropes while taking in the incident.

"Hey kids, are we having fun yet?" Taleeka said, not taking her attention off the Etheria statuary.

"If that's what you want to call it," Tantei replied.

"Your boss was pretty adamant I leave my nice warm bed and get down here," Taleeka said, eyeing the Etheria figure closely. "Now I see why."

"You know the victim?" Talib asked, glancing over at Folsom.

"Yeah, she helped me out on a job in Tannimore. I got her out before someone dropped an island on it."

"What's Chen Arador doing here?" Talib asked, looking over at the swordsman staring intently just outside the ropes.

Taleeka looked over at Chen and he smiled at her.

"Beats me," she replied with a sigh. "He's been following me around all cycle, looking like a lost puppy."

"Did you know he's Mazie's bodyguard?" Tantei asked cautiously.

"Was," Taleeka corrected. "It's a long story. Anyways…"

"The victim claims she doesn't know why she was targeted," Tantei said, watching Taleeka ignore Chen and circle the Gollum.

"Targeted is the right word in this case," Taleeka agreed with a nod. "This hardly looks like a random act of violence. Who put the hole in it?"

"Some young patrol guard that just happened to be passing by," Tantei said. "Poor bastard, it was only his second cycle on the job."

"Yeah, well, welcome to the mean streets of Zor," Taleeka said, kneeling by the blast field of black shards.

"That was from the second shot," Tantei reported. "The first one was in the chest, but it quickly healed up."

Taleeka gazed up at Tantei. "Oh?"

"Yep, both victim and guard said the opening just started to fill in. Even the blasted pieces lined up and reassembled on their own."

The last statement sent Taleeka's mind racing. This happened to be exactly what occurred when she smashed the Etheria tentacle that got ahold of Noorim in the crystal cave on Awa Island.

"Why didn't it reassemble again after the second shot?" Talib asked.

Taleeka picked up one of the black shards and held it up for the inspectors to see.

"Obsidian," Taleeka said confidently. "The second shot blew out this thing's psionic battery."

"What the fuck is this thing?!" Tantei asked frustratingly.

"I've got a vague idea and it's not particularly good," Taleeka said, standing. "I've dealt with something like this before. Have you taken enough renderings?"

"Yep, even up its ass. Which, by the way, it didn't have."

Taleeka smiled at Tantei's earthy humor which so reminded her of her mom. "Okay sit on this thing a little longer. I'll return with my ship. I want to get this to Landagar, where an expert I know can look at it."

Tor-Ga, the Penaber station chief for The Order of Kaplan, yawned watching the moonrise through the omnipresent dirty mist. It cast ghostly shadows across House Calden's most remote seaport.

The orange Tiikeri usually enjoyed the short morning walk from his modest bungalow to the listening post he commanded. The Tannimore Winter changed all that.

The mist, soot and ash from the destroyed city hung in the air, aggravating his nose and lungs. It made travel nearly impossible, creating a marked increase in the number of maritime wrecks, hackney collisions and air traffic crashes during the moonless due to the reduced visibility.

His secretive comrades, who arrived thirty cycles ago, were responsible, of course. He knew the destruction of Pa-Waga to be forefront in their charter, but he would have never gone along with such a dangerous plan had he known there would be such far reaching consequences. But then, no one asked him. He also found himself pleased that the two remaining perpetrators were now in custody, even though technically they were brethren of the same order.

Arriving at the nondescript, windowless, single-story structure, he saw his six mongrel team waiting for him by the front door, chatting amongst themselves. The moonless shift inside would no doubt be eager to leave and, for security purposes since Mukavar's recent incursion, they designated the incoming shift's chief as the only one who could open the door.

Nodding a greeting to his crew, he stepped up to the Etheria composite pad beside the featureless door and placed his nose against the smooth milk white surface. The MagiTech device identified the unique pattern on the tip of his snout and the lock clicked. When the door swung open the six mongrels eagerly pushed their way into the simple two room structure.

Hearing screams and cries of alarm, he rushed through the opening and froze in horror. His group stood amongst the bodies of the moonless shift littering the floor. The chief, another orange Tiikeri, had been suspended in the doorjamb to his office by a long spike through his chest. Blood covered the floors, walls and equipment all around them.

"Welcome to work, boys," Kai said with a raspy voice.

The petite, one-armed, human female stepped from the office, past the impaled manager and into the room. Despite her nudity, she appeared ghastly, with bone white skin, sunken eyes and a bald head. She scanned the room with a malevolent stare and, with a wave of her hand, a sudden gust of wind slammed the door closed. The mongrels realized they were trapped and panicked.

Kai extended three fingers on her still outstretched hand and flexed them twice. Six small blue bolts shot from her fingertips into the scrambling crowd of mawls, striking each of the mongrels in the head. They silently dropped all around Tor-Ga leaving only the terrorized Tiikeri standing amongst a field of corpses.

"Can you smell it in the air?" she asked, moving towards the station chief. "I can. It's the smell of hundreds of my dead brothers and sisters. They hang on in that accursed mist. The mist your people caused!"

"Please, wait, I had nothing to do with it. You have to believe me. I didn't even know about it."

Kai stepped in front of Tor-Ga and looked up at the much larger man-tiger.

"Oh, I believe you," she said with a hiss. "Where are the parties responsible?"

"They're gone."

"Where?"

"They were tried and sentenced to life at hard labor."

"Where?" Kai demanded impatiently.

"Lorovan Prison."

Kai knew Lorovan Prison. Located on Quell Island, it happened to be one of the farthest northern most points of human habitation in the Goyan Islands. The lone compound situated atop the rocky peaks on the northern point of the Island remained rightfully dreaded. The inhospitable weather, combined with the facilities remote location, made it absolutely escape proof. Run by the most brutal slavers House Whitmar had to offer, who took out their resentment of being stationed there on the prisoners. Anyone sentenced to that infamous detention facility was doomed to be literally worked to death in the weapon forges within or in the iron mines to the south.

"Thank you," Kai croaked before a long blue ghostly blade appeared from the stump of her missing arm.

The phantasmal weapon plunged through Tor-Ga's abdomen and out his back. The Satya, formerly known as Kai, yanked it violently downward and the glowing blue blade cut cleanly through the bottom half of the Tiikeri's body, exiting between his legs. Tor-Ga peered down with a shocked expression at his internal organs rushing out onto the ground, swept along by a flood of blood and gore.

"Your people killed mine. I return the favor," she said, watching him topple to the floor amongst the rest of the dead mawls, the blood seeping out of his lifeless body, mixing with theirs.

Senior Valdurian airship pilot, Tayaar de Atar, checked the controls one more time and performed a gentle bank around the Amarenian capital city of Mostas. She welcomed the last run of the cycle and looked forward to a layover in the vibrant City of Circles. Not that she could make a return trip even if she wanted to, since the low light of the setting moon, along with the dirty mist of the Tannimore Winter, grounded all aircraft.

"We're almost there, Private," she called back to the Valdurian Marine seated just behind her, in front of the cargo bay opening.

Normally, she did not need security on her deliveries, but on this particular run, she picked up a large shipment of salt, spices and sugar, three very sought after and expensive commodities. Any one of them would be a prime target for pirates.

"Hope you got your rest," she said salaciously, "because the Amarenians really know how to party!"

The young man scrunched his boyish, cleanshaven features and scoffed. "Even me? I hear they don't like men."

"First time in Mostas?"

"Yeah."

"It's not so bad anymore," Tayaar said, managing a reassuring smile. "They've still got their old timers, the real hard-liners who still call men 'dags'. That's mostly the High Amarenians though, the real pale ones, but the younger generation, now that's a different story.

A lot of them are real curious about us dark-skinned Goyans. A good portion of them are more than a little eager to experience some brown dick. Just be respectful and hope you don't get a Hill Sister... unless you're into that."

"A what?"

Tayaar gave an amused sigh. "Oh boy, you really are new at this. Hill Sisters have both a dick and a pussy. They tend to be a bit larger and more aggressive than your run of the mill Amarenian."

"Oh," the private replied weakly.

"Relax, you stand a much better chance of getting laid than me. I'm not into women."

"Well, part of the reason I joined the marines was to see the world."

"That's the spirit!" Tayaar said heartily.

She brought the ship around to hover just above the half dozen circular landing pads. Reaching up to the overhead console, she pressed the milk-white Larimar disk.

"Big Mo Control, this is Transport Two One Seven, requesting permission to land?"

"Transport Two One Seven," a young female voice crackled in her head. "You're cleared to land in Slip Twenty-three. I know you need the room."

"Roger that, Control. I got sugar and spice and everything nice, just for the good people of Amarenia."

"We appreciate that, Two One Seven. Slip Twenty-three is open and ready."

"Copy that, Mostas Control, Two One Seven heading in."

Descending through the mist, she caught sight of the ground crew when she reached fifty feet off the landing pad.

"You're with the cargo until the city guards relieve you, right?"

"Those are my orders."

"Well, if our paths don't cross in the future, it was good flying with you. Remember, relax and have fun this coming moonless."

"Yes ma'am, thank you ma'am."

"Well, okay, here we are," Tayaar said, guiding the ship to a stop and dropping the rear cargo hatch.

She watched the marine get to his feet, shoulder his carbine and march back to greet the six-woman unloading crew. Smiling at the private's naiveté, she spun back around in her chair and reached for her logbook. Recording the proper documentation of the trip would keep her busy while the ground crew unloaded the cargo and she could perform her post-flight inspection of the ship.

Tayaar smiled at her good timing when she heard the last of the boxes being unloaded and carted away just as she came to the final page of her report. She jotted down the remaining setting and considered raising the rear hatch when she felt a presence behind her.

Quickly pivoting, she gasped in surprise when she saw Mazie and Vozac standing behind her. Mazie smiled broadly, but the airship pilot's attention rapidly focused on the pistol in Vozac's meaty hand.

"You're not allowed to be in here," Tayaar blurted out, getting to her feet.

"Hi there," Mazie said robustly. "I'd like to rent you and this ship for a little while."

Tayarr's mouth dropped open. "The ship's not mine to rent."

Mazie continued with her cheerful demeanor. "Well now, let's not get all tangled up in rules. It pays really well."

Tayaar shook her head in disbelief. "That's quite impossible…"

"Hey, Captain!" the young private's voice excitedly interrupted from behind. "I've got a date already and…"

The marine halted at the hatch's opening when he saw Vozac with the pistol. He scrambled to unshoulder his weapon with flailing arms and a panicked expression. Vozac, with pistol already drawn, merely raised his weapon and fired. The swiftly moving projectile disintegrated the young man's entire torso, spraying the ramp with a fine red mist, while the head, arms and legs spun off wildly in different directions.

Tayaar cried out in stunned disbelief and Mazie returned her friendly attention back to the terrorized pilot.

"Now, about that rental?"

"I, I told you, I don't have the authority to do anything like that."

"Well then," Mazie said with a pout. "You're no help to me at all."

She then looked over at Vozac. "Can you fly this thing?"

The bull-necked thug merely nodded his bald head.

"Well," Mazie said, sighing and returning her attention to Tayaar. "You're of no use to me at all, so you can just run along."

Tayaar stood frozen in shock and relief at the thought of being released, causing Mazie to impatiently place her hands on her hips and tap her foot.

"We're in a bit of a hurry here, go, before I change my mind."

The last prompt spurred the frightened pilot into action. With a relieved look, Tayaar bolted for the open rear hatch. She had just made it to the opening when Mazie cocked her head and took the pistol from Vozac. She quickly raised the weapon, aimed and fired.

Very much like the marine before her, Tayaar's torso exploded and appendages went flying. When Mazie returned the pistol to Vozac, he raised a quizzical eyebrow.

"What?!" she asked defensively. "I changed my mind. I can change my mind! Besides, we would have had to kill her sooner or later. She saw our faces."

The nude older woman known as Seredina sat cross-legged, levitating several feet over an array of pillows on the floor, deep in a trance. Her short, plump body heaved, making her large pendulous breasts sway. Her thick, wild pubic patch, which had almost taken over her entire abdomen, still glistened from the stream of urine she had expelled upon making contact. She closed her eyes and threw back her head of greying, dark hair. Her mouth, open wide, displayed rotted teeth, but her lips didn't move. The voice of a panicked young girl streamed out of the psychic's mouth and into the room.

"Mommy, I'm lost in a maze. I can't find my way out. Help me mommy, please!" Her scream immediately followed the plea.

A young couple sat nearby in the simple one room hovel. The father, a young man in his twenties with short dark hair and a pencil thin moustache, held his wife's hand and stared intently at the floating medium. The young woman appeared to be the same age as her husband, with long brown hair framing the distraught look on her face.

The moment they heard the child's voice the young woman began crying. She opened her mouth to ask a question and her husband covered her mouth with his hand.

They had been sternly instructed not to disturb the medium once she entered her trance but hearing the voice of her recently deceased daughter proved more than she could take.

"Mommy," the voice called out again. "I want to come home! I don't like it here, it's scary!"

A distant growl and the child's scream broke the trance. The medium dropped onto the pillows breathing heavily.

"Where's my little girl?!" the young woman wailed. "What's happening to her?!"

Seredina sat up and waited until her breathing returned to normal. When she finally gazed over at the grieving couple, her wrinkled features betrayed no emotion.

"Your daughter's essence now resides on the Labyrinth Plain of the Middle Realms," Seredina said coldly.

The mother shot her husband a terrified grimace and then turned to Seredina with a pleading expression.

"It sounded like a terrible place!" she said shrilly. "What's my little angel doing there?! She was only seven grands old! What could she have possibly done to deserve being sent there?!"

"It was the sentence of Boran, Judge of the Dead," Seredina continued in her unemotional tone. "I do not know the reason. The gods' ways are mysterious."

"If you've found her and made contact, can we get her back?" the father asked desperately.

"Possibly," Seredina replied, "but it is a complicated and dangerous process."

"Can you do it?" the father asked hopefully.

"No," the psychic replied adamantly. "You will need a necromancer to guide you on that path, but I do not recommend it. Even if you are successful, reviving dead things will bring nothing but misery. Essences rarely return the way they departed."

"Still..." the father said, his hope draining away.

"I cannot help you."

"You got to her once," the mother said, desperation permeating her every word and motion. "Can you get her back again? I have to know if she's in danger!"

"I have shown you all I can," Seredina said curtly, getting to her feet. "Time for you to go."

"But I don't understand!" the mother moaned, tears filling her eyes. "Please…"

Seredina placed a hand on the mother's shoulder, not to comfort, but to interrupt another outburst.

"I have shown you all I can," she said, staring into the desperate woman's eyes.

The two continued staring at each other for a lengthy moment before the woman nodded her head in acceptance and peered over at her husband who gave a sad resigned smile then guided her towards the door.

"Thank you for your help," he said weakly, before opening the door and leading his bereaved wife into the dirty Kan fog.

Seredina sighed, walked over to the room's lone table and tore off a hunk of bread from the couple's food offering. Holding the piece of bread in her mouth, she removed her robe off the back of a chair and slipped it on. Grabbing the rope belt to tie the garment closed, she heard a weak knocking on the door.

"I told you! There is nothing more I can show you!" she said angrily.

She made her way over to the doorway and reached for the doorknob. Before she grabbed it, the top half of the door exploded, knocking her onto her back and showering her, as well as the room, with splinters.

Through the fog of shock and waves of pain, she saw a creature easily smashing through the bottom half and entering. It stood about six feet tall and appeared constructed out of a patchwork of interconnected crystals. It scanned the room dispassionately with its glowing blue eyes until it locked onto the prone figure of Seredina.

Still too shocked to move, she could only watch the creature calmly walk over to her. It reached down, grabbed her by the throat and lifted her up to its eye level. When she felt its cold, hard fingers begin to tighten, she knew this to be the end.

Through the numbing pain, Seredina heard herself gurgling frantically. In her last thoughts before her neck snapped, she came to the sudden realization this thing gave off no emotions whatsoever.

Quell Island is the northern most habitable piece of land in the greater Goyan Islands. The three small islands in the Goyodian Chain to the north of Quell were little more than jagged rocks jutting from the turbulent sea, used only for Kell breeding and EEtah Sunal training.

Even though Quell is technically habitable, it is far from hospitable. The barren rocky terrain is punctuated by prickly scrub and the occasional outcropping of boulders. The only thing making this cold windswept speck in the Shallow Sea of interest to sentients is its single natural resource, iron. The vein of this base metal runs deep and constitutes a good majority of the island.

What stout, hardy people would be willing to mine this valuable material from such a foreboding place? The governing body of the island, House Whitmar, provided the perfect answer, a workforce of conscripted labor—a practice the great human house was already well known for.

They built Lorovan prison five hundred grands ago and it barely served as shelter from the area's inclement weather for the unfortunate souls sentenced there. Being so close to an abundant source of iron, Quell seemed the perfect location to build forges and foundries. The lucky prisoners got assigned to work the furnaces. As dangerous and backbreaking as labor at the furnaces might be, at least you stayed warm.

Coming from the Land of Mists in Nocturn, Ruu-Da thought he knew cold. Damp cold had been a way of life for the white Tiikeri. Now, with his fur shaved off, he sat hugging his knees, shivering in a cage dangling over a sheer cliff, suspended hundreds of feet above the jagged rocks and the frigid waters of the northern Shallow Sea below.

They transported him here, along with the Yagur Geeorn, five cycles ago. Upon arrival, he informed his captors that he considered the work they wished him to perform beneath him. They promptly beat him, shaved his body and placed him in a disciplinary cage. With no walls to break the wind and the damp mist from the Tannimore Winter, Ruu-Da knew this meant a slow, frigid death.

"You look very uncomfortable out there," A female voice spoke from his right, near the edge of the cliff.

He glanced over and saw the nude, one-armed, human female standing beside the thick wooden arm suspending him in space. She looked pale and gaunt, but seemingly unaffected by the cold and wind.

Ruu-Da, too miserable to respond, weakly lowered his head back down between his knees.

"I'm about to extend to you something you don't deserve, mercy," the woman said with a sinister smile, "Your actions not only killed many of my brothers and sisters, but they also endangered all of humanity. For your transgressions against the Goddess Orad and the entire Annigan, you have been sentenced to death."

Her glowing blue blade lengthened from the stump of her missing arm, crackling in the cold wind. She quickly swung towards the thick wooden beam next to her. The phantasmal blade easily severed the rope suspending the cage. The enclosure and the Tiikeri plunged, disappearing into the dirty grey mist.

Kai heard the metal bars striking the rocks and the Tiikeri's anguished cry just before the splash of it entering the sea. She peered over the edge, hoping for a visual confirmation, but the mist obscured her view.

The undead assassin then turned her attention to the windowless metal box with a single heavy door which held the Yagur shaman. Its austere appearance stood out, located in the center of a small plaza between three very secure-looking buildings. She waited for a lone, shivering guard to pass, before making her way over to the cell specially designed to cut off the shaman from any elemental forces he might call upon.

Positioning herself on a rear corner, she placed her hand directly on the corner's edge and concentrated.

She then began muttering a phrase over and over, "She comes like the wind, taking whom she wishes. Her name is Orad, and she is death."

When the next flurry of howling winds whipped across the prison, rivulets of blue lightning flowed out from her hand, rapidly spreading so that it covered the walls. Within moments the metal glowed red. She could clearly hear the screams of pain and frantic scratching at the door coming from inside.

When the shrieking stopped, she caught the smell of burning fur and flesh. The lightning receded back into her hand, but the iron box continued to glow. She estimated it would probably take more than a deci to cool enough for someone to touch it.

So, the original perpetrators were now dead. It had become time for the Goddess' vengeance to fall upon the rest of the killers of her people. She didn't care how long it took, she had all the time in the world, but the group known as The Order of Kaplan would be rendered extinct.

"Come on boss," Tantei pleaded. "Who is she?"

Vanir sat back from his desk, took a sip of whiskey and cocked an eyebrow. "Who said it's a she?"

Tantei scrunched her face in disbelief. "Well anyways, *she* did a good job on your hair," Tantei conceded, nodding towards the neat braids on either side of his head.

An amused Talib sat beside his partner chuckling. "You know, Captain, we *are* investigators. We could find out if we wanted to."

Vanir rolled his eyes. "Sure, but the real mystery here is why you two are so interested in my personal life."

"That's the reason," Tantei said, amused, "You actually have one now. You never had one before and we're naturally curious."

"Tell you what," Vanir offered, before taking another sip, "let's put a pin in this conversation and revisit it later."

"That's what you said last time," Talib replied disappointedly.

"I'd rather be talking about those dead psychics and that... *thing*." Vanir said, pointing to the Larimar screen on the wall displaying a rendering of the Etheria Gollum.

Tantei sighed in defeat. "Four victims so far, and one almost. A lucky shot from a patrolman saved her. All the others' throats were crushed."

"And the mysterious killer?"

"It appeared to be some sort of machine," Talib offered, indicating the image on the screen, "but not like any machine I've ever seen before. It didn't require anyone to operate it."

"The statement from the sensitive that survived it said it first appeared as a weeping woman," Tantei said. "That's how it got her to get close enough to attack."

"She also said that she couldn't get a reading from it," Talib chimed in. "All the more reason to believe it's some sort of machine. She also said that during the attack it made no noise and showed no emotion."

"Where is it now?" Vanir queried, before draining his glass.

"Tally Konrad took it to Landagar to see what they could find out."

"Well, if anyone can figure it out it's the gearheads over at the Landagar Group. You think that was the only one?" Vanir asked both his detectives.

"I sure hope so," Talib said quickly.

"Me too," Tantei agreed, "but we don't have that kind of luck."

"Alright let's cross our fingers and hope this is the only one," Vanir said, reaching for his glass once more. "If any more turn up, you two are on it."

Both detectives nodded in agreement just before a hurried knock on the door. Not waiting for a reply, the desk sergeant poked his head through the opening.

"Captain Vanir," he said with a distressed look, "morning patrol just found the body of Ditord. An evidence team is enroute."

The news hit everyone in the room like a blast of cold water.

"Isn't that the new guy?" Talib asked innocently.

Vanir closed his eyes and nodded grimly. "He was on stake-out up in the Dhsni Plat, keeping an eye on our newest mob boss wanna-be, Mazie. You two get out there and take a look."

Both investigators gloomily nodded while getting to their feet.

"What did I tell you about our luck," Tantei said, heading for the door.

"This damn mist is a pain in my ass," Tantei ranted, maneuvering her hackney onto the shoulder of the road beside the roped off crime scene.

"Yeah, this can't be good for anyone," Talib said, getting out and surveying the area. "I wonder how long it's going to take to dissipate?"

"It can't happen soon enough to suit me," Tantei answered.

She placed the lanyard of her badge placard around her neck and then started towards the cordoned off area. Six members of the evidence team swarmed around Ditord's damaged hackney and several of them nodded at the pair of investigators as they passed the red ropes.

Tantei peered inside the shattered driver's side window. Ditord's headless body still sat upright with the partially unwrapped meat stick in his lap. Dried blood, bone and brain matter thoroughly coated the entire front seat and all the glass on the far side of the vehicle's interior.

"Looks like they got him on his dinner break," one of the evidence team said behind her. "Just walked right up and shot him at close range."

He pointed to a set of tracks in the ground. "He then took off in that direction."

"You get a cast of the footprint?" Tantei asked, returning her attention to the body.

"Yep," he confirmed and pointed to the corpse. "They used an expanding round. We pulled it out of the passenger door. The bolt ballooned open when it hit the glass. It was a good two inches in diameter when it pulverized his head."

"I'm torn," Talib said, stepping up to the gruesome scene and peering into the hackney. "It can't be a coincidence that this is so close to Mazie's place. On the other hand, I can't see them killing someone practically in their front yard."

"With the remoteness of the location and the Kan fog, you can bet nobody saw shit." Tantei lamented, staring over at the gate to the grounds of Mazie's estate. "Still, on the remote chance someone saw or heard something."

She then sighed and looked over at Talib.

"Okay, let's go."

Neither spoke on the short walk up the driveway to the tall wrought iron fence and elaborate gate. Finding it locked, Tantei pressed the Larimar disk beside the handle.

"Yeah, what do you want?" came a familiar voice.

Tantei shot Talib an amused glance before answering. "Why Drugo, I'd recognize that shrill voice of yours anywhere. Inspectors Talib and Tantei, there was a murder out in front of this place last Kan. We need to talk to you and your staff. So let us in and gather your people."

"I know who you are," the voice countered. "Nobody here saw nothing."

"Aw, come on Drugo," Tantei pleaded. "Why ya always gotta turn these little chats into pissing matches? Now, you can either talk to us here, or I send a brute squad to drag all your asses down to Judgement Square for questioning. The choice is yours my friend."

A moment of silence passed before the gate clicked open.

Both detectives entered the grounds to the sound of Drugo sneering in their ears, "I ain't your friend."

The moonless is hardly a quiet time in the Os'Oni Mountains of the Twilight Lands. Many species of creatures come out to hunt when the moon sets in the western sky. All must be guarded against by the first level of defense for the mighty Cevot empire. A Cevot guardian stood watch along the rocky slope, primarily against the Fudomi ram peoples, who would steal their silk and feed on their eggs.

So far this moonless, things had been quiet and she watched the dew on the webbing between mountain peaks twinkle in the starlight above.

Down below, The Plains of Taka-Vir stretched out to the horizon and she observed three family units of horses peacefully grazing, dutifully watched over by an On'Dara sentry and a giant Abani herd dog. The On'Dara stood as tall as the stallions of the three family groups. His equine head constantly surveyed his surroundings for threats.

A medium crossbow hung ominously across the shoulders of his humanoid torso. Crossbows had replaced their usual bow and arrows for herd guarding.

They also benefited from trade with the west. The silk they traded with the horse-men were traded again to the Bailians, who in turn bartered it for goods from the light side of the world. The system worked well, thanks to the proliferation of air travel since the end of the Etheria War. Items and people could now be transported around the Annigan which would never have been thought possible before. The Cevot spider people had no desire to travel. The safety and solitude of the webs and caves suited them.

She naturally looked up upon seeing a large shadow pass over her, blocking out the celestial light show above. It looked like a huge transport airship from Lumina. She had become used to seeing them; the On'Dara regularly chartered them to safely take their horses to market. She had never seen one flying during the moonless though. Thinking it strange, the humanoid spider scurried across the web for a better view.

The ship made broad circles over the horses below, slowly descending with each pass. When it got within fifty feet of the ground, the horses started to become spooked, the dog began barking and the On'Dara unslung his crossbow.

Suddenly, a massive cloud of glittery powder sprayed from the bottom of the craft. It floated down over the eighteen horses, causing them and their protectors to become extremely lethargic. Once sedated, the airship settled gently to the ground beside the dazed animals and the rear hatch dropped.

A human female and two males got out of the vessel and placed ropes around the now docile animals' necks, then led them inside. She couldn't really make out much about the airborne rustlers. Humans all looked alike to her. The only thing that really stood out was the female seemed to have a metal object tucked into the small of her back, which glinted in the starlight.

Once loaded, the ramp raised, the ship quietly lifted off and headed west. This needed to be reported. Of that she could be certain.

She drummed on the web with one of her insectoid legs and summoned a two-foot-long, work spider. The arachnid conveyed what she had seen by pounding her vibrational message on the web in front of the work spider. When finished, the creature scampered off.

She wasn't sure what needed to be done. That would not be her call. She just hoped it had been reported in time to make a difference.

"Exactly what was that called again?" Noorim asked Taleeka, exiting the newly renovated Divadlo Theatre.

"They billed it as performance art," Taleeka replied, still processing the bizarre show she had just witnessed.

"For Bailians, given their intrinsic natural beauty, these were quite hideously deformed," Noorim assessed, her eyes squinting to see through the dirty gray haze.

"They sure could dance though," Taleeka added with an impressed nod.

"Indeed they could. At first glance, with those club feet, I would not have believed them to be graceful at all."

"And how about that singer?"

The Amarenian smirked at the recollection. "A truly lovely, very powerful voice."

"Yeah, but all that drool, I'm sure glad we weren't in those first two rows."

"Yes, those patrons had a truly immersive experience."

Taleeka abruptly halted and stared in amazement at her friend. "Did you just make a joke?! You never joke!"

A sly smile crossed Noorim's pale face. "Perhaps my friends are rubbing off on me."

Taleeka smiled and gave an approving nod before starting off again. "Nice!"

"And you give this theatre money?"

"Yep, I'm a patron. That's why I've got my own private balcony box. It helps keep me away from anything that might fly off the stage."

This time, Noorim stopped and smirked at Taleeka who studied the thinning traffic in the streets.

"I wonder where Gidaria is with the hackney?" Taleeka pondered aloud, ignoring her friend's amused expression. "She's normally never late."

Her friend, tackling her to the ground behind a parked hackney, answered her question, while a hail of slugs peppered the wall behind where they formerly stood. Taleeka immediately rolled, pulling her backpack off and retrieving her pistol. The thinning pre-Kan crowds screamed and scrambled all around them to get out of the line of fire.

"I count three of them," Noorim said, rolling into a crouch. "They have carbines."

Taleeka nodded, raised her Mark Seven's clear Etheria sighting device and replaced the current magazine with one containing tracker rounds. She waited for the next volley of projectiles to fly, before popping over the hood of the hackney and lining up one of her assailants in the small round disk of clear Calcite. She ducked back down without firing because of a fresh unexpected barrage of shots.

"They have us completely pinned down," Noorim said.

"What say we reduce their numbers," Taleeka said, pointing the barrel of her weapon straight up and pulling the trigger.

The bolt fired out of the pistol with a soft woosh and did an immediate right turn over the hackney. The Calcite in the tip of the projectile locked in on the mobster she had just sighted and streaked towards its predetermined target.

She couldn't see the effect, but by the startled cries of his companions, Taleeka knew the seeker round found its mark. Another round of shots rapidly followed the shocked outburst. The projectiles ricocheted wildly around them shattering windows and sending people running. An unexpected and unusual silence followed, accented only by the Zorian Guards' alarm whistles in the distance.

"Hello," came a familiar male voice. "It's safe to come out now."

The two friends exchanged curiously relieved looks before cautiously coming to their feet. Chen stood over the three dead assassins, who lay crumpled and bleeding in the street. The moment he saw Taleeka, a love-struck grin crossed his face.

"You were right," he said, holstering the two Mark Five pistols he commandeered two cycles prior, cross-draw style. "These do come in handy but nothing beats a good blade."

"Thanks, I owe you one," Taleeka said, just before Gidaria pulled up in front of them.

"Sorry I'm late, Tally," Gidaria said, when Noorim opened the back door. "Traffic was terrible for so late in the cycle. So, what did I miss?"

"You can repay me by having dinner with me tonight, Tally," Chen called out hopefully.

"I don't think that's a good idea," Taleeka said, starting to get into the back seat. "We gotta scoot. I don't want to have to explain to the guards why people are constantly trying to kill me lately. I suggest you do the same."

Taleeka got in, closed the door and glanced into the front seat at Gidaria with her pet lizard seated beside her.

"Giddy, get us out of here, quick!"

"You bet!" she said enthusiastically.

Gidaria opening the sunroof, caused her lizard to excitedly fidget.

"Bang bang, Brzo," she commanded.

The lizard jumped out of the opening in the roof, ran down the windshield, across the hood, ending up in a special collar Gidaria released. The hackney took off at a blinding speed and Gidaria steered the lizard toward the nearest wall, where he scrambled up ten feet vertically. The Gyronite panel on the bottom of the vehicle righted it and it sped away.

"The man seems to be enamored by you," Noorim said questioningly. "For a male he seems very aesthetically pleasing."

Taleeka chuckled. "Yeah, he's prettier than most women I know. He just doesn't do anything for me. He's been following me around like a lovesick puppy since we met. Right now, I'm more interested in why certain people are trying to kill me."

No one was surprised to find the central meeting hall of the Zorian Forum filled past capacity. The entire high council took their respective seats, as well as their various aides and scribes. The sovereigns of the great human houses, along with their seneschals and bodyguards, sat in private alcoves off to the side of the massive chamber. The rest of the available seating, usually vacant, was filled with various dignitaries and nobles.

The sentient who would be addressing the assemblage happened to be the reason for the packed house. Everyone wanted to see the newest addition to the Annigan, a race who called themselves the Etherions. Six cycles after the return of Konaleeta, this special gathering promised the official first contact with its mysterious residents.

The Na-Kab representative, Krak, also attended the standing room only gathering, watching and listening. He watched the bipedal Etherion seemingly float onto the round stage in the center of the amphitheater.

It stood just a little over five feet tall, covered head to toe in light blue robes, which only revealed a humanoid nose and mouth. It wore a wide brimmed conical hat on top of its head pulled down to the blindfold.

"Members of the high council," a deep male voice filled the room, even though its mouth didn't move. "Members of state, and honored guests. On behalf of my people, I thank you for granting me this audience so that we may better get to know one another."

Krak noted the flat, lifeless, monotone it spoke in, making the words seem hollow and disingenuous.

"As you can probably surmise, we did not choose to be here, and yet, here we are. We regret any difficulties that have arisen from our untimely arrival but know our intentions are peaceful. To demonstrate our benevolence, we offer assistance in your fledgling ventures into the world of Etheria crystals. My people have studied them for thousands of grands and we will freely share what we have learned.

"We do not know why we were brought here or for how long we will stay. While we are here, for as long as we are here, we look forward to a peaceful relationship based on mutual trust and cooperation.

"Now I'm sure you have many questions..."

Krak tuned out the barrage of queries and issues posed by the various races present. He noted the four Avion ambassadors remained oddly silent, but keenly observant of the whole proceedings.

He, however, felt certain these Etherions were the beings responsible for the disruption and partial destruction of their hive. Vengeance would be dispensed, but he would need to be discreet, so as not to offend their human allies. Admittedly a delicate predicament, but in the end the Na-Kab's fiery retribution would be consuming and final.

Valindra Valdur hated running late. The smartly dressed brunette, in her crisp white blouse and calf length blue skirt, cut a striking figure moving quickly through the halls of the Zorian Forum. The high council's meeting with the Etherions, some of which had been heated, went on longer than expected.

Since her cousin Joc''s ascension to the Valdurian throne thrust her into the position of family ambassador to Zor, she felt like she always had to play catch up. Dryden might be the Valdurian seat of power, but business of the empire took place in Zor. She now had also come to fully appreciate all the situations and personalities her cousin Joc' had to navigate. Like the meeting that she was tardy for.

Entering her outer office, her Picean assistant, Katulong, peered up from her desk and smiled.

"They're waiting for you."

Valindra nodded, rushing past the humanoid fish. "And I thought only heads of state were long winded. They've got nothing on the nobles."

She grabbed the door handle to her inner office, paused and took a deep breath to compose herself. Opening the door and stepping inside, she noted the room to be full, but the distinctive livestock smell greeted her first. The On'Dara reclined at the far end of the room with its four legs folded beneath it on the floor.

*It's going to take me forever to get that smell out of this office*, she thought closing the door behind her.

Shurta's pale, impressive frame filled one of the two chairs facing her desk. Next to her, in stark contrast, sat a woman in her early twenties with light chocolate brown skin, delicate features and short black hair. She and Taleeka Konrad, seated casually on the corner of her desk, traded side glances at each other. Everyone but Taleeka stood when she entered.

"Sorry I'm late," Valindra began, making her way over to her desk, "Thanks for coming on such short notice, but we've got a situation."

Valindra paused in front of the still seated Taleeka and gave her an annoyed glance. Realizing the awkwardness of the situation, Taleeka quickly got to her feet with an embarrassed contortion of her face.

"Sorry," she said sheepishly.

The Valdurian ambassador said nothing, but rounded her desk and sat down, while the other young woman suppressed an amused grin at Taleeka's predicament.

"Be seated," Valindra said officially.

Once everyone settled in, she continued. "For those of you who don't know me, I am Valindra Valdur, the new

Ambassador to Zor. This is my lead mechanic Shurta de Ovora," she said pointing to the hulking Amarenian.

She then pointed to the young woman seated next to Shurta. "This is Zerga de Woon from the Quartermaster's Office and standing next to her is Taleeka Konrad."

"*The* Taleeka Konrad?" Zerga asked, looking up at her.

"Yeah," Taleeka said, peering down with a flirtatious glance. "I guess the word gets around."

"I'll say," Zerga replied, mirroring Taleeka's stare, both of their gazes lingering.

Valindra cleared her throat and brought both women back to the conversation. She then gestured to the On'Dara who had remained standing. His short brown and white fur covered his equine lower body and head, while his pale humanoid torso appeared smooth and chiseled.

"And this is, well, On'Dara don't have names, this is a representative from the Horse Lords of the Taka-Vir. He is one of the reasons you are all here today."

The humans and the On'Dara traded nods before he focused his attention back on the ambassador.

"Thank you for your help in this matter, Madam Ambassador," he said.

"This is obviously going to be a multi-jurisdictional operation and time is of the essence," Valindra began. "Two cycles ago a Carrega Class transport ship was hijacked from the Mostas Air Station in Amarenia. A farmer found it this morning, floating a few feet off the ground in a field outside the town of Woon, in Otomoria."

"And now I sorta know why you're here," Taleeka said to Zerga with a playful smile.

"I'm just a farm girl at heart," Zerga said, blushing at Taleeka's attention.

The ambassador gave a dirty look before continuing. "The ship appears to be empty and undamaged but the evidence team is still on scene. Initially the report I got said that there was quite a bit of horse manure in the cargo bay. This is where I turn it over to the On'Daran representative."

The humanoid horse stood a full head taller than Shurta and he stepped forward extending his hands. "Early last moonless, three family units of our prize horses were stolen, about eighteen in all. Their guard, as well as his Abani herd dog were killed. These horses were breeders and we must have them back!"

"Breeders?" Zerga asked quizzically, looking around.

"The horses my people sell to the rest of the Annigan are all alchemically sterilized," the On'Dara explained patiently. "It is the only way my people's way of life can be guaranteed."

"Not to mention a nice little hold on the market," Taleeka said flippantly, which drew another exasperated glare from Valindra.

"If that was not bad enough, one of the fifteen mares taken was a Dronning Mare."

Taleeka and Shurta groaned at the same time prompting another questioning stare from Zerga.

The On'Dara's face went melancholy. "We are an all-male race. Once a grand luna, a special mare is born into one of the various herds that is capable of mating with our clan chief and producing an On'Dara."

So, whoever did this isn't just messing with your livelihood, they're playing around with your race's very existence," Taleeka noted direly.

"Exactly," the On'Dara confirmed. "One Dronning Mare can give birth to fifteen On'Dara in their lifetime. It is essential we get her back!"

"If these Dronning Mares are so precious," Zerga asked hesitantly, "what was she doing out on the plains with such minimal guard?"

"She was not yet old enough to leave her family for the chief's harem."

"Ambassador?" Zerga asked. "Permission to task an Ironmark and petition House Nur for EEtah support?"

Valindra shook her head. "We don't have time. This is an extremely fluid situation. You all are the team."

"And there was a witness to the theft," interjected the On'Dara.

The statement perked everyone up and all looked around with relieved smiles.

"A Cevot guard in the mountains close to where they were taken, saw the whole thing," the On'Dara continued.

The elation rapidly turned to concern and everyone looked over at Valindra.

"We gotta deal with spider people?" Shurta asked with uncertainty.

"I'm guessing that's why I'm part of this merry band," Taleeka said with a chuckle. "I've got something going on right now, but this is important. I'll make arrangements."

"You *have* dealt with the Cevots before," Valindra said. "At least that's what the reports say."

Taleeka gave a resigned sigh. "Yeah, I have. It was quite a while ago, though. I guess I better dig up that 'free pass' into their caves. I think I remember where I put it."

The On'Dara majestically lifted his head. "Do this for us and you all shall be awarded the honored title of, 'Karja Kaitsea!'"

"'Defender of the Herd,'" Taleeka translated. "My parents carry that title."

"Your parents are great friends of the On'Dara," the man-horse proclaimed proudly.

"Alrighty then," Taleeka said. "In short, we gotta find us some horses. I guess I'm headed for the Twilight Lands."

She then glanced down at Zerga who peered back with an impressed stare. "You wanna tag along?"

"Sure," Zerga said enthusiastically. "I've never been to the Twilight Lands and I've sure never seen a Cevot."

"That means I'm bound for Otomoria to see what the evidence team has come up with, if anything," Shurta said, when everyone came to their feet. "If the Goddess smiles upon us, our thieves, whomever they may be, didn't disable the tracking chip and we can trace their route to see where they went."

"The Kan's going to be starting soon," Taleeka announced. "Nobody's going anywhere until morning."

She turned to Shurta and Zerga. "What do you say, dinner at my place? We'll put our heads together."

At Taleeka's invitation, her two dinner guests caught a ride with her from the Zorian Forum. Gidaria dropped all three out front of Konrad House West, while she parked the hackney in the first-floor garage.

"No handle or lock," Shurta noted, while Taleeka fished around in her pocket for the key fob.

"Helps keep the riff raff away," Taleeka said.

She pointed the Etheria crystal at the door until she heard the tell-tale click and the Ukko Wood barrier swung open. The inviting sound of laughter and the savory smell of cooking food greeted them. Both of her guests gave Taleeka an inquisitive glance.

"Sounds like the gangs all here," Taleeka said, stepping across the threshold. "Not to worry. We can speak freely. I would trust any of the people here with my life."

The reassurance seemed to calm the Valdurian mechanic, all the while Zerga looked on in wonder. Taleeka pulled off her backpack just as the door closed behind them and hung it on a coat rack just to the left of the entrance. All could hear soft whimpering coming from the hanging bag.

"Oops, almost forgot to let the dog out," Taleeka said, removing her cudgel from its side holster.

Both women looked on in fascination when Taleeka touched the baton gently against the door jamb. A small shower of blue sparks erupted the moment the two wooden surfaces touched. They heard two happy barks and panting when Defari's essence entered the framework of the house. The joy of the canine spirit rushing around the structure felt palpable. By the cheery greeting from the other dinner guests, they were as glad for the return of Taleeka's faithful companion as the dog spirit was to be home.

"Defari belonged to my dad," Taleeka explained to the two awestruck visitors, "she lived in his long sword."

Without further clarification, Taleeka led her guests into the dining room where Nibira, Noorim and Barr-Ani enjoyed a pre-dinner cocktail with Folsom at the dinner table.

When Peshk heard Defari rushing through the walls, she poked her head out of the kitchen grinning broadly.

"Ah, Mz. Tally, you're just in time!" she said, before disappearing back to the stove.

Everyone around the table greeted their host warmly and Taleeka made the appropriate introductions. Taleeka seemed pleased to see that, as requested, her seneschal had set an additional two places at the table.

"Okay kids," she said, sitting down and pouring a glass of wine from the decanter in the middle of the table. "Looks like we've got a bunch of stolen horses suddenly thrust onto the docket, especially one horse in particular."

"What about the current threat to Barr-Ani and Folsom?" Noorim asked.

"I should only be gone a few cycles," Taleeka assured. "Besides, we've got to wait on the report on that crystal creature from our friends in the Landagar Group to even know what we're dealing with. Barr-Ani and Folsom can hold up here. Noorim, between you and Defari, I think you can protect them."

All nodded in agreement and Noorim looked up at the ceiling. "Did you hear that girl. We have a job."

A solitary bark caused all at the table to smile.

"So where are you going?" Nibira asked, after taking a sip of wine.

"Zerga and I are headed over to the Twilight Lands," Taleeka replied. "We've got a witness to question."

"And I have to say, you're a lot cuter than the Ironmark I'm usually stuck with on assignment." Zerga added, just before catching herself and blushing. "I mean, uhh…"

Nibira traded a knowing smile with Barr-Ani before addressing her friend. "Oh, so when you said stolen, you meant from the source."

"Yeah, and the On'Dara are understandably upset about it."

"I'll bet," the librarian concurred watching Peshk walk to the table carrying a steaming tray of food, "but you've got to ask yourself, where in the name of the Goddess do you hide a herd of stolen horses? I mean, before air travel it would have been easy, but now…"

"Hopefully, that's what I'll be able to find out," Shurta said, reaching for a serving spoon.

Krak stared through the dirty haze at the simple one-story dwelling on the edge of the Seven Sisters. The Zorian streets bustled with the business of the High Holy City all about him. Venders in stalls along the side of the road hocked their wares to the throng of passers-by, while carts and hackneys made their way in the congested street in front of him. All the while in the distance, the pervasive sound of renovative construction resonated through the poorest neighborhood of the metropolis.

"You are absolutely certain?"

The thin, nude, middle-aged man standing beside him meekly bowed his head. The entire bottom half of his face appeared both shriveled and melted. Withered flaps of flesh barely covered a mouth of blackened teeth.

"Yes, oh great Na-Kab," he replied through the loose skin of hideously burn-scared lips. "I saw them change to their true form when they returned."

"You have done well," Krak said, facing him, "and you will be rewarded."

Krak touched the man's right nipple with the palm of his hand and it briefly glowed orange. The man threw his head back and reeled in an exquisitely painful trance, accentuated by the smell of burning flesh. When Krak pulled his hand away the nipple had disappeared, melted into the burnt shape of the Na-Kab's long three fingered hand.

"Now, go," Krak ordered.

"Yes mighty Na-Kab, thank you mighty Na-Kab!" the man rapturously said, rushing off to show his brethren that he had been marked by a god.

Crossing the street proved no easy task due to the volume of traffic, but Krak eventually found himself in front of the one-room windowless building. Its shabby wooden design seemed like the logical choice when it came to renovation.

Ignoring the passing sentients, he stepped up to the door and gripped the handle. Just like before, the palm of his hand glowed and the iron latch began to smolder, the smoke joining the already dirty gray mist around him. Within moments, the metal went soft and the handle broke off in his hand. He tossed it to the ground and kicked open the door.

Krak bounded inside, reverting into his mantis form. He found the small room devoid of anything signifying habitation. Instead, two large blue-green crystals floated three feet off the floor in the center of the room. The oversized gems measured about a foot wide and four feet long with faceted ends. They hovered several feet apart and dozens of delicate tendrils of blue lightning connected them, crackling with energy which lit up the darkened room.

With the burst of the door flying open and the sudden flood of light, the blue lightning bolts surged between them and a torrent of PSI energy shot out towards the intrusion. When the bolts struck him, spreading across his body, Krak let out a high pitch squeal of pain.

The Na-Kab opened its mouth, unleashing a massive column of flame engulfing the two Etherions in magical fire and abruptly halting their lightning assault. With Krak's second blast, they began melting and the structure quickly ignited. The Na-Kab kept up his stream of flames until it reduced the Etherions to puddles on the floor and the building burned intensely.

Resuming his human appearance, he stepped back out the open door, not before noticing the individual melted pools joining together into one large blue-green puddle. The wet patch quickly slithered over to a crack in the floorboards and poured itself through the thin opening and out of sight.

A crowd now gathered but Krak decided to stick around to see if his victims would reform. He moved in front of the building next to the burning one and heard the shrill whistle of the Zorian Guards.

The Fire Division of the Zorian Guards were the only group allowed to drive ungoverned hackneys and one quickly threaded itself through the slow-moving traffic and lurched to a stop in front of the blazing building. This typical unit consisted of two Zorian Guards of the Fire Division. One to rescue any potential people trapped in the burning structure and the other to investigate the blaze. A member of the Air Workers Guild also happened to be part of the team. They would be the one to actually extinguish the fire. A

Clerria accompanied in case there happened to be any injuries

In this case, with the structure entirely engulfed, there appeared no need for rescue. The residents of neighboring buildings gathered together out front, expressing their concern about their property mere feet away from the flames.

With no one to save, the guards immediately began canvasing the crowd for witnesses, while a shaman of the Air Workers Guild calmly climbed out the back of the hackney and studied the fire.

Like almost all Annigan air shamans she was nude or skyclad as they referred to it. The light of the blaze glistened off her petite frame and golden-brown skin. She absentmindedly stroked the only item adorning her smooth, taut body, a long necklace of multi-colored, three-inch diameter Etheria disks stretching down to her navel. Two of the magical gems covered her diminutive breasts, while the third hid her bellybutton.

Touching the black gem covering her right breast, she extended her arms and fingers out at a forty-five-degree angle towards the burning building. For the briefest moment, a shimmering opaque field surrounded the engulfed structure. She then touched the light blue gem on her stomach and, with the other hand still extended, she pulled it back and closed her fingers in an elaborate flourish.

A giant gust of wind followed the gesture of her arm when the oxygen sucked out of the contained field and blew across the crowd. The flames immediately died and the young woman lowered her hands to her side.

"The field will remain for a deci," she said to the crowd of concerned neighbors. "This will ensure everything is properly extinguished."

She then returned to the hackney where the two guards had finished their interviews. As per usual in the Sisters, nobody saw nothing.

Krak stood watching the burnt-out hull of a building. He carefully scrutinized the charred remains for movement but saw none. *Where did the Etherions escape to?* he wondered. *No matter,* he finally decided. The vengeance of the hive had begun.

Noorim's dinner companions headed home. Taleeka and Zerga left for the Twilight Lands at the lifting of the Kan, where they would drop off the On'Daran representative at his respective clan, before interviewing the Cevots. Shurta would soon arrive at her closer destination, the agricultural island continent of Otomoria.

Noorim felt a twinge of guilt leaving Taleeka unguarded, but Tally's instructions to protect Barr-Ani and Folsom were just as explicit as her single word command to Defari, "Guard!"

Earlier this cycle, she accompanied the two psychics down to the waterfront, where they visited the caves of the Otick's Temple of the Golden Avatar. Ever since Barr-Ani introduced Folsom to the crab people's isolation shells, she became hooked. Their mental health break took a few deci and Noorim passed the time by running through her Kovos forms on the beach. Now, they were back at Konrad House West, awaiting Peshk to return from the market to begin the evening meal.

Defari's low growl interrupted Noorim's letter writing. Setting the pen on the desk, she looked warily around. When the two sensitives quickly entered the living room with worried looks on their faces, the Amarenian grew concerned.

"Defari senses danger," Barr-Ani said, nervously biting her lower lip.

"Do you feel anything?" Noorim asked.

Both shook their heads. Noorim stood and surveyed the room. The dog growl seemed to come from everywhere. Both Barr-Ani and Folsom jumped at a loud pounding on the front door and Defari began barking angrily.

"Get down to the escape pod," Noorim directed when the second round of pounding assaulted the door.

"What about you?" Folsom asked apprehensively.

"Do not worry about me, go!" Noorim said forcefully.

The two psychics briskly headed for the stairs. Noorim grimly reflected that if they had to use the escape craft, it would be the first time since Taleeka had it installed two grands ago.

The pod barely seated a very cramped four and could only hover, but it would be enough to get someone who couldn't fly an airship out of the building in case of fire or assault, like now. It operated with a single lever, which ejected the simple craft out fifty yards into space, away from the danger. There, it floated until the threat passed or help could arrive.

After the next set of even more vigorous pounding, there came a brief period of quiet where Noorim said a prayer of thanks to the Goddess for the Ukko Wood door. Her relief, however, became short lived, with the creaking and groaning of the door being pushed on with considerable force. Ukko Wood naturally repelled forceful blows, but slow, consistent pressure proved to be another matter. Within moments, the door tore away from the jamb with the sound of wood splintering and the three-inch-thick door crashed loudly to the floor of the foyer.

Another crystal patchwork creature loomed in the now open doorway, identical to the one Noorim encountered on the street four cycles ago. It stepped into the house, searching the room with its glowing blue eyes.

Defari continued barking furiously and pushed over the coat rack just as the creature stepped forward. It tripped on the obstruction and landed on the door which bounced the creature off onto the tile floor.

Emotionless, it slowly rose up on its knees and Noorim charged. Struggling with limited mobility, the creature lashed out at the attacking Amarenian. Obviously designed for strength and not speed or finesse, Noorim easily caught the assaulting limb and she drove up on the elbow with her other forearm. A loud crunching and snapping sound reverberated through the foyer when she broke the being's entire forearm off at the elbow.

The creature showed no sign of pain or any alarm. It swiftly pivoted, striking Noorim on the upper arm with a crude stiff-armed blow. The force of the strike propelled the much frailer woman against the wall, where she dropped the crystal arm on the floor in a pain filled daze.

Sliding down the wall, the wounded Amarenian watched the creature pick up its detached limb and place it back on the end of its broken elbow. The various crystals all around the break point began shifting and mending. Within moments the arm seemed completely functional again and Noorim expected it to attack her. Instead, the creature merely flexed its formerly detached hand and moved off.

Defari launched a barrage of knives and utensils at it when it entered the kitchen. Some became lodged in its frame, others merely bounced off. It had just finished removing several large kitchen knives from its torso when Defari hurled a large, heavy iron pan at it. The pot struck with a resounding clang, knocking the skull violently to the side, partially breaking it at the neck.

A small cloud of blue sparks emitted from the break point and the creature grabbed its head on both sides. It righted its head, showing no signs of pain or fatigue. As with the other wounds, the surrounding crystal shards simply closed in to fill any gaps and conduct repairs.

A noise suddenly came from down in the garage and the creature's now completely repaired head snapped in the direction of the sound. Once it identified the location, it made rapid, determined strides for the stairs.

Noorim, her injured arm hanging useless at her side, bolted towards the crystal being. She caught it just as it began descending with a flying kick to the back. The force of the blow lurched the creature forward. Losing its balance, it toppled down the stairs crashing and banging all the way. The Amarenian quickly leapt three stairs at a time right behind it. The monster landed face first and attempted to stand.

It reminded Noorim of the crime scene with the remains of a dead crystal creature four cycles prior. She remembered the hole shot through its abdomen and the expelled black crystal shards on the street.

Launching herself off the third stair from the bottom, she executed a powerful double stomp heel kick on the creature's lower back. The moment both her feet made contact, she heard a loud shattering sound and the creature froze in position.

Noorim stepped down off the dead thing's back, breathing heavily and nursing her wounded arm. Barr-Ani and Folsom climbed out of the escape pod peering meekly at the violent scene.

"Oh my!" came Peshk's voice from the top of the stairs.

Glancing up, Noorim saw her standing on the top landing, still holding her shopping basket full of the ingredients for dinner.

"Well," she said, going into seneschal mode. "We better get you to a Clerria to get that arm looked at and I've got to get someone out here to fix that front door."

"What about that?" Barr-Ani asked.

She pointed at the prone, immobile figure at the bottom of the stairs surrounded by a pile of black shards. Peshk quickly assessed the situation, her gill flaps fluttering.

"Move it out of the way," Peshk said, "and we'll let Tally decide when she gets back. Something tells me she's going to want to see this."

Nibira knew something must be wrong. Karta always had a healthy appetite and now he moved the food around on his plate, occasionally putting a small portion in his mouth.

"Well, I know it's not the meal, because this is one of your favorites," she said, reaching across the table and gently placing her hand on his arm. "What's wrong?"

The barrister shook his head all the while staring down at the plate before him. "I can't talk about it."

"Baby, I can't help if you won't tell me what's wrong."

Karta finally looked up. She could see his clean-cut, handsome features were clearly troubled.

"No, you don't understand. I *can't* talk about it. This has to do with a client."

"If they're causing you this much grief, drop them."

Karta sighed and put down his fork. "It's not that simple. This client represents a lot of money, steady money. This is not the kind of client you easily walk away from."

"This is about that woman and her renovation of the Sisters, isn't it?"

Karta nodded weakly. "I don't know why this one bothers me. I mean, I've represented some pretty shady characters in the past. Banavor's people, for just a recent example. I'm not sure why this one is getting under my skin. Technically, what she's doing in the Sisters is a good thing. Isn't feeding and employing the poor a good thing? I'm just not sure I approve of her motivation or methods."

"What's her motivation?" Nibira asked, sipping her wine.

Karta paused, his eyes shifting from side to side, searching for the proper response. "Right now, power, pure and simple. Eventually, money and lots of it. She wants to ultimately be the one pulling the strings in the Sisters. She's playing the long game. I'll give her that."

"Is what she's doing *really* such a bad thing? Let's face it, she's cleaning up the worst section of town.

"Which brings me to her methods."

"Which are?"

"People who she perceives are in the way, have a tendency to disappear."

"Yeah, but you said you've represented... What did you call them? 'Shady characters,' before. The inhabitants of the Seven Sisters are some pretty rough and tumble personalities. You don't get people like that to behave by saying please. What's different here?"

"I guess it's the fact that she's organizing a criminal empire and I'm helping her do it. No one's ever been able to bring criminal elements together in Zor. Any attempts in the past have always been quickly squelched."

"Don't tell me the infamous Karta Lushi, *barrister extraordinaire*, is growing a conscience?"

"Very funny," Karta said, rolling his eyes. "For the first time in my career, I'm not sure what to do."

"Don't look to me for advice. I never liked her in the first place but she sounds more like a corrupt, ruthless politician than a mobster. And the Goddess surely knows we've got plenty of them throughout the Annigan."

"That's kinda been my defense tactic, portraying her as an assertive social entrepreneur."

"Personally, I think you should relax. You're a good person. You'll do the right thing. Once you figure out what it is."

"Are you sure you don't want a career in law?" Karta said, feeling his mood lifting.

Nibira gave an exaggerated flutter of her eyelashes. "Nope, I'm perfectly happy with the librarian's life."

"You were right," Karta said, giving her an adoring stare. "Talking about it did make me feel better, even if I wasn't supposed to. You always find a way to make me feel better."

A licentious smile slowly crossed Nibira's face.

"Yeah? Well, I've got something in mind that I know will lift your mood, as well as something else. And, as prior experiences of this nature have shown me, it stimulates your appetite too."

"Really?" Karta said amusingly, watching Nibira push back her chair, slip under the table and begin crawling towards him.

Tantei leaned forward with her elbows resting on the interrogation table. Directly across from her, Chen Arador sat looking uncharacteristically nervous. Beside her, Talib curiously eyed the scene, while a scribe sat patiently at the end of the table, pen in hand.

"Okay," Tantei said, extending her hands. "You wanted to talk. We're listening."

Chen grinned knowingly at the attractive, bald investigator. "First, I'm going to need some assurances that after you hear what I have to say, you're not going to come after me."

"Being a bodyguard isn't against the law," Talib said confidently. "Unless you killed or stole for her."

"She ordered me to kill Tally Konrad and I refused."

"Well, that shows you've got some smarts and you've probably got nothing to worry about."

"Probably?" Chen asked skeptically.

Talib shrugged and Tantei gave a heavy, frustrated sigh.

"Look," she said, "you were the one that called for this little meeting. If you don't start talking pretty soon, my partner here is going to get bored and start playing with himself. Trust me, *nobody* wants to see that!"

Talib rolled his eyes and shook his head at the statement while Chen cracked a slight grin.

"Toward the end of the last quinte," Chen said, sliding forward in his chair. "Mazie attended a meeting with the leaders of the three Silent Partner cabals of the western Goyan Islands."

"Where did this meeting take place?" Talib asked. "We never heard of it and the Silent Partners boss' are kept under pretty constant surveillance."

"It was done remotely. Facilitated by someone called a Legate."

Talib furrowed his brow. "A what?"

"Suicide messenger, no witnesses," Tantei said, leaning back in her chair. "So that's how they're communicating with each other."

"From what I understand, she is very interested in mimicking Lord Hanara's model of rebuilding Makatooa for here in the Sisters."

"Wait a minute," Tantei asked suspiciously. "From what you understand? You weren't in the room?"

"No, I gathered this from her conversations and orders to Drugo."

"So, why roll over on your old boss?" Talib asked.

"I held her in much less esteem after she ordered me killed."

"That'll do it."

"Anything else?" Tantei probed.

"Isn't that enough?!" Chen's voice cracked in incredulity.

Tantei nodded in agreement. "Ten grands ago I would have said 'yes,' but not today. You just gave us some valuable information, but that's all it is, a starting point. Nothing you told us would stand up in front of an Imperial Judge. Her barrister will tear your story apart as hearsay and conjecture.

Chen slumped back in his chair with a dejected look. "So, you don't believe me?"

Tantei scoffed loudly. "Are you fucking kidding me. I believed all of it. But believing something and being able to prove it, are two entirely different animals. The judge won't even issue an arrest warrant with what you just told us, much less try him. And then we would have tipped our hand."

"You did the right thing, thank you," Talib reassured. "This is valuable information. We now know how the Silent Partners' leaders communicate and Mazie's plans. All of which we didn't know before. Now, we can start building a case that hopefully Karta Lushi won't be able to shred right from the get-go. The best part of all this is, they don't know we know."

Blustery winds blowing off the tops of the Os-Oni Mountains buffeted *The Vastus* from side to side. Gidaria deftly maneuvered the wheel of the airship with one hand, while petting Brzo in the seat next to her, all the while consulting the projected map of the terrain ahead. The fact that the effects of the Tannimore Winter did not extend this far east pleasantly surprised the pilot.

The captain's chair behind them sat empty. Taleeka and Zerga, the only two others in the airship, sat close, with bodies angled towards each other on the row of seats lining the inner hull.

"So why did you decide to be an investigator for the Quartermasters?" Taleeka asked softly.

"After graduating Zekoff's class, I considered the Zorian Guards, but I didn't want to be confined to any one city. I wanted to travel. I grew up on a farm, so my experience with anywhere outside of Otomoria was non-existent."

"Well, you just jumped into the whole traveling thing with both feet," Taleeka said with a playful nod. "Dealing with giant humanoid spiders is about as different as it gets from farm life."

This caused Zerga to laugh and place a lingering hand on Taleeka's shoulder. "Yeah, I still don't get to travel much. Most of my time is spent inventorying the holds of ships."

"How long have you been with the Quartermasters?"

A little over a grand now," she replied, letting her hand slowly trail down Taleeka's arm.

Taleeka felt a tingling sensation with Zerga's gentle touch and her heartrate quickened, but she thought it best to let the feeling pass, for now.

"Well then," Taleeka said, deliberately leaning in closer. "I guess you weren't one of those Quartermasters chasing my mom around the shallow sea."

"A little before my time," Zerga replied, also leaning forward so their foreheads almost touched. "She never got caught, did she?"

"She got nabbed a few times, but they couldn't make anything stick," Taleeka said, catching herself speaking in a surprisingly husky voice.

"Hey boss," Gidaria called back from the pilot's chair. "We're coming up on it now and it looks like we've got quite the reception down there."

Zerga shot Taleeka a concerned glance.

"Not unusual," Taleeka said, and patted her gently on the knee. "Cevots can be very territorial."

"When were you here last?" Zerga asked, following Taleeka forward toward the cockpit.

"It was during the Etheria War, so, it's been a while."

"Wait? You were in the Etheria War?"

"Yeah, I was pretty young," Taleeka said, looking out the side window. "My mom convinced the Cevots to fight against the invading mawls."

"That's pretty impressive," Zerga said, coming up beside her. "By the Goddess!"

Zerga peered out the window and clutched Taleeka's shoulder. Down below, a massive spider web connected several mountain peaks. Hundreds of Cevots and their spider workers scurried about on the web. The humanoid spiders followed under the craft pointing upward at it.

"Yep, just like last time," Taleeka said calmly, giving Zerga's hand a reassuring pat.

"We're actually going down there?"

"Well, not down *there*. We're gonna by-pass the welcoming committee." Taleeka pointed to a cave entrance in the side of the nearby mountain. "Gidaria, get us alongside that entrance."

"You mean the one with all the giant spiders going in and out of it?" the pilot asked nervously.

"That's the one. Drop us off, pull away from the mountain and wait till you see us in the cave mouth."

"I'm not sure going in there is any better than down on that web," Zerga said, looking frantically at the humanoid arachnids and their brood.

"You can always stay with the ship," Taleeka said, playfully bumping shoulders with her.

Zerga swallowed hard and peered over at a disturbingly calm Taleeka. "No, I accepted this assignment. I'm going to see it through."

"That's the spirit!" Taleeka said cheerfully, watching the cave mouth drawing closer. "Relax, there's a trinket in my pocket that can get us in there. Besides, I've got someone on the inside."

"The inside of *there*?!"

"Yep, just stick close to me."

For the briefest of moments, Zerga's deportment transformed from anxious to flirtatious.

"That's been my plan all along."

When the side hatch dropped, the pair could see a dozen Cevots and twice that number of their spider workers waiting for them in the large cavern. The humanoid spiders stared quizzically at them, while their workers swarmed all about the web laced walls and ceilings.

Taleeka couldn't help but notice Zerga felt both captivated and repelled by the Cevots' humanoid torso set atop a spider's body. She also found disconcerting the four eyes on their forehead above the two normal humanoid eyes.

Taleeka reached into her pocket, pulled out a palm sized object and held it in front of her for all to see. The token, given to her by the Cevot queen ten long grands ago, consisted of an intricate pattern of webbing within a circle of quarter inch thick silk.

"Greetings, mighty Cevots. We come in peace," Taleeka said, stepping out of the airship and into the cave. "I am Taleeka Konrad and this is my companion, Zerga. We wish to speak with your queen and the Strasta."

Two of the Cevots stepped up to the humans, inspected Taleeka's token and exchanged anxious glances.

"What is your business with our queen and our Strasta?" one asked in their high-pitched hissing language.

"Your Strasta is a friend of mine and my business with the queen is private."

The Cevot first appeared as if it would challenge her. It then took another look at the pass and changed its mind.

"Wait here," it said, before scurrying off down one of the connecting tunnels.

"What's a Strasta?" Zerga whispered, stepping up behind her so close that their bodies touched.

"Sort of a prophetess, she has almost as much pull around here as the queen." Taleeka said softly, leaning her head back so she could feel Zerga's breath on her ear.

"And you're friends with this prophetess?"

"She was our pilot for a while." The stunned silence made Taleeka smile. "It's a long story. Remind me to tell you over a drink."

"It's a date," Zerga purred sensuously in her ear.

Taleeka had no time to respond before the Cevot returned.

"Follow me," it said, before leading them down the tunnel it had appeared from. "Fortunately, the queen and Strasta were in consultation together and in the same location."

They walked down wide corridors in virtual darkness. Taleeka retrieved her Etheria spectacles and took Zerga's hand to guide her. Zerga eagerly took her hand and interlaced their fingers, which Taleeka noticed tingled with excitement. She could see the web laced corridors swarming with the large work spiders. She smiled at Zerga wriggling her nose at the sour musky smell accentuated by the distinctive odor of rotting flesh.

The receiving hall appeared just as Taleeka remembered it, with its hundred-foot-high ceiling covered in dangled webbing. Webs angled upward like stadium seating on three of the walls. Unlike her last visit, the stands were now empty.

All about, a dim luminescent orange glow lit the room. Taleeka took off her glasses and let go of Zerga's hand. On the far wall rested the queen's elevated web, where the Cevot Queen, Kumo and the royal scribe rested.

Taleeka watched Zerga out of the corner of her eye, staring around in wide-eyed wonder, especially at Kumo, who stood a full head taller than the rest of the Cevots. She also looked stouter, with pleasing human features and full pendulous breasts on her human torso.

"Oh great Cevot Queen," Taleeka began, loudly and clearly. "It is an honor to be in your presence once again. May we approach?"

Raising her hand, the queen silently waved them over. Once in front of the web throne, Kumo rushed down from the raised web platform and threw her arms around Taleeka.

"Little Tally!" she said, her naturally meek voice bubbling with excitement. "Look how you have grown!"

"It's great to see you too, Kumo. So, how's the life of a Strasta?"

"A bit embarrassing," she admitted in a whisper. "They virtually worship me."

"Good work if you can get it," Taleeka replied. "How's the queen's mood?"

"It's good for now, but that could change now that you're here."

"Yeah, it's never just a social call with me, is it?" Taleeka said, chuckling. "Well, hopefully this visit won't piss her off too much."

Kumo returned to the queen's side and the Cevot monarch stepped to the front of her platform.

"Taleeka Konrad, I too am happy to receive you once more. I see you made good use of the pass I gave you."

"It is one of my most prized possessions. You honor me, oh great Cevot Queen."

The queen's demeanor quickly went serious and the four eyes adorning her forehead blinked in unison. "So, what do we owe the pleasure of your visit?"

Taleeka took a deep breath and shot a quick glance at Zerga who still seemed enraptured by the whole experience.

"Oh, great Queen, I regret that this is not a leisure visit. Three lunas ago, a herd of horses were stolen from your allies, the On'Dara. We were told that one of your outer sentries witnessed it. We would like to question that sentry."

The queen gave an inquisitive look at her scribe.

"It is so recorded in the archives, oh queen," the scribe said authoritatively.

"Bring her here at once," the queen ordered and the Cevot, which had led them, took off.

"With your permission, great Queen," Taleeka said, "this is Zerga, she is a friend of mine and an investigator. I would ask that she be able to ask questions too."

"Investigator?" the queen asked quizzically, turning her attention to a very nervous Quartermaster.

"Um, uh, yes your majesty," Zerga stammered. "I track down tax cheats."

The Cevot queen tilted her head enquiringly and the eyes on her forehead blinked furiously. "What are taxes?"

The question went unanswered when the Cevot sentry entered the room. The guard quickly approached the monarch and bowed its head.

"You wished to see me, oh queen?"

"These sentients have questions for you," the queen said, pointing at the two humans. "You will answer them."

"Yes my queen," it said, spinning to face the two human females.

"You witnessed some horses being stolen from the On'Dara three lunas ago," Taleeka said. "Please tell us what you saw."

Taleeka and Zerga listened to the recounting of the incident told in a high-pitched deadpan voice from the humanoid arachnid.

"And you say there were only three of them?" Zerga confirmed.

"Yes," the Cevot replied. "A female and two males."

"Can you describe them," Taleeka asked.

The Cevot shook its head. "No, too far away. Besides, all humans look alike."

The innocent, subjective statement made both women smile.

"The female did have something on her lower back that glittered in the light," the Cevot added.

*Mazie*! Taleeka thought. *Well, at least now I know who. All I need to find out is where they are now, and why.*

"Tell me again about this, whatever it was they dropped on the horses," Zerga asked, stroking her chin.

"It was a glittery powder released from the airship. It made the horses tame enough that the two males could easily herd them into the ship."

The clarification caused Taleeka to perk up.

"Take us there!"

Many considered Tresnat de Warton, code name "The Dwarf," a driven man. He earned a reputation for pushing his team, the Landagar Group, as hard as he pushed himself. Standing exactly four-foot-eleven and three-quarter inches, one might be inclined to disregard him because of his size. That would be a colossal mistake.

One intense look from behind his goggle shaped glasses and even royalty was known to back down. As the one person responsible for the founding and growth of House Valdur's research and development unit, Tresnat insured that the once smallest of the great human houses rose to be one of the most predominant.

Shortly after the Etheria War, he had taken on a brilliant Gila Etheriat by the name of Da-Olman and production went through the roof. Two grands ago, Da-Olman came into possession of an Etheria bible of sorts. Since that time, there seemed to be no limits as to the uses of the various Etheria Crystals working in harmony with each other.

Tresnat coined the term "MagiTech" and it took off, along with the devises it facilitated. It seemed like everyone in the Goyan Islands clamored for any kind of Etheria gadget they could get their hands on.

A little under a cluster ago, he started getting disturbing reports which began as a trickle, but with the latest statement in his hand, had reached tsunami status.

He stared out the window of the shuttle between the securely segregated sections of Landagar Station and scowled at the dirty gray mist of the Tannimore Winter. The mist's arrival coincided with the time MagiTech devices began malfunctioning, sometimes with deadly results.

Tresnat hurriedly hopped on the shuttle for the short ride from the Intelligence Pod to the Weapons Development Division. Quickly stepping out onto the landing, he eyed the armed guard standing beside the doors beneath a large green dot. The color corresponded with the security level on everyone's identification badges authorizing entry.

His badge contained a solitary red dot, granting him access to all six of the stations' various pods. Moving briskly through the various halls, he made his way down to the third level where Da-Olman maintained a large, dedicated research lab. Without knocking, he placed his hand on the green Etheria pad next to the handle-less door and it opened.

He found the Gila Etheriat alone in his spacious lab. He had replaced his famous floor length duster jacket with a white lab coat. The Etheria automaton, which Taleeka Konrad delivered, lay completely disassembled on a large table beside him. He had laid out each of the hundreds of multi-colored pieces in their respective positions.

The Gila's scaley, blue-green skin glistened under the bright lighting and he didn't acknowledge his boss's arrival. Totally concentrating on the task at hand, his bulbous eyes moved independently of each other. One scanned the objects on the table to his right, while the other remained fixated on his mounted Larimar tablet to his other side. The rustling of papers in Tresnat's hands snapped the Gila from his occupational trance and he looked up with an enthusiastic grin.

"This thing is amazing!" he said grinning broadly. "I've been studying this Etheria Bible since I got it from Tally two grands ago and my progress was glacial. This thing comes along and now everything is starting to make sense. This, I'll call it an automaton, is nothing short of genius!

"Of course, they completely destroyed the Obsidian battery, but it was located in the lower back to attach it to this multi-piece Diamond Etheria spine. That spine connects the limbs and head, powering all these various Etheria parts, each designed to work in unison under the direction of an Obsidian brain."

Tresnat stood on his tiptoes to get a peek and Da-Olman chuckled at his predicament.

"You need a boost?"

Tresnat tossed the Gila an unamused look.

"Why don't you just tell a short joke?!"

Da-Olman didn't miss a beat. "You're so short that..."

His voice trailed off when he saw his director's irritated expression. Something had to be really amiss for Tresnat to become angry over the usual good-natured ribbing which went back and forth between them.

"It's happened again," Tresnat said grimly, waving the paper in his hand. "This time a bunch of people died."

"What in the name of the empire happened?!"

"A Zorian Guard's Mark Six went off by itself while still in his side holster. The rounds ricocheted off the street, killing him, his partner and sixteen bystanders."

"How?!" Da-Olman replied incredulously. "The Mark Six is a stable weapons platform. It's been standard issue for grands now!"

"The same way Etheria's been acting up for the past cluster. If you ask me, it has something to do with that damn mist out there."

Da-Olman paused at the mentioning of the Tannimore Winter. A look of dire recognition swept across his face.

"No, no, no," he pleaded, turning to his Larimar tablet.

After rapid tapping and swiping on its surface, he gazed back at Tresnat. "The last entry in this book is called Kniha Viartannia, or 'Book of the Return.' The thing that I first noticed was that it had been written in a different format than the rest of the book, more of a prose style, and I couldn't understand what they were talking about. But now, now it's starting to make sense."

The Gila silently traced a few lines with his fingertip and then stared back at Tresnat with a grim expression.

"I'm going to have to read it through thoroughly, but, from the little bit I did understand, I think I know what's going on... and it ain't good."

Tresnat's questioning gaze prompted him to explain.

"Like I said," Da-Olman continued, "I still have to read it in full, but I'm pretty sure the Etherions have the ability to enter into and take control of our MagiTech."

Many people once considered Yeni de Tuath to be a beautiful young woman, with her delicate golden features and a head full of wavy blonde hair. She, however, had always seen her attractiveness as a detriment. A serious young person, she hated how men only considered her beauty and few could even hold a decent conversation.

Even at the university, the shallowness of the students and faculty had prompted her to drop out in search of a path with deeper meaning. She found it in the worship of the ones responsible for saving the Goyan Islands by ensuring the fertility of the entirety of the Shallow Sea, the Na-Kab.

The small, yet passionately faithful group warmly received her. Her zeal for the new religion prompted her to immediately receive her first burn mark. They allowed her to choose which location to burn on her body and she chose the area which had caused her nothing but resentment in the past, her face. Now, with a long burn scar running across the bridge of her nose and extending down her left cheek, she no longer worried about only being valued for just her looks.

Her parents hated what she had done and disowned her immediately upon seeing the abhorrent mark. Yeni didn't care, her new family welcomed her with open arms, giving her a place to stay and utilizing her gifted skills at operating MagiTech devices. When her family thought she had been college bound they bought her one of the newest Larimar tablets and a library of obsidian nodules crammed with information. They were Yeni's most prized possessions and she never went anywhere without her tablet.

The streets of Zor were alive with morning traffic. Sentients of all types, mostly human and Picean, rapidly passed her on their way to their respective occupations. She travelled to a small plaza in the Shimol Plat that the priest Kahin had designated as this cycle's location of worship. Because their services involved fire and attracted attention, the location changed with each cycle. There, they would proselytize to anyone who would listen and Kahin would put on his enflamed demonstrations until the city guards ran them off.

Yeni felt especially excited today, because they would be in the presence of one of the very ones they worshiped. She could scarcely believe her good fortune that one of the Na-Kab now walked amongst them, assisting in their holy crusade of vengeance. The singular hive which had facilitated their very way of life came under attack. The defilers must be punished and this morning she would finally be able to help.

She got off to a late start that cycle and, by the time she arrived, Kahin had already begun administering the morning nourishment. As promised, Krak the Na-Kab made his appearance to bless the meal.

Yeni quickly fell on her knees with the other dozen devotees. She removed her messenger bag and set it beside her, without taking her eyes off the priest holding the loaf of bread over his head standing in front of Krak. Everyone became so enraptured by the Na-Kab's blessing, no one noticed the small stream of blue sparkles rising from a crack in the plaza's cobblestones and slip rapidly through the bottom of Yeni's bag.

"We offer thanks to you, oh great Na-Kab," Kahin proclaimed loudly. "For this bounty which will sustain us, so that we may serve you and do your will."

Krak sternly nodded his approval and Kahin spun to face his brood. Stepping in front of the first kneeling parishioner, he broke off a hunk of bread and handed it to the naked man with burn scars across his chest.

"The light of the Na-Kab," he said, before moving on to the next one and repeating the ritual.

When all had eaten, they arose and Kahin called Yeni over to where he and Krak stood.

"You said you had a possible way to easily identify the defilers?" Kahin asked her.

"Yes, your reverence and mighty Na-Kab," she said, nervously nodding at each.

"Show us," Krak ordered curtly.

"Yes, mighty Na-Kab," she stammered, opening her shoulder bag and removing her Larimar screen.

She fished around in the pocket of her pants, retrieved a small black nodule and attached it into the channel running along the tablet's top edge. When nothing happened, she cocked her head with a quizzical look.

"I know I charged it this morning," she said, surprisingly.

Both Na-Kab and priest stared impatiently at the blank screen until they heard a loud pop come from the device.

Immediately following the noise, rivulets of blue lightning streamed out both sides of the tablet.

The bolts travelled up both Yeni's arms and into her body. The moment the blue energy entered her torso, she began violently convulsing. She opened her mouth to scream but only blue smoke billowed out, contrasting, then mixing with the dirty mist of the Tannimore Winter.

With a lightning-fast flick of his hand, Krak used his mantis reflexes to knock the Etheria device to the ground. The tablet clattered to the pavement, but the lightning persisted, convulsing through her body and the blue smoke now poured from her nose, eyes and ears.

The Na-Kab acolytes began panicking and screaming when Yenni levitated off the ground, seemingly suspended by the magical bolts of energy. When the young woman's eyes finally popped out of their sockets, several of the worshipers broke and ran through the growing crowd of repulsed onlookers.

Krak took a step forward with an angry bellow and opened his mouth wide, unleashing a torrent of flame at the possessed object. The crowd jumped back in surprise with several more screams following.

The glamoured Na-Kab kept up his assault until he reduced the Larimar into a molten pool. The lightning finally halted and Yeni dropped to the ground, her various orifices still smoldering.

Everyone gasped in shock when the milky white pool of liquid Etheria moved on its own, flowing between the cracks in the street and disappearing from view.

Krak realized he must have blown his cover, but the time had probably arrived to start working with the human authorities. He also now confirmed that the answer to the destruction of the Etherions would be holy fire.

Taleeka listened to the ringing of the Grand Turine in the Zorian harbor, indicating the end of morning, all the while brooding over the lethargic traffic they were stuck in. Zerga sat beside her in the back of the hackney, examining the white glittery powder in the vile she held up to the light.

"Are you sure this guy, Hemi, hem… is going to be able to identify this? There's not much left of it."

"If anyone can, it's this guy," Taleeka proclaimed. "Hemicar, alchemist to the criminal underworld. Everyone jokes he's got his own stocks in Judgment Square. I'm kinda surprised you haven't heard of him."

Zerga shook her head. "Like I said before, I'm a farm girl new on the job, who spends most of her cycles inventorying ship's holds and cargo bays. This is my first field assignment where I'm actually, you know, in the field."

"Is that why you're tagging along?"

"Well, you did say stick close," Zerga replied provocatively.

Taleeka gave a satisfied grin. "So I did."

"I mean especially when I saw what happened at your place last Kan."

Taleeka nodded. "One heck of a homecoming, I gotta admit. Something's out to get my two friends. That's why they're staying with me."

"Still, that thing got in anyways."

"Noorim and Defari took care of things like I knew they would and I should have a new door up by the end of the cycle. I'll have to get some extra perimeter security installed. As for that thing, we'll hold onto it until I find out what we're dealing with."

Sensing no movement, Taleeka glanced back up at her driver. "Gidaria, why are we stopped?"

"We just hit the Kampo Plat Tally. The university's in session. The traffics always like this around here and the mist isn't making it any easier." She reached over and patted Brzo on the head. "I can always get us there faster."

"That's okay," Taleeka said, sighing in frustration and plopping back in her seat.

Zerga gently placed a hand on Taleeka's knee and smiled reassuringly. Taleeka took a deep breath and smiled back before patting her hand.

When they finally crept through the university traffic, Gidaria pulled up in front of a nondescript, free-standing three-story building.

"Well, we finally made it," Gidaria said, getting out and opening the rear doors. "I'm going to park around the side and take Brzo for a walk."

"Alright, let's go see what an alchemist has to say about this stuff," Taleeka said, leading Zerga into the narrow foyer.

Off to their right, an open door led to a garment maker. From inside came the sounds of looms shuffling and the tapping of sewing machine pedals. The second story's lone closed door belonged to a jeweler. Taleeka guessed it would be locked for security purposes. They discovered the only third story door also closed. Taleeka reached for the handle.

"No knocking?" Zerga asked playfully.

Taleeka returned an amused grin. "If it's locked, we'll have to knock. Let me handle this, he doesn't know you."

"I'll just keep sticking close," Zerga said with an amorous tilt of the head.

Taleeka smiled suggestively. "Here goes."

The handle easily turned and they heard the latch click.

"What do you know," Taleeka said, opening the door.

The room measured thirty-foot square with rows of windows on the two adjoining walls. Worktables covered with jars and lab equipment lined all of the walls and ran down the center of the room. A man of average height, bald with a bushy black beard, stood at the middle table peering through an optical device into a shallow bowl. The knee length white lab coat he wore brightly contrasted against his dark brown skin. A young assistant in his twenties stood next to him jotting down notes as the alchemist dictated them. Both looked up when the women entered.

"Tally Konrad!" he said, his face lighting up. "It's been over a grand since I've seen you. How are your folks?"

"Loving retirement," Taleeka replied, hugging the slightly larger man.

"What, you mean they *don't* miss being shot at and all that other dangerous stuff?" he teased upon releasing her from his embrace.

"Not a bit," Taleeka replied.

"So, what brings you by?"

Taleeka held her hand out and Zerga handed her the vial.

"This is Zerga, she's from the Quartermaster's Office. I'm helping them out with a case. We've got this powder I need some information about."

Taleeka handed the container to Hemicar who held it up at face level and carefully examined it.

"I'm pretty sure I know exactly what this is," he said, pouring some on the table, "but I believe in being thorough."

Removing a test tube filled with a clear liquid from a nearby rack, he pulled off the stopper and let a drop fall onto the powder. The moment it hit the pile it fizzled and smoked.

"Just like I thought," he said triumphantly.

"You know something about this?" Taleeka asked, watching the effervesce subside.

"I know everything about it. I made it."

Both women shared a surprised look, then stared back at Hemicar.

"This is a weakened, powdered version of a horse tranquilizer I make," the alchemist said authoritatively. "It's normally a liquid, but I got paid quite a bit to alter it."

Taleeka's eyes narrowed. "Paid by who?"

"Come on Tally," Hemicar pleaded. "You know I can't give out client's names. Besides, they didn't give me one."

Taleeka gave an exaggerated sigh. "Look Hemicar, normally I would never ask you to reveal anything about your clients. But like I said, I'm working on a case with the Quartermasters. Now, you gotta ask yourself, which would be better, answering my questions and having me in your debt or Zerga arresting you for obstructing an investigation?"

Hemicar glanced quickly over at Zerga, who remained silent and then back to Taleeka.

"I told you; he didn't give a name."

"A description then."

"About six cycles ago, this guy comes in waving these gold notes around and says he's got a rush job for two casks of the compound. He was about your height with a wispy brown beard and wild eyes."

The name Drugo flashed through Taleeka's mind and she grimly nodded her head. There now could be no doubt, Mazie was behind this. Proving it to an Imperial Judge, however, was another matter, but that didn't concern her.

"Okay, thanks Hemicar, I owe you one," Taleeka said, before heading for the door.

"You know, given who your mom was, I'm kinda surprised to see you working *with* the Quartermasters," Hemicar said, watching Taleeka open the door.

"That was a lifetime ago. Besides, this is important."

Once out in the hall Zerga grinned villainously.

"Tally, I don't have arrest powers. I just…"

Yeah, yeah, I know," Taleeka playfully cut her off. "You just inventory ships' holds. He doesn't know that!"

A look of recognition, then amazed astonishment, flushed across the young Quartermaster's face.

"That's awesome," she said, with an impressed nod.

Shula, Queen of the Bailian Empire, sat back on her throne and watched the last of her official court file out of the narrow receiving hall. The moon would set soon and it had been a long luna. Much had changed in the Twilight Lands since the end of the Etheria War. It amazed her how much her workload substantially increased.

Her capital city, Immor-Onn, the Shining Jewel of the East, had grown rapidly with the municipal duties following suit. They formed an official defense militia protecting the western Twilight Lands. In the Os'Tor Forest, the huntsmen now banded together into a ranger force to protect the various hamlets, also growing quickly. After mutual defense treaties were signed with the Oases of the Dark Waste and the On'Dara of the Plains of Taka-Vir, Shula felt confident they could meet any future invasion with enough force to repel, or hopefully discourage it in the first place.

She stood and with a contented sigh, smoothed the front of her floor length gown. Lifting the delicate diamond adorned crown from her head, she handed it to her assistant and flattened any blonde hairs the crown had tussled.

"I think we're done for the luna," she said wearily. "You are all dismissed."

Aide, scribe, as well as Tam'Eez bowed their heads and followed the Royal Court out the doors. Shula took a moment and looked around her receiving hall with a satisfied smile. Despite all the work, things in the Bailian Empire were going well.

"You appear well, my queen," a familiar female voice rang out behind her.

Recognizing it, she froze and her eyes went wide in amazement. She spun and gasped with her hand across her mouth. Kai stood to the side of the throne's riser, looking much like she had when the Bailian queen last saw her.

"My little savior!" she squealed in delight. "You've come back!"

Opening her arms, Shula took a step towards her former spymaster only to have Kai raise her lone arm, stopping her.

"Do not approach, my queen. I am not as I seem. I am death incarnate. Any mortal who touches me will die."

Realizing the dire tone, Shula halted abruptly.

"What, what do you mean 'death incarnate?'"

"I have assumed this form so as not to distress you. I know longer look this way. I am Satya."

"I don't know what that means."

"Long ago, just before I lost my arm, I made a bargain with Boran, Judge of the Dead. Upon my demise, my soul would be at the beck and call of the Gods of Death, their instrument of judgement and vengeance, a Satya."

"Why in the name of the Goddess would you do that?"

Kai gave a sad smile. "It doesn't matter. I have returned to the Corporeal Reach in the service of Orad. Her children were slain and I am on my way to the Land of Mists to perform a death watch. I could not pass you by without stopping to say hello and tell you how much I miss you."

"I miss you too little savior, as well as your council and your friendship."

Kai nodded and looked away. "And now I must go. She comes as the wind and takes whom she wishes. Her name is Orad and she is death."

Kai looked once more back at her queen. "Today, with her children gone, I am her instrument of retribution."

Tears welled up in Shula's eyes watching Kai move away. "Please, let me see your true form."

Kai halted and faced Shula once more, shaking her head. "My form would be most disturbing to mortals. Please remember me as I was, not what I have become."

Shula, now openly weeping, managed to nod her head.

"Farewell my queen, I shall never forget you."

"You sure you want to put yourself through this?" Taleeka asked over her shoulder to Zerga, walking right behind her.

The smitten Quartermaster chuckled and placed a gentle hand on her shoulder. "Are you kidding? I wouldn't miss this for all the cows on Parin's Farm!"

Taleeka, unsure of the reference, gave a quick bewildered look before returning to her jovial demeanor.

"Okay, suit yourself."

Keeping her eyes locked on Zerga's, Taleeka knocked strictly as a formality and opened the door without invitation. Inside, Tantei and her partner Talib sat across from each other around the oblong conference table. Shurta sat directly beside the investigators, looking extremely uncomfortable squeezing her ample frame into the decidedly inadequate chair. Vanir, who sat at the head of the table took a swig off his flask and grinned at the Amarenian's predicament.

"They designed these chairs so you can't get too comfortable," he explained. "Wouldn't look good having people dozing off during a lengthy meeting."

A large Larimar screen, on the wall behind the head investigator, displayed Da-Olman's rendering of the disassembled automaton.

"Hey, the gang's all here!" Taleeka greeted cheerfully, leading Zerga into the room. "And I see the renderings from Landagar made it, good."

Pulling off her backpack, she headed for an empty seat when she noticed everyone staring at her companion.

"Oh, sorry," she said, sitting and indicating the chair next to her for Zerga. "This is Zerga; she's out of the Quartermasters office. We're working a case that may cross over to some of yours."

Everyone relaxed at the explanation and Vanir jerked a thumb over his shoulder at the screen behind him.

"Okay Tally," he said, "you've been talking with the MagiTech folks over at Landagar. What in the name of the gods is that thing?"

"The Landagar lab is calling it an 'automaton.' It's made up entirely of interlocking Etheria crystals. Everything is connected by that diamond spine framework. The spine itself holds an obsidian battery at the base and a small obsidian brain at the other end in the skull."

"Could they get anything out of the brain?" Talib asked, staring at the screen.

"Nope," Taleeka replied, shaking her head, "but they're still working on it."

"Well, you've covered how it's made but not what it's for," Tantei said, running her hand across her bald head.

Taleeka scoffed and peered over at the investigator. "Well, given its past actions, I'd say, nothing good. It appears to be able to follow simple commands built into its brain. It's like a highly advanced autonomous machine, hence the name."

"Yeah, but who gave it the initial orders?" Tantei asked.

"We'll probably have to get into the thing's brain to answer that question."

"I hope there was only one of them," Talib said. "According to the patrol guard who shot it, that thing was freakishly strong."

Taleeka and Zerga exchanged nervous glances before Taleeka cleared her throat.

"Uh, afraid I've got a bit of bad news on that front," she paused for everyone's attention. "There's definitely more than one."

The news caused all to sit forward in their seats with concerned expressions.

"How many more?" Talib asked anxiously.

"I don't know, but there's definitely more than one. I've got another on ice over at my place. It actually pushed in my front door to get to my friend, Folsom. It happened when Zerga and I were meeting with the Cevots over in the Twilight Lands."

"Anybody hurt?" Vanir asked, before taking another hit off his flask.

"Nope, my people took care of it. Made a bit of a mess though."

"At least we've got another specimen to study and compare," Vanir offered, attempting optimism. "Looks like all we can do is be vigilant. I'll get with Gasata over in patrol."

"I sure wish we knew how to spot them," Talib said frustratingly.

"You know," Taleeka said, playing with a ringlet of hair while contemplating. "Landagar might not be able to get into that brain, but I think I may know someone who can."

"Let's run with that," Vanir encouraged, then took another drink.

"Speaking of Cevots and Twilight Lands," Shurta said, shifting uneasily in her chair. "What if anything did you find out?"

"According to the witness, it was a three-person operation. Two males and one female with, get this, something shiny on her lower back."

"Hey!" Talib said in recognition, while Tantei lowered her head and exhaled, rubbing her temples.

Taleeka then reached into her pack, pulled out the half-filled vile of powdered horse tranquilizer and set it on the table. "They used this to pacify the horses so they could get them in your stolen transport ship. That's why they only needed three of them."

"Exactly what is it?" Shurta asked, picking up the bottle and examining it.

"It's weakened and powdered horse tranquilizer. I had it checked out. Hemicar said he made it. He sold two casks of it to a guy that looked amazingly like Drugo."

"That means Mazie is behind your whole horse rustling, smuggling thing," Talib said innocently.

Tantei shot her partner a weary look. "Tay, there ain't one swinging dick on this whole force that would be surprised if Mazie were behind things. My big question is why?"

Taleeka shrugged. "Maybe she wants to start breeding horses."

Shurta huffed. "Yeah, but she stole them using a Valdurian airship. That makes it *my* business."

"Did you find anything with the evidence team," Zerga finally felt comfortable enough to ask.

"Not much besides a bunch of horse poop. One big lucky break though, the hijackers neglected to disable the tracking chip." Shurta reached over and touched the screen of the Larimar tablet in front of her.

The screen on the wall now displayed a map of The Twilight Lands, Amarenia and the Goyan Islands. Connecting the continents, a red line traced the route.

"We may not know their exact destination, but we sure know the stolen vessel's path. This gives us a place to start."

"It sure does," Taleeka agreed, a bit of hope creeping into her voice. "Why don't we start at each end of the route and work our way towards each other."

"I like it!"

"Alright, sounds like a plan," Taleeka agreed. "You wanna start at the far end where they were taken? It's closer to your native land."

"Actually, I was born in the Goyan Islands. It was my mother's native land, but I take your meaning and sure."

"Zerga and I will start where the ship was found and work backwards."

Vanir took another jolt of whiskey, then recapped the flask. "We all know what we gotta do, let's get to it."

"Not to worry, Vanir," Taleeka said, coming to her feet. "I'll get my people working on that automaton's brain."

"Thanks, Tally" he said, watching the people file out of the conference room. "Hey Tally, can I have a word?"

Taleeka gave a curious look, then sat back down. "Sure, what's up?"

The head of the Investigations Division of the Zorian Guards leaned forward and his tone grew guarded.

"You still own controlling interest in the Dokana Pub?"

"My family is the bank, if that's what you're asking?"

'Well, I was wondering if you had any pull there?"

"Yeah, I personally know the owner and chef."

"Um, well, I was kinda wondering if you could put in a good word for me there?" Vanir then started to blush. "I was kinda hoping to take someone there and I wanted it to be special."

Taleeka sat back with a mischievous grin. "You mean like a date?"

"Yeah, I guess. I mean, I don't want anything for free, or anything like that! But if they could make things nice for us, it sure would leave a good impression."

"My friend, I can fix you right up!" Taleeka said, slapping him playfully on the shoulder. "My family has a private alcove there. I'll make sure they've got it all nice for you and you get the royal treatment."

"Really?!"

"Sure, that's what friends are for."

"Oh, and Tally."

"Yeah?"

"I'd appreciate you keeping this to yourself for the time being."

"Discretion is my middle name."

Vanir sighed and a look of relief flooded his face. "Thanks, I owe you one."

Both got up together and promptly exited the room. Vanir took off for his next appointment and Taleeka stepped up to a waiting Zerga who held a questioning look.

"Okay, let's get *The Vastus* ready to fly," Taleeka said, absentmindedly reaching out to touch Zerga. "Looks like we're starting back in your old stomping grounds."

Zerga gave a quick huff. "Stomping is right. Hey, what was that all about back there?"

The impish grin returned to Taleeka's face and she let her hand trail slowly down Zerga's arm.

"Just doing my part in getting two people together."

Zerga's smile immediately mimicked Taleeka's and she blushed slightly. "Oooh, I like the sound of that. Got anyone else in mind?"

Proceeding cautiously down the stairs to the garage level of Konrad House West, Barr-Ani anxiously eyed the prone automaton laying off to the side of the room, just where they left it.

"Are you sure this is what Tally wants?" Folsom nervously asked, following the Bailian and eyeing the creature which recently tried to kill her.

"I just spoke with her," Barr-Ani replied gripping the handrail, not looking back. "Her, and what I think might be her new love interest, are following some sort of trail left by that stolen airship. The Landagar people weren't able to discover anything and we're the only ones that can check out *this* thing."

"Are you sure Tally realizes her feelings about this 'love interest'?"

"Oh, they both know, the attraction between them is quite strong," Barr-Ani replied, reaching the bottom of the stairs. "It may just take a little while for both of them to acknowledge it."

"I sure hope so," Folsom said, joining her on the cool of the garage floor. "I can sense Tally's unhappiness at her recent break-up. Even if it was a long-distance relationship and both could see it coming. These things are never easy."

"Romance, break-ups and the messiness of sex makes me feel fortunate that my order avoids such things."

Folsom chuckled. "It's enough you can feel it in others, you sure don't need it for yourself."

"Precisely," Barr-Ani agreed, coming to a halt over the lifeless creature.

"Well, there it is," Folsom acknowledged hesitantly. "How should we do this?"

Barr-Ani put her hands on her hips and considered the task ahead when Brzo came bounding up to them followed by Gidaria.

"Hey kiddos, what's going on?" the driver greeted.

"We were just trying to figure out how to get inside this thing," Barr-Ani replied, not taking her eyes off the automaton.

Brzo crept up to the motionless figure, ran its long tongue over its chest, then looked up at Gidaria with a puzzled expression. The driver smiled at her pet's reaction, then turned her attention to the two psychics.

"Have either of you ever really worked with tools?"

They both answered, "no," and Gidaria shook her head.

"Okay you two, out of the way. Exactly what part do you have to get into?"

"The head," Barr-Ani replied. "Tally says there's a small Obsidian brain in there."

Stepping over to a workbench against the wall next to her hackney, she selected two prybars, a medium and small one. She then knelt down by the automaton's head.

Looks like there's a seam right here," she said, feeling around the top of the cranium. "Okay, let's see what we've got."

Using the medium prybar, she slipped one of the tapered edges into the seam and applied leverage. The top of the skull popped off with a snapping sound, revealing an intricate network of small, interconnected Etheria crystals of various shapes.

"It's pretty tight in there," Gidaria noted. "Looks like we've got another panel here on the back of the skull."

After another ratcheting motion, the rear plate of the automaton's head came off in Gidaria's hands with a click. They could now clearly see the top of the spine, composed of hundreds of small, interconnected Etheria diamonds. A tiny black cylinder, connected at the top of the spine, linked the eyes and ears.

"That looks like what Tally described," Barr-Ani said, "but what's that around it?"

She pointed at a blue sheath with red striations, open at both ends.

"Looks like some sort of shielding," Gidaria said. "Let's see how easy it comes loose."

She set down the medium sized tool and picked up the smaller one. Deftly manipulating the narrow, six-inch-long implement, she popped the cylinder loose from the tip of the spine and gently pulled it away from the thin diamond ribbons leading to the eyes and ears.

"And here we are," Gidaria proclaimed, holding the detached part aloft.

"Thanks, Gidaria!" both chimed happily.

"Anytime," she nonchalantly replied, handing the part to the Bailian.

Folsom and Barr-Ani both stared anxiously at the Etheria device knowing what they must do. Folsom stepped up close and Barr-Ani held the tube vertically while Folsom cupped her hands directly below it. Barr-Ani placed her forefinger into the opening and pushed at the sheathed black cylinder. It dropped into Folsom's waiting hands. Without delay, Barr-Ani discarded the sleeve and placed her hands on top of Folsom's with the Etheria brain between them.

Closing their eyes, the two psychics concentrated in unison. Both immediately opened their eyes and stared at each other with an expression of dread on their faces.

"So, it wasn't just after you," Barr-Ani stammered. "It wanted to kill me too."

"And any other sensitive out there," Folsom added. "They know we can spot them because they give off no emotions or feelings!"

"So, you really can fly this thing," Zerga said, taking her eyes off the Goyan countryside passing several hundred feet below them and gazing adoringly at Taleeka.

"Yeah, every now and then I like to give Gidaria some time off from carting me around," Taleeka said, peering out her side window. "Especially if there might be trouble. I don't want to lose her. Good drivers and pilots, like her, are hard to find."

"I bet, especially being able to run the sides of buildings."

"It does come in handy if you're trying to beat the traffic."

"I'm thinking the patrol guards aren't wild about it."

Taleeka smiled at the thought. "I try not to make it a regular thing. If they see me doing it, most know it's for a good reason."

"Still, it's kinda hard to get busy in the back seat if you're hauling ass along the side of a building," Zerga probed suggestively.

This prompted a sarcastic chortle from Taleeka. "Believe me, if I'm involved in a high-speed encounter, sex is the last thing I'm thinking about. Not that I've had any opportunity to even think about it, of late."

"And that, is an absolute crime," Zerga bemoaned amorously, quickly looking away out her side window.

Taleeka blushed and considered a flirtatious response, when Zerga perked up and pointed towards the ground on her side of the craft, where she saw movement in an expanse of trees and scrub separating two large clearings.

"Eh, thought I had something," Zerga said disappointingly. "It's just a small herd of deer."

Taleeka looked and shook her head in startled disbelief. Down below them, in the adjacent clearing an identical herd of deer ran in the same direction.

"Hey, check it out!" Zerga said, her attention torn between the two identical herds.

Both cried out in surprise when the herd on Zerga's side performed a sudden right turn, as did the deer below Taleeka, just before they disappeared into thin air.

"Did you see that?!" Taleeka stammered in astonishment.

"I sure did! What's going on down there?"

"I don't know," Taleeka said, banking *The Vastus* back around, "but we're not going to get any answers from up here. I'm going to put her down and we'll check it out from the ground."

Da-Olman hadn't slept much in the three cycles since he deduced the dangerous vulnerability in the MagiTech which society had come to rely on. The door to his lab remained closed with a marine guard stationed just outside. Lab assistants scurried in and out at all times during the cycle, while the Gila Etheriat worked feverishly at a solution. Finally, on the third cycle, a glimmer of hope emerged.

He sent an assistant to retrieve Tresnat, calling the short, slightly mercurial head of the Landagar Group out of a budget meeting with the administrators of Landagar Station. Though appearing irritated, Tresnat welcomed the reprieve from the tedious, yet necessary, conference.

When he reached the lab, he found Da-Olman seated at his worktable, shoulders slumped, staring off into space with weary eyes. The stagnant air throughout the room contained the sour smell of Gila body odor and stale tea. On the table before him, nestled amongst the pages of handwritten notes and delicate instruments, lay a one-inch square, multicolored crystal wafer.

"You've got something?" Tresnat asked expectantly, reeling from the stench upon entering.

The exhausted Etheriat silently nodded and pointed at the Etheria chip.

"I know you're tired," Tresnat said, pulling a stool over. "Brief me on this, then you can get some rest."

Da-Olman nodded again, picked up his latest invention and handed it to Tresnat.

"This is a triple Etheria compound."

He pointed to the milky blue center of the wafer.

"At its core is a Blue Opal, for its warding properties."

He ran his finger across a yellowish-brown strip along the top edge. "Here we've got Xenoti for removing parasites and poisons."

The Gila managed a weak smile and pointed out the dark green strip with black striations along the bottom of the chip.

"Here's the best part; this is Vivanite. It doubles PSI output. No matter how much energy they use to try and get past the Blue Opal and Xenoti Etheria, it will always double the warding power of whatever is thrown at it."

"Brilliant!" Tresnat praised with a rare smile. "What about its size? We must install it in some pretty small items."

"Completely scalable. You can make it as big or as small as needed."

"Excellent! I'll get this, along with your notes, down to production. I'm putting all other projects on hold. We're going to mass produce these babies."

The head of the Landagar research team stared around at the unkempt room and sniffed the pungent air.

"In the meantime, let's air this lab out while you get washed up and some shuteye."

"Would you just look at this place!" Zerga said softly, unable to contain her amazement.

Taleeka shook her head, just as surprised.

In what appeared to be an empty field from the air, a stable, a house and large corral actually took up the bulk of the clearing. The stolen horses milled about in the pen, grazing and occasionally whinnying. Through the gray haze, they could see lights burning in the house and open doors through the stables.

The pair knelt in the waist high grass so only the tops of their heads down to their eyes showed. A large shaft of light stretched from a break in the trees behind them and passed twenty feet directly over their heads. The beam travelled across the pasture and struck a large sheet of Larimar on the roof of the stables. From there, it projected an opaque shimmering canopy covering the field.

"They're projecting a reflection of the adjacent empty clearing," Taleeka said admiringly, "so their little horse ranch can't be seen from the air. This is some operation."

"How soon before Shurta and the marines get here?"

"Well, I just sent the word, so, soon I hope, but the marines have got a couple of hundred miles to cover, and Shurta's over in Otomoria, so it'll be even longer for her. They've got my signal, so they should be able to find us, but I'm going to make it a little easier for them. In the meantime, all we have to do is hang out here until help arrives and make sure they don't move the horses."

The pair settled to the ground cross-legged, disappearing below the tops of the grass. Zerga snuggled up close in front of Taleeka so both of their knees touched.

"Thanks for pairing up with me," Zerga said, reaching forward and placing a hand on Taleeka's knee. "I mean, I know I'm new at this whole field assignment thing and I was worried about being a burden."

"Not to worry," Taleeka replied, gazing into her nervous smile. "I like pairing up with you. And you're really in the field this time around, well, *a* field anyways."

Zerga lowered her head and snickered at the joke. When she looked back up, her face still contained a nervous grin.

"Tally, can I ask, kind of a personal question?"

"I guess, sure."

"Are you... you know... involved with anyone now? You know... someone special?"

Taleeka paused, charmed by the awkward question and she felt her pulse quicken. "Nah, in fact I just got dumped."

Zerga gave a sympathetic pout and leaned in closer.

"Oh, I am so sorry."

"Eh, it's okay. It was a long-distance thing with a Bailian. It was never gonna work."

"Uh, any prospects out there on the horizon?"

"Nah, most of the guys I encounter on a regular basis aren't what you would call *my type*. I mean, in case of trouble

378

you can count on them to back you up, mostly, but nobody I would want to get involved with."

"So, uh, what is your type?"

Taleeka paused again, reflecting that she hadn't really thought about it.

"Well, if I had to be honest, now that I think about it, being raised by a guy like my dad has set the bar pretty high."

Zerga's hand now insecurely fidgeted on Taleeka's knee. "Have you, uh, maybe ever thought about, you know, maybe something different?"

"A Bailian isn't different enough?"

This caused Zerga to give out a tense chuckle. "No, I mean, maybe, maybe girls?"

Taleeka patted her hand and gave a playful eye roll. "Well, I can't say I haven't thought about it, but..."

Taleeka found her explanation cut short by Zerga gently grabbing both sides of her head and pulling her in for a kiss. The moment their lips touched, Taleeka felt a wave of light headedness sweep over her. Although initially startled by the suddenness, she found herself returning the kiss, noting her heart thundering in her chest.

As their lips lingered, she found herself comparing kisses. Taleeka had never kissed a woman romantically before and, although she remained inexperienced at kissing men, she marveled at the difference. A woman's kiss felt less forceful and softer, even when done suddenly. Then, she had to admit the lack of abrasive facial hair felt nice. Additionally, in this instance, she enjoyed the novelly heady sensation of not being in control.

The kiss lingered and just as she found her lips parting, a male voice rang out in both their heads. "Recon one, this is mongoose, do you copy?"

The two pulled away from each other slowly and Taleeka kept her eyes closed, savoring the moment. When the message repeated, Taleeka opened her eyes, gave Zerga a warm smile before immediately transforming her demeanor.

"Mongoose, this is Recon One, I copy."

"Roger that, Recon One, we are approximately five centis out and have a lock on your position."

"Sounds good, Mongoose. I'm going to make finding us a little easier. There's going to be a stable and corral, concentrate on that, the horses will be *there*. I have a quartermaster on scene. Detain everyone else. Try and keep the shooting to a minimum, especially around those horses."

"Copy that, Recon One, we're coming in!"

Taleeka reached into her backpack and pulled out her Mark Seven pistol, gave Zerga a playful eyebrow waggle and a quick kiss on the lips.

"Alright, it's show time!"

Taleeka stood rapidly, aimed at the break in the trees where the projection emanated from and fired. Getting to her feet, Zerga heard the Larimar mirroring device shattering and crashing. The illusion above them vanished, leaving only the dirty mist of the Tannimore Winter.

"Things are about to get dicey," Taleeka cautioned. "You stay here and wait for the marines. Make sure no one leaves, especially with horses. I'm going around to cover the back.

"You're armed, right?"

Zerga nodded and retrieved a pistol from under her tunic.

"Standard field issue Mark Six."

"Have you ever used it?" Taleeka asked.

"Only in practice."

"Well, just try not to shoot *me*," Taleeka said, giving her another quick kiss and taking off running.

The shattering of the Larimar projection device spooked the horses and they immediately began bolting about in their confines, bucking and snorting. Taleeka had almost flanked the compound staying just beyond the trees, when the front barn doors flew open and a half a dozen men rushed out into the corral.

"Get the horses inside!" a female voice screamed from the stables.

Taleeka heard the shouting and commotion of the marines landing out front as she made it to the back of the building. She gasped in surprise when she discovered a small transport airship backed up to the rear of the stables, not visible from out front. Mazie and two guards stood next to the ship's open bay doors, funneling horses from the stable into the ship's cargo bay.

Taleeka bolted from the cover of the trees and headed towards the escaping group. One of the guards spotted her and began to raise his carbine.

With her weapon already drawn and in position, she fired off a shot at the top of the stable's open door. The slug blew off the top corner of the wooden barrier, spraying the guards with splinters and slamming the door shut from its velocity. Both guards screamed, dropped their weapons and bent over, wincing in agony from the splinter shrapnel.

Mazie pulled her cleaver and scowled at Taleeka.

"I knew I should have killed you when I had the chance," the female mobster spat, waving the cleaver menacingly in front of her.

Taleeka halted ten feet away and scoffed at the threat.

"You're bringing a cleaver to a gun fight?!" she asked. "*Really?* Look, I know what you're thinking, but I'm *not* here to stop you!"

"You're not?" Mazie asked, staring at Taleeka incredulously. "What about your pals out front?"

"Oh, *they* want to stop you, but you see, theirs and my agendas are only slightly aligned. Look, this feud between us is pointless. If you want to be Queen of the Sisters, I have no intention of standing in your way."

"Really?" Mazie's eyes narrowed, her voice awash in skepticism, but she began to lower her weapon.

"And I don't give a crap about you keeping the horses."

Mazie's cleaver was now completely lowered and her demeanor had changed to guarded optimism. "Why?"

"The On'Dara have had a lock on the horse market for too long. They could use a little competition."

"And you're just going to let me go?"

"Yep."

"What's the catch?"

"Well, there's a couple of things," Taleeka replied calmly, listening to the conflict drawing closer. "But it's a limited time offer."

The Valdurian scout craft *Hurtig* plummeted from the upper atmosphere, leveling off a hundred feet above the agricultural fields of the Goyan countryside. Shurta checked the blinking Calcite navigation stone in the dash and then glanced over at the young pilot next to her.

"It appears the signal is coming from that wooded area ahead," she said, pointing the way.

The young man nodded and sent the fast-moving craft on a course which took them directly over the besieged stables.

"Looks like we missed the party," Shurta said, noting the bodies scattered about. "Put her down by the stable doors."

The pilot landed the scout craft and Shurta popped the top hatch in time to see Zerga, pistol still drawn, emerging from the broken doors.

"You can take off after you've dropped me," Shurta ordered. "I'll catch a ride."

The *Hurtig* silently lifted off and sped away, once Shurta landed on the ground. The Valdurian mechanic approached the Quartermaster, who clearly looked amped up.

"You just missed this," Zerga said. "We're still securing the stable's interior."

Shurta gave a painful nod and rubbed her forehead.

"Are you okay?"

"Yeah, skirting the upwinds always gives me a headache."

"Quickest way to get around though unless you want to take your chances with a portal."

"Yeah," Shurta said flatly. "Horses? Tally?"

"She was securing the rear. No sign of the horses."

A marine with his weapon lowered, stepped through the open doorway causing a break in the conversation.

"Interior secured," he said. "No horses."

"Damn, how could they have gotten away?!" Shurta asked frustratingly. "You said Tally had the rear?"

"Yep," Zerga replied.

"Anyone seen her?"

"Now that you mention it," Zerga answered, expression turning quizzical, "no."

Both stared at each other for a brief moment, thinking the same thought, then they rushed through the empty stables for the back door. They found it broken with a sizeable chunk of the right corner missing. Out back, one of Mazie's henchmen lay dead in an area of crimson stained grass, a sizeable shard of wood impaled completely through his neck.

Ten yards away, Taleeka stood holding a rope attached around the neck of the Dronning Mare, who peacefully grazed beside her. It looked up when the pair approached. Shurta and Zerga couldn't help but marvel at its golden fur and perky reddish-brown tail.

"What in the name of the empire happened here?" Shurta asked, examining the colt. "Where are the rest of the horses."

"Gone," Taleeka replied, stroking the horse's mane. "They had just about finished loading them into a small transport ship they had hidden back here when I showed up. I tried to slow them down by shooting at the door to close it, but I was mostly too late. I did manage to save the important one, though. The On'Dara should be happy to get their Dronning Mare back."

"Mazie?" Shurta asked hopefully.

"No," Taleeka lied, with a shake of her head. "Just a bunch of goons like that one."

"Damn," Shurta said with a scowl.

"Well, anyways," Taleeka said, leading the horse for a clear area several feet away and reaching in her pocket for her fob. "I'm calling down the *Vastus* and get this little girl home. You coming?"

"I'll catch a ride back with the marines," Shurta replied.

"I'll be right there," Zerga called to Taleeka.

Stepping over to Shurta she traded a suspicious look with her Valdurian counterpart.

"What do you think happened?" Zerga asked softly.

Shurta watched Taleeka walking away and sighed.

"Personally? I think she cut a deal."

"I think you're probably right," Zerga agreed, with a resigned nod.

The Grand Turine in the Zorian harbor ringing out the lateness of the hour matched Zerga's passionate, labored breathing which slowly subsided.

"Damn girl," she finally gasped, smiling upward on her back. "You sure you've never been with a girl before?"

Taleeka giggled, raising her head from between Zerga's legs and began a series of soft kisses up her still trembling, naked body.

"I think I would remember something like that," Taleeka said, pausing long enough to kiss both of her nipples.

"Well, I just gotta say, you eat pussy like a pro!"

Taleeka giggled again and playfully nuzzled, then kissed her neck. "Thanks. What can I say? I'm a quick study and you certainly did furnish me with the right inspiration."

"I'm glad I could be so inspiring," Zerga purred, when Taleeka's face finally met hers.

Taleeka enthusiastically nodded with a broad grin, then passionately kissed her. When the kiss eventually broke, Taleeka plopped over onto her back, staring at the ceiling in a love-struck haze.

They laid there for a long moment with their shoulders touching, basking in the afterglow until Taleeka looked over at her newfound love. "I'm kinda hungry."

"Yeah, you didn't want anything when we got back."

"Oh, I wanted something, just not food. I was too busy succumbing to your, *inspiration*."

"I could eat," Zerga said, finally looking over at Taleeka.

Taleeka nodded and got out of bed. "Let me go see if Peshk left us anything in the kitchen."

"My legs still feel like wet noodles," Zerga said, watching Taleeka slip on a robe.

"That's okay, I'll bring you something."

"Thanks, whatever you're having is fine. Nothing like a successful... well... *partially* successful mission and hot sex to bring on an appetite."

"Partially successful?" Taleeka asked, tying her robe closed.

"We only retrieved one of the horses."

"Yeah, but it was the important one."

"Hey, are you ever going to tell me what *really* happened with the rest of those horses?"

Taleeka sighed and sat down on the edge of the bed. "If this relationship is going to work. You have to realize that, given my current vocation, there are going to be certain things I'm not going to be able to share with you. Given *your* vocation as a quartermaster, I would never want to put you in a compromising position."

A sly grin slowly crossed Zerga's face listening to Taleeka. "Relationship huh?"

"You don't think I go around eating just anybody's pussy do you," Taleeka said, winking and getting to her feet.

"You sure know how to make a girl feel special," Zerga said, watching Taleeka open the bedroom door and step out into the hall.

The walk through the quiet house to the kitchen comforted Taleeka. She heard Defari's happy panting through the wall following her and it made her smile.

Once inside the kitchen, she tapped the crystal on the wall beside the door and the room became bathed in a warm orange light. Stepping over to the preservation cabinet, she opened the Lakananite lined door and peered inside to see what leftovers might be available.

"You very much remind me of your mother," came a deep male voice from behind.

Taleeka gasped in surprise and spun, quickly scanning around for anything that she could use as a weapon. When she saw Lord Julius standing in the doorway, she heaved a sigh of relief and understood why Defari had not warned her of another's presence.

"Lord Julius?" she stammered. "How...? What are you doing here?"

The Avion's wings fluttered slightly, sending shivers through his body when stepping forward.

"Taleeka Konrad, I come to you this time not just as a Harbinger of Balance... well, let's face it, I never was just a

Harbinger of Balance, I've always been more complex than that. I'm not just any one thing, but I understand your thinking of me as just a Harbinger of Balance. That's pretty much all you've ever seen me be, but this time I am also... wait for it... an emissary of the Gods!"

Julius fluttered his wings for emphasis and shook his hands in the air.

"Okay," Taleeka said, closing the door. "I get the feeling something big is brewing."

"Really?" Julius said, perking up. "I would love a big beer. Is that what you got brewing?"

"It's just an expression," she attempted explaining, "meaning something big is going on."

"Not just going on, Taleeka, reaching the point of no return."

"The Black Mural?"

"Yes, and this time the threat is doubled." Julius then cupped his mouth and repeated the last line in the sentence like an echo. "Threat is doubled... threat is doubled.

Taleeka sighed and sat down at the kitchen table, reminding herself to be patient with Lord Julius' eccentricities.

"I'm listening."

"The first threat is what your people unimaginatively call the Tannimore Winter." Julius then changed his voice, awkwardly trying to mimic the Zorian dialect. "Look honey, it's the Tannimore Winter."

"Yeah, it's nasty out there."

"Yes, it is, but it's more than being just nasty. It already affects your crops, choking out the necessary sunlight. Then there is the effect it is having on sentients of all forms when they breathe it. And who knows what that might be, they had bad breath enough. Something must be done." The mad Avion cupped his mouth again, creating the echo, "Must be done... must be done."

Lord Julius moved in closer, looked around the room as if someone might be listening and lowered his voice, "The second threat caused the Tannimore Winter... the Etherions."

"Etherions, huh?"

"Yes, they are not what they appear to be and must be dealt with."

"No kidding. We just found out their automatons are trying to kill the psychics in the city because they can spot them while glamoured. I've got to get this information to Vanir's people."

"Have someone you trust deliver the information to the Zorian Guards. I need you to come with me now."

Alright," Taleeka said, extending her arms in a pleading gesture. "How can I help?"

"I have a plan. However, adversaries must become friends and villains must become heroes for it to work."

Zerga watched Vanir trade an uncertain glance with Tantei before he lifted the whisky glass off his desk.

"And you're sure this is what Tally's sensitives discovered?" he asked before taking a sip.

The young quartermaster nodded. "Yes, they want to kill all the psychics or at least as many as possible."

Tantei scoffed and furrowed her brow, "For the love of the Goddess why?!"

"From what I understand," Zerga explained, "psychics can spot glamoured Etherions because they don't give off any emotions."

"Why would they care?" Tantei asked shaking her head. "I mean, didn't they just appear in front of the high council with the whole, 'we come in peace' routine?"

"Yeah, it looks like the Annigan's newest arrivals are *not* to be trusted," Vanir said, taking another sip.

"So, what about the psychics, boss?"

Vanir sighed and set the now empty glass down on his desk. "Well, there must be hundreds in the city. It's a given we can't offer them all protection. We just don't have the personnel. I'm going to bump this over to Gasata in Patrol. There's no way we can keep tabs on all the independent sensitives, but maybe he can have his people keep an eye on all the psychics operating out of storefronts. Those are the ones they'll probably target first."

Tantei nodded at her boss then glanced back to Zerga. "And Tally's not here to tell us in person because she's got her own thing going with these Etherions?"

"Yes, an Avion visitor arrived late last Kan and she left with him."

"Didn't say where or what?"

"No," Zerga replied, shaking her head, "it all happened so fast."

Vanir sighed and reached for his glass before remembering he had already drained it. At that point, he heard a light knock at the door. It opened without invitation and an excited Talib stepped into the room.

"Mazie just resurfaced!" he said, slightly out of breath.

All three quickly gave the young investigator their full attention.

"What! Where?!" Vanir asked, sitting forward at his desk.

"She hit town a little while ago, made a beeline to Judgement Square, picked up her lawyer and took off again heading west."

"Horse country," Vanir said, staring past his detectives.

"Boss, I'm sure she was behind Ditord's death so no one would know what she was up to," Tantei said, scowling.

"Mazie's the one that keeps a cleaver in the small of her back, right?" Zerga asked.

All three Zorian Guards nodded.

"Then, I *know* she's the one behind the stolen horses!"

Vanir gave a frustrated sigh. "Yeah, well, knowing and proving it are two different things, especially since she has Karta Lushi on retainer."

The lead investigator became quiet and pensive for a moment. "Round up a list of all the registered horse brokers in central Goya."

"That could be some list, boss," Tantei said skeptically.

"Humor me. Start with the biggest ones. If she's trying to move those horses, they *can't* be cheap. Focus on the ones who can afford it."

"You got it boss."

Vanir looked back at Zerga. "This was initially your case with the quartermasters. You want in on this?"

Zerga shook her head and pouted. "Technically, this is no longer my jurisdiction. It *was* a smuggling case. *Now* it's rustling."

"She's right," Vanir confirmed, "and while I know rustling is against the law here in the Goyan Islands, the horses weren't stolen here. I'm not sure she broke any laws."

"I say we shove her ass in front of an Imperial Judge and let them decide," Tantei said defiantly.

"Agreed!" Vanir concurred vehemently. "So, the two of you go out there and get me something to work with that won't make me look like an idiot in front of a judge. Start with the horse brokers."

"You got it boss!"

Mazie sat back in her chair and gave Karta a confident grin before taking in the vista outside the picture window. Through the grimy haze, the grass covering the rolling foothills of central Goya gently waved in the spring breeze, mesmerizing her for a brief moment, before her attention returned to the meeting, now winding down.

Across their rustic dining-room table, the smiles of the two leaders of The Zaldi Ranch were a bit more subdued. Ronette Zaldi, matriarch of the largest and wealthiest family of horse brokers in the Goyan Islands had always been known for driving a hard bargain, but not today. The chance to purchase rare breeding horses just couldn't be passed up and she found herself in no position to negotiate.

Ronette's plain, but pleasant, light brown features took on a serious note when she peered over at Mazie.

"What assurances do I have this transaction will be kept confidential?" she asked.

"Yes," Ronette's eldest son, Berrat, agreed, "if the On'Dara get wind of this, they'll cut us off from the regular horse shipments. Until we get our own breeding operation up and running, that can't happen!"

Mazie gave a reassuring smile at the brash twenty-six grand old who greatly resembled his mother.

"I'm sure not going to say anything," she assured. "My reputation's on the line. As far as your own people talking, well, I can't control that. Horse breeding is hardly a one-person operation. A certain number of your people will have to be in on it."

"You let me worry about our people," Berrat said, scowling.

"That's all I'm saying," Mazie replied, still smiling.

"So, it's settled then," Karta proclaimed cheerfully, not wanting the deal to get sidetracked by bickering. "We have seventeen breeding horses consisting of three stallions, twelve mares and two female colts, all for the bargain price of twenty million."

"Hardly a bargain," Berrat grumbled.

"It takes money to make money," Mazie said, still grinning amicably, "and you're getting in on the ground floor. Start-ups always require more capital up front, but you've just purchased seventeen guaranteed money makers. A lot of money I might add."

Ronette's hand gently resting on his shoulder silenced Berrat's next statement.

"Please forgive my son's nerves," she said, returning Mazie's smile. "He's still learning the business and this is his first deal of this size. The terms are fine."

Something drew Ronette's attention out the window and her expression suddenly turned from happiness to surprise.

"It looks like we've got company," she said distantly.

Everyone focused on the Avion and Resistance Class airship settling on the lawn thirty feet away from the window.

"I recognize that airship!" Mazie called out.

"That's Lord Julius!" Karta exclaimed, eyeing the pale, bare chested Avion with long black hair. "He used to be an ambassador from House Pyre. They say he's quite mad."

When the side hatch to the airship dropped and Taleeka appeared in the doorway, the barrister knew this had to be serious. Julius then walked up to the window, pressed his face directly against it, distorting his nose and mouth and stared directly at the startled lawyer.

"Karta Lushi," they all saw the Lord Julius twisted mouth sealed up against the glass, but his voice seemed to come from everywhere, "don't let this disturb you. I hear voices in my head like this all the time. You learn to get used to it."

Karta stood dumbfounded and stared back into the Avion's crazed eyes.

"Your world is in peril and your skills are required!" Julius' voice emoted.

"What?" Karta said, finding his words. "Wait, what's going on? How do you know me?!"

"I know much about you, Karta Lushi. I know of your encounters in the Awa caves and your apprehension to propose marriage to your live-in mate because of your age difference, I know about the pimple which formed this morning on the cheek of your left buttock—a hot water compress will bring it to a head—however, it is because of your legal prowess that I now summon you into service."

Upon hearing Lord Julius recite his life's intimate details, Karta sputtered in surprise.

"How... How could you possibly know these things?!"

"The Harbingers of Balance are, first and foremost, watchers," Julius replied, authoritatively. "Okay, I get it, that sounded creepy... but you are a handsome human and should be proud of your body. Anyways, our observations have shown a great imbalance growing. You are *needed*."

Mazie, who had been looking on in awe, along with the Zaldis, suddenly grew irritated.

"Wait just one damn minute!" she snapped at Karta. "You work for me. I'm not about to let you..."

Julius, keeping his face pressed against the glass, raised his hand outward in a cupping gesture and orange sparkles appeared in his palm, cutting short the mobster queen's protest. Finding she couldn't speak, her eyes went wide, her hands covered her mouth and she looked around in a panic.

"What's a Harbinger of Balance?" Karta asked, overwhelmed by the situation.

"All will be explained," Julius said calmly, "and I'll do that just as soon as I get my face unstuck from this glass. In the meantime, Taleeka Konrad is here to transport you."

"It's legit, Karta," Taleeka called out from the airship.

Karta absentmindedly nodded his head while attempting to process what he had just heard.

"Yeah, yeah, okay," he finally said, after a long moment's deliberation.

Upon hearing his decision Mazie's eyes bulged in anger and she strained to speak, but her lips wouldn't part. Karta gave his client a helpless look.

"Look," he said, "the deal here is already done. I'd be heading back to my office now, as it is. I'll be back soon, I hope. Anyways, something tells me this guy isn't going to take 'no' for an answer."

"This guy is nuts!" Gidaria said from the cockpit of the *Vastus*, watching Julius performing pirouettes in the air.

After picking up Karta, the Avion led the airship steadily southeastward, over the livestock grazing and agricultural fields towards Mount Goya. The mountain represented so much more than Lumina's largest and oldest active volcano, serving as the epicenter of fire magic for the entire Annigan, as well as home to the hive of the fire mantis Na-Kab.

"Julius has always been a handful," Taleeka said, watching him descend to the foot of the mountain's western face. "My mom and dad could tell you some stories."

"Have you had many dealings with him?" Karta asked, joining them in the cockpit.

"Mostly through my parents. He never cared much for humans in general, my folks were sort of the exceptions. He mellowed after becoming a Harbinger and he always had a soft spot for me.

"Have you thought about what you're going to say?"

"Kinda," the barrister replied. "I think better on my feet."

"Well good, because we're here."

Gidaria guided the ship down to where Julius landed, next to a simple one-story stone structure butted up against the base of the mountain. A staging area surrounded the front of an open doorway where several humans with glowing eyes loaded a large lizard-drawn cart with boxes. From there, a lone, hardpacked road led westward.

"I see they've got a shipment of Na-Kab Carbon going out," Taleeka noted when the craft settled to the ground next to the waiting Avion.

"I never knew this place existed," Karta said, curiously eyeing the humanoids with glowing red eyes sending the loaded cart on its way.

"We humans needed someplace to trade with the bugs," Taleeka said. "We sure can't go down into the fire hive."

When the side hatch dropped, Karta came face to face with a broadly grinning Julius.

"Beautiful day for an audience with the queen of a giant magical bug race, don't you think?" he said, opening his arms widely.

"Uh, I guess," Karta replied, unsure how to respond.

"Okay, so don't let this intimidate you," Julius said, turning and facing Karta, "but the simplest mistake on your part could end up in the death of all of you. Now, before you ask me what a mistake might be. Nobody really knows. Their bugs after all. They think like insects for goodness sakes. I've been living with them for grands and I still don't really get them…"

Karta's face went pale at the statement and he just slowly shook his head.

"Well then, let's go," Julius said, spinning towards the open doorway. "We shouldn't keep her majesty waiting."

"Shouldn't we be announced?" Karta asked, when he and Taleeka approached.

"Oh, no need," Julius replied, leading them to the doorway. "The queen knows we're here. See those strapping fellows just inside the door with the glowing eyes."

"Yes."

"Well, as you can probably surmise, they're not human," Julius explained. "The Na-Kab use a glamour Etheria crystal when dealing with humans. Much like their cousins the Do-Tarr, they have a hive mind. Believe you me, the queen already knows we're here. Which is a good thing! If she wanted you dead for any distant genetic connection to some enemy in her past, they would have killed you already!"

"Alright," Karta said apprehensively. "What is the queen's name so I can address her properly."

Julius shot Karta an amused side glance. "The Na-Kab don't have names. They all belong to the hive. I like to call her, Queen Bee, but I'm practically fireproof."

The slightly unnerved look didn't leave the lawyer's face when they entered the simple structure. Karta immediately noted the temperature rise the moment he crossed the threshold. The perfectly square room had only two openings on the back wall. One doorway appeared wider than the other and contained a ramp. The other, much narrower archway led to stairs heading downward. The three glamoured Na-Kab nodded at Lord Julius and then indicated the doorway with the stairs.

"Standard rules of addressing royalty will do," Julius advised softly, while descending the steps. "She really doesn't care. If anything, she finds our protocols amusing... or maybe she just finds me amusing. Anyway, just be respectful. Address her as a noble superior."

Karta nodded nervously while wiping his sweating brow.

"She will seem abrupt," Julius continued. "She means nothing by it. They do not share our manners or etiquette. Just be honest, straight forward and you'll be fine... and don't make any mistakes *or we all might die*."

The stairway descended only twenty feet before opening into a small alcove with a three-foot-tall stone lip for a railing. It looked out over a vast cavern dotted with jagged rock formations and pools of magma throughout.

Standing regally in a large pool of lava at the cavern's center, the Na-Kab Queen watched the pair approach the railing above, while several of the fire mantis creatures moved in and out of the pool attending her. She towered over her brood, standing seven-foot-tall. The six teats with black nipples on her human torso caused a profusely sweating Karta to shoot Taleeka an uncertain glance.

"Don't look at me," she said softly, wincing at the sulfurous smell. "This is all new."

Thankfully, Julius took over and stepped forward. "Oh, illustrious queen of the mighty Na-Kab empire, we thank you for allowing us this audience. This is Taleeka Konrad and Karta Lushi who represent the humans at my request. Karta has a matter of great importance to bring before you."

Karta nervously swallowed when the queen's mantis head turned his way, before stepping up beside the Avion.

"What matter do you have for me to consider?" she asked in her language of pops and hisses, translated by the talking stones everyone bore in some fashion.

"Oh, queen," Karta began stiffly, "I know a great injustice was done to your hive by the new crystal creatures. I have been informed that the ones who caused the disturbance were destroyed, so, in the interests of peace, I would beseech you to look past this infraction and forgive this trespass."

The queen tilted her head in confusion. "What is 'forgive?'"

The question took the barrister completely by surprise.

"The Na-Kab, much like the Do-Tarr, have no words for forgiveness or accident," Julius whispered.

Karta nodded and then continued, "We would ask you to not exact vengeance on the crystal creatures."

"Our hive was violated. Our children killed," the queen said firmly. "Violators must be destroyed!"

Karta sighed and collected his thoughts. "I realize your traditions have served you well in the past, but I propose that your situation has evolved. You are no longer an isolated community in a remote part of the Annigan. You are part of a very diverse and heavily populated region. A war between the two of you would be devastating to us all."

"No war; Na-Kab fire will destroy them all!"

"Oh, queen," Julius interjected. "I have seen firsthand the effectiveness your fire has on them but consider the other sentient lifeforms that would be affected by such actions."

The queen paused and stared at the Avion for what seemed like an eternity before she spoke to Julius, this time decidedly more subdued, "The Na-Kab owe you a debt of gratitude we will never be able to repay. I would not be here if it were not for you. Upon *your* word, and only if these crystal beings agree, *a truce*, and only a truce may be called."

"Thank you, Your Majesty," both negotiators said in unison.

Karta resumed his lead role. "We go to speak with the Etherions next about living in peace with the rest of us."

"And if they refuse?" the queen asked, menacingly.

"Then, Your Majesty, I'll personally fly an army of your people to their homeland so you can destroy them," Taleeka said, stepping forward.

Silovik watched one of the many mid-cycle corpse carts appear out of the dirty grey mist from the top of the Pyramid Temple of Jalaana. He hated the haze, as if the Kan fog wasn't enough to obstruct his view of the Holy Mount Goya.

He followed the cart making its way up the incline to the River of Fire, which channeled the molten magma from the volcano out to the Shallow Sea. Volcanic vents dotted the large, grooved berm, smoldering noxious gasses into the air.

Constructed above each vent hovered a pully system, many extending winching chains downward into its recesses.

The cart stopped when it reached a row of six openings. Two robed acolytes, wearing heavy soled boots and gloves, stepped up to meet it. One pulled a small cart carrying a stack of X shaped wooden crosses in its bed.

They met the corpse cart and, while one unloaded six bodies, the other attached the wooden crosses to the empty pully systems. Both then affixed the dead bodies to a cross and lowered them into the smoking opening.

Without speaking, they rolled both carts over to another row of six holes and winched up as many bodies which had been curing for a cluster. The bodies were petrified in the spread-eagle position and appeared withered and dark brown in color. They were then removed from the crosses and placed in the corpse cart to be delivered to the temple. The cross cart then rolled to a position where it would meet the next returning corpse cart from the countryside, now rolling up the road from the south.

Silovik nodded in satisfaction, six more offerings for the Festival of Lights two cycles from now. They had almost filled the top of the temple with the human torches. He assessed that there should be no problem filling the rest of the spots marked by black soot stains from prior festivals held once a grand. Four bodies constantly burned on each corner of the temple's roof. The bodies generally took several cycles to burn up and mourners often remained at the base of the temple, at the corner their loved one had been offered from.

The festival, however, would be a grand spectacle, with the attached town of Zolene filling up with religious pilgrims. All considered it a great honor to be burned at the festival and offered up in such a grand fashion to the fire Goddess Jalaana.

Silovik also felt honored this grand as the official Lighter of the Flames. He smiled in satisfaction, grateful to his boss,

Lord Hanara, in Makatooa, who allowed him time off from serving as his fixer to attend this cluster-long religious event.

He had just finished watching another cart being unloaded when something drawing near in the sky caught his attention. Instead of the usual airship traffic heading in and out of Zor or a herd of Kells being driven across the sky, it appeared to be a lone Avion leading an airship.

The Cleric of Jalaana found it most odd that they were heading up from Mount Goya. He gasped when the Avion landed mere feet from him with a serious deportment and the airship hovered just off the roofline of the temple.

"Silovik de Zolene, I am Lord Julius, Harbinger of Balance and your services are immediately needed."

A startled Silovik gave a nervous grin. "Hello, Lord Julius, Harbinger... whatever. A couple of things. One, I can't leave. The festival is in two cycles out and I'm instrumental in it. And two, you're not supposed to be up here. This is holy ground."

"I apologize for the infraction. Being from House Pyre, I try to be respectful of all fire deities. The task will be brief and you should be back in plenty of time for your festival."

Silovik's pregnant pause prompted Julius to stress the seriousness of the situation. "Silovik, this task is consequential in the extreme and *time is of the essence!*"

With Gidaria skirting the upwinds, the *Vastus* made it to Konaleeta in a little over a deci. Reaching the upper atmosphere truly revealed the expanse of the Tannimore Winter. It covered the entire Goyan Islands, the Narrow

Lands to the west, the Ice Lands to the north, the Wild Lands to the south and all the way to the Nocturn border.

"It's huge!" Taleeka noted, shaking her head in wonder.

"And it must be dealt with," Julius announced, when the airship began its descent into the mist, "but first things first, we must now go to the epicenter of this plague."

Taleeka peered back at Karta. "You know what you're going to say to them?"

"I'm going to wing it," the barrister replied confidently.

"Really?!"

"I have absolutely no idea what to expect," the lawyer said, shrugging, "so, yeah. I just figured Lord Julius will get the ball rolling."

"That's if they'll talk to you at all," Silovik said. "Exactly why am I here? I'm hardly the negotiating type."

Julius indicated Krak seated next to him.

"Yeah, well I hoped between Magma Mantis, here, and a cleric cremator like yourself, you would serve as our protection in case things get heated… so to speak. We don't know much about Etherions, but we do know magical fire is effective."

"Speaking of which," Taleeka said, reaching behind her captain's chair where her backpack hung.

Placing the pack in her lap, she fished around inside and pulled out her Mark Seven pistol and an additional magazine. Pressing the release button on the side, the magazine already in the weapon popped out and she replaced it with a new one.

"Trinilic rounds, just in case."

"We're coming up on the island now, Gidaria reported. "Let's get a better look."

She reached over to the console and pressed a button bathing the front windshield in orange, but nothing appeared.

"That's odd," she said, shaking her head. "I'm getting no heat sources down there, I mean, *off anything*."

"Blink blink, Brzo, blink blink," she commanded the lizard in the seat next to her.

The lizard extended his neck and pressed the Etheria button on the console in front of it, activating the Croquis and the blue phantom globe projected from it. Gidaria reached over, spun it to the proper section and zoomed in, but still no heat signatures.

"Okay, I'm getting nothing. So, we're going in blind," Gidaria said worriedly. "Now that I think about it, this only makes sense. We knew, from the psychics, that Etherions have no emotions. I'm betting they don't give off heat signatures either. The reason the Croquis isn't seeing anything, is that this island is a new arrival. It has no point of reference."

Taleeka sighed in frustration. "Okay, just find us a clear spot to set down."

Passing over Konaleeta proper, Taleeka noted the similarity between the monoliths beneath them and the ones in the Etheria caves of the Awa Mountains. She peered back over her shoulder, about to let everyone know, when she saw a long tendril of blue lightning shoot out of a massive monolith just ahead of them.

The electrical field enveloped the *Vastus* in a web of crackling energy, jolting it to a stop and rocking the craft violently. Everyone inside the airship was shaken about, but unharmed. Except Julius, who gripped his chest, eyes wide, and toppled to the floor.

"Holy crap!" Taleeka yelled, bolting from her chair and rushing over to the fallen Avion.

"What is it?" Karta asked, when the others gathered round the prone body.

"I think that lightning attack affected his heart.!"

"Speaking of which," Gidaria said from the pilot's station, "this isn't good for this ship either!"

"Blast it!" Taleeka ordered, rushing to her command seat.

Gidaria popped a protective cap revealing four orange Trinilic buttons on the overhead console. Without waiting, she quickly tapped both front buttons. Immediately, two grapefruit sized fireballs shot from the two forward Trinilic rods under the ship.

The fireballs exploded on contact, setting the corner of the offending monolith aflame and melting it. The attack ceased and the molten corner of the monolith toppled to the ground with a crash.

Scowling, Taleeka reached up to the overhead console and pushed the Larimar button. "Etherions, this is the *Vastus*. We mean you no harm, we're here to talk, but we *will* defend ourselves."

Silence greeted her from the other end, but there were no further attacks.

"Okay, put her down there," Taleeka said, indicating a nearby intersection.

Gidaria did as ordered and set the craft gently to the ground. Taleeka then turned her attention to the unconscious Julius. If the task had any chance of success, he was an integral part of it. Now, with him out of the picture, Taleeka grew concerned about the mission's outcome.

"Uh, Tally," Gidaria's worried voice cut through her internal assessment.

Taleeka snapped her attention out the windows to find her ship surrounded by the Etherions in their humanoid monk appearance. They stood silently in their light blue robes, wide conical hats and blindfolds, facing the intruders.

"I tell you, I 'm going stir crazy!" Folsom said, plopping down on the sofa after her third trek around the living room of Konrad House West. "We've been cooped up in this place for cycles!"

Barr-Ani, sitting across the room, looked up from her schoolbook and smiled sympathetically. "You can always help me study. I've got finals in a couple of clusters."

"What I want to do is take a walk, get a bite to eat and spend some quality quiet time in one of those Otick isolation shells."

The Bailian set the book down in her lap and smiled. "Yeah, those are nice. I could use a little quiet time too."

"So, why not?"

"You heard Tally. It's way too dangerous for us out there."

"Well, we can't stay cooped up in here forever. I mean you've got finals coming up. I've got to get back to the harbormaster's office. That's if I've still got a job!"

"It shouldn't be much longer. I mean, Tally left last Kan with that Avion, saying something about the Etherions. I'm sure they'll take care of things."

"Me too!" Folsom said in frustration, "but how long will it take?!"

"Wow, you really do need the isolation."

Folsom sighed and rubbed the bridge of her nose. "I really do."

"Well…" Barr-Ani said, her resolve cracking.

"You got nobody to blame but yourself. You turned me on to the damn things. Now it's the only way to clear the voices from my head."

"Well…"

Folsom, now on her feet, quickly became animated. "Look, we quietly slip out of here, grab a hackney, stay low, and slip into the Otick caves. A deci or so later, we emerge a lot more sane, all before Tally gets back."

"I don't know…"

"I'm paying."

"Let's go!"

Once down on the street, the pair stayed in the recess of the front door until Folsom saw a hackney pull onto Kassada Drive and head their way. Folsom discreetly stepped into view and raised her hand to hail it. Once in the back seat, both heaved a sigh of relief then slumped down.

"Where to?" the cabbie, a balding middle-aged man with light brown skin, asked over his shoulder.

"Northern Docks," Folsom ordered and the vehicle pulled out at its typical lethargic pace.

The ride went slowly and methodically through the busy streets of the High Holy City until he turned off of Meridian Street in the Bogat Plat where everything ground to a halt.

"Eh, accident ahead," the driver grumbled, smacking his palm against the steering wheel. "You know, lately, with all the traffic it doesn't even pay to take Meridian any more..."

The driver continued his unhappy diatribe, but Barr-Ani concentrated on the blue flash she noticed several cars ahead of them. The azure burst of light lasted only the briefest moment and wasn't noticed by anyone until it converted into a long blue rivulet of energy. The crackling tendril passed harmlessly through the three hackneys in front of them heading their way.

"Get down!" the Bailian warned, ducking her head.

When the bolt struck their vehicle, it brilliantly lit up the cabin, but quickly dissipated. When Barr-Ani slowly looked up, she saw her friend and the driver, seemingly unharmed.

"Is everyone alright?"

"What in the name of the gods was that?!" the driver bellowed.

Folsom sat speechless, her eyes wide and mouth tautly open. The Bailian sensed something had gone wrong. She could only feel part of Folsom's presence within her body, along with something else.

Folsom quickly reached out and grabbed both sides of the cabbie's head with a murderous roar. The possessed human psychic then wrenched it savagely around with inhuman strength, loud crunching and tearing sounds preceded the unfortunate driver's head being completely turned backward. It stared back at them from its unnatural position with a look of utter shock.

Barr-Ani screamed and slid to the farthest end of the seat by the back door.

*"Thieves! Usurper of worlds!"* came a deep male voice from Folsom's open mouth.

Barr-Ani stammered in a panic and the haunted Folsom began inching towards her.

"I didn't steal anything!" the frightened Bailian tried to reason.

*"You are the children of the Avatars!"* the voice growled menacingly. *"The world was ours, Etherions once ruled, until the Avatars wrenched it from us, soiling its pristine crystal surface with its filth!"*

Barr-Ani sputtered in a shocked panic. Could it be true? Was everything she had ever come to know a lie? Were the current residents, in all their diversity, really, including her, the evil doers?

*"We have returned from our long banishment in the Middle Realms to take our world back,"* it said, grabbing Barr-Anni and shaking her.

"Please, I don't know what you're talking about!"

*"Soon the world will be returned to its rightful form, with its rightful inhabitants."*

The Bailian could feel Folsom's grip tightening on her when the human suddenly began convulsing.

Barr-Ani screamed, trying to pull herself free, when Folsom shuttered and toppled to the back floorboard of the hackney. Whisps of blue smoke trailed from her nose and still gaping mouth.

The Bailian sensitive sat against the back door trembling and crying, listening to the Zorian Guards' whistles approaching. Looking down at her dead friend, she felt waves of guilt wash over her for agreeing to the outing turned deadly.

Guilt or not, she recognized the gravity of the Etherion's accusation and knew Tally needed to be informed immediately. With trembling hands, she reached in her pocket and retrieved her Larimar talking stone.

Julius opened his eyes and stared upward at a featureless light gray sky. He sat up and took in his surroundings. The land seemed a darker grey than the sky and just as unremarkable. It stretched out in all directions until it met the horizon line. In the distance, a large wide monolith rose from the bleak, featureless terrain. Beside him, a forty-foot-wide waterway filled with a calm black liquid, extended past the monolith and off into the distance in both directions.

Julius knew he had ended up in the Land of the Dead Plane of the Middle Realms, next to the Ghost River. He identified the structure in the distance as Serma, City of the Dead. There, Boran, Judge of the Dead, determined the final destination of all sentients' essences in the multiverse.

He remembered the jolt of psionic energy striking the ship and the sudden pain in his chest, but little else. He surmised that since he had not arrived via the traditional voyage down the river, he must be still teetering on the precipice of death and not yet remanded into Boran's bosom.

Julius easily rose to his feet and felt no pain or discomfort. He then noticed two figures in the distance approaching from the city beyond. They traveled in a jerky motion, advancing large distances at a time without appearing to touch the ground they hovered just above.

When they finally came within visual range, Julius gasped in surprise but had no time to react before the two figures abruptly halted before him. His eyes filled with tears and grief wracked his heart. He dropped to his knees and turned away weeping, covering his head with his wings and his face with his hands.

Just mere feet away, close enough for him to reach out and touch, stood two versions of his dead sister, Drucilla. One appeared just as he remembered, his beautiful smiling sister with her long wavy dark hair and pale complexion.

When he looked at her through his fingers, his mind flashed back to her death. Falling from the sky, her wings just out of his grip, crashing into the frenzied school of Perrikin fish, the water boiling with gore and feathers.

He turned away and looked at the other Drucilla. It appeared with the body of the Ash-Ta bat creature she had been force resurrected into. She also smiled, but it carried a more sinister quality to it.

His mind threw at him the images of her ravaged victims, drained of blood and ripped to pieces. He saw the moment that Kai put her down and he covered his face again.

"Hello Brother," they said in unison.

"I'm so sorry, Dru," he said between sobs. "I'm so sorry."

"We have come to offer you a choice, Brother," the Ash-Ta announced.

"That's more than you had," Julius said sadly.

The Ash-Ta kept her sly smile. "I offer you rest, Brother. The Harbingers have kept the Black Mural from falling for thousands of grands now. For every tilt of the scales towards balance, something always happens to tip things towards destruction. You must be exhausted. You need not return to a never ending and thankless job."

Julius slowly nodded and stepped towards his Ash-Ta sister. The Avion Drucilla, who had listened patiently to her Ash-Ta counterpart, gently placed her hand over his heart stopping him and gave him a sympathetic look.

"My Brother, you know what to do. Your friends and your world need you right now. To abandon your duty and your true self would be disastrous for all and you could be judged harshly for it by the one who resides in that city on the horizon. Rest assured, when your labors are done, there will be a place for you with me in the endless sky."

Julius hugged his Avian sister, she leaned close and whispered in his ear, "More important than anything else you do, Brother, you must…" her voice faded away, replaced by the increasing sound of his heartbeat.

When the twin versions of his sister blurred and spun, he felt unconsciousness coming on and everything went black.

Taleeka looked up from kneeling over Julius' prone body. "What are they doing now?"

"They're just standing there," Gidaria replied, staring out at the sea of identical figures surrounding the craft.

Brzo also watched the silent welcoming committee from the seat next to her and then gazed back at its master with a puzzled expression.

"I know Brzo," she said, baby talking while patting its head. "Scary people. Yes they are, aren't they? Mommy won't let them hurt you."

Taleeka became truly torn between getting Julius to some help or continuing their plans without him. She stood and peered over at Karta.

"You think you can get this done without him?"

The barrister cocked his head and exhaled loudly. "I don't see as we have much of a choice. What about *him*?"

Both then gazed down at Silovik, still kneeling over the unconscious Avion.

"There's a faint heartbeat," the Fire Cleric reported, "and the breathing is shallow, but he's still with us."

"Well, we're here," Taleeka said. "We've got to try something."

She stepped back into the cockpit and checked on the crowd outside, which appeared to have grown.

"I guess it's time for me to put on my best diplomatic hat and see what I can do," Karta said with a resolute nod. "I'm certainly glad your psychic friend was able to get us the information they discovered. I think I've got an angle on how to approach the situation."

"Use it well," Taleeka said, "that information came at the cost of another friend's life."

"I just wish Julius was here to smooth the way for..."

Almost on cue, Julius shook and sputtered, then abruptly sat up, looking straight forward with a thousand-mile stare.

"Julius!" Taleeka cried out. "You're back, are you alright? What happened?"

The Avion lord did not acknowledge her questions and continued to stare into the distance. Taleeka and Karta shared a concerned look as the awkward silence hung in the air. Taleeka frowned and knelt beside Julius. She slowly reached out to touch him when he suddenly turned and smiled at her.

"Well, answering in order," Julius said, slowly rising to his feet. "Yes, I'm back, slightly weaker but I feel fine physically. I just attended a little family reunion with my sister... sisters... er... sister. So, let's just say, my inner child in cowering in its happy place, demons rule my subconscious and I'm operating in a highly unstable, emotional disconnect mode. So, yeah, I'm good to go.

"Now, what's going on?" he asked, shaking his wings.

"We're on the ground and the Etherions have the ship surrounded."

"Splendid!" Julius said buoyantly. "It saves us the trouble of looking for them. What say we have a chat? Are you ready, Karta?"

"Are *you* ready?" Karta asked back, eyeing the Avion with eyebrows raised.

"Believe me, young human," Julius said with a wink, "I'm ready for anything."

Gidaria dropped the side hatch. The two negotiators stepped onto the ramp, flanked by Krak, Silovik and Taleeka bringing up the rear. They stepped away from the airship and found themselves enveloped in a crowd of identically robed figures.

*"You are a Harbinger,"* the words reverberated in all of their heads, though clearly meant for Julius.

"I am," he answered.

*"Why are you here and why did you bring them?"*

Julius' eyes crinkled in amusement.

"Apparently, some of your folks have been causing a bit of mischief with some of their folks. So, they're here to discuss that with you.

"Karta?" Julius stepped aside and the barrister stepped forward, nervously clearing his throat.

"Etherions, I have come to discuss the proposal of our two cultures peacefully coexisting."

*"You would lecture us on peace when you are all the product of the Avatar's treachery."*

"I am aware of your position on the Avatars, but we must find a way to coexist in the world."

All of the blind monks now faced Karta. *"We ARE the world, human! Just below this filthy façade created by the Avatars, is our world, the one we have been exiled from for far too long. It is beautiful, colorful and pristine. Below us, this world's liquid crystal center still swirls and flows. That*

411

*constantly flowing crystal gives your mages their power, you call it PSI. When it rises to the surface, it crystallizes into what you call Etheria. If it rose to the surface on our island, another of our kind is born. So you see, YOU are the invaders, you are the ones not supposed to be."*

Karta nodded that he understood. "Tell me, how did the Avatars come to be?"

*"Something struck the moon. Pieces broke off and fell all across the pristine surface. We surrounded them with the Avatars so as to purge and isolate the offending pieces."*

"So, what you're telling me is, this world actually created the Avatars?"

*"To keep our world pure and protect it, yes."*

A sardonic smile played at the corner of the lawyer's mouth. "If your world created the Avatars, then they are a *natural* phenomenon. It sounds like they were very much meant to be."

*"Their influence spread too fast,"* the voice protested. *"Especially when they started singing. That is when the world you know came into being."*

"That is completely immaterial. We are the natural evolution of this world. We didn't steal anything, we evolved. All the more reason for us to live harmoniously. Speaking of which, those of you who are misbehaving must be dealt with."

*"We cannot be expected control all of our facets."*

"Yeah," Karta said, chuckling, "something tells me that whatever is in the works is decidedly bigger than a few bad actors. You've already made dangerous enemies. I would hate to see things escalate."

"Yes, and do remember," Julius said, his voice taking on the full authority of a Harbinger of Balance. "Anything catastrophic and the Black Mural will fall. It will spell all of our doom, yours and ours. I find the whole matter highly ironic, seeing how you were the ones who created it in the first place!"

There was an extended silence before the Etherions replied, *"We will consider this a truce while we contemplate your reasoning."*

Vanir looked up from the paperwork on the desk before him, just in time to see Talib and Tantei march through his open door. Both carried frustrated expressions, however, Tantei actually grimaced. She walked over to the shelf behind the desk and grabbed Vanir's liquor bottle and a glass. Talib plopped down in one of the two chairs facing Vanir, shaking his head hopelessly.

"I take it your inquiries were unsuccessful?" Vanir asked, watching Tantei pour a healthy dram, down it and then pour herself another.

"Nobody seems to know anything Boss," Tantei said, sitting next to her partner. "If they did, they sure aren't eager to share it. Let's face it, those horses are long gone by now."

Vanir nodded. "Well, keep your ears to the ground. We might get lucky. Any psychics turn up dead today?"

"All quiet on that front," Talib said. "And our stakeout people report that Mazie got back last Kan. She's been checking in on her newest soup kitchen."

"Alright, keep up the surveillance, sooner or later she'll slip up. I want us there to capture the moment, as it were."

Vanir pushed his chair away from his desk. "The cycle's almost over. I'll give the On'Dara the bad news tomorrow."

The *Vastus* lurched violently to the right, causing its passengers to sway back and forth in their seats.

"Sorry about that," Gidaria called back from the pilot's station, "unexpected updraft."

Taleeka gave a reassuring smile to her three nervous passengers. She really had no cause to complain, Gidaria had proved herself an exceptional driver, extremely adept at high-speed maneuvers. When she voiced an interest in piloting, Taleeka enrolled her in the elite Valdurian Air Scouts School.

"Julius has it worse than us," Taleeka said, taking a quick glance out the side window. "The weather in the Twilight Lands can be a real challenge."

"Yes, but the skies are clear over there," Karta said with a touch of exasperation. "We've got a Tannimore Winter over here."

"We're working on it," Taleeka replied. "Julius had a two-part plan. The first part was tamping down the Etherions. We pulled that off by the skin of our teeth. Now, for the second part. We've got to get rid of this dirty mist before bad things start happening."

"And exactly how do you plan on doing that?" Silovik asked skeptically.

"Julius is headed towards the Os'Oni Mountains and The Ghas' Tor," she explained. "He's going to try and convince the Nalesh to help."

"I've never heard of either of those things," Silovik said.

"Unless you hang out in the Twilight Lands or practice Air Magic you probably wouldn't," Taleeka replied. "The Ghas 'Tor is the highest mountain in the Annigan. It's also the epicenter of Air Magic. The Nalesh are fanatical practitioners of said Air Magic. They live an isolated life along the slopes of their magic mountain. My part in this plan is in Zor with the Air Workers Guild. The object is to get these two groups to work together."

"Do you think they will?"

"I sure hope so."

"We're coming up on Air Station Three," Gidaria announced over her shoulder.

"Hey, we can afford to be a little optimistic, can't we?" Karta said. "I mean we got the Etherions to back down."

Taleeka scoffed loudly. "As my mom would say, 'I trust those fuckers about as far as I can throw them.'"

Krak's eyes suddenly glowed red with anger and the temperature in the cabin rose. "If they go back on their word, even a little, they will meet a fiery death."

The headquarters for the Air Workers Guild is located in the upper Shimol Plat of Zor, within walking distance of Air Station Three. At five stories, it is one of the tallest buildings in the High Holy City, with every floor lined in large sliding glass windows and a bright blue Planchite Etheria tower on the roof for channeling Air Magic. Most days, the windows were open to the air, but now had to be closed to escape the effects of the Tannimore Winter.

Gidaria guided the hackney out of the early morning rush of traffic. Taleeka stepped out of the back seat, eyeing through the dirty gray mist, the river of pedestrians sweeping past her.

"Hopefully this won't take long," she said, leaning through the hackney's open door.

"I'll pull around to the side. I've got to take Brzo for a walk," she said before scratching the lizard under its chin. "Isn't that right? Mommy's got to take you to do your business, doesn't she?"

"Wish me luck," Taleeka said, before closing the door.

The first floor appeared open and spacious, with small chair and sofa groupings scattered throughout. A ten-foot-wide clear tube led upward through the ceiling at the far end of the room. Taleeka found herself staring with an amused grin at two nude male air mages levitating down the tube to the floor while casually chatting.

She recognized Jauhari de Tuath, owner of one of Zor's largest jewelry operations, in one of the seating groups. The man would be difficult to miss, with his deeply furrowed, angular face and head full of short, snow-white hair. He chatted with a thin, nude Bailian woman, with light brown hair streaked in purple. The two smiled amiably and nodded, before Jauhari reached into his coat and handed a hundred Secor gold note to her. They shook hands and then stood.

On his way out, he passed Taleeka and they nodded at each other. The female Bailian handed the money to a nude human female, who walked over to the tube and ascended upward, accompanied by the sound of rushing wind.

"That's a pretty impressive security system," Taleeka said, approaching the Bailian woman.

"Thank you," she said with a warm smile. "Only Adepts are allowed on the upper floors. The Transit Tubes ensure privacy."

"I'll say," Taleeka replied, watching another nude man gently land and walk over to one of the seating stations.

"I couldn't help noticing that you and Si. Jauhari greeted each other."

Taleeka nodded. "Yeah, we've dealt with each other before. I was just a little surprised to see him here. Jewelers rarely need Air Magic."

"Si. Jauhari is to be one of our first clients in our new Laudation services we're starting next quinte."

"Laudation?"

The Bailian seemed barely able to control her enthusiasm. "Oh yes, we're all very excited. You've no doubt noticed the blue monoliths going up on rooftops throughout the city?"

"Yeah, they look just like the one on the top of yours."

"They're made of the Etheria Planchite, which helps channel Air Magic. With them, we can control the Aikin so that they travel in patterns we choose over the city. We've developed a way to project information about our client's business on the exterior of the clouds surface, effectively lauding for the client."

"Interesting," Taleeka said impressively. "Are you by any chance Hava-Dada?"

"I am," she confirmed with a curious tilt of her head.

"Taleeka Konrad," she said, offering her hand.

"Well!" Hava-Dada said in impressed recognition, taking her extended appendage. "What can the Air Worker's Guild do for a Hero of the Realm?"

"Well, I was hoping we could work together to improve the air quality around here."

The Bailian gave a sad smile. "If only we could. The mist makes any type of incantation much more difficult and because we work sky-clad, it irritates our skin. We, however, are a relatively small group. Not nearly enough to affect any noticeable change, even with the help of Etheria."

"What about working with the Nalesh?"

Hava-Dada scoffed loudly. "The Nalesh will not help us. They look down on us as unrefined hacks."

A mischievous twinkle lit up Taleeka's eyes. "But you *would* work with them if they agreed?"

"Yes, of course, but I can assure you, they won't."

"What makes you so sure?"

"Because before I was expelled, I was a Nalesh of the Ghas' Tor. It is me they hate for forming the Air Workers Guild."

"In the name of the Goddess, why?!"

"Because I proposed the outlandish notion that we could use our craft to make money."

Julius wasn't fond of being kept waiting. Whether as prince of Avion House Pyre, or as a Harbinger of Balance, leaving the mad Avion with time on his hands usually ended with calamity. In this instance, however, with the visit being unexpected, the wait seemed entirely understandable, sort of.

Pacing the length of the receiving area, which was completely open to the elements on one side, he peered down the side of the mountain. All down the eastern face of the Ghas' Tor he could see the lights from the various keeps twinkling in the Nocturn darkness. The various outposts played an essential part in the training of Nalesh Air Mages. The beginners were located at the base of the mountain, which, in itself, could be dangerous enough. Its surrounding Os'Oni mountain range teemed with dangers, ensuring any who made it that far to apply would be highly motivated. As the adepts, mostly Bailian, increased in skill and power, they ascended the mountain in increments.

Not wanting to have to deal with lesser ranks, Julius flew to the highest keep and his arrival caused quite a stir. Few dared to intrude unannounced into the lair of such a powerful group of shamans.

On his one hundred-twenty-sixth pass of the room, the door opened and a nude Bailian male gestured for him to enter. "Lord Julius, the Mistral will see you now."

"Excellent," Julius said, grinning broadly. "As it is, it's going to take forever to get my hair untangled. I do hope the Mistral doesn't mind the wind-blown look?"

"Uh, no sir, we're all quite used to it."

"Yes, I would imagine so," Julius said, following the young Bailian down the hall.

They led him to another bare room which contained a large oblong obsidian Etheria frame mounted on one wall.

The blueish grey cloud of a captured Aiken peacefully swirled inside the frame. As Julius examined it, the Aiken began swirling faster.

Moments later, three nude and quite beautiful Bailians, a male and two females, stepped out of the cloud. The females had short black hair and the male sported a shoulder length golden mane contrasting and complimenting his pale blue skin.

"Lord Julius?" the male greeted stepping forward. "I am Wushi, and we are surprised to see you. We have our own Harbingers here."

"Mistral Wushi, today I come to you not as a harbinger, but as a representative from the peoples of Lumina."

"Oh?"

"Yes, I don't know if it has come to your attention, but better than half of Lumina is now covered in a dirty gray mist from a giant explosion. It is starting to affect daily life and I fear if it's not cleaned up there will be serious long-term harm."

"I am truly sorry to hear that."

"Well, if you're anything like me you're probably saying to yourself, Lumina, humans, no big deal. However, there are many other races over there that will also be affected, like mine."

The elder shaman held out his hands palms up in a questioning gesture. "Once again, I am truly sorry, but I don't understand why you are telling me."

"Mistral, I have a plan for clearing the air but it's going to require you to partner with The Air Workers Guild in Zor."

Upon hearing the name of the renegade faction, the Mistral's mood became icy. "I am afraid that is quite out of the question."

"Mistral," Julius pleaded. "We're talking about a lot of sentients' lives here."

"And as I said before, I am truly sorry, but we will not work beside inferior mages. The risk is just too great."

"But Mistral…"

"The matter is closed," he said, turning and stepping back through the portal with his two adepts following.

A dejected Julius turned to go. He brooded about the decision all the way back to the receiving area. Before taking off from the open section, he reached into the pocket of his Kell pants and touched his Larimar talking stone.

"Taleeka," he called out defeatedly.

A brief moment later, Taleeka's excited voice resonated in his head. "Hey, Lord Julius, I've got good news. The Air Workers are on board with the plan."

"Yes, well, The Nalesh wouldn't even discuss it. They actually walked out of the meeting, how rude!"

"And you told them that lives were at stake, a lot of lives?!"

"I did. They consider the air workers inferior mages and it would be too dangerous to work with them."

A lengthy pause at the other end prompted Julius.

"Taleeka?"

"Yeah, I'm here," Taleeka said both calmly and somberly. "Unbelievable! They would let potentially millions die over a pissing contest. As my mom would say, 'this fucking bullshit is going to end!' If we can't convince them to help, I know who can. Lord Julius, get word to the Gods of the Air, I'm calling in my Pa-Waga marker!"

"An excellent idea! And I happen to be in the proper location to do just that! You know, for a human you're not half bad."

"Thanks, I think."

"Well, I'm off. This should be interesting. I've been summoned *by* the gods before, but this will be the first time I've tried summoning *them* to me."

Without waiting for a reply, Julius unfolded his wings and leapt into space. Catching a thermal updraft, he rapidly soared to the top of the mountain. He had never been this close to the Ghas' Tor before and he found himself surprised that the oxygen had not become thin at this height.

Several hundred feet down from the summit, a fifty-foot-tall section of the mountain had been removed and the entire mountain top now seemed to be supported by hundred-foot-thick pillars carved from the mountain itself, forming a giant portico. The columns were placed in the cardinal directions and both the floor and ceiling were smooth and polished.

Julius circled, about to land, when he saw a blue grey mist seep up from the floor and form into a cloud. The Avion had communed with the Aiken many times before, but this would be the first time he had seen one forming. Once created, it floated out past the east pillar on its own power.

The moment Julius landed and his boots clacked on the hard flat surface, the Avion felt a tingle of electricity pass through him and the foreboding feeling of trespassing swept across his mind.

Dropping to one knee, a whirling cyclone surrounded him sending his long black hair flying wildly about.

*You do not belong here*! A stern female voice rang out in his head and he knew he now directly communicated with the living embodiment of the Mistress of Storms, the epicenter of Air Magic in the Annigan. Physical manifestations were rare and always took on the appearance of a stern beautiful woman, but that happened almost exclusively to her mistrals. In this case, her authoritarian voice betrayed her presence.

"Oh, Mistress of Storms, forgive me for intruding on this sacred place, but I call upon the Gods of the Air. The situation is dire!"

*Who are you to dare summon the Gods of the Air*?!

"I am Julius, Harbinger of Balance. As I said Mistress, the situation is dire! Unless immediate action is taken the Black Mural will fall."

Once he identified himself, the cyclone slowly dissipated into cold mountain air. From the floor at his feet, an Aiken began forming around him. Once consumed by the magical cloud, he could see blue sparkles floating around him and tingling on his skin, making him slightly lightheaded. An instant later, he became aware of the overbearing presence of dozens of powerful entities surrounding and silently scrutinizing him. Julius decided the sensation felt much like an unsettled child being called in front of their parents or some other authority figure for a yet unknown infraction.

Summoning his courage, he lifted his head and called out into the Aiken. "Gods of the Air, I have called upon you on behalf of one, Taleeka Konrad."

The Avion cautiously looked around when met with silence, but he could still feel their overbearing presence, so he chose to continue.

"Taleeka Konrad now calls in your debt to her!"

Punetor de Orta slowly swung the arm of the winch over the side of the transport ship and gently hand lowered the large crate onto Wharf Number Six of Zor's Southern Docks.

"Alright, that was the last one," the deck foreman yelled down with a wave.

Punetor nodded and waved back, scowling at the blistering itchy rash on his thickly muscled forearm. The permanent cloud they called the Tannimore Winter affected just about everyone he knew who worked outside. It started as just a single blister on the back of his hand and had gotten progressively worse with each cycle spent unloading ships in the filthy grey mist. If it continued to spread, even the whores wouldn't come near him. Not that Punetor had any attributes worth looking at in the first place. Being short and squat with a brutishly protruding brow line and bowl-shaped haircut, all but ensured any affection he received would have to be paid for.

His current task now complete and without the distraction of work, he had to fight the urge to scratch. The last time he succumbed to the itch, several of the blisters opened up and a foul smelling puss ran down his arm followed by searing pain. He didn't want a repeat of that, so he sighed deeply and tried to ignore it.

Punetor prepared to swing his winch around to greet an arriving transport hackney when he felt the wind pick up from the east. This, however, felt like more of a sucking sensation rather than blowing. When people along the docks began gasping and pointing, he spun to see the nature of the commotion.

He quizzically cocked his head at the recently erected, blue air workers towers on several rooftops. Squinting through the fog, he could just make out that they now strobed and gave off showers of blue sparks.

The sucking wind from the east rapidly picked up, jostling clothing and tossing about anything not secured. He heard cheers erupting throughout the city when the Tannimore Winter began to rise. The citizenry's joyous outbursts reached a fevered pitch when it cleared the rooftops, but their revelry turned into a hushed reverential awe when the wind, now at gale force, carried the offensive mist swiftly eastward.

A rare smile crept across Punetor's face watching the sooty grey cloud leave. It took the better part of a cycle for the skies to clear but at least it wasn't dangerous to work outside anymore. When the wind began to die down, he peered back at the rash on his arm and hoped a trip the Clerria House would take care of it.

Julius knew the plan worked when he saw the sun in the western sky blocked out by the rapidly approaching cloud. Hovering just off the north face of the Ghas 'Tor's summit, he fought to maintain control in the high winds rushing through the mountain's large portico. If not for the deafening roar, he would have been able to hear the chanting coming from the Nalesh Keeps all down the mountain as every one of the air shamans worked in unison channeling their PSI through the magical mountain.

When the cloud reached several miles away, he saw the leading-edge taper into a point. The entire brume formed into a column the width of the manmade fissure at the mountain top. Julius couldn't help but laugh when the stream of sooty mist poured through the portico, whistled past the pillars, and emerged clean and clear on the other side.

He remained aloft for the duration, transfixed on the massive cleaning of the air. When it finished and the wind finally resumed its normal tempest, he considered going down to congratulate and thank the shamans but thought better of it. The Gods of the Air had to force the Nalesh to do the right thing. That did not warrant recognition.

Still smiling, Julius banked east, fully extending his wings, and headed home.

The crowd filled Imperial Judge Sudac Tuomari's chambers to capacity. Traditionally, the miniature courtrooms rarely ever hosted an assembly. The people came to listen to a full day of testimony from Taleeka, Shurta, Talib, Tantei and the alchemist Hemicar, as well as a host of other witnesses.

The judge, an elderly man with short grey hair and beard, patiently listened to the prosecutorial witnesses and Karta's cross examination maintaining an unreadable expression. Most of the crowd consisted of Mazie's ardent supporters, who the judge had to silence several times for their rowdy approval of Karta's defense. Nibira, who sat beside Taleeka, watched her live-in boyfriend rise from his station with a stone-faced Mazie seated beside him. Glancing down at a few notes, he prepared to deliver his final arguments.

"Your Honor, if it please the court?"

The judge silently gestured for Karta to approach.

"Your Honor, quite frankly I'm astounded that the Zorian Guards would waste both the court's and your time, listening to a case built on sand. As my cross examination has amply demonstrated, no human witnesses saw my client steal those horses. We have only the word of a Cevot spider creature, who saw someone from a great distance and has openly admitted to Mz. Konrad that all humans looked alike.

"Then there's the powder that the alchemist says Mazie didn't buy. There were no witnesses to whoever stole the transport ship allegedly used to transport the horses.

"Your Honor, there simply is no case against my client. Furthermore, I would argue that she is a pillar of the community who is personally funding the restoration of this city's most blighted regions. Through her soup kitchens, she is feeding the most vulnerable of our city and she plans to open more.

"Your Honor, please give this woman her good name back and throw out these preposterous charges.

"Thank you, Your Honor."

Karta sat back down and the judge sighed. "I'm afraid I'm going to have to agree with Si. Lushi on this one..."

Mazie's followers erupting in cheers and squeals of delight interrupted the judge's verdict, prompting a sound rapping of the gavel. The judge gave a stern look at the ragged, overjoyed crowd of Seven Sisters citizens and contemplated clearing the courtroom, but with the trial almost over, he continued.

"The Zorian Guards have failed to present anything that could convict this woman. I hereby order Mz. Mazie released and all charges dropped. This tribunal is adjourned."

The small courtroom immediately took on a celebratory mood with the judge's final rap of the gavel. A taut lipped Karta peered over at Nibira who stared at him with the most disappointed look he had ever seen. His heart sank, and a profound feeling of guilt swept over him. He had once again thwarted justice and let the bad guy go free.

Slowly coming to his feet, he stepped over to Mazie, who stood at the end of his table, greeting well-wishers.

"This is my last case for you," he said softly but firmly. "I quit!"

Kai sat cross-legged, floating inches off the ground so that just her eyes appeared above the mist. Twenty yards in front of her, the road leading to the Unaligned City of Shun-Dra stretched from the city out into the Land of Mists. Six mawl corpses lay just off the side of the road rotting away.

The stench of death permeated the entire area, but to Kai it smelled like perfume. She had sat there for a cluster now, waiting. The six dead mawls happened in the first few lunas of her vigil. Word quickly spread through the city's mawl population that stepping from Shun-Dra's protective boundaries constituted a death sentence. No mawls dared to venture out to retrieve their dead, lest they join them. The other races that travelled the only road in or out from the sanctuary city, merely moved the bodies off the road. So, there they lay decomposing, just under the mist and out of view.

The mawls died quickly, just as her people had. Kai had no interest in torture, but sooner or later, the ones called the Order of Kaplan would all die. Receiving refuge there only meant her vengeance would take longer. Because of the city's potent, unyielding anti-violence magic, she could not enter and get it all over with at once.

She had heard that there had been another which had set up a death vigil here. A human female by the name of Okawa who also sought vengeance against the cat people. She gave up however, for reasons unknown.

Giving up did not enter Kai's mind. Being already dead, she had all the time in the world to wait and no mortal could stop her. The mawls could either die of old age in their secure, comfortable prison, or come out to her, for a quick, painless end. It really didn't matter. Time was on her side.

Once the front door closed, Rafel turned off the effects of the shrouding stone and he, as well as the two Legate carrying Mukavar on a stretcher became visible. The Zorian spymaster had anonymously rented the small unassuming bungalow in the outer Shimol Plat of Zor as a place where he could give him constant care.

Clerria House had run out of long-term beds and he needed to be moved. Here Rafel would be able to work remotely and keep a watchful eye on Mukavar.

"The bedroom is over there," he instructed the litter bearers.

They trundled off to the adjacent room, placing him on the lone bed. When they returned to the common area, they stared quizzically at the wall containing six large Larimar screens before turning their attention to their employer.

"Will there be anything else sir?" a bald young man with badly trembling hands asked.

"No, that will be all," Rafel said nonchalantly. "Thank you for your service."

"No sir, *thank, you*," he replied with a broad grin, reaching into his pocket.

Both he and the older man pulled out small vials and began to open them.

"Uh, would you mind doing that somewhere else?" the spymaster asked, not wanting to have to get rid of their bodies.

"Of course, sir."

Both pocketed their containers and silently left. Rafel bolted the door behind them and heaved a weary sigh. He had to stay positive. His love would pull through this. He wouldn't allow himself the notion of a negative thought. He couldn't stand the thought of losing two loves.

The life of a Zorian sword instructor is hardly as glamorous as it sounds. This is especially true if you are the newest instructor saddled with conducting the entirely dreaded but highly profitable children's class.

Chen Arador heaved a weary sigh watching ten preteens pile noisily out the front door of the training hall and into the Zorian streets. He only wished that they could display the same enthusiasm in class.

Locking the front doors behind him he heard the Grand Turine in the Zorian Harbor ring five bells, indicating the Kan would start soon. He felt glad there had been no evening class scheduled and he could get some rest.

He had no sooner turned to leave than he heard a gull squawking just above him. It circled twice, landed a few feet away and made its way to where he stood, navigating through the flow of pedestrians eager to get home. Picking the bird up, he retrieved the message attached to its leg and cast it back into the air.

Chen couldn't imagine who it could be from, so he stepped into a doorway out of foot traffic and eagerly opened it. He cocked his head in surprise when he discovered it was from his uncle Argos.

> *Dearest Nephew,*
> *I hope this letter finds you happy and healthy. I have wonderful news for you. Your three cousins are with child and they are so happy you are the father. The plantation is abuzz with excitement planning the wedding. It should be a grand affair. We all look forward to your immediate return for this happy occasion.*
> *Affectionately,*
> *Uncle Argos*

The bustle of the street faded away with him focusing on the life altering correspondence. Chen read the note two more times making sure he had not misread it, but no, he would be a father three times over. The swordsman stared off into space considering his options, of which there were none. He would not be a pariah to his family. He would do the honorable thing. Marriage and children were now in his immediate future. There seemed nothing left to do but inform the master of his immanent departure and pack.

Everyone knew Patrol Sergeant Parek de Zor as a bull of a man, with a clean shaven, ruddy complexion and long stringy black hair. Standing over six-feet-tall and weighing in at two-hundred-fifty pounds of solid muscle, hardly any situation arose he couldn't control. He needed the intimidation factor too, because the ten grand veteran of the Zorian Guards patrolled the Seven Sisters Slums.

Parek loved walking the beat, keeping his finger on the pulse of the streets. He had turned down taking the test for lieutenant three times in his career, for fear of being shoved behind a desk to move paperwork around. On the streets of the Sisters, he had developed a reputation as tough but fair and absolutely not one to be trifled with.

For the last quinte, he had been partnered with a rookie to break in named Tahala de Tuath. The wiry young woman in her early twenties had delicate features and light brown skin, contrasting against her head of short thick white hair. He found her a bit quiet and shy, prompting him to try breaking her out of her shell, lest the streets of the Seven Sisters chew her up and spit her out.

"I tell ya kid, you gotta pick your battles," Parek said, eyeing a pair of suspicious young men following a well-dressed woman with a shoulder bag. "You're gonna see multiple crimes committed every cycle. There aren't enough decis in a cycle for you to chase after every one of them."

He motioned to the two young men, one of which had peeled off and attempted a flanking maneuver on the woman they stalked. "Now right there, that's something to pay attention to."

"What is it, Sarge?"

"The kid with the bad haircut over there."

"Yeah?"

"His buddy just ran off around the corner of that side street. They're trying to trap that Imperial Tax Collector. They probably think she's got money. Why the Imperial Bank would send a collector into the Sisters without an escort is beyond me. Come on, let's go, you take the far end of the street. Stay sharp."

"You got it, Sarge."

Tahala took off at a trot and Parek made his way across the busy main road to the smaller side street. Once he rounded the corner, he scowled, suspicions confirmed. The two young thugs had the woman trapped in a recessed doorway. They advanced menacingly with daggers drawn. The trembling woman cowered against the door clutching her bag.

"I tell ya what," Parek said, walking towards the calamitous scene. "My shift is just about over and I really don't need the paperwork. What say you boys put away the toothpicks and skedaddle before I mop up this alley with your sorry asses and then arrest you."

The two turned towards the Zorian Guard and sneered. Parek had to admit to himself, the kids had balls. Normally at this point, they would have taken off running. Instead, one lifted his face to the sky and gave out a loud warbling call.

"We are with the Kaya Militia and we have business with this person," the young man with the bad haircut said.

The sergeant scoffed and continued advancing. "Militia huh? I didn't know Kaya Plat needed its own militia."

"Yes, we protect the soup kitchen and new construction. We have no time for city workers, leave us!"

Parek chuckled and halted five feet away. "Protection huh? See, the problem here, is that protection is *this* city worker's job. I'm the law on these streets. So, I won't say it again. Put the knives away and trundle off."

Parek peered over his shoulder when he heard a commotion behind him. Entering the street were five other young men, grouped together.

Parek noted their similar grey tunics. "Ah, I see the rest of your little *militia* has decided to join us."

"You really think you can take us all on?" The young man said with confident condescension.

A wide knowing grin crossed the guard's weathered face and he shook his head. "Yes, but then again, I don't have to."

He then stepped to the side so all could see Tahala standing just inside the streets entrance thirty feet away, aiming her Mark Six pistol at the rag tag militiamen.

"She may be new," he said calmly, "but she's a really good shot. She'll splatter all of your buddies. Then we're just back to us."

Parek put one large fist inside the other and loudly cracked his knuckles. "Okay, so who dies first?"

With the defeated looks on their faces, the combination of the pistol trained on them and the sergeant's assertiveness took the fight out of the belligerent group. The five new arrivals slinked off quickly, while the two threatening the tax collector put their blades away and passed Parek with arrogant sneers.

In a sudden, solitary outburst, Parek lashed out with a ham sized fist that tagged the boisterous one on the side of the jaw. The young thug's head lurched violently to the side accompanied by the sounds of bones cracking. He dropped to the street, teeth and blood spewing from his mouth.

"You're under arrest, you arrogant little prick!" Parek said to the unconscious hoodlum, then addressing his stunned friend, "Now, get out of my sight! If I run into you again…"

The thug needed no more prompting and took off at a dead run before Parek finished his sentence.

"What was that all about, Sarge?" Tahala asked, holstering her pistol.

The tax collector still trembled and looked at both Zorian Guards with tear filled eyes.

"They said something about a tribute," she sobbed.

"Tribute huh?" Parek scoffed. "Are you alright ma'am?"

The woman nervously nodded. "You got here before they could do anything."

Parek bobbed his head. "Good, we're going to need you to testify when this clown appears before an Imperial Judge. That will probably be next cycle. So, make sure you're down at Judgement Square bright and early."

The woman acknowledged the request, then sighed. "In the meantime, there's a large glass of wine with my name on it. These papers can just wait to be delivered."

"I understand," Tahala said sympathetically when the woman passed her.

"He said something about being part of a militia that protects the soup kitchens and new construction," Parek said when Tahala joined him and they peered down at the crumpled body in the street.

"You don't think Mazie's putting together her own private security force, do you?"

"It sure looks like it," Parek said, pointing at the body, "and check out what he's got on under that tunic as well as his hands. He's one of the Sister's street people. So that means she's got a pretty large pool of people to call on."

Parek then exhaled loudly in frustration. "Dammit, and I was hoping I could get by without having to file any reports!"

A new member of Taleeka's inner circle now joined the regular, once a cluster, dinner meeting at Konrad House West. Zerga de Woon sat close beside her new girlfriend. Holding hands under the table, she stroked the inside of Taleeka's thigh, all the while laughing and giggling with her new group of friends.

"So, everything's good between you and Karta?" Taleeka directed her query at Nibira.

The young librarian grew animated. "Oh yes. You know that he quit working for Mazie the moment he got her off from stealing those horses? Right?"

All around the table nodded.

"Well, he no sooner quit than the Zorian High Council ruled that an office of Imperial Prosecutor be formed. They were tired of the bad guys having access to the best barristers while the Zorian Guards had to rely on their investigators. And guess who they offered the job of Lead Prosecutor to?"

"Nibira, that's wonderful!" Taleeka said, amongst the congratulations which erupted from around the table.

"And, I've got an announcement," Taleeka declared to a table full of inquisitive faces. "We're gonna have to move these meetings down to the Dokana Pub for the next few clusters. I'm sending Peshk out to secure properties across Lumina and you sure don't want to eat my cooking."

"What's going on, Tally?" Nibira asked.

"I need to secure bases of operation that aren't halfway around the world while travelling."

"Won't that be expensive?" Nibira asked.

Taleeka softly scoffed. "Honestly, with the investments my folks set me up with, as well as the several business ventures in progress, I'm making money faster than I can spend it."

A sarcastic, "Aww," quickly swept around the table.

Taleeka rolled her eyes and then continued. "After she secures the property, she'll then oversee the installation of a security system, much like I have here. If any one of us needs a safe house, one will only be a short distance away."

"Where are they going to be, Tally?" Zerga asked, before putting a fork full of food into her mouth.

"Up in the Goyodian Chain. I want apartments in all four human house's ancestral capitals. So, that's one in Rophan, Aris, Dryden and Brinstan. That should be enough to keep an eye on anything they may be cooking up. She'll then secure full, free-standing residences in Tewa-Ta, Makatooa, Modetto on Goyo, Tetrath on Wou, Danteia on Wou-Late', Faul on Lurd Island in the Outer Zerians, Simara on Moreen Island in the Otoman Group, Oramor on Zer-Tal Island in the Zer-Tal Twins and Penaber in The Narrow Lands."

She then glanced at Barr-Ani "There's also going to be a full residence in Immor-Onn."

The Bailian flushed at the gesture. "Really?"

"Yep," Taleeka confirmed. "Anytime you want to visit home, you'll have a safe place to lay your head."

"What about Amarenia?" Noorim asked.

The question prompted a wry chuckle from Taleeka. "Are you kidding?! If my mom found out I was in Amarenia and didn't stay at Konrad East, she would soundly kick my ass and I'd deserve it.

"Ahh, maybe in Durik. It's on the other side of the continent and I've heard they've got warlord troubles all throughout the Dor. I should keep an eye on things, so, yeah, maybe there."

"Speaking of Amarenia," Noorim said, hesitantly, "I have an announcement of my own."

All eyes at the table immediately fixed on the bare chested Amarenian.

"I will be returning to Amarenia," she said in her usual austere manner.

A collective gasp passed around the table.

"Why?" Barr-Ani asked sadly.

"My schooling is complete. I now return home to teach the Mahaila and Queen's Envoy what I have learned. It is my fondest hope for Amarenia to join the Society of Whispers. I also go for further training. Geta Kennari Napp has agreed to take me on as a student.

"Taleeka, I will be training beside your father."

"No kidding!" Taleeka beamed. "I mean I hate to see you go, but this is exciting! Something also tells me that if you're involved with the society over there, we'll be running into each other."

"Where will you stay?" Barr-Ani asked, a touch of melancholy still detectable.

"I could always stay at my family's plantation. That, however, would mean a lengthy trip for training. Kennari has offered to allow me to stay with her."

"Yeah, she's got a couple of spare bedrooms," Taleeka noted grimly.

"With all this shifting around, what about Mazie and the Etherions?" Zerga asked.

Taleeka picked up her fork and gave a shallow shrug.

"Mazie and I have an agreement. I don't care what she does in the Sisters, as long as it doesn't affect me or any of my operations.

"As for the Etherions, whew, talk about your fragile peace. The Na-Kab are just twitching, waiting for them to screw up."

"Do you trust any of it to last?" Zerga asked, raising an eyebrow.

"Not a bit," Taleeka replied, stabbing a piece of meat with her fork. "That's why I'm acquiring those properties. It's time I increased my sphere of influence."

# GLOSSARY

*Spoiler warning: The following is a master glossary for all the books in this series. Reading beyond a specific word or phrase searches could result in spoilers.*

**Adad Sunal** – EEtah war collage belonging to House Bran, specializing in conducting internal security for House Bran.

**Agress** – A green Etheria Crystal with red striations which opens and closes doors, windows and hatches, negating any locks but not traps or wards.

**Aiken** – Semi-sentient clouds sent out across the Annigan from Mount Ghas-Tor, recording everything they witness on the ground and in the air. They are indistinguishable from other clouds against the backdrop of a blue sky. Aiken constantly send visuals back to the mountain, but recent images remain in their limited memory. Those possessing psychic abilities can access their recent memories by flying through and communing with them.

**Akina** – Humanoid fox creatures native to the Barrens in the Twilight Lands. Often sly and excellent thieves.

**Amarenian** – Female human race formerly noted for their hatred and slavery of men and piracy.

**Angona** – Roasted eel on a stick. Sold from vendors' carts all over the City of Immor-Onn.

**Annigan** – The name of the world which is the setting for the various stories in the Tales of the Annigan Cycle. It includes the two hemispheres of Lumina and Nocturn separated by the Twilight Lands.

**Anointed Sister** – The title for the Amarenian Queen.

**Aquamarine** – Pale blue Etheria Crystal which reveals something's true nature.

**Ara-Fel Party** – Political party of Amarenian farmers.

**Arapa Fish** – A large fish native to the back waters and tributaries of the Otoman River. Their tough scaly skin is coveted among the Dreeat as armor. The scales by themselves are so abrasive they are also sold as nails.

**Ash-Ta** – Avion term (winged monster) for the widespread colonies of humanoid bats inhabiting the rocky crags stretching across of the Spine of the World. Avion scholars record six tribes: the Molossi, Acero, Chiro, Ptero, Diaemus and Desmodus. The Ash-Ta allied with the Tiikeri due to their shared enemy, the Do-Tarr.

**Astute Sister** – Amarenian title for high level politician.

**Aur-Quaz** – Iridescent Etheria Crystal stimulating energy.

**Available Regions** – Uninhabited areas of Immor-Onn waiting for the residents displaced by the recent Black Pearl Revolution to return and inhabit.

**Avion** –Proud sentient rulers of Lumina's sky. Incredibly beautiful and graceful to behold and unabashedly elitist, especially towards their distant cousins, the Humans. Avions refuse to wear any armor and yet have led the way in almost every major war fought. Their scholars contributed a great deal to the knowledge of Lumina. Their four Great Houses occupy the airspace and mountain tops of the Goyan Islands.

## Avion Great Houses:

**House Azar** - Avion House inhabiting the City of Mitar, on the Island of Dal, in the Tellasian chain, ruled by Queen Averin. Their territories include the skies over the Tellasian Chain, Otomoria, Zer-Tal Twins, and the Zerk Atoll. They are known for their healing Clerics of Neami and their beautiful music.

**House Eacher** - Avion House inhabiting the Island of Wou, City of Picon & surrounding airspace. Ruled by King Sindil.

**House Solas** – Smallest of all the Avion houses. They inhabit the city of Adean on the Island of Temil in the Outer Zerians and control the surrounding airspace.

**House Pyre** - Eldest, largest, and most powerful of all the Avion Houses. They inhabit the skies above the Island of Goya. Their city stronghold, Darmont Keep, sits on the north face of volcanic Mount Goya. Unlike the other Avion Houses who utilize Air Magic, they mastered Fire Magic drawing their power from the volcano.

**Awal** – First of the ten Quinte Grand Cycle, Spring.

**Azurite** – Purple Etheria Crystal which connects to the Middle realms.

**Bailian** – Predominate race of the western Twilight Lands. Descended from the Piceans, they are a beautiful humanoid race with pale blue skin and large eyes.

**Banja** – The seventy-seven Amarenian noble families, eleven for each of the various seven provinces called Dors.

**Banok Atoll** – Island ring in the Southeastern Ocean of Lumina housing one of the largest permanent Flavian portals. Its psionic ripples extend out hundreds of miles and affect the entire southeastern Deep Ocean of Lumina.

**Banok Run** – The final test for admittance to the elite Brightstar Sailors where they must navigate a tight circle around the turbulent seas surrounding the Banok Atoll without being pulled into its giant Flavian portal.

**Bespoke Lords** – Members of prominent families who have Bespoke Names and serve as advisors to the sovereign in a respective noble human house in the Goyan Islands.

**Bespoke Names** – Honorary family names only bestowed by a Goyan Island governor or higher as reward for exemplary service to the crown.

**Black Mural** – A magical record of the Annigan located deep in the Rod-Ema Trench in the Ocean Deep of Nocturn. It slowly grows in size as it records every act of imbalance on the planet. If it grows too large, it will penetrate into the planet's core, killing all life and allowing it to start anew.

**Black Talon** – Special forces of the Aramos Army, the Fosvara Guard.

**Boustian Mage** – Bards who perform magic by singing, playing music and storytelling, found predominantly in the larger cities of the Goyodian Chain of islands.

**Brightstar** – Elite sailors of House Calden qualified to sail the Deep Oceans and the storm-tossed seas of the Twilight Lands. Captains in the Calden Navy must be Brightstar qualified. Brightstar only allows acceptance to their ranks upon completion of the treacherous Innaca or Banok Runs.

**Brom** – Horse size dragonflies inhabiting the steep southern foothills of the Amaren Mountains.

**Calcite** – Clear Etheria Crystal which aids in navigation.

**Caldani** – Privateers hired by Human House Calden to patrol their waters.

**Calden Intelligencer Service** – House Calden's elite spy agency and secret police. They draw recruits mostly from the Calden Maritime Legion.

**Calden Maritime Legion** – Marines for House Calden

**Calisma** – Main library in the University of Marassa.

**Cali** – Branch libraries and scriptoriums in the five Human capital cities in the Goyodian Island Chain.

**Carbana** – Chewing tobacco rolled into a tight tube.

**Cavernite** – A pale green Etheria Crystal with pink striations that can increase the physical dimensions of the interior of any structure it is placed within. The size increase depends on the amount of Cavernite used and the level of PSI used to power it. Without a constant supply of PSI power, the dimensions revert back to their original size. Often used with an Obsidian PSI battery backup.

**Centi Elipse** – Called a Centi for short. Unit of time in the Goyan Islands equaling a minute.

**Celot** – Amarenian term for a priestess.

**Cevot** – Large sentient spider creatures known for their silk, inhabiting the Os-Oni Mountains of the Twilight Lands.

**Ched** – Seventh of the ten Quinte Grand Cycle, Autumn.

**Chanakans** – An ancient race of sentient octopoids dwelling in vast underwater cities in the Ocean Deep of Nocturn. They worship the ancient ones of the abyss and practice a powerful water magic.

**Cluster** – The name for ten cycles, the Annigan's version of a week. There are five clusters to a Quinte (month).

**Cobalcite** – Deep pink Etheria Crystal used for healing.

**Code of Tisina** – Mobster code of silence in the City of Zor. Because of Zor's zero tolerance for organized crime, the various independent criminals adopted a "no cooperation" rule with city officials. The slightest violation of this code is punishable by death.

**Common** – The Common Tongue, a spoken only language used mostly by humans and those in business with them.

**Cocoonessa** – Cocoon city of the Tinian Moth people on Mount Natal in the Land of Mists. Also called the Silk City.

**Corporal Reach, The** –The prime material plain of the middle realms where the Annigan resides.

**Coxeter** – Both the language and magic system of the Tinian race based on a complex form of three-dimensional geometry. The written language is made up of cryptic mathematical notations using lines and dots. Tinian minds perceive all math as the three-dimensional mapping, best displayed in their silk weavings of intricate geometric patterns. When combined with Etheria Crystals, these patterns can be used to perform spells.

**Croquis** – Magitech mapping devise projecting a scalable three-dimensional holographic image of a desired location, including the other planes of the multiverse.

**Cub Prince** – A rare black tiger heir to the throne of the Tiikeri Empire. Once every generation, the Tiikeri king must breed an heir. All prominent Tiikeri families offer their most eligible daughters for breeding, but only one will conceive of a black tiger. All other cubs produced from this royal union are killed at birth. They move the complete family of the female who gives birth to the Cub Prince into the palace and considered them nobility. They immediately begin grooming the Cub Prince for the throne, and, when he comes of age, he must kill his father to take it.

**Cul-Ta** – Humanoid rat creatures found in almost every City in Lumina.

**Cycle** – Time period equivalent to a day.

**Dag** – Amarenian term for a common slave. A derogatory slang word for a male.

**Darek Witch** – Amarenian earth shamans acting as midwives and performing other shamanistic duties.

**Darian Silk** – High quality silk spun by the Cevot Spiders traded to the On'Dara.

**Darwan** – A cross between the Balians and the Fudomi, this race is the most prolific humanoid native to the Barrens. They situate their villages around Ghorn temples and must pay tribute to the Onay hordes of the region. Villages close to the borders of the hordes remain under constant threat. Darwans raise a herd animal called the Ng'Ombe which provides the major staple food in the Barrens.

**Dasam** – Tenth of the ten Quinte Grand Cycle, Winter.

**Deci** – Time unit equivalent to one hour.

**Derde** – Third of the ten Quinte Grand Cycle, Spring.

**Diamond** – Clear Etheria Crystal which transfers power.

**Doggin** – Derogatory term used for slave dock workers in the city of Aris.

**Dolin** – Etheria gem hunters, mostly of the Gila race, traveling the Barrens in small caravans and harvesting raw Etheria Crystals to sell to the Zadim lapidaries of the Oasis in the Dark Waste Desert.

**Dor** – Title of the seven various provinces in Amarenia. Taia-Dor, Denat-Dor, Mivira-Dor, Amoso-Dor, Kinning-Dor, Rackam-Dor, Durik-Dor.

**Do-Tarr** – Sentient, hive-minded mantid creatures from the Land of Mists in Nocturn. They comprise two large hives in the north and south with precise subterranean tunnels connecting them. They are expert builders and remain neutral in all forms of politics.

**Dreamer in the Lake** – Demi-God of the Os'Tor Forest and a Harbinger of Balance. She rests at the bottom of a large lake encased in mud and manifests herself on the lake's surface as a multicolored lotus. Her accolades, sentients from every race, sleep around the lake's shore, sending their ethereal bodies out into people's dreams and guiding them.

**Dreeat** – Humanoid crocodilians inhabiting the end of the western fork of the Otoman River in Otomoria. They grow sugar cane and make magical healing candies from it. They harvest river fish as a major part of their diet. For thousands of grands, ever since the arrival Human race, the Human families have tried to eradicate them.

**Dronning Mare** – Female horse chosen to breed with the On'Dara chief.

**EEtah** – Large, powerful and aggressive sentient humanoid shark creatures trained in martial schools known as Sunals to become the professional warriors of Lumina. After their egg birth in the hatcheries and their first year in the nursery, they are sorted into one of the various Sunals of their House. Females enter House Nur and the males go through a highly competitive Sunal scouting and recruiting process with the nursery's called the Garess. Sunals hire out bodyguards, sentries, mercenaries and virtually anything martial. This, along with weapon manufacturing and sales, provides the main revenue stream for the great houses.

**EEtah Great Houses:**

> **House Nur** – This Noble house is female only. Co-ruled by a secular Queen Mother and spiritual High Priestess.
>> Temple of Drulain headquartered in the High Holy City of Zor.
>> Specialty: Scribes, Clerics, Healers, Politics, Domestics.

> **House Crom** – Three Sunals in the Tellasian Chain.
>> Sedar Sunal on Roe Island. Specialty: Bodyguard.
>> Boril Sunal on Uma Island. Specialty: Crom Internal Security.
>> Zorod Sunal on Tel Island. Specialty: Castle and Town Defense.

> **House Bran** – Four Sunals in the Goyodian Chain.

Garf Sunal on Quell Island. Specialty: Long term inland duty.

Tukk Sunal on Mobis Island. Specialty: Shipboard Security.

Adad Sunal on Creos Island. Specialty: Bran Internal Security.

Farak Sunal on Roust Island. Specialty: Bounty Hunter, Vengeance.

**House Zed** – Three Sunals in the Wouvian Islands.

Dakor Sunal on Owling Island. Specialty: Shock Troops.

Jut Sunal on Tor Island. Specialty: Zed Internal Security.

Morrak Sunal on Billow Island. Specialty: Police, Executioners.

**Elipse** – A unit of time equaling a second.

**Ellie** – Slang and abbreviation for an Ellipse.

**Esteemed Sister** – Amarenian title for Ambassador.

**Etheria Crystal** – Crystals containing magical properties mostly found in crystal trees in the Barrens of the Twilight Lands. Residents of the Dark Waste Desert harvest and process the oases' crystals. These crystals provide the primary form of magic in Nocturn.

**Flavian Portals** – Portals through space making different points in the Annigan instantaneously accessible by passing through the inter-dimensional Middle Realms. Each portal is different. There are several large, fixed portals on both Lumina and Nocturn and hundreds of smaller dedicated Flavians. Certain animals, intoxicants and magical items can open smaller portals.

**Frozen Sea** – The vast expanse of ice flows covering the majority of Nocturn and the largest centrally occupied area in all of Annigan. The ice ranges from a slushy mixture with icebergs near the land masses to several hundred feet thick in the eastern areas.

**Forsvara Guards** – A rank-and-file foot soldier army of House Aramos.

**Fudomi** – Sentient humanoid ram creatures inhabiting the western Os-Oni Mountains of the Twilight Lands. They steal and sell the Cevot Spider broods' silk and eggs, which they consider a delicacy.

**Galeb** – Sea Gulls with a psychic connection to a handler. They are used to transport messages across Lumina.

**Garf Sunal** – EEtah War college belonging to House Bran. Their specialty is long term inland duty.

**Gar-Kal** – Fish head humanoids living on the ocean floor of Nocturn. They are of low intelligence and aggressive.

**Geta** – Amarenian title for a master at a skill or craft, especially if they teach it.

**Ghas-Tor** – This is the tallest peak on the Annigan. It reaches upward 32,000 feet in the Os'Ani Mountain range of the Twilight Lands. More than a mountain, it is a sentient being and the epicenter of Air Magic in the world.

**Ghorn** – Necromancers of the Barrens in Twilight Lands.

**Ghost Suit** – A gray, skintight jump suit used mostly by Valdurian forces to blend into the Kan fog.

**Ghosts of the Kan** – Mariner's term for Rayth raiders. Due to their ghost white chalk covering their bodies and acting as camouflage when they attack during the Kan fog.

**Gila** – The main sentient race populating the Dark Waste. Hybrids comprising Bailian pilgrims and a now long-gone sentient lizard native to the region. They are an advanced race occupying the three large oases of the desert.

**Golden One, The** – Otick term for the Golden Avatar.

**Goy-Ardia** – Goyan fire mages trained at the University of Marassa.

**Goyan Calendar** – Method of time keeping found only in the Goyan Islands. It consists of a Grand Cycle (year) which is comprised of ten Quinte (months) named; Awal, Teine, Derde, Kvara, Peto, Sesto, Ched, Merve, Tisa and Dasam. Each Quinte is divided into fifty Cycles (days) with each cycle being divided into fifty Deci (hours) twenty-five in sunlight and twenty-five in Kan. Ten cycles equal a Cluster (week) with five Clusters per Quinte.

**Goyan Rise** – A 300-mile-wide sea mount in central Lumina acting as the floor of the Shallow Sea. Its volcanic vents fuel the volcano of Mount Goya.

**Grand** – Short for Grand Cycle. Unit of time equivalent to a year.

**Grass Eater** – Singa insult

**Gustare'** – Amarenian bath house and tavern.

**Hackney** – Etheria driven floating carriages found throughout the major cities of Lumina.

**Hand of the Wind** – The Assassin's Guild of Annigan. All members worship Orad, goddess of death. The upper levels are clerics of Orad.

**Hakim** – A judge in the High Holy City of Zor.

**Harbingers of Balance** – Sentient creatures of all types called to a secret society monitoring the balance of the Annigan and warning when something upsets it.

**Hasteen** – City of the Dreeat crocodile people.

**Hill Sister** – Hermaphroditic warriors inhabiting the northern foothills of the Amaren Mountains in Amarenia. Though they possess both male and female sex organs, they cannot procreate. Popular with Amarenian nobility as seneschal/bodyguards partly because they can have sex with them and not violate their "no man" pledge.

**Hoon** – Word used in Zor to denote a pimp or the manager of a brothel.

**Howlite** – Gray Etheria Crystal used for glamour, disguise and polymorphing.

**Humans** – The Human race descended from the Avion race. In 5070 PA, the rebellious Avions which joined Xandar the Mad's doomed Great Kraken Incursion had their wings severed as punishment before being banished and scattered to the Goyodian Chain. 171 years later the Seventh Avatar sang the "Song of Rebirth" evolving them into a separate race. They formed their Great Houses, spreading out across the Goyan Island Chain and beyond the Shallow Sea.

**Human Great Houses:**

**House Aramos** –The largest and wealthiest of the great human families directly descended from the First Men. The capital city of Aris is located on the Island of Vakai in the Goyodian Chain of Islands in the Northern Shallow Sea. They control banking and finance in Lumina and constantly hatch Machiavellian plots to expand their power over the other houses.

**House Calden** – This great house controls the seas with the largest military and commercial fleets. Their Capital City of Nader is on the Island of Tarla in the Goyodian Chain, but they command the island chain of the Zerk Atoll where their sailors are trained.

**House Eldor** – This great house controls virtually all the agricultural islands of the eastern Goyan Islands. Their Capital City of Rophan is on the Island of Tolle in the Goyodian Chain of Islands in the Northern Shallow Sea.

**House Valdur** – This house is known for their incestuous practices to keep the family bloodline pure. Their capital city of Dryden is on the Island of Atar in The Goyodian Chain of Islands in the Northern Shallow Sea. All but destroyed in a surprise invasion by House Eldor called the Unification War, only the discovery of lighter than air travel and a fleet of war balloons saved their home island. They lost the rest of their agricultural lands to Eldor. Their entire culture revolves around their powerful air guild, the Valdurian Air Service.

**House Whitmar** – This family runs the organized and sanctioned slave trade on Lumina from the City of Nier on the northern Goya coast. Their Capital City of Brinstan is located on the Island of Umin in the Goyodian Chain in the Northern Shallow Sea.

**Immor-Onn** – Large city known as "the Shining Jewel of the East" located on the western coast of the Twilight Lands. Home of the Bailian Empire.

**Idonian Philosophy** – The Avion prejudice that Humans are a scourge which should be wiped out. The driving belief of the Idonian Cabal of Avion House Pyre and Solas.

**Innaca Deep** – Giant whirlpool in the Northwestern Ocean of Lumina housing one of the largest Flavian portals. Its psionic ripples extend out hundreds of miles.

**Innaca Run** – The final test for admittance to the elite Brightstar Sailors where they must navigate a tight circle around the turbulent seas surrounding the Innaca Atoll without being pulled into its giant Flavian portal.

**Ironmark** – Brutal enforcers of the Quartermasters in the Goyan Islands of Lumina. Each island chain has their own Ironmark specializing in their own unique form of torture.

**Itori** – Insect Shamans found throughout the agricultural western Goyan Islands. Although they control mostly locusts, they can command any insect and are immune to all insect venoms and stings.

**Jangwa** – Elite desert commandos defending the outer parameter of the two civilized oases in the Dark Waste Desert. Capable of traveling under the sand and rapidly over the surface of the desert, they make frequent scouting missions to the untamed Qua-Raman Oasis and the Buried City of Nof-Saloom.

**Kaefom** – Traditional Amarenian breeding ritual overseen by the Darek Witches.

**Kan** – Period of the day in the Goyan Islands when the thick sea fog rises blotting out the sun, used mostly for sleep. It is an effect caused by geothermal activities only found in the Goyan Islands and Shallow Sea.

**Kel** – Flying lizards bred and tended by Avions for food and as beasts of burden.

**Kharry Institute** – Tiikeri medical facility located outside the Tiikeri capital city of Hai-Darr and run by the brilliant and ruthless Dr. Met-Ge, specializing in crossbreeding Mawl races to produce Mongrels for specific duties. The Institute created Cheepas and the Ves-Lari.

**Kinjuto Dominator** – Sex mage using BDSM techniques.

**Konaleeta** – Called the Island of the Lost. The entire island is caught in a permanent Flavian Loop. It bounces around from location to location across any of the planes of the Middle Realms, never staying in anyone place for very long.

**Kusars** – Mawl bandits from the Dasos region in the Land of Mists.

**Kvara** – Fourth of the ten Quinte Grand Cycle, Summer.

**Ky-Awat** – Sentient rat creatures of the Dark Waste Desert. They have bred them up from the Cul-Ta and are larger and more aggressive, but no smarter. Various factions use them as cannon fodder. They breed quickly and are plentiful, especially around the three main oases.

**Land of Mists** – The largest land mass in Nocturn. So named because the mixture of cold temperatures in the air combined with the warmth of the ground results in a uniform constant low hanging fog over the entire continent. Three distinct landscapes cover the surface of the land, separated by the Kel-Raku Mountain range and dimly illuminated by bioluminescence, outcroppings of Etheria Crystals and the moon and stars. The thick rainforest of Arboro lies to the north, and the vast savannah of Rovina runs to the south. They're connected by the Bor-Kaa Pass. The dense jungles and swamps of Dasos lie to the east.

**Landagar Group** – Research and Development Division of the Valdurian Air Service located in the balloon city of Landagar high in the mountain peaks of the Valdurian home island of Atar.

**Larimar** – The "Talking Stone," a milky white Etheria Crystal with blue striations, used for psychic communication between parties within proximity of the gem.

**Learned Sister** – The title given to Amarenian teachers, scribes & academics.

**Legates** – Suicide messengers hired through House Whitmar. Candidates are usually elderly or terminally ill. Upon their death, House Whitmar agrees to care for their surviving family for their remaining lifetimes.

**Lor-Danta Oasis** – The eastern most major oasis in the Dark Waste Desert. The large Obsidian field stretching from its shore contains six Tanum Charts of the skies used by the Arron-Nin Astrologers dwelling there.

**Lumina** – The hemisphere of the world in constant sunlight.

**Luna** – Term for the lunar cycle used by every culture in the Annigan except the humans in the Goyan Islands, who cannot see the moon.

**Luroh** – Bolo/sash weapon used by the Mahilia. The sash contains the person's rank and record. The two metal balls at either end become an effective weapon when twirled.

**Magitech** – The fusion of magic and technology. Mostly referring to the use of Etheria Crystals and specific mechanical items. i.e., Airship engines.

**Mahilia** – City guards in Mostar, the capital of Amarenia.

**Makari** – Inter-dimensional race of sentient spiders from the Pasture Plain of the Middle Realms. They seeded the Cevot race in the Os'Tor Mountains in the Land of Mists. The males resemble hairy wolf spiders, the females resemble black widows. The females have been known to allure any male of any race. They compulsively kill after sex.

**Malachite** – Light green Etheria Crystal, absorbs energy.

**Marassa** – A professor at the University of Marassa.

**Masha** – Amarenian for master.

**Maudo Grass** – Tall grass with a bright blue flowering tuft growing in the Land of Mists. The flowers are a favorite intoxicant for Mawls and especially coveted by the Tiikeri.

**Mawl** – Overall name for the humanoid cat races of the Land of Mists. It is also the term used for the common language they share.

**Medikua** – Medical officer aboard Calden naval vessels.

**Merve** – Eighth of the ten Quinte Grand Cycle, Autumn.

**Middle Realms** – Constantly shifting inter-dimensional plane between worlds. Sometimes referred to as the Fairy or Dream Realms.

**Mongrel** – The product of cross breeding between the Mawl races found all over the Land of Mists. Pure breeds mostly shun them and the Tiikeri use them for slave labor.

**Moonfall** – Period of the cycle when Nocturn's main illuminating body, the moon, dips below the horizon issuing in the Moonless

**Moonless** – The "night" period of the cycle when Nocturn's main illuminating body, the moon, orbits around to the Lumina side of the Annigan.

**Mora** – Term used for teacher or master in the Whovian Sword Schools of Rohina Takki.

**Morasian Puff Boy** – Male prostitute from the Port City of Moras on Goya's west coast. Known for their distinctly feminine demeanor.

**Mostas** – Capital City of the Amarenian Empire on the western shore of Amarenia.

**Najuka** – Amarenian emasculation ritual performed on all males except those used for breeding purposes in the Kaefom Ritual.

**Na-Kab** – One of the three insectoid groups originating from below the Land of Mists. They occupied the easternmost hive closest to Mount Natal. Their exoskeleton is made up of fire magic. Their tail has a penis shaped stinger capable of impregnating any living thing they sting.

**Namesake** – Term used for spouse when they share a bespoke last name.

**Narrows, The** – Remnants of an old iron mine forming the slums of the Hidden City of Toriss in Otomoria.

**Nocturn** – The hemisphere of the world in constant night

**Nolton Boat** – Ships made of Ukko wood in a secret shipyard on the Island of Zer, mostly used by Brightstar sailors. Hovering less than an inch above the water, their Ukko rudder guides and propels. The specific construction of the hull makes the boat unsinkable.

**Noma** – Poison from the Noma Viper.

**Nurian Edicts** – EEtah rules of conduct set down by House Nur forming the basis for all Sunal laws. The various Sunals add their own individual laws to this baseline.

**Nyanja** – Large seahorses ridden as sea cavalry by the Calden Navy.

**Obsidian** – Black Etheria Crystal storing psychic energy.

**Ocean Deep** – Name referring to any of the deep oceans of Lumina or Nocturn.

**Ol'daEE** – Person able to cast spells while having sex under the influence of Oldust.

**Oldust** – Hallucinogenic powder derived from the spores of the rare Impia Mushroom, increasing magical abilities and is essential for individual travel to the Middle Realms.

**Onay** – Humanoid wolf men of the Barrens, banding their various packs together in three distinct hordes.

**On'Dara** – Sentient horse creatures living on the Plains of Taka-Vir in the southeastern Twilight Lands. They raise and train horses, trading them for silk with the Cevot Spiders and selling them to the rest of the Annigan.

**ooD** – Shell worn on the back of the male Otick warriors as armor. They mark the warrior's rank and house on the outside of the shell and inscribe a record of their deeds on the inside. They place the ooD over the entrance to their homes in the sand.

**Oracle of the River** – Demi-God who dwells in the cypress swamp at the end of the western fork of the Otoman River for thousands of grands. It appears as a partially submerged giant catfish with its many whiskers sunken into the water. These whiskers perceive anything happening in, on, or around the waterway.

**Orad** – Air goddess of death and predominate deity of the assassin's guild, the Hand of the Wind. Her creed: *She comes as the wind. And takes whom she wishes. Her name is Orad. And she is death.*

**Orad Dex** – Initiates to the Orad priesthood. Street/entry level assassins.

**Orad Con** – (Taker of the Divine Wind) These are full priests of Orad. Their special skills are the Kiss of Death, the Poison Breath and the Phantom Dagger.

**Orad Sto** – (Giver of the Divine Wind) High priests of Orad who can also restore life.

**Otick** – Humanoid crab people inhabiting the Shallow Sea. Among the first sentient creatures to rise from the ocean floor they evolved into a proud, deeply spiritual and noble race. Goya's volcanic warmed waters provide home to the Otick's prolific oyster beds littering the floor of the Shallow Sea. From these beds arose the five great Pearl Avatars, creation gods whose songs brought life and sentience to Lumina. Otick society is divided into a highly structured caste system: Worker Class, Warrior Class and Mother Class, and organized into two main categories: domestic and military. The Shelled Triad, the three Otick Great Houses, tend their own oyster beds and compete for the birthplace of the next Avatar.

## Otick Great Houses:

**House Awa** – Home of the last two avatars. Located in the Tellasian Chain, in the capital city of Hidet on the Island of Zod. Mother Class specialization.

**House Pewa** – Located in the Goyodian Chain, in the capital city of Oniack, on the Island of Zak. Worker Class specialization.

**House Sensu** – Located in the Otoman Group, in the capital city of Sunico, on the Island of Lakia. Warrior Class specialization.

**Otomoria** – Large Island continent in the western Goyan Islands. The main grain producing agricultural island.

**Outer Clan EEtah** – Humanoid shark creatures smaller in stature than regular EEtahs and cast out from the three great EEtah Houses hatcheries. The survivors band together into loose clans, contracting themselves out as deck hands or recently volunteering in the Valdurian Marines.

**Padi** – Regional demi-god of water worshiped in and around the High Holy City of Zor, associated with the peace and calming effect of water and represented by a calm pond.

**Palu EEtah** – Rare hammerhead EEtahs. They are as big as the Outer Clan EEtah but extremely intelligent. They tend to be reclusive loners.

**Pappia** – Members of the child street gangs of the Hidden City of Toriss in the slum section of The Narrows.

**Pa-Waga** – Lawful evil god of greed worshiped mostly by the Tiikeri. Its clerics practice binary blood rune magic comprised of the letters "X" and "I."

**Peace Babies** – Children born of a union between any of the five major Human noble houses.

**Peto** – Fifth of the ten Quinte Grand Cycle, Summer.

**Piceans** – Humanoid fish people of Lumina. Capable of breathing above and below the water and impervious to the ocean's depths. They have gill flaps large enough to fold over their ears and when the vocal sound waves pass through the membrane, it translates it. This makes them valuable translators in the seaports of the Goyan Islands.

**Piety Watch** – Militant, religious police faction of the Pa-Waga church. They arrest anyone caught begging, idle, or not being productive. Minor offences are punished by a beating with thin cane rods. They wear red shirts under black capes with high pointed collars resembling cat ears.

**Pisar** – Bailian title for a scholar.

**Pomaku** – Humanoid leopard people (Mawl) native to the Arboro region in the Land of Mists, Nocturn.

**Protocol 13** – EEtah House Nur code phrase requesting a meeting between an intelligence asset and their handler.

**Qua-Raman Oasis** – An oasis in the central Dark Waste Desert. Due to its location just south of the Tur-Qua Pass, it serves as a major trading post for gems harvested in The Barrens to the north.

**Quartermaster** – Collector of taxes and tariffs in the Goyan Islands who use the Ironmark to enforce their rule.

**Queen's Envoy Service, The** – The Amarenian Empire's spy service and member of the Society of Whispers.

**Quinte** – Time period equivalent to a month.

**Ramu** – A gambling dismemberment game banned everywhere in Lumina, except the Free City of Tannimore.

**Rayth** – Pirate faction of the Amarenian people in open revolt and attempting to form their own nation.

**Rod-Ema Trench** – Massive abysmal fissure running along the equator in the western ocean floor in Nocturn. At its head is the Agar Goyot and the Black Mural is found on its north wall dipping into the ocean depths.

**Rohina Takii** – Sword school originating on the Island of Wou. Known for its strike while drawing technique.

**Sardor** – Amarenian title for a female warlord.

**Salar Winds** – Turbulent winds surrounding the peak of Mount Goya which must be navigated to enter the Avion City of Darmont on the mountain's northwestern face. Avion term of exasperation, "By the mighty Winds of Salar!"

**Secor** – Street name for the Imperial Gold Ingot equivalent to ten struck gold coins.

**Sesto** – Sixth of the ten Quinte Grand Cycle, Autumn.

**Shallow Sea** – The body of water surrounding the greater Goyan Islands covering the Goyan Rise. The depth is no more than thirty feet deep at its lowest point.

**Si** – The term for "mister" in the Common Tongue spoken in the Goyan Islands.

**Sikari** – Female Singa hunter/killer squads, traveling in groups of two or more. They arm themselves with crossed bandoleros covering their chests and filled with sickle shaped throwing blades.

**Silent Partner** – Seven cabals of organized crime families in the Goyan Islands.

**Simikort** – Round engraved coin acting as an Amarenian noble's calling card.

**Singa** – Humanoid lion people (Mawl) inhabiting the southern Rovina area of the land of Mists.

**Skirting the Upwinds** – Dangerous maneuver practiced by few airship pilots. It involves taking the airship up to the edge of the atmosphere and then plummeting down to your destination. Allowing long-distance travel in a short period.

**Society of Whispers** – The general intelligence cooperative of the five Human noble houses, the Zorian Spymaster, the Calden Intelligencer Service, Suusho, and the Queen's Envoy Service.

**Spice Rat** – Smugglers operating in the Spice Islands chains (Zerian Reef Chain and Outer Zerians) and occasionally in the entire western side of the Goyan Islands.

**Spooks** – Street term for spies and operatives in the Society of Whispers.

**Strasta** – Ancient prophet in the folklore of the Cevot spider people of the Os-Ani Mountains.

**Sunal** – EEtah war college specializing in martial skills.

**Suusho** – The Bailian Empire's spy service and member of the Society of Whispers.

**Szoldos Mercenaries** – One of several small private armies for hire on the Goyan continent.

**Taking it Upstairs** – Airship slang for skirting upwinds

**Tanum Charts** – Six maps of Nocturn's night sky. The Arron-Nin Astrologers use them for divination and sometimes the opening of Flavian portals.

**Teine** – Second of the ten Quinte Grand Cycle, Spring.

**Ten/Fifty**— Cliché phrase in the Goyan Islands referring to the ten cycles (days) in the cluster (week) and fifty decis (hours) of the cycle (day). The equivalent of 24/7.

**Tenable Sister**—Title given to Amarenian lawyers.

**Tiikeri** – Sentient humanoid Tiger creatures of the Dasos region in the eastern Land of Mists.

**Tisa** – Ninth of the ten Quinte Grand Cycle, Winter.

**Trinilic** – Orange Etheria Crystal, fire magic connection.

**Turine** – Tidal clocks used in the Goyan Islands.

**Twilight Lands** – Area between Lumina and Nocturn in constant state of Twilight. Due to converging hot and cold air masses its weather remains perpetually stormy.

**Ukkonite** – Bronze Etheria Crystal with natural repellant properties. It is the crystal equivalent to Ukko wood found only in Nocturn.

**Ukko Wood** – Magical wood from the World Tree, harvested only on the Island of Zer in the eastern Goyan Islands. Its natural repellant properties are used in shields, weapons, Brightstar Nolton Boats and used as currency.

**Ulana** – Chaotic evil sea goddess worshiped by a small sect of Amarenian Rayth in the province of Durik-Dor

**Unification War** – Conflict started by House Eldor in 2 P.A. against the eastern agricultural islands of House Valdur. It ended as quickly as it began when House Aramos forced them to the negotiating table by threatening to freeze both houses' accounts in the Imperial Bank.

**Valorous Sister** – Amarenian title for heroic acts which affected the realm.

**Vedette** – Small fast Nolton Boats crewed by a single ex-Brightstar sailor and used for fast, anonymous travel around the oceans of Lumina.

**Velocomite** – Pale blue Etheria Crystal with red bands, increases or decreases an object's speed travelling.

**Veros Pearls** – Highest quality pearl cultivated in the Otick oyster beds. They are capable of holding a magical charge.

**Ves-Lari** – Mawl mongrels bred by the Tiikeri for rowing and poling. They are a combination of Pomaku (leopard) and Duma (Cheetah). Crews can pole or row for hundreds of miles at a time without stopping.

**Vurr Carts** – Carts used by the Vurr Clerics to collect the City of Zor's dead and garbage. There are two types: stationary carts situated on every major street where citizens can deposit their waste and roving carts mostly dealing with collecting the bodies of the dead.

**Vurr Clerics** – Accolades of the Free God Vurr serving as waste disposal in the City of Zor. Once maintaining constantly pyres burning everything from corpses to ordinary refuse. The city upgraded the pyres to full crematoriums. Vurr clerics smell of smoke and generally work nude, wearing only a simple cloak.

**Wraith** – Deep cover agents for House Aramos drawn from the elite Black Talons unit.

**Yagur** – Humanoid jaguars (Mawl) from the Arboro region of the Land of Mists. They are seers, healers and shamans, serving all the various Mawl races.

**Yudon** – Harpoon with a rifled the shaft for throwing accuracy. The standard weapon of every Sunal EEtah.

**Yupik** – a.k.a. the Ice Clans, one hundred and sixty-five clans divided into three major groups. The nomadic wanderers of the Western Flows compete for resources while the Ash-Ta constantly hunt them as prey. The largest group inhabits the vast Eastern Flows with semi-permanent settlements surrounding the Ice City of Mos-Agar'.

**Zadim** – Lapidaries operating in the Dark Waste Desert.

**Zerian Rangers** – Woodsmen fighters belonging to any of nine different clans occupying the forests of the Island continent of Zer in the Goyan Islands.

**Zoldak Group** – A private mercenary army comprised of former Black Talons of House Aramos.

**Zorian Monetary Council** – A ruling body founded in 3850 P.A. controlling all banking in the High Holy City of Zor. The council coordinates with the Calden Commodities exchange to regulate the exchange of money, goods and services, and uses the Quartermasters Guild for the collection of taxes and tariffs.

# MAPS

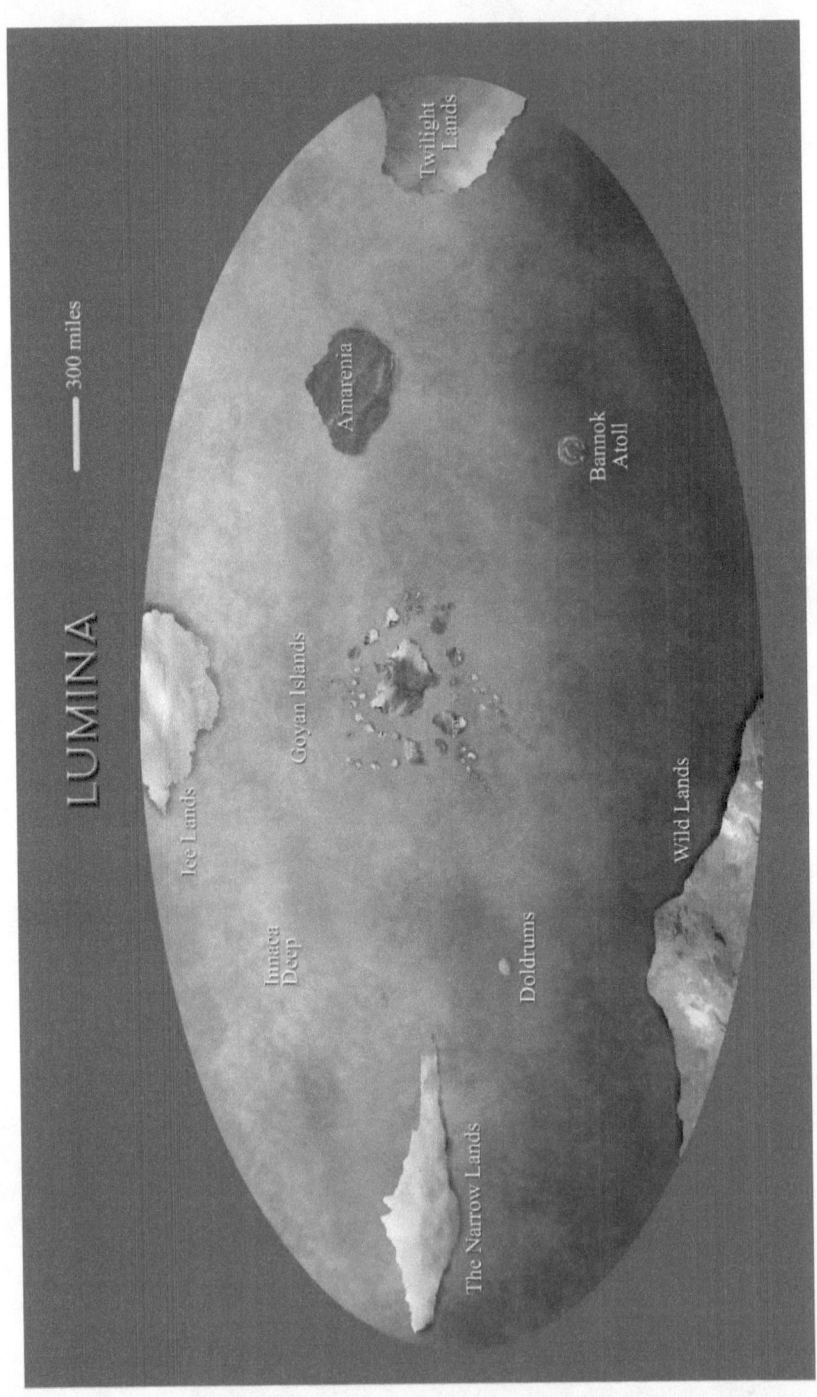

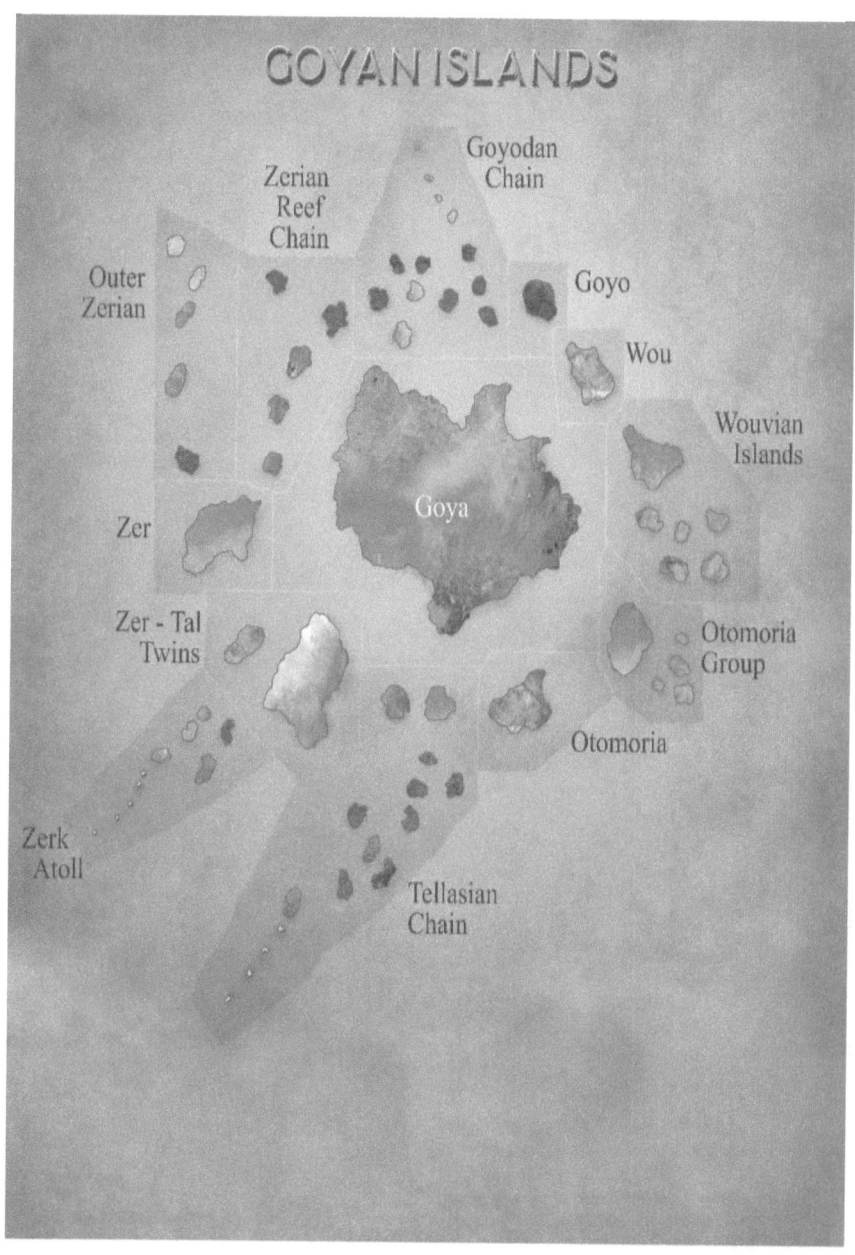

GOYAN ISLANDS

Goyodan
Chain

Zerian
Reef
Chain

Goyo

Outer
Zerian

Wou

Wouvian
Islands

Goya

Zer

Zer - Tal
Twins

Otomoria
Group

Otomoria

Zerk
Atoll

Tellasian
Chain

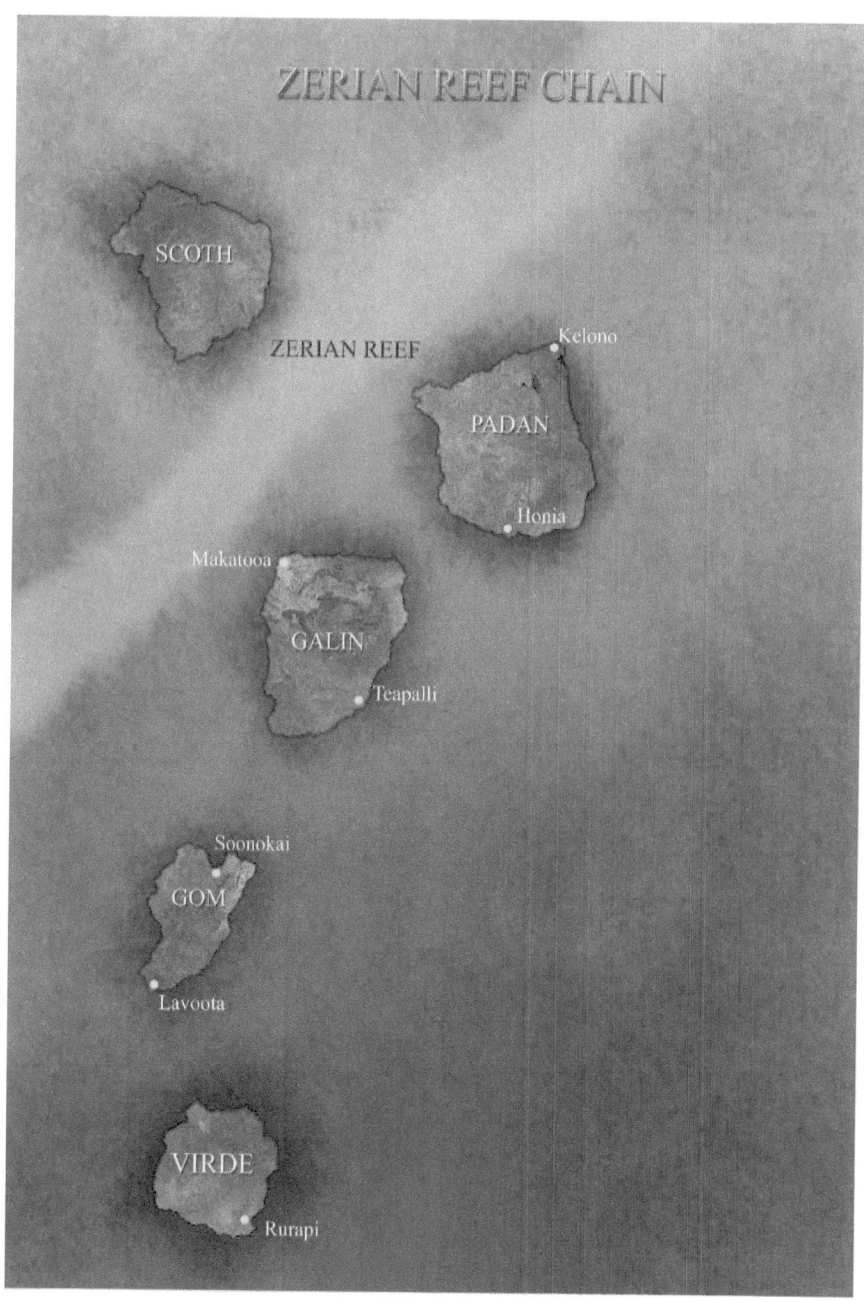

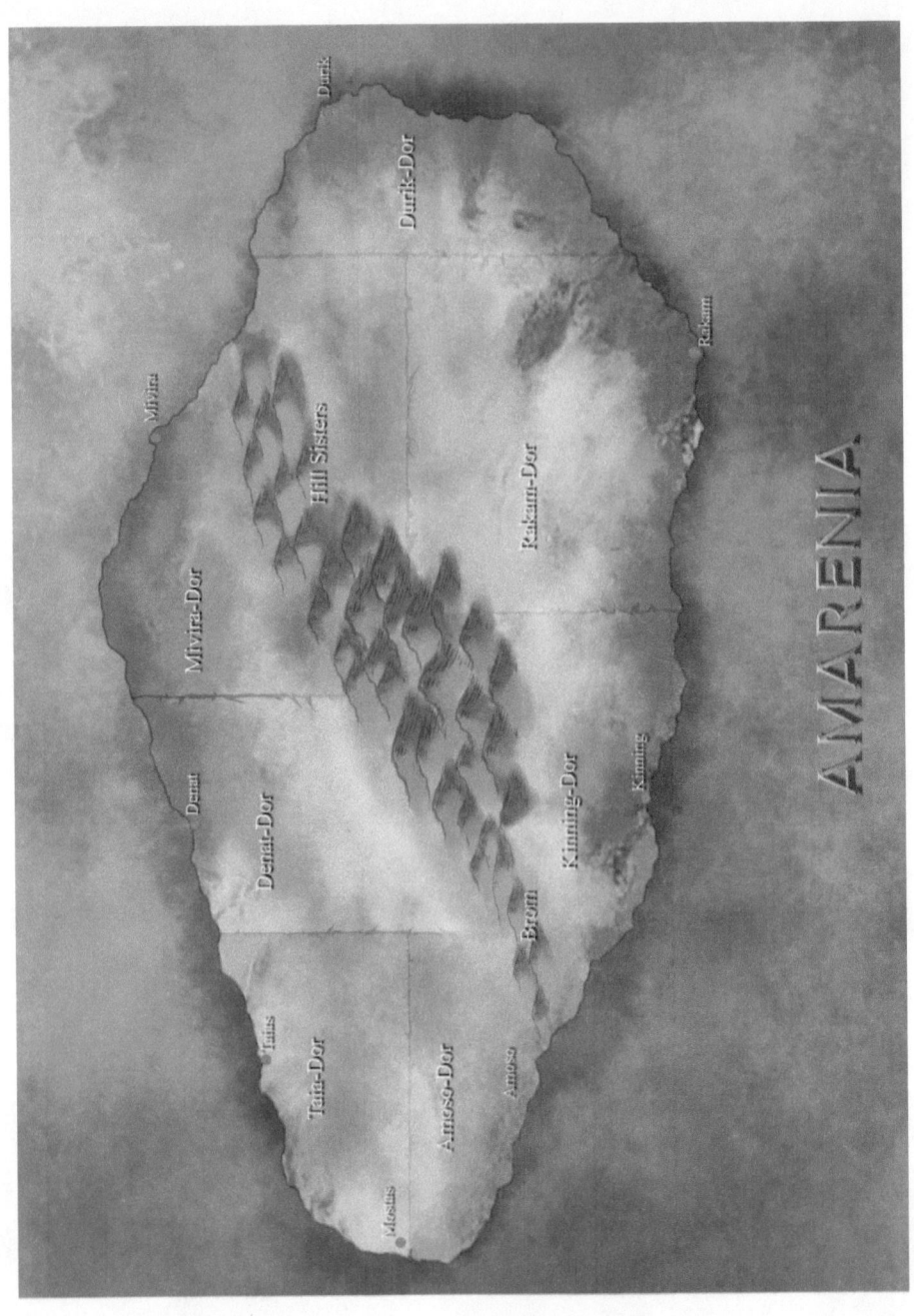

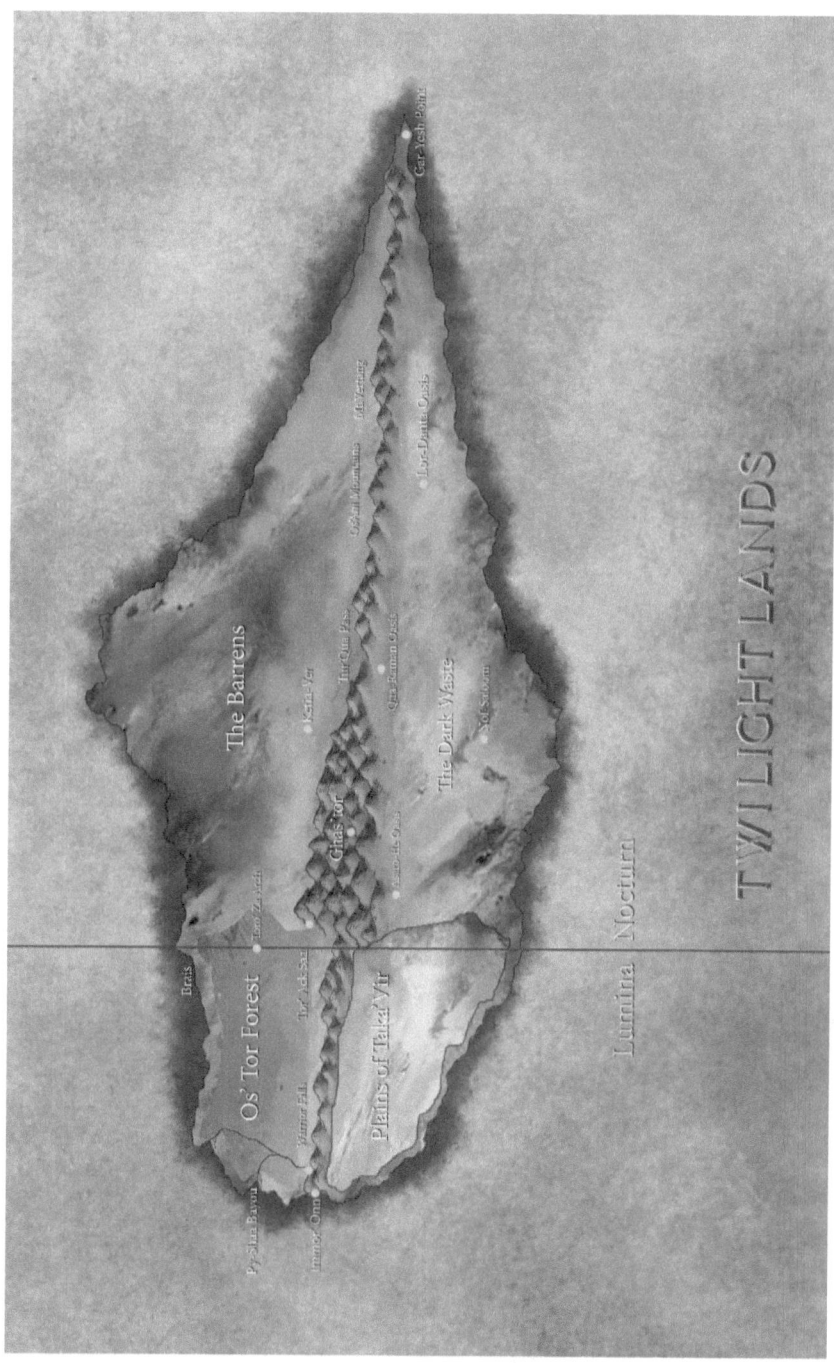

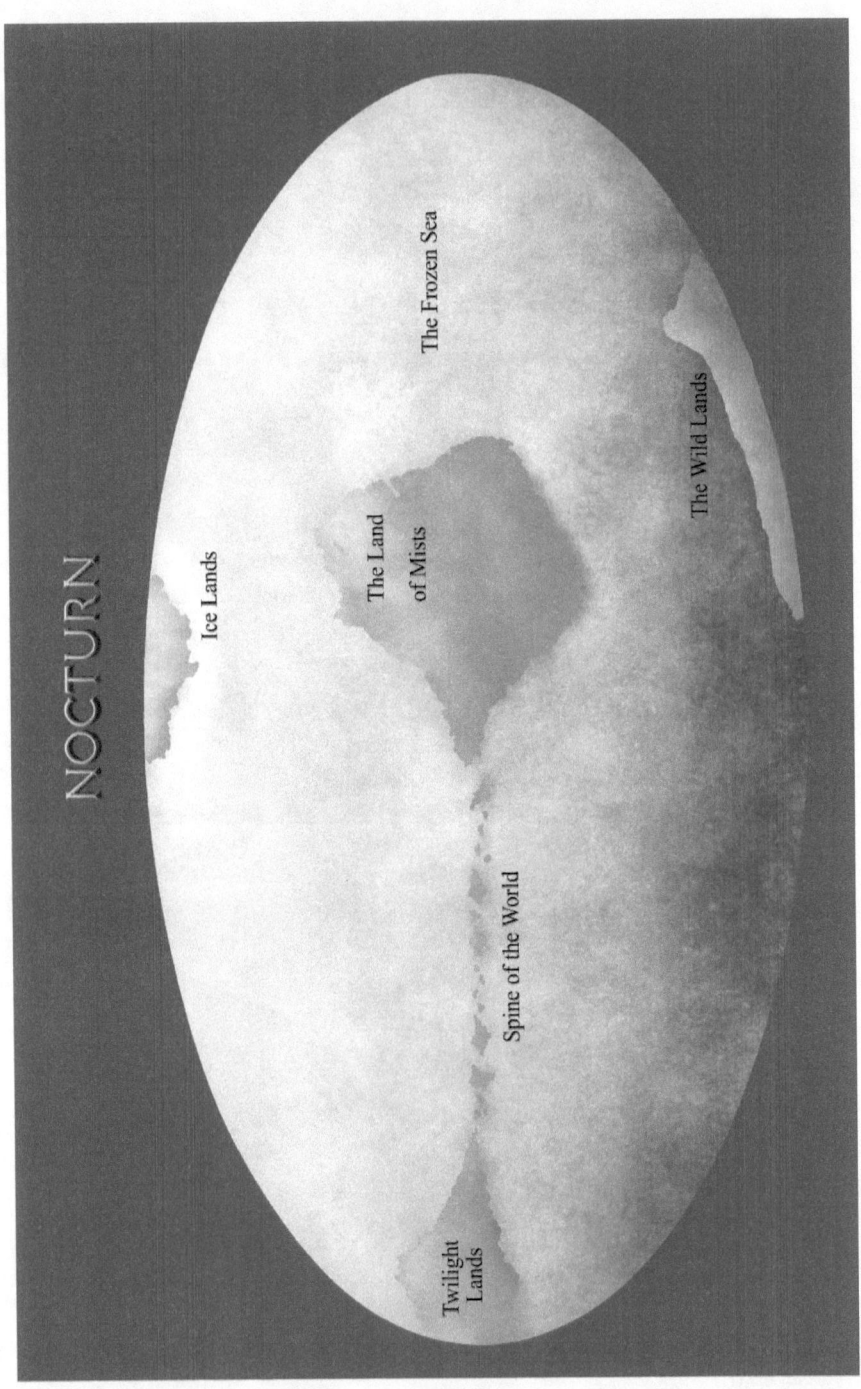

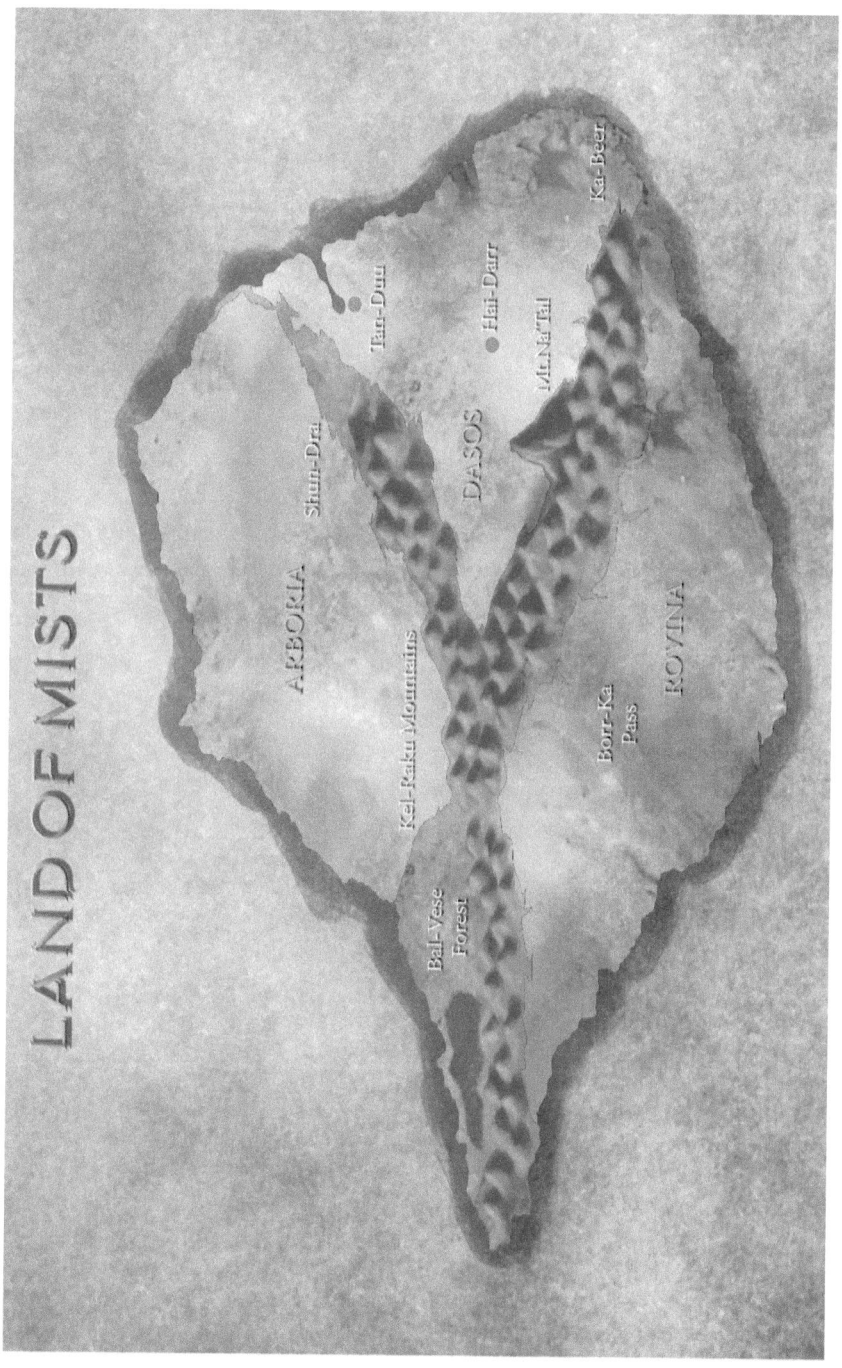

# ABOUT THE AUTHOR

R.W. Marcus spent most of his life selling books. Along the way he managed to become a Falconer, 3rd Dan Black Belt in Yoshukai Karate, Freemason, Freelance Photographer, Ad Copywriter and WMNF Radio Disc Jockey. Marcus' radio commercials and freelance photography won numerous awards, including Best of Shows and Best of the Bay Addy Awards for work with Creative Keys and Laughing Bird Productions. R.W. Marcus was also Founder and Creative Director of United Game Masters, where he cowrote the UGM Universal Gaming System which he used to create and playtest a role-playing game based in the world of the Annigan Cycle. He formally held the title of Director

of Incunabula at Griffon's Medieval Manuscripts, where he penned his first nonfiction title, *The Ship of Fools to 1500*, which Amazon called "an authoritative guide to one of the most popular works of secular writing." Now retired, he created a new genre of fiction— Pulp Fantasy Noir—to exorcise the darker side of his good nature.

## CONNECT

WEBSITE: https://AnniganCycle.com
FACEBOOK: https://www.facebook.com/noirrwmarcus/
TWITTER: @NoirRWMarcus
EMAIL: RWMarcus@yahoo.com

**SPHERES OF INFLUENCE**
**TALES OF THE ANNIGAN CYCLE**
**BOOK NINE**
**FROM LAUGHING BIRD PUBLISHING**